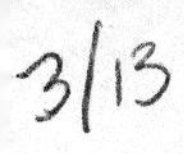

I've gone by many names, but it's always been me.

I met Anne Frank before she wrote her diary. I consulted with Churchill on political doctrine. I crossed the Potomac with Washington. I even polished Napoleon's shoes in the streets of Charleroi, once, though it's not a story I like to tell. I've been in too many places to name, and done things I never thought I'd do. All in the name of saving history, and saving the world we call home.

I realize that these boasts won't be taken seriously, but I must remind each of you that at one time the earth was flat, the atom unbreakable. And the thought of reaching the moon was just as ridiculous as the idea of jumping through time.

I know, because I was there.

My name is Jason Evans. I'm ten days shy of my fifteenth birthday, and this is my story…

KEEPER OF THE BLACK STONES

Stone Ends, Book 1

PT McHugh

SAN DIEGO, CA

SAN DIEGO, CA
sales@glasshousepress.com
www.glasshousepress.com

This is a work of fiction. Apart from well-known actual people, events, and locales that figure in the narrative, all names, characters, places, and incidents are the products of the author's imagination or are used fictitiously. Any resemblance to current events or locales, or to living persons, is entirely coincidental. The publisher does not have any control over and does not assume any responsibility for author or third-party websites or their content.

Published in the United States by Glass House Press, LLC, 2013

GLASS HOUSE PRESS and colophon are trademarks of Glass House Press, LLC.

Library of Congress Cataloging-in-Publication Data
McHugh, P T, 1969-
Keeper of the black stones / PT McHugh. -- First edition.
pages cm
Summary: Shy fourteen-year-old Jason must travel through time to the Middle Ages to join Henry VII's fight against Richard III and stop the man who holds Jason's physicist grandfather captive.
ISBN 978-0-9816768-0-7 (trade pbk. : alk. paper) -- ISBN 978-0-9816768-1-4 (ebook) (print) [1. Time travel--Fiction. 2. Middle Ages--Fiction. 3. Grandfathers--Fiction. 4. Orphans--Fiction. 5. Great Britain--History--Richard III, 1483-1485--Fiction.] I. Title.
PZ7.M478637Ke 2013
[Fic]--dc23
2012031556

ISBN 978-0-9816768-0-7 (paperback)
ISBN 978-0-9816768-1-4 (ebook)
Printed in Canada on acid-free paper
16 15 14 13 12 1 2 3 4 5 6 7 8 9
First Edition

To my wife, Tatiana, for her unwavering belief in me.

To Katherine, whose hugs and smiles cheer me up, even on my worst days.

And to Cristina – your name might not be used for any of the characters, but your personality shines through in all of them, and that matters just as much.

I love you all.

Finally, in loving memory of my oldest and dearest friend, Natalie.

ACKNOWLEDGMENTS

Writing a book is an adventure unto itself, and getting it published is a whole different story. I've been very lucky to have come so far, but none of this would have happened without some very important people. I would like to start off by thanking Cynthia, David, and Maureen for their patience and assistance in editing my first manuscript (which seems as though it happened a lifetime ago).

To the Stilley family, for their overwhelming encouragement and support early – your assistance was crucial in getting this book off the ground!

To my father, who introduced me to his love of history early in life, and my mother, for encouraging me in anything and everything I pursued.

To Barbara, John, and Andrea for putting up with me, my Clancy & Theys family in Raleigh, and my HMH family in Sacramento.

To Glass House Press, for giving me the opportunity to put this book into print and find out what it has to offer. And last – but certainly not least – my special thanks to Carrie White, the best editor in the world. This book is as much yours as mine. You have been a friend, a therapist, and my greatest supporter.

Thank you all!

June 14

The Ribbon Theory ... it's something I've been working on for years, and now it looks like we have proof. This both frightens and fascinates me. When something that has always been abstract – a theory – becomes suddenly solid, it is as though the world turns on its side. Exhilarating, and yet terrifying, no matter how 'right' it makes you.

What then, is the Ribbon Theory, you may be asking yourself. Well, I shall tell you. It started as a dream ... an idea that time was a force of its own. An alternate dimension, if you will. The Ribbon Theory follows this dream, assuming that the fabric of time is imprinted on a dimensional ribbon. Think of music or film, imprinted on tape as it was years ago, before the microchip. Now imagine that the tape actually holds time rather than 007 or The Wizard of Oz. This, then, is the ribbon of time.

If time is a ribbon, folding back on itself again and again, and there are – as we know there to be – black holes that are rips in the fabric of space and time ... if these holes exist where the ribbon folds back on itself, and the fabric becomes weak ... does that mean that there are worm holes between different parts of the ribbon? That there are, in fact, holes that lead from one time plane to another?

Could there be doorways, so to speak, into our past? Into different parts of our history, depending on where and how and when the rip or tear takes place? Could these doorways be manipulated? Used to transport us anywhere we wished to go? Could these holes take us back in time, if we wished to go there?

You may be asking what the Ribbon Theory has to do with our real lives. You may also be asking what holes in space have to do with our physical world, and what we see around us.

What you should be asking yourself, dear reader, is what the Ribbon Theory – and the idea of time travel – have to do with history itself. What if we did have that power to travel through time? And what if that power, God forbid, fell into the wrong hands?

Doctor Richard Evans
John de Vere, 13th Earl of Oxford
Keeper of the Black Stones

Prologue

Abergavenny, England
August, 1485 A.D.

The old soldier's horse thundered across the plain toward the small village of Abergavenny, and death rode with him. The people of the village didn't deserve to die, but within the next several hours, many of them would. For all the soldier knew, many of them may already be dead; Dresden's men had arrived hours earlier, and did not have a reputation for mercy. It was very important that he get there as quickly as possible, not only for himself, but for the people of Abergavenny. For the entire country, truth be told, and for the world itself.

The Earl of Oxford pushed his horse forward at the thought, the bulk of Henry Tudor's army at his back. The road here had been long, difficult, and trying, but they'd landed successfully a week earlier, in the Welsh coastal city of Milford Haven. The army's goal – and the Earl's – was simple: overthrow the current king, Richard III, and replace him with Henry Tudor. Now the Earl snorted to himself. Simple. It was an ambitious plan, and it had always been a long shot. If they were successful, they would change the course of the country, uniting the people for the first time in generations. It was an enormous task, and it was the reason the Earl was on his current path.

He straightened in his saddle and squared his shoulders. Today's battle, in Abergavenny, had absolutely nothing to do with Henry Tudor or his war. To the Earl, though, this particular mission was just as important.

He glanced at the sky and cursed quietly to himself. Today was not a day for fighting such a battle, and he would have delayed it if he could. The sky was low and dark, with harsh winds to match. Rain had been driving down since early morning, leaving the ground around them a hazardous marshland. They had lost several horses in the last hour as a result; animals that had gone down in the treacherous mud and been unable to rise. They'd been forced to leave the wagons behind for their own safety, and his soldiers were traveling light, with few weapons and minimal armor. He could only hope that they would find Dresden's men unprepared or similarly armed. The fighting would be messy and dangerous, with mud below and armed men above, but he had little choice; the window of opportunity opened today at sundown, and closed a heartbeat later.

The Earl crested the rise above the village and slid to an abrupt halt. The hillside below him had fallen out, a river of mud and water flowing over what should have been his path, and delaying his entry into the village. He grunted in frustration and turned to seek another way down, but found his way blocked by his lieutenant.

Trigva, son of Halvor, was a massive warrior, measuring well over 6 feet in height. He wore a steel helmet, affixed with a brass nose plate and painted with a wolf's head. The painting was appropriate; the Earl knew the Danish soldier to be both fearless and unendingly loyal. Today, the man wore nothing more than a leather jerkin and a set of chain mail. His left arm bore several silver rings – signs of his wealth, Nordic heritage, and skill on the battlefield. He was an imposing force, and the Earl's best ally. He was also the only person the Earl truly trusted in this time and place.

He did not look happy, though the Earl had never seen the man actually smile.

"I have just come from the Archbishop's camp, my Lord," Trigva said, bowing, and raising his voice over the wind. "He is not pleased with your decision to invade the village."

"The Archbishop may hang himself, if it please him," the Earl growled. "This is not his army to order. I have no obligations to him." He paused. "And I have no choice. I must control that village. And quickly."

They turned to face the buildings below them, and the Earl sighed. The village contained fewer than thirty structures, housing around fifty families.

These were farmers, uninterested in war or politics. They hadn't earned the battle that came to them, or the soldiers who had already invaded. In the center of the village, a crude stone-and-mortar tower rose roughly two and a half stories from the ground, anchoring the north end of the town's church. The remaining structures stood in a loose rectangle around the tower, using the church as a connecting point and their walls and roofs as shields. Together, the tower and homes created a small but formidable fortress. They were well defended, the Earl knew, and ready for battle.

"You're going in?" Trigva asked quietly.

"I must."

Trigva shook his head. "Why did Lord Dresden send his troops to protect this town? It seems of little consequence."

The Earl smiled wryly. "They are here to steal the very thing that I need," he replied. "I must pray that we are in time to save it."

Instead of replying, Trigva shouted out a warning and vaulted out of his saddle toward the Earl. He hit his commander in the shoulder, knocking him roughly off his horse and to the ground. As they fell, the Earl glanced up to see a volley of arrows cross the space over his saddle and fly into the forest beyond. Arrows that had been meant for him.

"It appears, my Lord, that they know of our arrival," Trigva said drily. He groaned and pulled himself off the Earl, who grunted in response. He turned to look at the ridge line, and saw that his men were already lined up and prepared to charge.

"Very well. They leave me little choice, then." He pulled himself back onto his horse and looked to the sky to judge the sun's location behind its dark bank of clouds. An hour before sunset, he thought; that gave them just enough time. If his calculations were right. "We must finish this quickly, my friend. There is no time to waste."

Trigva nodded curtly, remounted, and spurred his horse toward the men on the ridge, shouting orders in both Nordic and English. The Earl galloped after him, looking anxiously for a way down the hill below. He would leave the initial charge and fighting to the men, but would have to enter the village himself – soon – to find what he sought. To get there, he would ride directly behind the force, fighting if he must, but keeping out of harm's reach as well as he could. It was a risky proposition, but was his only chance.

He glanced again at the sky, then back down to his forces. Trigva had reached the small group of soldiers and given them their orders. The men began to move rapidly down the liquid hillside, their horses slipping to their knees when they couldn't find purchase, but regaining their feet when they could. Turning his horse, the Earl growled deeply in his throat, ducked in time to avoid another arrow, and plunged after them.

The sky opened as the men raced down the hill toward the village, their horses throwing mud and stones up in their wake. The wind was picking up, its velocity g rowing to match the intensity of the rain, until the Earl could hear little more than the storm around him. His men flowed across the ravine that surrounded the village, and thundered to the base of its outer walls. There, the defending force – forty armed men, dressed in leather, mail, and steel plate – launched their first volley of arrows. They pierced the air, their long wooden shafts armed with steel tips meant to tear through leather armor. The wind caught the arrows as they flew toward the invading force, though, sending them wide and long. The Earl, joining the fray from behind, breathed a sigh of relief at the continued safety of his men. He looked to his right for the reinforcements he knew would be coming from that direction. The men in front of him, now erecting their ladders against the wall, were merely the distraction.

On the other side of the village, a modest infantry of twenty men, with eleven more on horseback, emerged from the westward tree line. They raced without fanfare to their own side of the village. There, the wall would be left unguarded, as Dresden's men had rushed to defend against Trigva's forces on the eastern side of the wall. There, the wall – and the village beyond – would be easily invaded.

The Earl sprinted toward this second force and rode in behind them; this was where he would enter the village. The new troops threw their own ladders up against the walls of the outer buildings and began to swarm up the rungs. The Earl looked up to the top of the buildings and allowed himself a small smile. The defenders had seen the second force, but were now dividing their own forces between the two groups of invaders, panicking at the double attack. They would never see the Earl's third attack coming, hard on the heels of the second, along the now fully unattended southern rampart.

A roar went through the Earl's men as they rallied with the third group to climb the ladders and invade the town. The man in front of the Earl threw himself from his horse and lunged up the closest ladder, his large blade free in his hand. The massive soldier swung the steel sword over the top of the wall and pulled himself past two of the rampart's defenders before they noticed his presence. He quickly cut both men down, then moved out of sight. Another man followed him, and then another. Looking along the ramparts, the Earl could see that the enemy was failing. Quickly. He jumped from his horse and made his own way up one of the ladders, anxious to fight for himself.

As he stepped forward, though, the defenders unleashed their hidden weapon. Several loud thunderclaps sounded from the village, followed by a cloud of black smoke. No fewer than six of the Earl's men went down under the barrage of lead bullets, falling from the ramparts to the cold mud below. The other men froze and dropped to their bellies. This wasn't the first time they'd encountered this weapon. The men of this period called it the Devil's Flame. They couldn't comprehend the mechanics or technology behind it, but they'd seen the results.

The Earl knew it to be nothing more than simple gunfire. He knew also that it should not exist – and had not existed – in this time period. The fact that Richard's men had this weapon was Dresden's work. This was part of the Earl's personal battle against the man, and was a source of some worry. It was not, however, the reason for today's battle. And it would not stop the Earl of Oxford's men.

Within seconds his men had recovered their poise, and several new soldiers replaced their fallen comrades. The defenders had only a handful of the modern weapons at their disposal, with only one or two men knowledgeable enough to use them, and the Earl's men far outnumbered the defending force. No further gunfire erupted, and within twenty minutes the battle was finished.

The Earl strode quickly toward the edge of the wall, anxious to get inside and find the artifact he sought. When he dropped to the ground, he found

Trigva waiting for him.

"What's the butcher's bill?" he asked his lieutenant quietly.

"Seven dead, five wounded, two seriously, my Lord."

The Earl closed his eyes briefly in regret. "How badly?" he asked.

"Two will not make it through the night, my Lord."

The Earl nodded. He had never accepted this particular aspect of his role – the knowledge that his decisions and actions meant both life and death to so many people. His only justification was the mission, which was more important than any single human life. More important even than his own, though his continued survival was necessary, for now. He sighed and stood a bit straighter. This was not the time for fears or regrets. Besides, a show of compassion was too easily seen as weakness in this day and age.

"Has your brother found it yet?" he asked tersely, looking around the village.

Trigva had expected the Earl's question, and shook his head. "Not yet, my Lord. But I have all of our men searching for it."

"Very well. Tell them to make haste, and take me to the wounded."

Five men lay on their backs next to a well in the center of the village courtyard. Two of them had flesh wounds on their arms, and one had taken an arrow to his leg. These three would survive, unless infection set in. Two men, however, had taken bullets to the chest and abdomen. These were undeniable death sentences. One of the men was unconscious. The other was alert, and very much aware of his impending fate.

The Earl knelt down beside the conscious man and took his hand. "Is there anything I can do for you?" he asked softly. This was not standard behavior from a lord, but his was a heart that sought to share itself with others. He would not pass a wounded or dying man without at least one kind word.

The man smiled, genuinely pleased with the offer. "Watch over my wife and children, my Lord. Do not let them suffer, or forget me."

"They will be well cared for. I give you my word. Rest now, my boy." The old warrior rose and motioned for one of his priests to kneel in his place and administer last rights. He stood watching for a moment, then turned at a shout behind him.

"My Lord!"

"What is it?" the Earl asked. One of his men approached him, holding a dark object in his hands.

"I found it on one of the defenders, my Lord. It is the Devil's Flame!" The soldier held the object out apprehensively, as though it might explode at any moment.

The Earl accepted the heavy object, and glanced quickly at it. It was a gun, roughly 14 inches long, and crafted out of wood and iron. The weapon was crude by any stretch of the imagination, with limited efficiency and range. These pistols existed in the fifteenth century, and the weapon itself was no cause for concern. The object inside the gun, though, touched off an icy knot of fear in the Earl's stomach. The old soldier reached into the barrel and extracted a small metallic object, no larger than his smallest finger. Crude guns – nothing more than small cannons – were common. This single metallic cartridge, which was a self-contained firing chamber, was not. How had Dresden done so much with so little, and so quickly? The Earl swallowed heavily, then jumped at another shout from one of his men.

"My Lord, please come quickly!" the man shouted. He stood near the church, motioning to his leader.

"The stone?" he asked sharply.

At the soldier's nod, the Earl exhaled softly. They had found it, then. But was it in one piece? And was there time? Glancing at the sky, he saw that the glow behind the clouds had moved toward the horizon more quickly than he'd realized. Some rapid calculations gave him an estimate of ten to fifteen minutes before his window of opportunity opened; enough time to get to the stone and prepare. If it was still whole, and functioning. He dropped the bullet in his pocket and strode quickly toward the church, Trigva following closely behind.

"Take me to it," he ordered.

The Earl and Trigva followed the soldier, Par, through the stone archway that led from the courtyard into the church. They made their way past several wooden benches, which were currently operating as makeshift gurneys to support the dead and dying. Two silver cups and a small golden crown still lay on the cloth-covered altar at the far end of the church; the Earl was right in assuming, then, that Dresden's men had been here for something other than riches. His gut clenched in fear. Had they found it or destroyed it already? Stolen it? Was he too late? Had this entire journey been in vain?

Before him, Par parted the heavy red curtain behind the church's altar, and pointed through the exposed opening. "There, my Lord!" He stepped aside to reveal a set of stone stairs descending steeply downwards.

"Are we in time? Is it safe?" the Earl gasped. He brushed past Par and ran down the steps to enter a small, dank cellar, exhaling sharply in relief at what he saw. A large, polished stone lay in the center of the small room, absorbing the light of the six torches on the walls. The stone was wide and long enough to accommodate a man twice his size; smaller than some of the stones he'd seen, but large enough for his need. Symbols ran along the borders of the stone, their grooves harboring what was left of the torchlight. As the Earl watched, the shadows of the symbols rose off the rock, dancing and twining together in a reflection of both shadow and light. Calling the Earl, beckoning him forward. Calling him home.

He stood for a moment and smiled in profound relief, then made his way slowly toward the stone tablet, staring down at it with both affection and reverence. The stone began to glow softly in response, putting off its own form of light and power as the symbols around it intensified. A soft hum filled the air, accompanied by the vibration of the impending jump. These changes meant that the Earl had only a few moments before it was time to depart. He was just in time, then; if he had missed this opportunity, it would have been weeks before he'd had another. But he had made it. And it was time to go home.

"Richard's soldiers did not take it despite our presence? Why, my Lord?"

Trigva asked, startling the Earl out of his thoughts. The soldier referred to Dresden's puzzling habit of collecting the stone's brothers as he found them. In doing so, he restricted the Earl's movements, and his ability to return.

"The village priest must have refused to tell them where it was. We may have come upon the town before the soldiers could find it, or before they could tear the confession out of him." The Earl paused for a moment, and looked back over his shoulder. "Perhaps Lord Dresden wished to keep it for himself, and we arrived before he had time to move it."

"I see. Is there anything else my Lord?" Trigva asked.

The Earl smiled. Trigva did not understand the stones or their meaning, but he had seen them before. He knew that the Earl needed time alone with the stones, and did not accept questions or arguments on that point. To his credit, Trigva had questioned the Earl only once, and maintained a stoic silence afterward.

"No," the Earl replied, shaking his head. He knelt down and began to sweep the accumulated dust and dirt off the perimeter of the stone. "Give the men my thanks and let them drink, but not too much. Be prepared to leave at any time."

"What of King Henry, my Lord?"

"He'll make camp where he is if he knows what's good for him, and wait for my arrival," the Earl answered. He traced the symbols on the stone's face, and felt the power begin to flow through his own blood and bones.

"Of course, my Lord," Trigva said. He bowed his head once again, then strode out of the room, closing the door softly behind him.

The Earl of Oxford waited for a moment to ensure that he was truly alone before standing and removing his belt and scabbard. He smiled as he laid them gently aside; he would not need these where he was going. He rolled his right shirtsleeve to the elbow to expose his forearm and the pocket-sized portable computer strapped to it, then pressed the red power button on the bottom of the device. The LCD screen jumped to bright, electric life, and lit up the room. The Earl used the small keyboard to quickly record the location of the stone as best he could, typing in a description of the terrain and rough position of the village. He would need to locate this stone again, if it survived, and this was his best and only method for doing so.

The Earl finished typing, turned off the computer, and took a deep breath. The stone was glowing brightly now, and it was time to jump. He dropped to his knees on the stone and brushed away the remaining dust and debris. His cloak dropped to the floor near his sword, followed closely by his boots and chest plate. Finally the Earl reached for his leather bag, kept under his surcoat, and lay down with it, stretching his tall frame atop the black stone, and making sure that both his feet and head lay within the perimeter of the stone. He'd never broken the boundaries of the stone before, and he wasn't going to start now. He closed his eyes and took several deep breaths; simple exercises that he'd learned over time to assist both body and mind during the transition. He waited only a moment before the familiar feeling of vertigo, combined with an anxious adrenaline rush, filled his chest and stomach. The world swayed violently and went dark, and he jumped.

When the world stilled again, he took a deep breath and counted slowly to one hundred before reopening his eyes. He lay motionless for several seconds, willing himself to breathe normally and reconnect with his physical body. The air here was different – thicker, and more difficult to take in. But it was familiar.

The Earl of Oxford was back home. Here, though, he was not known as John de Vere, Earl of Oxford and eldest warrior of the Lancaster bloodline. Here, he was Dr. Richard Evans, recent widower to Patricia Evans, and grandfather to Jason Evans, denizen of twenty-first-century New Hampshire. Here, he was simply a retired physics professor, virtually invisible to the world at large, with nothing more to think about than paying the mortgage and making it to the market once a week. He rose quickly from the stone and climbed the ladder standing next to it, on his way into the modern world.

PART I

1

LEBANON, NEW HAMPSHIRE
PRESENT DAY

"Jay .... Jason, are you listening to me?" Paul asked abruptly.

"Yeah, I heard you," I lied. Of course I hadn't *really* been listening. If I listened to everything Paul said, I'm pretty sure I'd have gone insane by now. Don't get me wrong, he's my best friend and all, but everyone has a breaking point.

"If you stack your rotation with right-handers and no lefties, you're screwed, right? How come I'm the only one who can see that?" Paul asked impatiently. By his tone of voice, I thought, this must be the second or third time he'd asked.

I cringed. This was Paul's newest obsession: second-guessing the decisions of the Red Sox coaching staff. Personally I couldn't be bothered, and I didn't know why *he* bothered, but I played along with his disgust. "I don't know, Paul."

The truth was that I hadn't been paying attention. Not even remotely, if I was being honest. Which I usually was. I loved Paul like a brother, and I'd usually go along with his crazy self-important fantasies, but my grandfather had just returned from yet another out-of-town conference, this time in Ithaca, New York, and I was busy trying to figure out where he'd actually gone. He was doing that a lot lately – disappearing for days on end, to a place that didn't get cell phone coverage. Or mail, evidently, since he never left hotel information, or a forwarding address. How could the city of Ithaca not have cell phone coverage? It was a university town, for God's sake, and yet I hadn't been able to reach him for three full days. It wasn't like I needed to know where he was at all times, I argued against myself, but I'd be lying if I said it didn't bother me. And asking Mrs. Grey, our neighbor, to check in on me several times a day – as he was wont to do – didn't make it any better. She was nice and all, but her never ending need to know *everything* about where I was or what I did was getting annoying.

Suddenly I realized that Paul was talking to me again. I gave myself a mental slap and turned back to the real world. I could worry about my grandfather later. Right now I had some real life to handle; namely, getting to school on time. I looked around, trying to remember where we were, and paused at the scenery. It was late October in New Hampshire, which meant that the leaf-peeking tourists were long gone. The leaves on the trees had all but disappeared as well, giving the dark gray mountains that surrounded our little town of Lebanon free range over the landscape. The sky was low and gray, and the air already felt cold and wet. It was actually a little sinister, I thought. The smell of burning wood filled the air, announcing the approach of winter as much as the remains of the brightly colored foliage. Everyone in New England said they loved the fall, but what they really meant was that they loved the two weeks of bright autumn foliage. After that, it was downright depressing.

"I'm cold … it's colder out than usual, don't you think?" Paul asked. He tucked his hands deeper into his jacket pockets and glanced at me. Not that it would have mattered what I thought. I caught a smile at the corner of my mouth and stifled it. Paul's questions were never actually questions. He was used to me agreeing with him about pretty much everything, and even when I didn't agree with him, and said so, he chose to hear what he wanted to hear.

Still, he had a point. It was only October, but it wouldn't be long before the town was buried in snow and practically hibernating. From then on it would be short days, early nights, and mornings so cold that you couldn't feel your feet when you got out of bed. With my luck, we wouldn't get a thaw until May. I'd spent my entire life in this town, and I still wasn't used to the cold. I definitely didn't like it. Snow was okay until Christmas. That was about it.

That was my life, though. Boring. Pointless. Cold. Like any other kid, I had dreams of doing something more. Going somewhere. Meeting someone. Having an adventure. Having anything at all, for that matter. Not that it would happen. I'd probably be stuck here forever. I bit my lip, pulled my jacket tighter around me, and trudged forward. It was 7:30AM on a Friday, and my job right now was to get to school. Just like every other day of the year.

"What do you have planned for your birthday?" Paul asked abruptly. This was another of Paul's trademark moves: changing topics abruptly, taking everyone else by surprise.

I shrugged my shoulders. "I'm pretty open." No doubt Paul already had something in mind.

"How about bowling?" Paul casually bent down, picked up a rock, and tossed it across the street into the woods, as though nothing mattered. Which was what made me suspicious. That and the fact that we never went bowling.

"Bowling?" I asked, matching his casual tone. "Since when do you like bowling?"

"I don't know, I was just thinking it was something you'd like to do, that's all."

I started to laugh. "Yeah, sure. Tell you what, how about we hire a clown as well?"

Paul's face drew down into a frown. "Hey, I was just asking," he snapped. "I didn't know you were going to over react about it." He turned away abruptly.

I sighed. Despite his outgoing demeanor, Paul was actually pretty sensitive. And extremely insecure. If you disagreed with him, he took it personally. Which was why I generally tried to play nice. Fighting with Paul was

… unpleasant, at best.

“I didn’t say I hated bowling,” I said, trying to make it up. I wasn’t in the mood to fight this morning. “I just think you have to be under ten to have a birthday party at a bowling alley, that’s all. I mean, I think it’s a rule or something.” I was trying to stop laughing, really. Granted, I wasn’t succeeding.

“You’re an ass, do you know that? I was just asking!” Paul ducked his head and marched ahead of me, pouting the way he did any time I didn’t agree to his plans.

Then it hit me. “Wait a minute. This doesn’t have anything to do with Heather Woods, does it?”

Paul looked at me with puppy dog eyes, “I don’t know what you’re talking about,” he deadpanned.

I snorted. “Yeah, right.” Paul had been obsessing about Heather Woods for weeks, if not months, and I knew for sure that she’d recently started working at the bowling alley. Besides, Paul never offered something like a party without having an ulterior motive of one sort or another.

I laughed again, then grew quiet. His question got me thinking. My birthday was only a couple of weeks away. I wasn’t really looking forward to it, to be honest. Not that I was opposed to turning fifteen … I was actually pretty excited about being a year older. But my parents had died three years earlier, two days before I turned twelve, and my birthday never failed to bring those thoughts and feelings back. They had died in a traffic accident, on their way home from a conference in Boston. I had blamed myself for their death at the time and had never quite gotten over it. I knew I wasn’t the one that physically hit them – a drunk driver had taken care of that – but I *was* the one that had begged for their early return. They hadn’t been scheduled to drive back until the following morning, when bright sunlight and a decent hour may have saved them. I’d been in love with my parents, though, and desperate for them to return. They had, of course, given in. And died satisfying my selfish wish. Counselors and friends – and my grandfather – had spent the last three years trying to talk me out of it, but I’d clung to the truth; it had been my fault that my parents were killed, and I would have to live with that burden for the rest of my life.

Birthdays always reminded me of that fact. It hadn't exactly made them happy occasions.

Paul and my grandfather – Doc, to me – would want to celebrate my birthday, though. They always did. And I would go along with them, like I always did. Who was I to argue? I'd smile and laugh and pretend that the whole thing didn't conjure up bad memories. Like it always did.

"Now that you mention it, I guess bowling doesn't sound so bad." I picked up my own rock and tossed it into the woods after Paul's, then saw him smile out of the corner of my eye and turned to grin at him. He always won our arguments. It didn't really bother me anymore.

Neither of us spoke as we walked toward Harvey's Truck Stop. This was our standard route to school, with our standard stop. Paul went inside and bought himself a large cup of coffee while I waited outside, watching the trucks come and go on their way to bigger, better places. Paul was the only kid I knew that drank coffee. He didn't actually like it – and that was a fact – but it was another part of his persona. Another attempt to look and feel older than he actually was.

I looked long and hard at the storefront window as I waited, and studied my reflection. I was a good 4 inches shorter than Paul, but not quite as thin. I grinned at that. Paul had the general size and dimension of a flagpole, so I would have had a lot of trouble being any skinnier than him. I turned to the side to view my profile, and sighed. Undersized kid. Messy, unkempt hair that would have made my mother cringe. Button-up shirt – buttoned to the top, of course – with skinny jeans and a coat that was about two seasons out of style. I wasn't ugly, but I didn't think I was ever going to break any hearts. To be honest, I thought I was probably the sort of kid that people overlooked. I blended in, flew below the radar. This was partially natural, and partially my own mask. I'd been working on it for about three years now.

Evidently, I'd done a good job. My grandfather had told me that I was the perfect model for the average American boy. "A Rockwell painting," he'd said. I knew who Rockwell was, and I knew Doc had meant it as a compliment. In a way, that was what I wanted. But lately there had been a voice in the back of my head, whispering in my ear, asking me if I really wanted to be average. Overlooked. Unimportant. Wasn't that like picking vanilla ice cream as your favorite flavor every time you went into the ice cream parlor? Preferring vanilla over the million and one other exotic flavors available?

Ironically enough, vanilla was my favorite flavor. But it was starting to lose its charm.

"Any plans for the weekend?" Paul asked from behind me.

I jumped, and realized he'd probably been watching me check myself out in the window for a while now. I hunched lower into my worn-out jacket, embarrassed at having been caught. And at the question. Paul knew perfectly well that I didn't have any plans. I never had plans. Sometimes I thought that his asking was a form of pointing that out. Then again, maybe that was just my bizarre mood.

"Nope," I muttered, stepping past him and heading up the driveway to school.

This was always the most interesting part of the walk, as it took us directly through the entire student body. Everyone who was anyone hung out in front of the school until about fifteen seconds after the last bell rang, displayed in all their group mentality glory. Paul and I made our way past the upper classmen, who stood clustered together in cliques. The jocks stood outside the gymnasium doors to the right of the main entrance, while the 'untouchable girls' huddled around a handicapped parking sign just to the left. The emo kids stood next to the bike racks at the end of the parking lot, smoking cigarettes, talking in low voices, and doing their level best to look mysterious. The techies, armed with Apple's latest and greatest creations, were content to hang out beside the recycling dumpster on the opposite end of the entrance. For a moment I wondered what it would be like to be in one of those groups. To be honest, though, I knew that none of them would accept me, and I didn't belong with any of those kids. I was the smartest kid in school, brought up on physics and history. I lived with my grandfather, a well-known genius and world-famous college professor. I dressed like a thirty-year-old computer programmer. I was, for all intents and purposes, a self-admitted nerd.

Paul, who I didn't think ever worried about these things, shoved past me to throw away his (untouched) cup of coffee. I laughed and looked beyond him, to the entrance of our school. A large, ugly concrete staircase led up to four empty glass doors. The only attempt at decoration was a sign that read "Future Leaders of the World." Somewhat self important, if you asked me. Having known these kids for most of my life, I also hoped that it was a huge exaggeration. Otherwise our world was in a lot of trouble.

I kept my head down as I made my way through the crowded hallway, trying to avoid eye contact with both teachers and students. In my experience, making eye contact encouraged people to talk to you, and that was usually the last thing I wanted. The result, of course, was that I generally got knocked around like a ball inside a pinball machine when I was in the hall. I also got stepped on at least three times a day, and always by someone taller than me. Through some bizarre twist of fate, though, I never managed to run into any girls. Only guys. Large guys. Sometimes I had a real problem with Murphy and his laws.

I got to the refuge of my locker – which I shared with Paul – bruised, battered, and disheveled, and heaved a sigh of relief. I opened the locker, then opened my bag and started shoving books into the compartment. I could never understand why we needed so many books for school. Most of them were worse than useless, and the physics text I had right now was juvenile at best. The thing was, though, you had to have your books in every class or –

"Damn," I muttered, pulling my hand out and peering down into my bag. Nothing left there, and I hadn't found the book I needed yet.

"What's up?" Paul asked, looking up from the copy of *Johnny Quest* in his hand.

I slammed my hand into the door of my locker in frustration. This turned out to be a mistake, as the locker swung back, hit the locker next to mine, and rebounded right into my forehead, causing Cristina Patterson, who stood across the hall from us, to laugh. This, of course, just made the whole situation even worse.

"Nothing, other than the fact that I grabbed Doc's bag again, and I don't have my Spanish textbook." Damn it. This was the third time I'd done this. My grandfather's bag looked exactly like mine, and I had a record of grabbing his bag, stuffing some of my books into it, and ending up at school with only half of the things I needed. This time I had ended up with Doc's personal journal rather than my Spanish text.

"Not like it matters," Paul said with a smile. "You don't understand the textbook anyhow."

"True," I replied. I pulled the journal out of my locker and blew the dust off the leather-bound cover. At least it was the same color as the Spanish book – a deep blood red. I shrugged. "I'll just bring it to class. Maybe Senora Caswell won't notice."

"That seems like an awfully big gamble," Paul replied, grinning. "Good luck."

Paul turned away, laughing at his own joke. I cringed, but shook it off. Paul Merrell had been my best friend since I was five, and he'd always been this way. He wore hand-me-down clothes from his brother, and they never fit his lanky frame like they should. His mom cut his jet-black hair for him, so he usually looked like he'd had a run-in with the business end of a weed whacker. He was also the underdog in a screwed-up family. His mother was rarely home, and when she was, she was asleep or ignoring him. Or forcing a haircut on him because she didn't want to pay for one. Paul's dad had disappeared several years earlier, leaving him at the mercy of a clueless mother and monster of a brother. He made up for these physical shortcomings with intelligence, a sense of humor, and an independent streak that bordered on suicidal. He also said what he thought – all the time – and cared very little about whether he hurt anyone. And that included me. Paul was even more socially awkward than I was. I had never figured out whether this bothered him or not.

I snorted. "You're a funny guy. I find it hard to believe that no one likes you."

Paul shook his head and shut his locker, then headed down the hall. I followed him to class, my hand in my bag. I was in for a tough time if the teacher noticed that I didn't have my book. But this was the third time I'd grabbed Doc's journal by mistake, and my mind flew back to his recent prolonged – and mysterious – disappearances. As long as I had a book full of his private thoughts, and nothing better to do…

Hey, I said I was smart. Not perfect.

2

My capabilities in Spanish had always been less than stellar. I wasn't stupid, by any stretch of the imagination, but fifty fruitless minutes of Spanish every day did little for my self confidence. It didn't help that the teacher didn't like me much.

An involuntary shudder ran down my spine as I entered the ugly classroom. It was painted mustard yellow, and the walls were littered with Spanish phrases painted on white cardboard cutouts. Colorful photos of matadors, castles, and Spanish villas decorated the walls haphazardly, many of them peeling at the corners. There was a large whiteboard on the wall at the front of the class, and a television sat atop a moveable metal table lodged in the corner. The desks were neatly arranged in four rows of five, and Senora Caswell's desk sat in the far corner of the room beside the whiteboard, where she could see everything that went on in the classroom, at all times. The room looked like every other classroom I'd ever been in – pretentious and over decorated.

I took my usual spot in the back, right behind Rachel Wheeler. My mission for the next forty-eight minutes was simple – I would try my best not to make eye contact with Senora Caswell, while trying to look as though I didn't care if she called on me. If she noticed me avoiding her eyes, she'd call on me for sure, and then realize that I didn't have my book. Then I'd be sunk.

"Hola class, como estas?" Mrs. Caswell asked. It was her usual greeting. Standard fare. No problem.

"Hola, muy bien," we all replied, emotionless. Now everyone in the class held their breath; the game of calling on students for individual answers was about to begin.

I began praying that she wouldn't call on me.

Spanish, and every other foreign language, had always been Greek to me. I was good at math, but I honestly couldn't take credit for that. I'd grown up with a physics professor as a grandfather, and had heard mathematical and physics equations tossed around ever since I could remember. My talent in that particular realm was purely a product of good genes and exposure. Then again, being good at it never made me love it. My real passion was history.

Both of my parents had been high school history teachers, and they had read to me endlessly about ancient civilizations, wars caused by power-hungry dictators, and battles that destroyed entire civilizations. My parents and I had done a lot together – fishing, camping, trips to the beach – but the nights when the two of them sat on the edge of my bed, reading tales by Shelby Foot about the Civil War, or Medieval novels by Bernard Cornwell … those were the memories that I treasured. Those were the times I missed the most, and they had colored my development. I was good at math and physics, but I was a history buff at heart, and no mistake. The blood and guts, the mystery, the adventure…

Unfortunately, I had to focus on my Spanish lessons at the moment. Senora Caswell wheeled the TV into the center of the room and announced in Spanish that we would be watching another episode of ***Senda Prohibida*** (***Forbidden Path***). It was a Mexican soap opera, and was supposed to teach us about their culture. Personally I thought the only reason we watched it was because Senora Caswell actually liked it.

At least it would keep me out of trouble, for the most part; no textbooks for watching a soap opera, after all. The television came on and half the class promptly dropped their heads onto their desks to go to sleep. Predictable as clockwork. I leaned back in my chair and flipped open my grandfather's diary. This was exactly the chance I'd been waiting for. I knew I probably shouldn't read the journal, but that certainly wasn't going to stop me.

Not that I was expecting much. Doc was a physics professor, after all. Pretty dry stuff. I figured I'd find some long equations that I couldn't understand, or a scribbled definition of a theory that would fly right over my head. I was quite surprised when I found a real diary entry on the first page.

The writing jumped right in, without any preliminaries, as though I'd come into the middle of a conversation in progress. What I saw shocked me.

June 3

My oldest and dearest friend, John Fleming, surprised me greatly earlier this week. He has asked me to view a relic that his son Nicholas discovered in the Middle East. I am by no means an archeologist, nor am I a treasure hunter as the Flemings are, so I'm not sure what to expect. I've been told that the object has symbols inscribed on the surface, which may be linked to the language of mathematics rather than linguistics. If this is true, I suppose that I am in fact better equipped than the average historian. That doesn't mean that I like it.

I'm looking forward to seeing John again, though. It's been a long time. I hope I'm able to help in some small way. And I have to admit at least a small amount of curiosity.

I frowned. This didn't sound like the Doc I knew at all. This sounded more like the plot of an Indiana Jones film. And a good one. What on earth was Doc into? I flipped the page over and read the next entry.

June 15

Met John and his son at Dartmouth College earlier this morning, at Nicholas' private research facility. It would seem that John's personal fortune has gone a long way toward funding his son's research! I doubt that the school knows about half of the equipment in this particular part of the building.

I snorted at this. My grandfather moved in a very specific crowd. All of his friends were physics geniuses, and like peas in a pod. Except that from what I could tell, some of them had more money than God. Evidently this John was one of those friends. Doc's finances were generous but were also a bit more … earthbound. I went back to the journal, smiling at the metaphor.

John and Nicholas signed me into the building and led me past two security checkpoints (I later learned that the security was more of John's private staff, which made me wonder), and into a basement. There I saw something that affected me in a way I don't think I can explain. I'm not sure whether words can express my feelings, but I'm absolutely determined to try. For the sake of my own peace of mind, if nothing else, and because I think that it may be important.

Two large black stones lay on the floor of the office. They were flat slabs of dark, glossy material, almost like obsidian, and possessed an other-worldly beauty. I don't mind telling you that they gave off a distinctly ... unsettling vibe. Each was marked in exactly the same way, and was exactly the same size – twice as large as I am, more or less. Large enough for a grown man to lie upon. It wasn't the size that drew me, though. It was the humming. The stones sang, as though they were calling out to me. My blood thrummed in my veins until I thought my heart would burst. Before I knew what I was doing, I had crossed the room to lay my hands against the first black stone.

The stone's touch electrified me, as I think I knew it would. The texture of the top was smooth to my fingers, polished to a fine finish. The sides and underside were rough, though, almost like sand paper, like the stones had been chiseled from a larger slab. Each stone had carved on its smooth face a set of characters – lines of unfamiliar symbols and signs. John was correct to assume these to be mathematical, although I couldn't have said what they meant. I thought for a moment that they resembled Mayan formulas I'd studied, and then the whole world blurred. The symbols suddenly began speaking to me, and revealing what they meant ... and the power they possessed.

I paused, took a breath, and went back to the start of the entry. Reread the words. This time I slowed down and concentrated on each word, to be sure that I was seeing what I thought I was seeing. The passage read the same way the second time. And the third. My heart skipped a couple of times, and I turned the page. I was skipping passages now, anxious to find out what had happened.

July 23

After all these years of research and speculation, we have proven my Ribbon Theory to be right. And in the most unlikely of ways! Of course I'm overjoyed, can hardly contain my excitement, and yet ... Nicholas' suggestion that we go public with this information ... that we consider actually using these Stones ... frightens me to my very core.

We have been over the information – the facts – at least a million times over the past few days. We've gone over what we know to be true time and again, and have a very rough idea of how the process works, how the ... jumps ... take place. But there is still so much that we don't know. So much that could go wrong. And if it did? I have to assume that it could mean the destruction of something very important, possibly time itself, and therefore our very world.

Nicholas, I'm afraid, can only see the fame, fortune, and ... power that the Stones represent. Of course that's what he sees. His father made his name and fortune seeing those very things, and now Nicholas wishes to make his own mark on the world. But at what cost? He's far too reckless for my liking, and I don't trust him. I'm afraid that he's spoken to others about his discovery, and I believe there's even a chance that he's sought buyers for these Stones. Internationally. John, of course, denies it, but I wouldn't put it past the man. Despite our long friendship, I've never been truly comfortable with his brand of ethics.

July 24

*Now that we've confirmed my Ribbon Theory, I've started working on something new. The question is, if time is a ribbon, bending back on itself, and there are windows through which one may pass, what happens when one does? More specifically, is there a time change between the two ... planes? I believe that there is, and I believe that I've found an answer to that question. The equation I've been working with is DT*C*365 (solar cycle) = TE.*

TE= Time Elapsed

DT= Duration of time (Present Day – Distance in past traveled)

C= Constant variable is .1440 (.001% of minutes in a day)

There are problems, of course. This isn't a true answer. The formula, although sound in its mathematical form, is still missing a variable that I can't quite understand. The Stones allow me to anticipate the approximate arrival of my comings and goings between present and past, and physics – mathematics – demands that there must be a reason for that. The equation should be the answer, and yet it doesn't quite work. It seems to collapse in short increments of time. Something is not quite right.

I shook my head, trying to clear it of that jumble of physics and mathematics, and drew back from the journal. What on earth *was* this? Was my grandfather actually losing it? This last entry certainly didn't encourage faith in his … rational mind. Though it fit in with some recent odd behavior. To say that Doc had been acting strange lately would have been an extreme understatement. He'd been constantly preoccupied. Staring off into space, talking to himself … I'd had full conversations with him, only to realize at the end that he hadn't heard a word I'd said. I thought at the time that he was simply having trouble with his hearing. That had been shocking enough, since I knew quite well that I could mumble a comment under my breath 20 paces away and he'd make a point of telling me what I said. As if he was proving how good his hearing was. I would bet a year's worth of physics homework that he could still do just that.

So that left two explanations for this so-called journal and his recent lack of attention. His seeming descent into absent-minded professor. One: it was some sort of creative writing exercise for a retired – and bored – physics professor. Two: Doc was going absolutely, certifiably, and irrevocably insane.

I looked up quickly to make sure that the TV was still on and that Senora Caswell was otherwise occupied, then bent back to the journal.

August 5

Today, everything went wrong. Nicholas insisted that I was withholding information from him. We have a basic idea of how the Stones work, but not why, or even when. I've told him that I do not have any further information, but he doesn't believe me. He believes, in fact, that I have better communication with the Stones than he does – which is true – and that I can manipulate them – which is not. For himself, Nicholas cannot fully read the Stones, and must depend on me for translation. This does not sit well with someone who is accustomed to getting his way in all things. When I told him, again, that I could not tell him how to jump through time, he lost his temper. John intervened, but not until Nicholas threatened me, as well as my family, if I didn't reveal the secrets of the Stones. To be honest, I believe that John wants to know as badly as his son, and held himself in check for as long as he could, hoping that I would reveal something. It's hard to convince both father and son that I don't know how the Stones work, when I don't know my own role in the situation.

On a side note, anyone reading this journal (I gulped, and had to stop myself from glancing over my shoulder) will notice that I have begun treating the Stones as proper nouns, with capitalization. I assure you that this is not a mistake, nor an oversight on my part. I do this intentionally, for the simple – or not so simple – reason that the Stones seem to me to be living, breathing, and even feeling entities. I do not believe that they are just slabs of rock. I believe that they are something ... more. What that is, I cannot yet say.

I slammed the journal shut, and sat staring at it for several minutes. As though that would make the words unsaid. Or reality less true. It was official: Doc was losing his mind. He actually thought he was living in some crazy sci-fi film. He was inventing conspiracy theories, and casting himself as the hero. Ridiculous. What would I find next, aliens attacking?

I realized that my breath was coming fast, my chest heaving, and forced myself to calm down. Fiction. It was all fiction. Something in Doc's imagination, that was all.

I still found myself holding my breath when I opened the journal again. Something about it…

June 23, 1481

I have done my best to reason with Nicholas, both in person and by messenger. I have tried everything within my power to bring him back. In return, he has made no less than two attempts on my life, that I know of. Dresden, as he is known here, continues to be convinced that I know how the Stones work. He has proven that he will stop at nothing to obtain that information. I do not know whether he plans to return to our time period. His last comments lead me to believe that he seeks to reshape the world to his liking, through the Stones. I have little doubt that the man has gone completely insane. I do not believe that I will be able to convince John of this. John is, as ever, convinced that his son is harmless.

I glanced at the date of the entry again. Did it really say 1481? What did that mean? What was Doc thinking? And what exactly was he into? I looked up, wondering, and noticed that Senora Caswell was looking directly at me. My heart dropped several inches.

"I hope you are following along, Cisco." She used my Spanish name, of course; a name that I'd found when I Googled 'Mexican Restaurants' at the start of the year. A name that I now found ridiculous.

"Si Senora … muy bien!" I said with an emphatic nod of confirmation.

I turned and pretended to watch the television show while I waited for Senora Caswell to direct her attention back toward the TV, and away from me. When the coast was clear, I opened the journal to the end and found the last entries. I had to know what had happened. In Doc's imaginary story, I mean. I needed to know exactly how far the delusion had gone.

July 2, 1482

Nicholas Fleming arrived in this world only seventeen years ago, by this time period's reckoning. In that short amount of time, he has managed to obtain the trust and loyalty of the York family, which in turn gives him direct access to King Richard's land, gold, and army. Nicholas, or Lord Dresden, has the opportunity to rewrite at least this part of history as he sees fit, by leading Richard to victory over Henry Tudor. It would eliminate the Tudor dynasty and a large part of England's history, and change the modern world irrevocably.

I am convinced that he's trying to find the remaining Stones, just as I am. I do not know whether he shares the same knowledge or connection as I do, though I can say that the last time we spoke, he did not. I do not believe that he shares his knowledge of the Stones with the York family, though I cannot be sure.

August 9, 1482

We have discovered a third Stone. It was in Carmarthen, as I foresaw. Lord Dresden's men arrived at the village first and fought hard to protect it, but we broke through the defenses and secured the town. Unfortunately, Dresden ordered that the Stone be removed before I could lay hands on it. He seems to be collecting the stones, though I do not understand why. I do not know where he takes them, or what he does with them. Unfortunately, his men also destroyed the village. It was burnt to the ground, along with the men, women, and children living there. I have felt the loss of the stolen Stone in ways that are difficult to describe, and the destruction of the town compounds those feelings. I feel as though a piece of me has died. What does this mean?

August 14, 1485

I landed in Milford Haven, Wales one week ago, with the bulk of my forces and those of Henry Tudor. We have less than two weeks to double our forces and confront Dresden, who rides with King Richard's army, to take the crown. The Battle of Bosworth is about to take place, with a new set of rules. Dresden will try to alter the outcome, for reasons I still do not understand. I have put myself in a position to block him. To balance the scales, so to speak. I can only pray that I am enough. Henry must win this fight. History depends on it. If we fail, I have little doubt that history, as well as the future, will fail with us.

The journal ended there.

I sat back in my seat, and let the breath I'd been holding whistle through my front teeth. There was a small gap there, and the sound of air rushing through the opening usually helped me settle down and figure out how to deal with a bad situation. I liked to think of it as one of my trademark moves – something I relied on to help me out of a tough spot.

This time, it didn't work. The thoughts that were rushing through my head flat out refused to settle, and they were carrying me with them in a virtual flood of panic. Was my grandfather truly losing it? If so, what did that mean for me, and for our life? And wouldn't I see more signs of it at home? Then again, maybe the signs were there and I was simply ignoring them. That didn't help much, because what kind of grandson did that make me? Ignoring my own grandfather, abandoning him when he obviously needed me to be stable. Was Doc going insane, or at the very least senile, without me realizing it? After reading the journal, I didn't think I needed any further proof, but what was I supposed to do about it, exactly?

The first bell rang and I looked up just in time to see Senora Caswell wiping a tear from her eye. That soap opera must have been terrific today. I should probably have some thoughts prepared about that, just in case. I tried to get my brain back in gear, but the class around me seemed suddenly … irrelevant.

"Okay class, make sure to read Lesson 6 by Wednesday. I'll see you all on Monday," Senora Caswell said in English. Most of the kids around me rubbed their eyes to wake themselves up and started to file from the room. Just another boring day, as far as they were concerned.

I closed the journal slowly and looked at the battered leather cover, then glanced at the dust that covered my hand. Something flitted across my brain, and I started putting pieces together. Slowly, at first, and then more quickly as the panic set in. How long had the journal been lying in Doc's bag? Long enough to collect dust, so several days. How much dust can you accumulate in a hotel room in downtown Ithaca? Had he been anywhere else? I'd heard Doc's pre-dawn arrival this morning, but had been too tired to get up and welcome him home. Now I wished I had. I glanced at the journal again, thought about the prospect of Doc traveling alone in this state of mind, and rose to stumble out of the room. The nightmare feeling that I was losing my grandfather stumbled after me.

3

I gripped the journal tightly to my chest as I walked toward my locker, then forced myself to stuff it into the bag. It wasn't like I was holding onto Doc, for God's sake. Though it almost felt like it. My head was swimming with all that I had just read, and for a moment I thought about simply going home. I didn't know if I'd be able to handle the rest of the day.

As usual, though, the world – embodied by my next class – had other ideas. We had a "surprise" quiz every other Friday in Physics, and I couldn't afford to miss it. I got to my locker, stuffed my book bag in, and grabbed my physics book and notebook. I was one of only two freshmen in AP Physics, and was pretty good at it, for all the good it did me on the social ladder. That didn't mean I would get away with being late to class, no matter what the family emergency. I closed the door on the journal firmly, and walked toward Physics.

"Good morning, Jason!" The voice echoed across the hallway before I got to the door of my classroom. I stopped, shocked, and turned slowly.

"What – what are you…?" I stuttered.

Paul, who had run into me after my abrupt stop, had no such problem. "Good morning, Doc," he grinned. He stepped past me, gave me a shove, and strolled over to shake my grandfather's hand. "What brings you here?" he asked.

"I'm here by invitation," Doc answered. He looked over and grinned at me.

I groaned. My grandfather, who I had called "Doc" ever since I could remember, was hard to miss at 6 feet 4 inches, and stood out in the hall full of high school kids. His appearance was even more imposing next to the teacher he was walking with – Mr. McGregor, my vertically challenged Physics teacher. My grandfather was also more impressive than any man I'd ever met before. He had an air about him that I had failed to inherit – the bearing of an old Hollywood star. He was thin, but fit and healthy, and had more physical energy than anyone his age had a right to. His solid, square jaw sat under a slight Roman nose on a face topped off with a thick crop of grey – always slightly disheveled – hair. The most notable feature, to me, was that my grandfather had very few wrinkles. He looked like he was about fifty, instead of his real seventy-one years. And he definitely didn't look old enough to be crazy. Not even slightly senile.

I finished my mental catalog of his appearance and shook my head. Of course, appearances could be deceiving. And a fit exterior didn't mean an able mind. I hadn't imagined what I'd read in his journal.

"I've been begging your grandfather to speak in my class for years. He was kind enough to accept my standing invitation this morning," Mr. McGregor said with a proud smile.

Paul, of course, was quick to jump to the point. "Sweet! Does this mean that we can forego the surprise pop quiz?" he asked.

Mr. McGregor smiled and nodded. "I suppose it does," he replied.

I groaned quietly. Doc, speaking in my Physics class? I would rather have taken the quiz, myself. Though I shouldn't have been surprised. Doc and Mr. Macgregor had been friends for years, and the teacher was a regular dinner guest at our house, staying up late to talk physics theories and philosophy with Doc. But having Mr. McGregor over for dinner in the privacy of our home was a hell of a lot different than having Doc visit Mr. McGregor in my class.

I grimaced and turned toward the classroom. If Doc was going to be lecturing in my class, this was going to be a tough day. After what I'd read in his journal, I had no idea what he was going to say – or how crazy it would sound – but I didn't really have much choice in the matter. The sooner we started, I figured, the sooner it would be over.

"Jason," Doc called, stopping me in my tracks. I turned slowly to see him advancing toward me. "Dinner this evening?"

"Yeah," I said, nodding. "I'll be home early." I wondered what that was about; I was always home for dinner, and he was coming with me to my Physics class. Was it really necessary for him to ask me about dinner *now*, in the middle of the hallway? I glanced around quickly, wondering how many people were watching us.

My grandfather nodded and smiled, ignoring my furtive glances at our surroundings, then gave me the "aha" look he used when he was trying to be subtle. He grabbed the leather book bag that hung by his hip and held it up.

"I almost forgot. It appears we got our bags mixed up again, young man." He chuckled and handed the bag to me. "We should really find a way to get more organized. Do you mind if we head back to your locker and retrieve mine?"

And there it was. That was why he'd come to school today. He knew I had the journal, and he wanted it back. Speaking to the class was just the excuse for coming after his bag. He might be venturing into some crazy theories, but he was certainly sane enough to know that he didn't want me – or anyone else – reading those entries. That left me wondering, though … did he realize that those entries were nuts? Or did he just know that other people would think they were? Where, exactly, was the line?

I shuffled my feet, thinking. "Um, can it wait until after school?" I asked, hoping to gain more time with the journal. I didn't want to read more, I didn't think, but I might change my mind later.

My question didn't sit well with Doc. His smile disappeared, and his face fell. He didn't look upset, precisely, but he did look worried.

He shook his head firmly. "I'm afraid not, but I promise I won't take long. Your locker's just down the hall anyway, isn't it?" His mega-watt smile returned at this seemingly simple solution to the problem.

"I, uh…" I stalled.

"I'm sorry, Jason, but I really must insist. I left something in the bag that's very important to me. I promised a friend I would retrieve it," Doc explained.

"Yeah, sure," I said, realizing that I'd lose if I tried to fight him on this. I turned around and led him back down the hallway, toward my locker. Suddenly I wondered whether or not I had already put the journal back in Doc's bag after Spanish class. Had I left it out? Bent any pages? Smudged the ink? Left any clues, in short, that I had read the thing? I thought I was safe, but I felt my palms beginning to sweat. What would Doc say if he found out that I'd read it? What would he do? Would it be better just to tell him that I had? Perhaps he could give me a simple explanation and put my fears to rest, once and for all. Then again, what if he couldn't? Or didn't?

By the time we got to my locker, my head was spinning. I reached in nervously, fishing around for the bag, and released a breath when I found it. I slid my hand into the bag to search for the journal and felt it there as well, present and accounted for.

"Here you go," I said with a nervous smile. I pulled the leather book bag out and handed it to Doc, journal intact.

Doc smiled with what I could have sworn was relief. "Excellent. How does pizza sound for dinner tonight?" he asked.

Paul chose that moment to step between us. "Pepperoni?" he asked.

I snorted. For the past two years, ever since Paul's dad left, Doc and I had played Paul's surrogate family. He didn't even ask permission to come over for dinner anymore. I didn't mind, of course, but sometimes I thought it would be nice to spend some time alone with Doc. Tonight might have been one of those nights. Then again, I thought ruefully, maybe spending time alone with Doc wouldn't be such a great idea. With everything I'd learned in the past sixty minutes, I was bound to be at least a little awkward around my grandfather. Having Paul around would lighten the mood.

"Of course Paul, I wouldn't have it any other way." Doc smiled and took the bag from me. "I'll see you boys tonight," he said. He gave me another look, as though he'd just remembered that he forgot something at home, and gestured toward our Physics classroom. "I've just remembered that I have an important appointment to keep. Can you boys let Mr. McGregor know, and give him my apologies? I'm afraid I can't stay to talk to the class today. I…" Instead of finishing, he shrugged apologetically. He turned and walked away before I could answer.

I watched him walk down the hall, and was still watching when he opened the leather bag and stuck his hand in. He must have found whatever he'd been seeking, because I could see his shoulders relax. It didn't take a genius to figure out what he'd found in the bag.

"Well that was strange," Paul observed, watching Doc as well. "Why would he tell McGregor that he could talk to the class, then suddenly change his mind?"

I grunted in response, not yet ready for conversation. Besides, I didn't have an answer for him. I couldn't exactly tell him the truth – that Doc hadn't actually come to school to speak to the class. That he'd come, instead, to collect his journal, which seemed to detail his mental journeys into the past. I watched my grandfather as he made his way down the crowded hallway toward the front door. He was easy to spot, at least a head taller than most of the students, and with a regal bearing that most high schoolers lacked.

"No idea at all," I replied quietly. It occurred to me suddenly that I didn't have a clue about a lot of things Doc did. Or at least the things he thought he did. I saw him first thing in the morning, and of course when I got home from school in the afternoon, but had no idea what he did during the time in between. I didn't know where he went lately, when he was gone for hours and even days at a time. It made me feel a bit lost, and more than a little suspicious. There was obviously more going on than I had ever considered. What those things actually were … well, that was what I needed to find out. As soon as school finished for the day.

The final bell rang, releasing us from seventh period, and I made my way upstream through the hall, navigating wave after wave of students to reach my locker, where I shuffled books from the locker into my bag without paying attention to what I was doing. My mind had already moved on to the night ahead of me, and my options. I'd been thinking about them all day, and now was the time for making a decision.

"Wait up," Paul said. He brushed up against me and threw his own textbooks into the locker. I turned to walk away before he'd finished, hoping to avoid the company.

"What's your hurry?" he asked, grabbing my arm before I could get away.

I didn't have an easy answer. I had a terrible need to get out of school, to a quiet place, where I could think and try to figure things out. I had no idea what I was going to do about anything yet, but I knew that I had to come up with a plan, and quickly. I couldn't get Doc's journal out of my head, no matter how hard I tried, and I wasn't going to be any good to anyone until I figured out my next move.

I couldn't say any of that, though, so I settled for a shrug. "Just ready to go home, that's all."

Paul grabbed his backpack and threw it over his shoulder. "Well, what are we waiting for then?" he asked brightly. He slammed the locker door shut and shoved past me toward the closest exit. I smiled and slid after him without answering. Paul might have been difficult, but he usually supported me when it counted. And if I didn't want to talk about why I was doing something, he wasn't going to make me.

We walked past Camp's field, then sliced our way along the dirt path that separated the football field from the soccer field. We always took a different route home than we did on the way to school – it took more time, but provided better scenery. I wanted to get home, but still didn't know what I was going to do when I got there, so I didn't argue with the path.

After a few minutes of walking in silence, Paul got tired of letting me be. "Hey, did you hear about the substitute teacher who took out Derrick's friend Hunter today?" he asked. I shook my head, but didn't answer. Derrick was Paul's older brother, and the biggest bully in school. Anytime anything happened to him or one of his friends, Paul gloated over it for at least a week, which meant that I would probably hear this story about ten times between our walk home and our arrival at the house. Still, it took my mind off Doc, and that was a blessing. I looked at him and lifted both eyebrows in encouragement.

Paul smiled, warming to his subject. "Yeah, I was there. Saw the whole thing. This Mr. Slayton is subbing for Fulton in History. It was amazing. This kid was shouting from the back of the room, just giving the sub nothing but crap. So the guy gets up, real smooth and no-nonsense, walks over to the kid, and makes his point. Ends up taking the kid's wrist and twisting it around behind his back." Paul breathed out in a low whistle. "Real Special Forces move, you know? Never even broke a sweat. But I swear he scared the hell out of everyone in the room."

"Impressive," I answered, despite myself. "That kind of move takes some serious skill. What happened?"

Paul snorted. "Hunter was mouthing off, as usual, and the sub wasn't having any of it. He walked up and said so, and Hunter actually took a swing at him. That's when the sub grabbed his wrist and twisted his arm around his back. Smooth and easy as you like. And get what he told the kid." Paul's voice dropped, to better imitate the teacher. "'Beating kids up on the playground isn't the same as taking a swing at a grown man. You're out of your weight class, boy.'"

I whistled in appreciation, and Paul nodded emphatically.

"I know, right? He towed the kid out of the room and directly to the principal's office." Paul finished the story triumphantly, as if it had been his own personal accomplishment.

"Sweet," I grunted.

We continued on in silence, considering the actions of the new Special Forces substitute, and heard a car pull up behind us. Turning, we saw two girls from our school sticking their heads out the car's passenger-side windows.

"Hey dorks, *catch!*" someone inside the car shouted, amidst heavy laughter. A plastic cup flew out of the car and landed at our feet. Before I could answer, the driver punched the car's accelerator and screeched away. We were left standing in a cloud of smoke and gravel, a puddle of Mountain Dew at our feet.

I looked down at my sneakers, disgusted.

"Well, that was classy!" Paul yelled at the quickly receding car. We heard faint laughter, but got no other response.

"Did you catch who it was?" I asked.

"Boothie was driving. Another charming friend of Derrick's," Paul replied, shaking his head. "Another gift from my lovely older brother. What an ass!"

"Still feeling so bright and shiny?" I asked, annoyed.

Paul snorted. "Of course. You're not letting those losers get to you, are you?"

I shrugged, but didn't answer, and Paul snorted angrily. "Forget them. Someday they'll be working for you. They don't have half your intelligence or drive."

I snorted back. I wasn't too worried about anyone working for me. I'd settle for just getting out of this town and doing something with my life. But I didn't think now was the time to outline that subtle difference. Even if I had, I didn't think that Paul was the type to understand what I was talking about. I was saved from the thought of explaining by the sound of another car slowing down behind us. I turned around, grinding my teeth and trying to harden myself against the insults I figured were coming.

I was surprised, though, to see a car I knew very well pulling up next to us. "Gentlemen, may I offer you a lift?" my grandfather asked. We were already almost home, but Paul and I jumped into the convertible without a word and sat down. My grandfather had screeched back into the road before we had time to put our seat belts on. He was always in a hurry to get somewhere, and today seemed to be more of the same.

We drove in silence for several minutes, watching the scenery fly by, before Doc decided to focus on us instead of the road.

"Did we have a good day today?" he asked cheerfully.

The phrase 'monumentally confusing' entered my mind, but I bit my tongue.

Paul nodded with excitement. "Yeah, there was a new sub in History, and he totally beat the..." His voice faded as we pulled onto Patriots Drive, where we lived, and came on a scene straight out of a cop movie.

"What the hell..." he breathed.

My eyes scanned the street and I nodded in wordless agreement. At least four police cars were parked in and around our driveway, along with a State Trooper SUV. Men in bulletproof vests and black jumpsuits lined the driveway and filed in and out of our house. Police tape covered our lawn, the black words "crime scene" stark against a bright yellow background. Above it all, the constant din of the police radio screeched in the background. I stared around, completely shocked. Everyone in our town knew that at least two police cars responded to every call – even if it was just a cat in a tree – but this was ridiculous. Unless the President of the United States was lying dead in our living room, there was no need for this many cops in one place at one time. Especially at our house.

Doc parked the car on the opposite side of the street to give us a moment. We watched the activity wordlessly, then started to slowly unbuckle our seatbelts. Before we could get out of the car, a cop came out of our house, looked in our direction, and turned to walk directly toward us.

4

The officer was young and overweight, and his legs looked to be both too short and too thin for his torso. In a less serious situation, I might have laughed at him. As it was, I just watched silently as he walked up, pulling a heavily starched sleeve across his sweaty brow.

"Are you Mr. Richard Evans?" the officer asked breathlessly. He placed his hand on the driver's side door and leaned forward until his head was halfway through Doc's window.

Doc leaned back slightly, his mouth turned downwards. "I am. What seems to be the trouble? I certainly hope that you people have a good reason for being in my house."

The officer huffed defensively. "I'm sorry, sir. We received a call from one of your neighbors. She reported some suspicious activity at your residence. It appears that someone broke in this morning."

"In broad daylight?" Paul asked, shocked.

My grandfather grunted and attempted to open his door. "Are they in custody?" he asked curtly. The cop stayed put, and Doc pushed against the door again, harder this time, and with an air of intensity that seemed rather ... well, odd. After several quick attempts, he finally dislodged the cop from the side of the car and climbed out. When the officer tried to block him off to finish his statement, Doc shoved past the man and darted across the street.

Paul and I watched in awe, then jumped out of the car and ran after him. Doc was standing in the driveway, gazing intensely at the house, when we caught up with him. The overweight cop waddled up a few moments later, grumbling.

"Unfortunately, sir, the perpetrators left before we arrived. We did get a license plate number on the vehicle, thanks to your neighbor."

Doc glared at the man, his face growing bright red with frustration, his mouth compressing into a grim line. I moved to stand in the space between him and the officer, worried about what he might do.

"Mrs. Grey," I said, glancing at my grandfather. Mrs. Grey was the neighborhood's busybody, and everyone here knew it. Nothing went on without her noticing, and she usually followed up with an opinion or advice. Sometimes both. Though the way Doc was acting, her attention was less than welcome this time. He looked like he wanted to pin someone to the wall and take shots at them with his new dart set.

He shot the officer another angry look and moved toward the house, evidently intent on getting in. I grabbed his arm and held him in place, then turned to the officer.

"May we go inside?" I asked quickly. I was freaking out; someone had broken into our house and gone through our stuff, and now the place was crawling with cops and who knew what else. I couldn't figure out why there was so much police action over a break-in. But Doc had already been inexplicably rude to this guy and the last thing I needed was for him to walk in when no one was expecting him and get arrested. Or shot.

Instead of accepting the white flag, though, the officer decided that he was going to play hardball.

"Actually, son, we're still working on our investigation." He spoke slowly and clearly, like he was afraid that I wouldn't understand him. My fists clenched in response, and I bit my tongue. This wasn't the time for brash actions.

Doc took a more vocal route and growled deep in his throat, leaning toward the cop as though he wanted to shake him. The cop backed up a step, startled, and looked toward the house for help. Another police officer appeared at the front door at that point, looked in our direction, and waved us forward.

The cop next to us coughed, embarrassed. "Okay, well it looks like you're free to go inside. Please take your time and look very closely to see if anything's missing." He paused and allowed a moment to pass. "I'll be back in the morning to take a police report, which you'll need for your insurance claim. Make sure that you're careful with that report or you'll have trouble."

Doc jerked angrily past the officer, and Paul and I ran past him to enter the house. As I darted through the front door, I looked back to see if Doc was following us, and couldn't find him. I shrugged, sorry for whoever had delayed him now, and turned to survey our house.

We passed quickly through the mudroom, where the bench, chairs, and coat rack sat undisturbed. My Wellies were still lying under the bench, where I'd left them the day before. For some reason, this made me even more nervous, as if this room's innocence predicted even worse for the rest of the house. I gulped and shoved past the cop standing in the mudroom doorway to rush into the kitchen. Doc had redone our kitchen two years ago, and it still had that sparkly, freshly painted feel. The cabinets were a sharp, clean white, and the countertops were sedate slate-gray granite. The oven and refrigerator were brand new, and white to match the cabinets. The colors lacked a certain creativity, and were definitely those of a confirmed bachelor, but the room always seemed orderly and clean.

Now everything in the kitchen was wrong. Pots and pans lay scattered on the countertop, and canned goods rolled across the floor. A broken bag of rice littered the stove. Stacks of dishes were spread across the kitchen table like decks of cards. All of the cabinet doors were left open to reveal empty shelves.

I turned around wordlessly, too shocked to respond. These were our things. Granted, they weren't overly valuable – food, glasses, dishes that Doc had owned since the '70s. But they were ours, and someone else had gone through them, tossed them around, and disposed of them. The sense of violation was overwhelming. It started to dawn on me that this might not be the safest situation. What if these guys were still here, waiting? If they could do this to our kitchen…

Paul had stepped ahead of me and gone into the den. "Holy crap!" I heard him say. I snapped out of my thoughts and followed slowly, unwilling to see what they'd done to the den, which had been my favorite room in the house.

It was in worse shape than the kitchen. This was our haven; the place where we kept our treasures. The walls were lined with floor-to-ceiling bookcases, complete with a sliding ladder (my idea). Doc's desk dominated the center of the room with its deep mahogany presence, and the worn leather chair he kept was older than me. Leather-bound history books sat next to physics tomes, biology texts, and the classics of literature, along with my personal collection of comic books and graphic novels. One shelf was dedicated to knick-knacks and figurines from our travels. The room had always been warm, cultured, and welcoming.

Its current state made me want to turn and run away. Every book, every figure, even our old globe had been ripped off the shelves and thrown into the center of the room. It looked like someone had been trying to build a campfire.

My heart lodged in my throat as I bent down to pick up my copy of ***Robinson Crusoe***. I gulped and set it back on the shelf, as if one book in its place could cancel out the chaos on the floor. Then we continued on into the living room. The shelves next to the TV had been emptied, their contents spread out in the middle of the floor. The three large oil paintings of our home in the winter lay on the floor. But the flat plasma television still hung on the wall next to the fireplace, and the stereo and DVD equipment were untouched.

"So they left the expensive stuff, and made one hell of a mess with the rest of it," Paul observed. "Why bother?"

I shook my head and looked down just in time to keep from stepping on the picture frame on the floor. Lifting my foot, I saw that the frame held a wedding photo of my mom and dad. I bent and lifted the photo, careful not to cut myself on the broken glass. Suddenly the break-in was even closer and more personal. Painfully real. I must have made some sort of sound, because Paul stopped in the doorway and looked back.

"Hey, are you okay?" he asked.

I shrugged, unwilling to admit how close I was to crying. "Let's just go upstairs," I said. I put the photo carefully on the coffee table and walked toward the staircase. This was no time to get emotional.

My grandfather's bedroom was the first room on the second floor. His door was open and the scene was more of the same – bedcovers stripped, mattress turned, and all of the contents of Doc's desk on the hardwood floor.

Paul glanced at Doc's room but didn't stop. Instead, he continued down the hallway toward my bedroom. His shout pulled me out of Doc's room and toward my own.

It hadn't been spared; everything I owned was on the floor.

"Someone was looking for something," Paul said quietly. "What could you guys possibly have that someone would want?"

I gasped. Paul was right, and I had completely missed it. Everything was on the ground, and in complete disarray. But I was willing to bet that everything was still here. They'd been looking for something specific, but hadn't had any idea where it would be. I wondered what it was, and whether they'd found what they were looking for. Then, for reasons I couldn't fathom, I wondered if it had anything to do with Doc's strange behavior.

"Maybe someone thought you guys were loaded," Paul said, interrupting my train of thought.

"Oh yeah, I can see why. Doc installed new gutters over the garage this summer," I replied sarcastically.

Paul laughed, but without any humor. "What a friggin' mess. I'll call my mom and tell her I'll be late."

I stopped going through my stuff and stared at him. "Why?"

"Someone's got to help you clean up," Paul replied matter-of-factly. He reached into his backpack and pulled out his cell phone.

I smiled in response, thanking whoever was in charge of these things for a friend like Paul. I wouldn't have considered asking him to stay, so the fact that he was volunteering meant more than he probably realized.

I turned from him to gaze around my room again, overwhelmed. Books were everywhere, and my desk drawers were emptied out on the floor. The mattress and box spring from my bed were upside down, and it looked like every scrap of clothing from my closet had been pulled out. I closed my eyes in disbelief, and turned to my bedroom window. I half expected it to be covered in graffiti or broken, but it was intact, and I moved toward it instinctively, wondering what had happened to the yard.

Everything seemed to be in order out in the yard, though, and I almost turned my eyes back to the room. Then a movement caught my eye. Doc was slowly walking around our garden shed, going over the walls with his hands. I did a double take. Was he looking for damage? On the garden shed? Before I could say anything to Paul, Doc grabbed the padlock on the door and unlocked it. He looked secretively over his shoulder, then disappeared into the garden shed. My jaw dropped. What on earth was he doing? And in the garden shed, of all places?

I turned back to the room, where I found Paul on his phone.

"Mom, I'm good… I'll be home in a few hours… Everyone is okay, I just want to help clean up… Yeah… Okay… Bye!" He hung up the phone and made a face. "She never cares where I am or what I'm doing, and suddenly she wants to know when I'm coming home. As if Derrick and I are going to sit down for dinner, say grace, and talk about our day." He shook his head in disgust. "My mother, ladies and gentlemen."

He finished his tirade and glanced at me again, registering the look on my face. "Hey, are you losing it on me? You haven't moved from that position in at least five minutes. You aren't catatonic with fear or something, are you?"

I didn't answer, but turned back to the window and waved Paul over. He got there just as Doc was leaving the shed. We watched as he closed the door and quickly replaced the padlock. He looked around again, presumably to make sure that he was alone and unobserved. In any other situation it would have looked staged. And corny.

I turned to face Paul. "Why in the world would Doc spend five minutes examining the contents of our garden shed before coming inside to check out what happened?"

"What?" Paul asked, looking more closely at Doc.

"Why would Doc care about four shovels, a bag of mulch, and some rakes? He went in there instead of coming into the house with us. The house, where we keep the valuable stuff. Don't you think that's a little … odd?" I asked.

Paul shrugged his shoulders. "I guess the man loves to work outside." He shoved me with his shoulder. "Maybe we should go help him out."

I nodded and watched my grandfather walk around the corner of the house. I didn't know what he'd been doing, but he'd lost the tension in his shoulders, and didn't look as grim as he had before. I guessed that meant that he was relieved, or at least satisfied. But satisfied about what? What was so damn important in the garden shed? From his actions, I was willing to bet that whatever was in there was also what certain people had been looking for. Or at least Doc thought it was. And judging from his obvious relief, they hadn't found it. Did this have anything to do with his journal, or was I letting my imagination take over again? This was all more than a little odd, but based on the already-odd day I'd just had…

I sighed. Too many questions and not enough answers, and that never sat well with me. I wanted to get to the bottom of this, and there was only one way to start doing that. I had to read the rest of that damn journal. Get a better idea of what Doc was up to, and how deep he was. Then maybe I could figure out what to do about it. That meant that I'd have to get my hands on it one more time, and tonight was as good a time as any.

By 10PM, the pots, pans, and dishes were mostly back in their proper places. The books, DVD's, and CD's were on their shelves, and the picture of my parents had a new frame. It had taken us six hours to put the house back in order, throw away the broken stuff, clean the floors, and make the beds. My sense of self was a bit scattered, and our house still felt a bit off, but at least things were back in place. We'd been too busy for me to put my plan into action, though I'd spent several hours planning how I would do it. When we were done cleaning, Doc ordered a pizza for delivery and Paul chose a movie: ***Close Encounters of the Third Kind***. It was one of his favorites – born of a lifetime obsession with movies – and he was thrilled to find it on TNT. It also gave us some much-needed distraction. Communicating with aliens via flashing lights was, if nothing else, a break from the complexities of the real world.

Two hours later, and well past midnight, the three of us stumbled upstairs to turn in for the night. Paul pulled out the mattress that lay beneath my bed, retrieved an extra pillow and comforter from my closest, and collapsed. He was asleep before I could say goodnight, and well before I got to my own bed.

Paul was like that – he could fall asleep anywhere, at the drop of a hat. He wasn't a pretty sight when he slept, though, by any stretch of the imagination. His mouth was always open, and he never closed his eyes all the way. He also snored. Not loud enough to wake me, but loud enough to keep me up if I wasn't really tired. Tonight, his snoring and my racing thoughts had me wide awake. I looked at the clock for the hundredth time at 2:15AM and sighed. Time to get moving.

"Now's as good a time as any, Evans," I whispered to myself. "Quit stalling and get it over with."

I pulled my legs out from under my covers and placed my feet on the cold floor, trying to avoid the squeaky board that always gave me away. Getting past Paul was simple; he was out for the count. Getting past Doc wouldn't be so easy. He slept lightly, and I was willing to bet that he was sleeping even lighter than usual tonight. I kept to the side of the hall and walked as slowly as I could, holding my breath as I crept past his room, and praying to any guardian angels in range. When I finally got to the stairs, I exhaled as quietly as I could, and made my way down to the living room.

We didn't have night lights in the house, but we'd never needed any. A lone streetlight stood just outside our home, right in front of our porch steps. The light, in my opinion, was twice as strong as it needed to be, and three times as annoying as any other light anywhere. Instead of illuminating the patch of street directly in front of our home, the damn thing lit up half the block. Light from the lamp poured through the kitchen and den windows all night, despite the fact that the blinds were closed and the curtains were drawn. It was absolutely impossible to sleep in either of those rooms, or get through them without casting shadows and drawing attention.

Tonight, though, that lamp was my best friend.

I made my way through the living room and den to reach the kitchen. Doc was brilliant, but he was also a creature of habit. And it made him easy to track. He always left his book bag in the kitchen beside the mudroom door, right next to the refrigerator. Unfortunately, I too was a creature of habit; my bag always sat right next to Doc's. Today hadn't been the first time that I'd grabbed the wrong bag or set of books in the morning. I had planned for this tonight though, and my book bag was sitting safely upstairs, in my room. Doc's bag was here, all alone. And what I sought was still inside. I'd checked on that earlier, when I came to get my bag.

I took a knee on the floor beside the book bag and glanced over my shoulder to make sure that I was alone. I knew that what I was doing was wrong. Trust was a virtue that Doc valued above all others, but this was important. I absolutely had to know what was inside the journal.

I took a deep breath and reached into the bag. There was the journal – right where it had been earlier. I let my breath out again, with both relief and fear, and pulled out the leather-bound volume. Reading this journal may or may not answer my questions about Doc's sanity. The bigger question, though, was whether I actually wanted to know those answers. Either way, something told me that I needed to read the book. *Something* was going on, and Doc knew at least part of it. I eased down to sit against the wall and stilled, listening. Just the groaning and creaking of our old home, though there was a deep thrumming coming from somewhere … a thumping in the ground, almost as though someone was playing heavy drums a few houses down. I paused, listening, and felt the beat enter my bones, and then my heart. Something was there, I could feel it, though I shook the feeling off. I thought I heard footsteps from upstairs, then, but decided that it was my overactive, guilt-ridden imagination playing tricks on me. I wasn't used to sneaking around like this, and my nerves weren't taking to it like I'd hoped they would.

For a second I thought about returning the journal and walking back upstairs. But only for a second. I was in too deep to back out now, and my curiosity would never let me sleep. Besides, now that I was here, there was no reason to let the opportunity go to waste. Nowhere to go but forward. I opened the journal to the beginning, resolute on reading it cover-to-cover instead of skipping around like I had earlier, and tilted it toward the light from the street lamp. Bending down, I began to read. Slowly at first, and then more quickly as the story caught me and held.

For over an hour and a half, time stood still. I read every word of the journal as it unfolded. I read many of the entries two and even three times, to make sure that I had it right. My heart raced the entire time. Not from fear of being caught, but from the story itself. I knew without a doubt that the journal was real, at least in my grandfather's mind. These were not the words or emotions of some creative writing assignment. Whether that meant he was losing his mind was a different question altogether. I still had my doubts about his sanity, but as I read, I began to believe, despite myself. What if he had found a way to do it? What if these happenings *were* real? But if it was actually going on … if the journal entries were recorded as fact, and not as the incomprehensible raving of an old man, then everything I thought I knew – everything I thought important in my life – had been turned upside down and inside out. This would rip apart the fabric of reality as we knew it, and the basic bindings of my everyday existence. I leaned my head back against the wall and closed my eyes. What in the world was Doc hiding? And did the break-in mean that other people knew about it too?

I felt rather than saw the presence of someone walking into the kitchen, directly across from where I sat in the mudroom. I gulped and opened my eyes, my thoughts frozen. My sixth sense hadn't lied to me. He was standing in the kitchen doorway, staring back at me.

5

A light blue minivan pulled into the Lebanon High School parking lot and rolled to a stop beside the beige sedan. The parking lot was dark and deserted for the night, with only one lone streetlight to illuminate the expanse of blacktop. It was well off the main roads, and away from prying eyes. The perfect place for a meeting of this sort. When the van pulled up, a passenger got out of the sedan and walked quickly toward it.

This man went by the name of Briegan. He had a runner's build – tall, broad in the shoulders, and thin in the waist. Certainly a person that appeared to take good care of himself, the driver of the van noted. He wore a pair of jeans, a loose sweater, and a pair of hiking boots. His hair was cut short and his eyes were cold, gray, and quick. They darted around the parking lot, taking in every inch and drawing conclusions about safety and security. He paused and straightened, then opened the van's passenger door.

"Anything?" he asked, climbing in. He settled himself down into the passenger seat, but maintained a stiff, formal posture. The lines around his mouth bespoke a tense, stressful life, with very little laughter to dull the work, and a deep groove ran between his eyebrows.

The man seated behind the wheel of the minivan had his Mets baseball cap pulled down tightly over his eyes. His light blue t-shirt was a size or two smaller than it should have been, and stretched tightly across a well-muscled torso. He had no outstanding features, nothing useful for identification. His face was that of an everyman – relatively attractive, pleasant, and easily forgotten. People who saw him in the market almost never remembered seeing him, and couldn't have described what he looked like afterward. He had been born with the face, but had worked long and hard to learn this subtle trick of disappearing in broad daylight. This was what made him so good at his job.

When he answered Briegan, though, his voice was low and rough – frightening rather than subtle. "We didn't find anything that looked out of the ordinary. Books, photo albums, CD's and DVD's, computer hard drive … you name it, we looked through it." The man shook his head. "We didn't take anything, but we didn't find anything either."

Briegan grimaced. This wasn't the news he'd wanted. "Were you spotted?" he asked. He looked out the window toward the poorly lit high school, as though he would rather be anywhere but with the man next to him.

"I'll pretend you didn't ask me that," the other man growled.

Briegan nodded. "I appreciate your patience. I wouldn't have asked, but my employer is paying us both well. I need to be sure that we're doing all we can, and in the absolute best way. This is not a mission that allows for failure."

The man grunted in agreement. "Perhaps we would have had more success if you'd been more specific," he noted dryly. "'A diary of some sort' isn't exactly … descriptive."

Briegan snorted. "If you'd needed more information, obviously I would have shared it. All I've been told to share is that there's a journal, and that it has important information in regard to the old man and something that he might possess. My employer learned this directly from the … contact, so we have no reason to question the information."

The man behind the wheel smiled. "Is this a government job or a real government job?" he asked sharply.

"Excuse me?" Briegan replied.

The man grunted, unwilling to respond.

Briegan turned from the high school to fix the other man with his gaze. The conversation turned deadly serious, and the other man sunk further into his seat. Briegan worried him, and he wasn't interested in making trouble with the man.

"You're not paid to be curious, or ask questions. You're paid to get results," Briegan said quietly.

The driver of the van nodded and cast his eyes down. He didn't know exactly who Briegan worked for, but he knew that it was a powerful organization. He couldn't afford to be too cavalier. "Yes sir. So what now?"

"Watch the house. Follow the old man," Briegan said. He kept his gaze on the other man, pinning him to the seat with his eyes. The driver of the van didn't have to ask – the look promised terrible punishments for failure.

"And the boy?"

Briegan looked back to the school. "Nothing for now. We don't move against the boy until we're told to do so. At this point, we don't think that he's involved or … important to our mission. We need the old man, his journal, and whatever else he's hiding in that house." He got out of the van and closed it firmly, ending the conversation.

6

A gasp of air exploded from my mouth like a gunshot, and I gulped another down. Paul. It was only Paul. He stood in the doorway with his eyes wide open, staring at me. Following his gaze, though, I realized that he was actually looking at the refrigerator. I started to say something, then remembered that Paul had a habit of sleepwalking. At the most random times, and for the oddest of reasons. He had told me once not to wake him up, as it just confused him, so I watched quietly and tried to calm my pounding heart.

Sure enough, Paul walked right past me and opened the refrigerator door. He grabbed a bottle of orange juice, took off the cap, and chugged nearly half the bottle, then put it back on the top shelf. Before I could move to stop him, he'd shut the door, turned, and disappeared back into the living room. A few minutes later I heard him stumbling back upstairs.

I shook my head, thankful that sleepwalking didn't run in my own family. Talk about inconvenient. Paul had done me a favor though, and snapped me out of my trance. The hours had flown by, and Doc was an early riser. It was high time to get this journal back where it belonged, before I really got caught. I'd read all there was to read, and couldn't get any other answers from the book itself. The next step was going to have to be a bit more … active. I slipped the journal back into Doc's book bag and made sure to leave both the book and bag exactly as I remembered finding them. I didn't know whether Doc kept track of things like that, but there was no harm in being careful and covering my tracks.

As I made my way upstairs and crawled back into bed, I allowed the argument to take shape in my head. Facts. What were the facts? As the grandson to a physicist, and son of two historians, I knew that the truth – the real story – always started with the proof. So where to begin? I still couldn't believe that what I'd read was real. No proof there. But the other option – Doc going stark raving mad – was just as bad. My mind and heart both refused to believe it. My instincts, those surreal feelings that had always guided me before, were in turmoil. I wanted to believe Doc, wanted to allow the possibility of his story. The dreamer in me wanted to believe that it could be true, and something deeper was pulling at me, telling me to accept the story. The real question was whether that was the right move, though, or just more wishful thinking and denial.

After what felt like hours of arguing with myself, but was probably only moments, exhaustion overtook me. I felt that humming again, and it began to lure me into a stupor. I dropped into a fevered, disturbed sleep, and dreamt of ancient armies, time travel machines, and losing Doc to both.

By noon on Saturday the house was, for the most part, put back together again. We'd finished organizing and moved on to cleaning. Nothing was missing, so it looked like the thieves had missed whatever they were seeking. Not that Doc was admitting anything of the sort – he maintained that we were lucky they hadn't taken anything, and left it at that. The garbage cans, though, were full of broken glass, frames, CD cases, and light bulbs. We even threw away the old globe, which had cracked in the chaos. Paul finally left around 2 that afternoon, though he made it clear that he would return later that night to check on us and make sure that we were okay.

It was downright gorgeous outside, but I was in no mood for sunshine or singing birds. Instead, I retreated to my bedroom and cranked out my physics homework. I wasn't looking forward to the work, but I needed a distraction, and the painstaking logic and step-by-step process of physics was the most distracting thing I had available. I lost myself to it, and then went on to the final act of Shakespeare's ***Richard III*** for English Lit. By 5PM I'd put in three solid hours of work and was paying the consequences; my stomach was protesting, my head hurt, and I was bored out of my mind. I got up, stretched, and walked down the stairs and into the kitchen, toward the mouthwatering smell of food.

I paused at the dining room table and looked down. "Three plates? Are we expecting someone?" I asked quietly. I didn't want to startle my grandfather, still unsure how much I trusted his sanity. If I scared him, I thought, there was no telling what he might say or do. And I wasn't prepared to deal with that quite yet.

Doc turned from the stove, where he'd been stirring some sort of sauce. "Out of hibernation I see," he answered with a smile. "Yes, actually, my old friend John Fleming is going to join us for dinner. Have I told you about him? We were best friends from grade school through college. Absolutely inseparable. We've been close ever since."

John Fleming … I knew that name, though it took me a moment to remember where I'd heard it. Then it struck me – this man featured largely in Doc's journal, along with his son Nicholas. They had taken Doc to the infamous stone, and started the entire chain of events. The question was, though, whether this John Fleming was actually real. Did he truly exist, or was he part of the imaginary world of the journal? I had never heard of or met the man, which seemed odd, especially if he and Doc were so close. Did Doc really expect someone to show up? I didn't think I could handle sitting down for dinner and watching Doc talk to an imaginary friend.

"Does he live far away?" I hedged, wondering about this imaginary best friend.

"He lives in Woodstock, so not very far at all," Doc replied. He walked past me and placed three wine glasses on the table.

I took a breath and asked the question foremost in my mind. "Why haven't I met him before?"

"Excellent question," Doc replied. He shrugged casually. "Unfortunately I can't give you a very good answer. We both have busy lives. A poor excuse, I'm afraid."

I grunted. That response was a little short on the detail, and didn't answer the question at all. Hardly an assurance about this John Fleming's existence. I walked into the den and looked out the window, thinking, then did a double take.

"Someone must be lost," I mumbled, staring.

"Why's that?" Doc asked from the kitchen.

"There's a limo parked outside," I replied.

Doc gave a shout. "Ah! That would be John."

I looked back at Doc in shock, then turned back to the window. So this John Fleming was real. And rich. My curiosity went up several notches, and I went to answer the door.

Doc's personal-recipe pot roast was great.

The company was slightly … odd.

I was happy to see that Mr. Fleming was, in fact, real. According to Doc, he and Fleming were the same age, though I never would have guessed it. Doc was tall, fit, and lean, while Mr. Fleming stood several inches shorter and carried a good 60 to 70 pounds more than his frame required. He was going soft around the face, and looked worn out. And his behavior seemed off, like he had a secret that he didn't want to tell, or didn't actually want me there. I had the distinct feeling that he wanted me to leave him alone with my grandfather, though I had no intention of doing so. I didn't trust the guy.

I wondered again why I had never met this man before. I'd lived with Doc for nearly three years now, and had never heard of John Fleming. Was Doc keeping him secret for some reason? Did he and Doc have some sort of sordid past? And what about his involvement with the infamous stone? Doc's journal had an entry about how he distrusted both John Fleming and his son, and now the man was here in our house. Were we in some sort of danger? Why was he here now, suddenly having dinner with us?

One thing was obvious – they weren't going to talk about anything even remotely interesting. The conversation ranged from playing baseball in Shepard's Park when they were kids to remembering old friends who had passed away. As the evening wore on and the shadows outside grew longer, the conversation between the two became very stale. After two and a half hours I had lost interest in Mr. Fleming's arrival, and completely forgotten about the journal. I was bored out of my mind, and beginning to wonder if dinner would ever end.

Doc glanced at me and coughed. "Jason, you look distinctly unhappy. Do you have plans?" he asked.

I jumped at being directly addressed, then flushed. "I was going to go hit some golf balls with Paul, but it can wait," I lied.

Doc chuckled. "Why should it? If I were fourteen years old, I wouldn't want to sit and listen to two old men talk about their sixty-year-old exploits and triumphs. Take off and make sure to thank Paul again for his help." He waved his hands in my direction in a shooing motion, giving his blessing.

I didn't wait for him to repeat himself or change his mind. I stood up so quickly that my chair fell over, and rushed to the other side of the table to shake Mr. Fleming's hand. "Itwasnicemeetingyou, sir." I could hear my words coming out in a jumble, but I was beyond caring.

"Son, the pleasure was all mine, I assure you," he answered, his mouth turning up in a faint smile.

Nodding, I turned and left the room. I grabbed my golf shoes on the way through the mudroom and slid my baseball cap on, then darted out the front door. Twenty feet down the street I realized that I'd forgotten my golf clubs and skidded to a halt. Paul and I didn't actually have plans to play golf, but the excuse wouldn't hold up if I didn't make it believable. I turned and ran back toward the house.

Like most basements, ours had both indoor and outdoor access. This always came in handy when I wanted to get in undetected. Or avoid more boring conversation. I ducked past the front door, raced around to the side of the house, and opened the bulkhead door to the cellar. I had stashed my golf clubs down here at the start of the winter.

Our basement looked like any other basement in New England. A wood-burning stove sat at the far end of a large, open room, and exposed concrete walls matched the floor's stark gray surface. The room ignored the concept of 'décor' for the most part, the one exception being a painting of five dogs playing poker. This was a purely functional area. No one came down here unless they were searching for something or looking for a place to store it.

For this reason, the basement contained a strange array of goods: three bikes, two bags of salt for the winter, an unused weight set, kitty litter – despite the fact that we had an outdoor cat – and roughly three thousand cardboard boxes in various sizes. Three small, thick windows sat at the top of the outer wall, complete with a lot of cobwebs, and a set of several vents ran into the walls of the house. These allowed heat from the wood-burning stove to rise up and dissipate throughout the main building. They also, of course, carried noise from the basement up into the house. And vice versa.

I swear on all things holy that I didn't mean to hear the conversation between my grandfather and Mr. Fleming. I suppose I could have tuned it out if I'd been so inclined. It was such a stroke of luck, though, that I couldn't ignore it. Given Doc's recent behavior, listening to a suspicious conversation should have been the first thing on my list. I wasn't a natural spy, though, and I hadn't thought of it. Now I got my answers through so much dumb luck.

"Jason reminds me of my granddaughter, Tatiana," Fleming said. It was the first thing I heard, mostly because of the radar that always detects your own name being mentioned. I froze, thinking for a moment that he was in the room with me, and glanced around for him. Then I spotted the registers and realized what I was hearing.

"How is she holding up?" My grandfather's voice became hollow and supernaturally deep as it echoed through the registers.

I put my golf clubs down and moved quietly toward the nearest register, where their voices were emerging.

"Better than I am. She's tough like her mother, God rest her soul."

The two men remained silent for a moment and I reached over to lift a box of Christmas ornaments away from the register. This, I wanted to hear.

"You're sure it wasn't discovered?" Fleming asked now, lowering his voice.

I pricked my ears and leaned closer. Lowered voices were harder to hear, but they were also more intriguing. Lowered voices meant secrets. And – perhaps – answers to my questions.

"Yes, John, I'm sure," Doc replied. His voice sounded suddenly very tired.

"We can't keep this secret forever, my friend. Even from our families. I'm afraid it's only a matter of time," Fleming said. "This break-in confirms that someone out there already knows."

My breath caught in my throat. So the robbers *had* been looking for something. And this John Fleming character knew all about it, and thought that we might be in danger. I thought back to Doc's journal entries, and the pieces started to fall into place. Doc let out an exaggerated sigh, as though he were annoyed with his friend's concern, and had heard it all before. He must have made some sort of gesture, because Fleming changed the subject.

"What's my son been up to?" he asked unhappily. "Have you seen him lately?"

Doc paused for a moment before answering. "He's trying to crush Henry Tudor's army."

At that, my blood ran cold. This was exactly what Doc talked about in his journal, and just served to confirm my worst fears. Fleming was in on it, then, and was either leading Doc on intentionally or involving him in some very risky business. Neither possibility made me very happy.

"Well I already knew that," Fleming answered. "Has he acquired another stone?"

"No, and you don't sound very concerned about my declaration," Doc replied, frustrated.

"Change the outcome of the War of the Roses and make the end of ***Richard III*** inaccurate," Fleming said with a trace of amusement. "I still don't understand why you're so concerned. It's secondary to our true objective of bringing Nicholas home."

"It's more than that, John, and you know it," my grandfather snapped. "We've been over this before. Nicholas, for reasons I can't begin to fathom, seems to be hell bent on distorting history and recreating it in his own image. We cannot let him succeed! It would jeopardize our entire world."

"What happens if he does?" Fleming retorted, too quickly. "We may, in fact, be better off with a different version of history. Henry VIII was not a nice man. He killed hundreds of his own people, not to mention a few wives. And what his offspring did to the country ... to Europe as a whole..."

Doc groaned, as though he'd repeated this conversation more times than he could count. I wondered at the argument, and at Doc's frustration. If this man was one of his best friends, why were they fighting this way? Why was this Mr. Fleming causing so much tension, making himself intentionally so difficult?

"You're not hearing me, John. That is not our decision to make. We don't have the right, and we don't know what will happen if we attempt to exert such influence. Nicholas is taking us down a path that will destroy us all. Henry VII and his line led England out of the Dark Ages. When he took power, England found peace under one monarch for the first time in nearly eighty years. Henry's line, and the various wives involved, made great strides in art, music, literature, and science. Much of the country's Enlightenment occurred as a direct result of this war's outcome. I'd hate to think what would have happened if things turned out differently." By the end of this speech, Doc's voice was ragged, hoarse with strongly felt emotion and belief.

"Beyond that, what are the repercussions on the world, on time itself?" he continued. "If history suddenly changes course, our entire reality will change in the beat of a heart. Will the world survive this sudden change in direction? Will we?"

Fleming had gone quiet. He evidently didn't have an argument for that bit of logic. I couldn't believe what I was hearing, although possibilities were flooding through my brain. My grandfather and one of his close friends were sitting in our kitchen discussing how to manipulate Henry VII's future. As easy as discussing the weather. I was historian enough to know the man's importance to history, and the possible repercussions of his death. His line led directly down to Queen Elizabeth, and from there to almost every good thing in that country. Not to mention the future of our own. This meant … I released a quiet breath. Either the journal was telling the truth and our entire world was in danger, or both of these men were destined for the loony bin. Part of me was starting to believe that the journal was real. All of it. But I wasn't quite ready to admit it yet. Not without proof.

Finally Fleming spoke. "What else is it, Richard? I know you well enough to know that something else has you worried," he said.

"He's a well-educated man, John." My grandfather paused to take a deep breath. "And he went back prepared. I've heard rumors that he's already introducing Richard and his troops to advanced techniques in metallurgy."

"Metallurgy? You mean guns? He wants to make guns?" Fleming asked. This must have been news to him. His voice was now quite serious.

I heard someone reach into what I assumed was a paper bag, and something heavy clanked onto the table. For a moment, no one spoke. I held my breath, locked into a conversation I could only hear. What was on the table? I drew closer to the register and stared at it, as though I'd be able to see through to the table above me.

"We found these on several of the defenders in Abergavenny," my grandfather finally said. His voice was low, and unutterably sad.

Fleming grunted. "Fifteenth-century soldiers had crude forms of firearms," he said. "Perhaps this is one of their own making."

A gun, then. My grandfather had found a gun in fifteenth-century England. Fleming was right – they had existed, in limited forms, but…

"True, but cartridges didn't," Doc said. I heard something hollow drop onto the table, as though Doc had scattered several nuts across the surface. A long pause followed his words.

"But why?" Fleming asked quietly.

I didn't have to see my grandfather to know that he answered with a slight shrug. He used it anytime he ran across a problem to which he didn't have the answer.

"He's sick, John. He's trying to change the path of history. If given time and allowed to succeed, he'll push the technology of warfare forward, to a society that's not ready for it, and the results will be catastrophic."

The two remained silent for a moment and I sat, stunned. I had tried to convince myself that I was misunderstanding, at first, but the more I listened, the clearer it became. At this point, all signs pointed to these being real events, rather than some elegant farce. I couldn't image two grown men discussing something so seriously if it wasn't important. And I definitely couldn't imagine Doc going into such detail over something that was a figment of his imagination. He spoke with the emotion and knowledge of a man who was intimately involved. But how did it actually happen, this jumping through time?

And when would it happen again?

Doc interrupted my thoughts. "There's something else I need to tell you, John. It won't be easy to hear."

"How much worse could it get?" Fleming asked quietly.

I moved closer to the register, intent on the lowered voices and what they were saying, and leaned in. I had to be careful not to brush against any boxes in the basement; this was my chance to hear the truth about what was going on, and I wasn't going to waste it. I was moving carefully for a second reason, too – for all I knew, sound traveled up to the kitchen just as easily as it traveled down. Any noise might signal to Doc and Fleming that they had an audience, and end the conversation. This worried me enough that I'd been holding my breath throughout, hardly daring to exhale.

I was settling into a more comfortable position next to the register when something suddenly grabbed me from behind. I felt claws dig into my back and pull at my shirt, and sat up too quickly, scared out of my wits. The box underneath me gave way and I fell to the floor, grunting, then rolled to my stomach. My eyes flew around the room, searching desperately for my attacker. Who was down here? Were they going to give me away, or was it one of the men who had broken into our house? As I thrashed on the floor, our cat Milo walked self-importantly from behind the box and gave me a wide feline stare. I released my breath in a soft laugh, both at myself and at the situation.

The cat. Of course, it was just the cat.

"Damn it Milo, you scared the hell out of me," I whispered. I turned back to the register, wondering how loud we'd been. If Doc or Fleming had heard that ruckus…

"Nicholas has a son named Sloan. He's about the same age as my grandson," Doc was saying.

I sighed in relief. They hadn't heard me, then.

"So I'm grandfather to a child that's roughly five hundred years my senior. Fascinating," Fleming said sarcastically.

Doc grunted.

"And your plan, how is that progressing?" Fleming asked.

"The gold you gave me has equipped me with an army equal to the task of stopping Richard's."

I grunted. This, I had read about in Doc's journal. He had gone back looking for a way to stop this Nicholas character, and fallen into the perfect situation: a title without an owner, easy for the taking. Along with a small fortune, a couple of castles, and a large army. The Earl of Oxford had died in his twenties, without an heir, and his estate had fallen into chaos. Doc had purchased the title and *become* the Earl of Oxford, according to his account. Now he was using his position as the Earl of Oxford to support Henry Tudor's bid for the throne. Against Richard III and this Dresden character. Standard fare for England in the 1400's, I supposed.

I realized suddenly that Doc and Fleming were still talking, and leaned toward the register, unwilling to miss any of the conversation.

"But I have researched this man," Fleming was saying, bewildered. "By all accounts, he lived into his seventies. One of the oldest noblemen in the Lancaster bloodline."

Doc laughed. "I've read the history books, John. The old versions and the newer versions. I did my research before I went back."

"So you're telling me that if you didn't go back in time, John De Vere, the Earl of Oxford, would not have existed?" Fleming said incredulously.

"He would have existed. But not as we know him today," Doc replied.

"So if you or my son had not gone back in time…"

"The Earl of Oxford may not have registered in the history books. At least not in the way he now does. He would not have thrown his lot in with Henry Tudor. But, as the history books now read, the Earl is the only reason that Henry Tudor defeats Richard III to become King of England."

My head spun. I was familiar with the story, of course. We'd read about it the month before in History. Henry had been a bastard claimant to the throne of England, and had traveled over from France, gathered an army, and taken the throne for himself. The Earl of Oxford had supplied the bulk of that army, if my memory was right. That was the history I had read, and I knew to be true. Was my grandfather actually claiming to be that earl? Claiming that he had helped – or would help – Henry Tudor become King of England … hundreds of years ago?

Fleming was having as much trouble as I was, from the sound of it. "Does that mean that we already know how the Battle of Bosworth turns out?" he asked. "Do we know that you – and Henry Tudor – will defeat Richard and Nicholas? That's how history now stands, isn't it?"

"Unfortunately, no. The conclusive battle between the York and Lancaster clan is set to be re-fought, based on the changes Nicholas and I have made to history already. Its outcome isn't … set." Doc paused for a moment. "The ribbon of history is still moving forward. There's a good possibility that the history books may be rewritten. Again."

"Simply unbelievable," Fleming said in little more than a whisper.

I gulped in agreement. The two grew quiet and I took the opportunity to stand up and walk around for a moment. But my knees buckled before I went far, and not because I was tired. I was overwhelmed with excitement, fear, and disbelief, and still couldn't wrap my head around the idea. If Doc was telling the truth, which I now believed he was, that meant that a mad man living in the 1400's was about to destroy the world. I wasn't sure whether that was better or worse than the reality of Doc losing his mind. I did think that it was infinitely more dangerous. If, of course, I truly believed it.

"Richard, this entire situation concerns me. Yesterday's break-in confirms that our secret is getting out. You must realize that whoever broke in was after the stone, or you." Fleming cleared his throat. "That said, you are my oldest friend, and I worry for you. I've taken the liberty of hiring someone to help you. You're doing so much, and I hope that you'll allow me this one small token of … help."

I heard the sound of paper changing hands, and silence reigned for a full minute. I assumed that Doc was reading whatever it was Fleming had handed him.

"Why? I don't require a body guard. I get along quite well by myself, and I'm better at self-defense now than I ever was before. I don't need protection," my grandfather finally replied.

"I would note that yesterday's events say otherwise," Fleming answered quietly. "And think beyond yourself for a moment. You have family again, and you're sitting on the historical equivalent of a nuclear bomb buried under Fort Knox. People, corporations, historians … entire governments would do anything to get their hands on that stone. And on you as well. I know people like this, Richard, and they wouldn't think twice about hurting your grandson to get what they want."

My fingers clenched on my jeans at that, and my whole body grew tense. Governments … wanting to get to Doc? To me? Wanting to get a hold of what Doc had? This stone … the break-in. Pieces of the puzzle were crashing together so quickly that I almost missed Doc's response.

"Jason. You believe that he's in danger?"

"Look around you," Fleming replied. "Think, man. Use your brain."

"I don't know, John."

"I hope I'm wrong, Richard, but can you live with yourself if I'm right?"

Doc let out a long breath. "A body guard, then. For Jason. Agreed. When will I meet him?" Doc asked.

"You've taken on boarders in the past. It's the perfect cover for having a strongman in the house. He'll drop by tomorrow, and stay. He'll remain as close as possible to you and your grandson. He already has his orders."

"Does he know about the..."

"I haven't told him anything about that, and I would suggest that you keep quiet about it as well. It appears that too many people know already."

Doc grunted in agreement. "You're right, I don't want anyone else involved. And that includes my grandson. What do you suggest I tell him? You seem to have planned everything else for me."

"Just looking out for my dearest friend. You spend too much time with your head in the clouds, and forget to take care of reality. Rather, you spend too much time in the past, and forget to watch the present. I'm simply taking care of it for you. Tell Jason the truth – you've taken on a boarder. A nice guy who needs a place to stay. You've got the room, and you can always use the money."

There was a long pause, and then the scratch of chairs against the floor. Someone stood up.

"I'm glad we can at least agree about that, Richard. Now, I believe I've had as much as I can handle for one night. Your new roommate will be along tomorrow. I spared no expense; the man is the best at what he does, I assure you." Fleming cleared his throat, then continued. "Richard, if there's anything else I can do ... I realize that we disagree on some points of this plan, but if I can help at all..."

Doc laughed, though he didn't sound happy. "You've done enough as it is. You've spent a fortune."

Fleming let out a rough laugh of his own. "I've unleashed my son on the world and turned your life upside down in the process. Put you in jeopardy, and your grandson as well. I am no hero." He paused. "When are you going back again?"

"The next window opens on Monday morning. I'll go then. I hope that this will be my last time," my grandfather answered.

"I have no right to ask you this, but if there's any chance to save my son, any way to make him see reason..." Doc must have shaken his head, because Fleming stopped mid-sentence.

"He's not coming back, is he?" he asked quietly.

Doc cleared his throat before he spoke. "John, I've tried. You know that I've tried. I don't know what he's doing, or why. But I truly believe that your son has made his decision. And I think that his actions are probably going to change the course of time."

I waited until Doc and his friend left the house, then stumbled up the stairs to the surface. The vibrations in the ground were back, and it was freaking me out. They beat through my body, and made me feel likeas though my heart wasn't my own. It also felt as though something was calling to me. I didn't know what it was, but I didn't like it. I wanted to get away from the house, as quickly as possible. The basement opened up on the side of the house, so I didn't have to worry about running into them in the driveway. I looked around anyhow, wary of any sign of my grandfather, and quickly started the short walk to Paul's house. My mind was reeling, and my knees didn't want to support my legs. The passages in the journal might just be real. Doc might not be crazy, but completely sane. And shockingly casual about the reality he faced – government conspiracies, break-ins, a hypersensitive historical secret. A gateway into history. And a madman intent on taking advantage of all those things.

While my mind raced through the dangerous possibilities, and my place in the situation, my feet found their way down two blocks and over to the next street. I arrived at Paul's house without any memory of getting there, and found him in the yard raking up the leaves.

Paul glanced up at my dazed face, then did a double take. "What's wrong with you?" he asked.

"I just heard the most unbelievably bizarre conversation of my life. And the scariest part is that I believe it's 100 percent true."

Paul raised both eyebrows in surprise. "I assume you're going to give me a bit more to go on."

"I overheard my grandfather talking to a friend of his a few minutes ago."

"And..." Paul paused, waiting for an answer.

"Give me the most outrageous thing you can think of."

"Like you actually hooking up with Beth Alger?" Paul asked. He smiled at the joke, but his grin died when I didn't smile back.

"Not even close," I muttered. I proceeded to tell him everything, my words coming quicker as I talked. I started with the journal and went on to my conclusions, then pulled that into Doc's unexpected visit to our school today. I described what I'd heard in the basement. Every word of it. On the walk over, I'd decided that I couldn't handle something like this on my own. It was too big. Too complex, regardless of whether it was true or not. I needed Paul's quick mind and easy logic. Most of all, I needed his support. And I thought I might burst if I didn't tell him quickly.

"I don't know what to do," I finished, fifteen minutes later. "But I think that I have to do *something*."

Paul stood back and nodded his head, cataloguing the diatribe. He took several minutes with it, his eyes on the ground, in the trees, anywhere but on me. I held my breath, wondering if he was going to believe what I'd said.

Then he smiled again. "Time travel would not have been my first guess. I think you got me on that one."

I shook my head, but felt a reluctant smile tugging at the corner of my mouth. "Well at least I caught you off guard. But what am I going to do?"

Paul threw his arm around my shoulders and tugged me back toward my house. "I have absolutely no idea. But we'll figure something out. We always do."

7

Doc watched his friend's limousine drive out of view, then turned and made his way back to the kitchen table, where he sat down heavily. He poured himself a cup of coffee from the carafe and leaned back in the comfortable chair. His conversation with John Fleming had brought up a range of unwelcome emotions. When first introduced to the stones, he had thought that they promised proof of his Ribbon Theory, grand adventure, and an opportunity to touch the world as he never had before. To know the truth about what had happened in history, not just opinions distorted by time and personal bias, but actual fact. Now … everything had happened so quickly over the past three and a half months that he hardly knew what to think. For him, time had lost all meaning. Rather, it had taken on a whole new meaning. The most recent trip had marked nearly seventeen years spent in the past, though it had been only four months here. He still didn't understand the time conversion, though he was working on it. Either way, it meant that he had spent years in the past, compared to only months in the present. In many ways, he felt more comfortable there than he did here, at this point. There he had men, an army, power … a mission. There, he was working to save the world. Here, he was just another retired professor. A smart one, but still no one important. These were things that he could not explain to John, no matter how many times he tried. The confusion, the responsibility, the exhaustion…

Doc took another sip of coffee and examined the porcelain cup closely. This small teacup, so simple and unimportant, was just another example of something he'd always taken for granted. Something that John Fleming still took for granted. Simple forms of wealth. He looked around the small kitchen, noting the refrigerator, stove, and coffee maker. Integral parts of everyday life in the present, and yet people had survived quite well without them, once. Once, things had progressed without that technology, according to a natural order.

The old man closed his eyes for a moment and took a deep, steadying breath. Everything was so different in the past. John thought that he was asking simple questions: how is my son? What is he doing? Can he be saved? Yet the truth … the truth was far from simple. Nicholas Fleming had changed his name to Lord Dresden several years ago, and had long forgotten his father and family. He, too, had stepped into a position of power, and used it to manipulate and twist those around him. He wanted to manipulate time itself, to serve his will. Doc hadn't been able to uncover the man's ultimate plans, but even if he did, he knew that he'd never be able to explain them to John. He also knew that he'd never be able to save Dresden. The last time the two met – the last time Doc had tried to save him – Dresden had almost succeeded in killing him. Doc closed his eyes and remembered. On that day, he'd thought that his luck had finally run out.

47 MILES SOUTH OF YORK, ENGLAND
MAY, 1481

It was raining, but the heat rising from the ground made central England feel more like the South Pacific. The forest, which had received twice as much rainfall as usual in the past two months, was choked with overgrown brush and mud. Tree limbs flush with leaves arched skyward, creating a heavy canopy. The resulting gloom made following the small path nearly impossible. The Earl slapped at an insect the size of a small bird and cursed fifteenth-century travel, wondering about his decision to hunt down Lord Dresden. Then he shook his head. Second-guessing himself was becoming a bad habit, and it would get him in trouble at some point.

Suddenly Trigva brought his horse to an abrupt halt and held up his right hand. All forty-seven of the Earl's men followed Trigva's lead, and the column came to a shuffling halt. For nearly a minute no one spoke or moved, while Trigva remained rigid and vigilant, listening.

The Earl took the moment of silence to put his emotions in check. As the leader of the men he had to remain calm, no matter the situation, no matter the place. No matter how fiercely he questioned himself. He glanced up at the treetops, and saw that the clouds had moved on toward the south. Water continued to spill off the leaves, giving his men – and their horses – no respite, but at least they would get no more rain.

A twig snapped to his left, and he jumped. He had been warned on numerous occasions not to venture this deep into Chelmsford Forest, but on this occasion he'd had little choice. Sometimes risks had to be taken, the request of a friend had to be met. Sometimes blood had to be spilled. Fleming had asked him to save his son, and he felt that he had to try. Just once more.

After several minutes of waiting, the old warrior legged his horse forward several feet to reach Trigva.

"What do you see, my friend?" The Earl pitched his voice low, knowing the danger of the situation.

Trigva kept his eyes on the path in front of him and continued to listen, alert for any change in the scenery. "We're being watched, my Lord," the large Dane replied quietly.

The Earl said nothing, though the hair on the back of his neck rose. Trigva was only telling him what he'd already realized – in trying to do the right thing, he'd walked right into a trap. There would be no escape from this forest. Not without bloodshed. He tried to look into the woods, but could see only swaying branches and tree trunks. He didn't have Trigva's senses as a tracker, and could hear nothing more than the hollow sound of the wind passing through the leaves and rushing over the path. Trigva's instincts were uncannily accurate, though, and the Earl hoped that his lieutenant knew where the enemy was. This man could smell trouble a mile away, and had saved his commander more than once.

"Dresden?" the Earl asked, speaking more to himself than to Trigva.

"Someone," Trigva said with certainty. He continued to stare into the trees.

"Why don't we –"

The Earl's words were broken by a sharp whistling as arrows suddenly sliced through the air. A horrific scream sounded through the forest, and the Earl turned to see one of his men grab his chest and tumble backwards off his horse. Before he could register what had happened, another arrow cut through the evening air to rip through leather, cloth, and armor, and bury itself in the rib cage of one of the squires.

"SHIELDS!" the Earl shouted instinctively. He reached over his knee to grab his own wooden shield and pull it from the saddle. The heavy object came up to cover his chest and head just before another volley of arrows arrived. He felt the impact of at least four arrows as they met the surface of the shield.

"DISMOUNT and COVER!" someone shouted from the back of the column.

Horses screamed in panic as the men shouted warnings to one another. The Earl swung his leg over to dismount, but felt his horse stumble and rock back under him. The mare thrashed and began to fall, two arrows lodged deep in her neck. She was dead before she hit the ground.

The Earl jumped free of the animal as she fell, and found two of his knights already at his side. They grabbed his arms and ran for the cover of the forest, shielding his body with their own, and holding their shields before them.

When they got to deeper cover, the Earl saw that most of his men were already there. Trigva, along with several other knights, organized the soldiers, while the medics – new to this world and trained by the Earl – tended to the wounded. Arrows continued to rain down on the Earl's men for several minutes, peppering the path that they'd just traveled. Then they stopped, quite suddenly. No one moved or breathed. The trap was sprung, but now they must wait on their enemy to show himself.

The Earl crouched with Trigva, waiting for Dresden's next move. The fall had unsettled him, and he was breathing heavily. He'd just started to relax when a voice boomed through the trees.

"Richard!"

The Earl cringed. Hearing his twenty-first-century name in fifteenth-century England could mean only one thing. Lord Dresden. His worst enemy, and the man he'd been asked to save.

"Come out, come out, wherever you are, Richard!" the voice mocked.

"There my Lord! A white flag," one of the Earl's men said. He pointed toward the far end of the path, where the trees swallowed up what little light remained. A white handkerchief swung slowly in the wind, a sign of peace and good will. *Or trickery*, thought the Earl.

"They want to talk," Trigva said skeptically. He looked at the Earl, his face full of suspicion.

The Earl nodded. "It's Dresden. He wants to speak with me. Alone, it would seem." Privately, he wondered what kind of game Dresden was playing. He knew better than to trust the man. His one-time associate was full of deceit, and cared only for his own goals and power. He had refused to meet numerous times in the past. Why was he willing now? And why in this manner?

The Earl rose to his feet, sweat pouring down his back and sides, and considered the path before him. The situation. The repercussions. Finally he decided that he had little choice in the matter. His men were surrounded, and wounded. Some of them were dead. As their commander, it was his job to save them if he could. Even if that meant risking his own life.

He walked to one of his men and accepted his horse, nodding once to the man. Reaching one hand up, he rubbed the horse absently on the nose, then mounted and turned back to Trigva.

"How far back was the bridge we crossed at the river?" he asked.

"Perhaps as much as a full thirty minutes, my Lord," Trigva replied.

"That's if you follow the path my friend," the Earl said. He looked past Trigva to the hill on his right. "Find a faster route to the bridge, and then think of a way to get the men out of here. Quickly." He smiled faintly. "I will try to give you as much time as I can, but I cannot guarantee that I will be joining you. I do not trust this situation, and fear that I may be walking into a trap. Wait as long as you can. If things begin to get ugly, run. Save yourselves."

Trigva nodded, unquestioning, and the Earl turned and spurred his horse forward, toward Dresden's waiting horsemen.

Doc shook himself out of his memories. And particularly bad memories, at that. That day had nearly cost him his life. The peace flag had been a trap, as he'd suspected. Men had descended on him as soon as he'd entered the woods. They had seized his reins, dragged him from his horse, and blindfolded him, then led him, shaking, blind, and cursing, to Dresden.

The scene itself was no worse than Doc would have expected from the man. Dresden had accused him of terrible things, insulted his family, asked him questions he couldn't answer, and finally threatened his life…

Doc shook himself again, and heaved a sigh. He had escaped, though it had cost him the lives of several of his most trusted men. Men that had laid down their lives willingly for a man they hardly knew. He shook his head in wonder before his mind turned back to the image of Dresden. That man didn't forgive, and he didn't forget. Doc couldn't be caught again, because Dresden would be more careful, more brutal, next time. This time … this time he had to win. He had to finish things, because he wouldn't be going back again. He had promised himself that much, and he always kept his promises.

8

"Would you please leave it on one channel?" I snapped, my eyes struggling to adjust to the television screen. Paul was rolling through all two hundred-plus channels again and again.

I, on the other hand, was doing what I did best – drawing up a list of facts. Things I knew to be true, at least as far as I was concerned. Doc was into something heavy. It was definitely dangerous, and not only for him. From what I could tell, the entire world as we knew it was depending on his success. I might be quiet, and I might not speak out in class if I didn't have to, but I wasn't stupid. And I sure wasn't the type to sit back and watch while someone else had an adventure or did something monumentally stupid.

Doc had said he was jumping again on Monday morning. Today was Sunday, so that meant that I had only one day to come up with a plan. Paul's obsessive channel changing wasn't helping me think. I wanted to be alone, or at least in a quiet environment, to lay out the facts and figure out what my next move was.

"There's nothing on," Paul complained.

"Paul, you're not helping me here. Remember all that stuff I just told you about? All that jumping through time stuff? I'm trying to figure out what to do about it. And you're worrying about what's on TV?"

Paul grunted. "You know, buddy, I've been thinking about that. Don't you think it's all a little strange?" He turned down the TV and looked at me. "I don't mean that your grandfather's crazy or anything like that, but don't you find the whole situation a little … farfetched? Maybe you're a little too quick to believe in fiction. Reading too many comic books, these days." He grinned.

I felt my mouth tighten in frustration. Paul was my best friend, and I loved him like a brother, but some aspects of his personality really drove me crazy. This was not what I needed from him right now. I needed him to take me seriously, not play devil's advocate. Or joke.

"What exactly do you mean?" I asked quietly.

Anyone who knew me knew that I was generally pretty easygoing. I didn't fight with people, didn't usually throw around threats, and almost never got angry. When I did, though, I got very quiet. It was something I'd inherited from my mom, who'd had a hot Irish temper, and had trouble keeping it. She'd never shouted, though. A drop in her voice was how you knew you were in trouble.

Paul evidently missed my voice, though, since he kept going. "I just think you should chill, that's all." He turned the TV back up. "Watch some TV. Return to reality. Forget about all the time travel crap. There's no way it's true, so why bother thinking about it?"

I sucked air through my teeth to give myself a moment to settle down. Then I counted to ten. When my anger still hadn't cooled, I held my breath for twenty seconds. Paul was just trying to give me good advice. Trying to be a friend, and help me settle down. Calling my grandfather's story into question was the wrong way to do it, given my defensive reaction, but…

Before I could find a reply to Paul's statement, someone hammered on the door.

Paul and I stared at one another for half a second, then jumped up and ran toward the front door. Doc had been reading the paper in the kitchen, and met us in the mudroom.

"Must be that new boarder," he said, smiling. He tucked his newspaper under his arm, and the three of us made our way toward the front door together.

Paul got there first, and swung the door open. "No way," he mumbled quietly. "Mr. Slayton?"

At the name, I stopped next to Paul and stared. Mr. Slayton? The Special Forces sub Paul had told me about? What was he doing at our front door?

"Yes. Have we met?" the man asked, puzzled.

"Boys," Doc said, nudging the two of us aside, "where are your manners? Please come inside, Mr. Slayton." He opened the door wider and stood aside to let the man in. "I'm sure the boys don't mean to stare." He gave us a quick, hard glance, and we both looked down.

The new boarder stepped past us and set down his bag, then turned back. "Thank you, sir, and please call me Reis." He smiled and turned to Paul. "Now I remember you. History class, fifth period, right?" He held his hand out.

"Yes sir," Paul replied. He accepted the offer and shook Reis' hand, then turned to me with a dumbstruck look on his face. "This is that substitute I told you about." He looked toward Doc. "He's been filling in for Mr. Fulton, Doc."

Doc chuckled. "Ah, a man after my own heart. Nice to meet you, Reis." The two men shook hands.

I just stared. So this was the guy John Fleming had hired to watch after us. More precisely, to watch over me. Keep me out of danger. Presumably, then, to get in the way when I wanted to do something. I didn't trust John Fleming, and didn't really know what he had to do with my grandfather's situation. I'd had a long talk with myself about this body guard person, and had already decided that I wouldn't trust him, wouldn't let him in. He was here to guard me, and that alone rubbed me the wrong way. Beyond that, though, this guy was taking his orders from Fleming, and if I didn't trust Fleming, then I couldn't trust his employees.

So I was shocked when that little voice inside my head – the one that always judged someone as good or bad, within five seconds of meeting them – started telling me that I could trust this guy. Reis had a genuine, relaxed charm about him. He looked around confidently, assured of his place, but didn't look down on us like he could have. He smiled warmly at me in greeting, nodding gently in my direction. His easy manner made me feel like I'd known him for years. He looked to be just over 6 feet tall, and had a lean, hard physique; the type of muscular body I'd always wanted and would probably never have. He had dark green eyes, short blond hair, and a small scar on his left cheek. I thought he was in his late twenties until I looked into his eyes. Those eyes had seen too much to be that young. I'd never met a Special Forces guy, but if I had, I was willing to bet he'd have had eyes just like that.

Damn, I thought. I'd been so ready to hate this guy. And instead, here I was already liking him, and trying to figure out where he'd been. So much for making my mind up ahead of time.

"Listen, I really appreciate you guys letting me stay here," Reis was saying. "I'm new in town, and I don't know anyone. Looks like I might be here for awhile, so I hope this works out."

"Well, you come highly recommended, and this house is obviously large enough to accommodate all three of us." Doc glanced at Paul. "Well, sometimes four. But Jason and Paul effectively share a room." He grinned at Reis and leaned down to pick up his bag. "I've got your room all set up. Let me show you where it is."

Reis' hand jumped out to stop Doc's. "I've got it sir, if you don't mind." He bent over to retrieve his bag himself.

Doc shrugged. "Sure. Do you have any more luggage?"

Was it my imagination, or did Reis' mouth harden just a fraction? I blinked, and looked again; if I'd seen a change, it disappeared as quickly as it came, because he was smiling now.

"I have a couple others, but I can get them later. I generally carry my own bags. Personal quirk. Is it okay to park on the street?"

"Oh, that's fine. But we also have plenty of room in the driveway, if you want to park there. It's totally up to you." The two of them made their way back through the mudroom, through the kitchen, and out of view.

I shook myself and closed my mouth. I felt an odd urge to follow Doc and Reis to spend more time with the man, but restrained myself. I'd be seeing plenty of him, and I wanted to gather as much information as I could first.

"That's the guy who manhandled the kid in class?" I asked.

"Yup."

I whistled. "I believe it. He certainly knows how to fill up a room. I wouldn't want to mess with him."

"Told you," Paul quipped.

"It's weird, though." I shook my head. "I like the guy. He seems … like a good guy, I guess." Then I laughed. "Man, this is getting stranger by the minute. Last week I was worried about my Physics midterm. Now I've got a body guard."

"It's bad ass," Paul replied with a smile.

"I'm glad you think so. Except now I also have to worry about people trying to kill me because my grandfather travels back in time to stop a madman who wants to change history. I have enough people after me that I need a body guard."

Paul shrugged. "I have to admit, this does help your story. I don't want to believe it, because it's crazy, but this Reis character showing up…" Paul shook his head. "Well let's just say that's one hell of a coincidence. Sort of clinches it, I guess." I got the feeling that Paul didn't want to admit what I already knew. I didn't blame him – once you admitted that the crazy story might be true, it was a little hard to deal with. Still, if he was starting to consider it, then that meant that he was on my side.

"No joke." I paused. "One thing's for sure, though. There are still too many questions. This is one piece of the puzzle, but there's a lot more. We need more answers."

"What do you have in mind?"

"When Doc was talking to Fleming at dinner, they talked about there being a stone here. If there's one here, then that's where it all starts. And I want to see it with my own eyes," I replied.

Paul snorted. "Well that'll be a neat trick. You don't know where it is."

"Actually, I've got a pretty good idea," I said.

"Then let's go," Paul replied. He took a step toward the door.

I shook my head and grabbed his arm. "No, Doc can't see us searching. He doesn't want me to know about it, which means I have to find it without *him* knowing that I'm looking. He leaves in the morning, and I want to know what's going on before then. We'll go tonight, when everyone's asleep."

"Thank you for coming on such short notice, Mr. Slayton," Doc said, watching as Reis laid his green canvas duffel bag on the bed.

"Please, sir, call me Reis."

"Of course, of course. As long as you'll stop calling me sir." Doc smiled. "I must admit, Reis, that this is all a little unexpected. I'm not used to having a…"

"Body guard?" Reis finished with a reserved smile.

Doc nodded. "Exactly."

"Well, Mr. Fleming has paid me a lot of money to make sure that you and your grandson are safe. I don't know why he thinks you're in danger, but his convictions are very strong."

Doc nodded again. "You must understand, Reis, that my personal safety means little to me. My grandson's safety, however, means everything. The only reason I'm agreeing to John's plan is that I think he may be right about the danger. I didn't want to believe it, but I'm afraid that I may no longer have a choice."

Reis took a deep breath. "Doc – may I call you Doc? – Mr. Fleming was awfully vague about why he felt you were in danger. I realize that there are things you might not want to tell me, but knowing what I'm up against –

and who we're fighting – would sure give me a better shot at doing my job."

Doc studied Reis for a moment, then nodded slowly, having made his decision. Something about the man made him feel that he could be trusted. And as long as he was going to be protecting Jason, Reis was right – he needed to know everything. Regardless of John's reservations.

"Well, Reis, I suppose you might as well know. I can hardly keep it from you, and it may help you at some point. The fact is, I'm in possession of an object that allows me to travel back in time. Unfortunately, there are others who know about these objects. And others who use them. One of these men is in the past now, attempting to derail history for his own – questionable – reasons. I'm the only one who can use the objects to stop him. In short, I've been entrusted with the fate of the world. John Fleming believes that this fate may bring my grandson into fairly ... unique danger."

Doc stood absolutely still as he finished speaking, and watched Reis carefully. What would this man do? Believe him? Ridicule him? Storm out? After all this time, to tell someone the whole truth, without censoring the facts, and expect belief...

Reis stared back blankly for several seconds before shaking his head. "Listen, Doc, I didn't mean to offend you by asking the question. If you don't want to tell me the real reason that I'm here, you can just say so."

Doc snorted, then barked with laughter. He didn't know whether Reis truly didn't believe him, or was acknowledging and accepting the situation and secrecy with a code of his own. Either way, it appeared that the secret and the stones – and Jason – were safe for the moment. He nodded in relief, smiled, and strolled casually out of the room.

Behind him, Reis sank slowly onto the bed and began to breathe again. He watched Doc leave the room, closed his eyes briefly, and turned to unpacking.

9

I rolled over and looked at my alarm clock. It was past midnight – 1:14AM. That was it, it was time. I hadn't slept a wink all night, waiting for this, and I wasn't going to wait any longer. I reached for the pretzel that was lying on my nightstand and threw it at Paul, who was sleeping at the foot of my bed.

He jerked awake when the pretzel hit his forehead. "What the hell?" he grumbled.

"It's time," I whispered as softly as I could.

He groaned and cracked one eye open. "I'm up, I'm up. I hope you appreciate this."

I laughed. Paul was complaining now, but he'd been beside himself with excitement when I first told him about my plan. Paul loved an adventure more than anyone I knew, and as far as he was concerned, doing it in the middle of the night just made it better. We got up and slipped on our sneakers, which were sitting ready next to my door. I opened the door as quietly as I could, and poked my head out into the hallway, listening. Dead silence, though the house was half-lit with the shine from that damn street lamp. Most importantly, the hallway was empty. I had half expected Reis Slayton to be standing guard outside my room, and was relieved to see that he wasn't. Luckily, his room was on the opposite end of the house, away from the stairs. I didn't think he would pose any problem to our plan. Doc's bedroom, on the other hand, was directly between my room and the stairs. And his door was wide open.

I paused. Doc never slept with his door open. Why tonight, of all nights?

If he woke up and saw us, it would throw a very large wrench in the works.

Paul and I glanced at each other, then took a couple of steps forward. The squeak of a floorboard reverberated through the house, and we both froze. When nothing happened, we crept forward again, sticking to the walls and stepping carefully.

"Like walking on explosive eggshells," Paul breathed quietly.

I glared at him and pressed my finger firmly to my lips. If we got caught now, just because he'd felt the need to make a clever remark…

I got to Doc's door and peeked around the wall. Inside, my grandfather's comforter rose and fell with his slow, steady breathing. Still asleep, then. I darted past the door, and motioned for Paul to follow me. We descended the carpeted stairwell as quickly as we could, nerves rattled but intact, and sprinted through the living room and kitchen. In the mudroom I stopped, collapsing onto the bench in relief. It was working. We weren't out into the shed yet, but we were almost out of the house. So far, the plan was going exactly like I'd hoped. I'd honestly expected to be caught by now, though, so the thought of actually going forward was a bit daunting. Still, that was what I had planned to do, and turning back wasn't an option. I breathed slowly, trying to collect myself.

Paul glanced at me. "What are you doing?" he hissed.

I grimaced at being caught. "Nothing, I … nothing," I finished lamely. "Let's go."

We grabbed our coats and the flashlights I'd left out, opened the door, and stepped into the night.

"Holy God, it's freezing out here." Paul's breath turned white and foggy as he spoke, and I shivered.

He was right – it was cold, and indefinably spooky. The air was dense with mist, and a full moon above turned the entire world white. The thick air muffled our steps and crept down my throat. I couldn't see a thing. I could feel a slow, steady pulse around me, and didn't need my sight to know where we were going. I'd heard that beat before, and I knew what it was now. It was leading me forward, toward the garden shed.

"This way," I whispered.

Paul stifled a yawn. "This all seemed like such a good idea when we were inside…"

"Shut it, Paul," I grunted. "Doc's leaving in the morning. I want to know what's going on, and this is my only chance to find out."

We stumbled forward, tripping over rocks and bushes in the fog. It was a wonder that we didn't wake up the entire neighborhood, with as much noise as we were making. When we finally reached the garden shed, I handed Paul my flashlight and reached for the combination lock. Doc liked to keep things consistent, and I knew from experience that he only ever used one combination – my dad's birthday. The lock clicked open the first time I tried, and I pushed the heavy door inward.

"Looks like a regular old shed to me," Paul said. He handed me back my flashlight and we ventured inside.

Our flashlights shone quickly along the floorboards, walls, and ceiling. Dusty and unused, with a generous scattering of cobwebs and a spider or two, but nothing appeared to be out of place. Or out of the ordinary.

"What exactly are we looking for?" Paul whispered.

I shook my head. "I'm not entirely sure. I'll start looking at the floor boards, you concentrate on the walls."

"The walls?" Paul asked skeptically. "What am I supposed to do with *them*?"

I ignored Paul, who talked too much when he got nervous, and looked around. There was nothing here. "It must be under the shed itself," I said quietly, thinking out loud. It was the only possibility. I dropped to my knees and started poking at the wooden planks of the floor. The pounding in the air, or in my head, got louder.

Paul walked toward the back of the shed and began to move things out of the way while I crawled around on my hands and knees, periodically blowing the dirt and sand from between the floor boards to find any trace of an access door. After a few minutes, I stood up and brushed the dirt off my pajamas. The two of us looked at one another, lost.

Paul spoke first. "I'm freezing. What makes you think it's hidden in here anyway? Maybe it's in the garage."

I shook my head. I knew we were looking in the right place. It was in here, somewhere. "Remember Friday afternoon, when we came home? You and I went right into the house to look around, but Doc made a beeline for the shed. It didn't make sense at the time, but now … It's got to be here somewhere," I said. I looked around in frustration. I couldn't tell him about the further proof – the sounds, or feelings, or signs, or whatever they were. The bone-deep knowledge of the stone, and the fact that it was here. "We're just not looking hard enough –"

I stopped talking in mid-sentence, overcome with a sensation I had never experienced before. I was dizzy for a split second, and then a cold chill ripped through my body. The hair on my neck and arms rose, and my stomach dropped. Everything grew familiar, as if I were having a deja-vu moment, and it stuck. I knew exactly where the stone was, and how to find it. I knew, because it was calling to me. Giving me directions.

"Are you with me?" Paul asked. He directed his flashlight to my face. "You okay?"

I nodded and pointed toward the back of the shed. "I know how to find what we're looking for. That empty peg next to the rake."

"Yeah? What about it?"

Without bothering to explain, I took three steps past Paul, reached up, and placed my hand on the empty peg. "You'd probably better move," I said, looking at his feet.

Paul glanced down and shuffled back several steps. I waited until I knew he was far enough back before pulling the peg down. When I pulled it, a small door dropped quietly open, creating a 2-foot hole in the center of the floor. A ladder led down into the darkness below.

"Holy crap." Paul redirected his flashlight onto my face. "That's a real James Bond move. You knew that was there the whole time? Why'd you wait so long to open it?"

I shrugged, coming out of my trance-like state. "I didn't know… until now," I replied.

Paul paused for a moment, then shook his head. "Whatever," he mumbled. "You're starting to creep me out." He turned his flashlight down to the hole in the ground and coughed. "So, uh, who goes first?"

I straightened up. "I'll do it. It's only fair. Keep your light on, though. I don't want to fall."

When my feet hit the ground a couple minutes later, I looked up at the trap door. "Okay, your turn," I called up. I heard a moan, and the creak of the ladder above me. In less than a minute, Paul was by my side.

"What is this place?" he asked breathlessly. We were in a dark underground room, much smaller than our basement. The room was lined in thick concrete blocks. There was no light coming from the outside, and I guessed that the room was probably soundproof as well. Not a room built for entertaining. A room built for keeping secrets.

Paul found a cord in the ceiling and pulled it. We both jumped as several light bulbs clicked on and flooded the room with harsh artificial light. The light revealed a small metal desk with an old wooden chair against the back wall. A computer monitor and hard drive sat on top of the desk, along with several pens and pencils and one red three-ring notebook. Beside the desk stood two wooden bookshelves, filled to bursting with books. Next to those, a large map of England was taped to the concrete wall.

I ran my eyes over the map to the floor on the left, and froze. The desk and map were odd, but at least they were everyday items. The large black slab of stone lying next to them was not. The cold chill ran down my spine again, and I shuffled backward several steps.

"Oh my God, is that it?" Paul asked nervously.

I ignored the question and inched my way forward, toward the stone.

It was large, perhaps 7 to 8 feet wide and 10 to 11 feet long. Easily 3 to 4 inches thick. Hundreds of symbols were etched into the dark surface, in a language I'd never seen before. The stone was glossy, but didn't reflect light the way it should. Instead, it seemed to suck the light from the room around us, building its own dark aura. And it hummed. I could feel the pulse of the stone in my bones, like a giant, steady heartbeat. It beat again and again, matching my own heartbeat, and I forgot to breathe. Doc hadn't been lying, then. The stone did speak to him. And it called to me the same way it called to him. I'd been hearing it for days. I just hadn't realized it.

As I stood there, transfixed and listening, the writing on the stone began to glow. I blinked and looked again, to see that the glow was gone.

"Did you see that?" I gasped, reaching for Paul and taking my eyes off the stone for the first time.

"See what?" Paul whispered. "The only thing I see is that creepy stone."

"The symbols … I think they moved," I said, surprised that Paul hadn't seen it.

Paul shook his head. "Didn't see anything like that, buddy." He took a step toward the stone and bent over to look at it.

I followed slowly, wondering if I'd been seeing things. Then the humming started again, louder than before. This time it went straight to my head, and I gasped and fell to my knees. The stone thrummed louder, and took on its eerie glow, burning brighter and brighter until the symbols themselves lifted up off the surface. They hovered just above the stone's surface, ghostly, fiery reflections of their physical counterparts. Then they began to move, dancing around the edges of the stone to the humming rhythm of its heart.

"Holy…" I breathed. It was one of the most beautiful things I'd ever seen.

"Hey, what on earth are you doing?" Paul asked nervously.

I stood, keeping my eyes fixed on the dance in front of me. "You're honestly telling me that you can't see that?" I whispered.

"See what? This isn't funny anymore."

Paul grabbed my arm, and the dance ended as abruptly as it had begun. The symbols fell back into place, and the stone lost its glow. I moaned quietly. The symbols had been strange, eerie, and frightening, but they'd also been surprisingly familiar. Losing them was almost physically painful. I focused on the stone, trying to bring them back, or make the slab glow again.

"So how exactly does this thing work?" Paul asked, breaking my focus.

I cleared my throat and tried to find my voice. "Doc didn't exactly leave directions in his journal. He just said that the stone ... spoke to him."

"Well what the heck does that mean? That stone doesn't look like it has any kind of speech capabilities."

I smiled. "Actually, I think I know exactly what it means."

Paul didn't hear me, and reached out to touch the stone. "So this is it," he said, bending down. "This is the stone that can take us into the past."

"Stop! What are you doing?" I grabbed his hand and pulled him back.

"I'm just touching it. Why?"

"I don't know. Who knows what might happen? Maybe you're not supposed to touch it," I answered.

"Ah." Paul nodded. "Good point." He shoved his hands back into his pockets.

As he spoke, though, a jolt of energy shot from the stone into my bones, and the unearthly glow returned. I felt an irresistible urge to put my own hands on the stone, and allow the symbols to race across my skin. Confused, I closed my eyes, trying to focus and clear my head. All I could feel, all I could hear, was the stone's humming, drowning out all other sight and sound. Drowning out thought. Then it was gone, leaving in its place a feeling of calm contentment. Of readiness. And a clear, precise light in my mind.

I could feel the stone beneath my hands, as though I were already touching it. My mind explored the deep, cold grooves in the surface, and felt the light touch of the symbols as they moved. A shot of heat moved from the stone, through my hands, and down my spine.

"I wonder what the symbols mean," Paul said quietly.

I heard him through the haze of the stone, like he was standing on the other side of a wall, or under water. I suddenly became acutely aware of my surroundings – the smell of mildew and garlic, the friction of a cricket rubbing his back legs together outside. I could taste the sodium that clung to the salt water embedded in the concrete of the walls around us, and felt Paul's heart beat as if it were in my own chest. I heard sounds that didn't make any sense. Horses running, and the sound of metal screeching against metal. Men yelling, or cheering.

Looking down, I saw a hazy, half-formed path in front of my feet. Listening closely, I heard exactly where it would lead. And when.

I opened my eyes, breaking the spell, and turned to face Paul. His face had gone slack and white as he stared at me.

"I know exactly what the symbols mean," I said quietly.

"How do you know that?" Paul asked.

"Because," I replied slowly, "the stone just told me."

Reis Slayton jerked awake, then lifted his head and sat up. He looked around, confused at the unfamiliar surroundings, and then remembered. The Evans family – grandfather and boy. One odd friend. Mission – protect against unknown threat. Reis sat still, waiting for his heart rate to return to its normal rhythm. His bed sheets were wet with sweat, despite the cool temperature inside the house, and he sighed. How many years, and he was still waking up like this. The logical part of his brain tried to remind him that the dreams couldn't hurt him – those things had happened in the past, and couldn't come through to his current reality. After all these years, and the continuing nightmares, he was starting to wonder if that were true. If his subconscious – his own personal ghosts – would ever forgive him, and let him rest again.

He moved instinctively to place his right forefinger on the left side of his chest, searching for the built-up scar tissue just above his heart. These scars were painful reminders of the three 9-mm bullets that had torn into his body nearly three years ago. There were nine other visible scars over his chest and abdomen, wounds he'd been lucky to survive. But none of the physical wounds were as painful as the wounds and nightmares he still carried in his head. Those were scars that ran much deeper than Reis cared to admit to himself, even in his frankest moments. To Reis, the scars were a form of penance. A reminder of someone he had once loved, and the price he had paid for failing to save her. He had survived for a reason, he thought, though he couldn't understand what that reason was. Why had fate led him here, to protect a kid in the middle of nowhere?

He sighed, then stood up and made his way to the window, seeking to put his mind at ease with the dark of the night. He poked his finger through the blinds and looked out, searching for nothing in particular. Sudden movement in the yard below drove all thoughts of the past out of his mind.

A stray light appeared under the garden shed's door, shooting out into the heavy fog in the yard. Someone was inside the shed, and about to come out. Reis glanced at his clock, and saw that it was 1:47AM. No one had any good reason for being out there at this time of night. He was reaching for his 9mm Browning automatic, which he always kept at the ready, when the door to the shed opened and two people stepped out.

Reis jerked his gun up, then recognized the boys and set it down slowly. Below him, Jason turned and put the lock back on the shed's door, then turned back toward the house. Reis stepped closer to the window and watched the duo creep back toward the house, and through the door.

"What the..." he mumbled to himself. What the hell were the boys doing in the shed this late at night? And why were they sneaking around like they'd just murdered someone and hidden the body? Reis turned from the window when he heard the door shut in the mudroom below, and listened closely. No excited whispers or nervous laughter. Whatever the boys had been up to, it had scared them enough to keep them quiet. Probably served them right. Reis grunted thoughtfully and snapped the blinds shut behind him.

He had no idea why Fleming was paying him to babysit the old man and his grandson, and that lack of knowledge made him distinctly nervous. If this kid was prone to sneaking around in the middle of the night, it would make his mission even more difficult. He sighed, shook his head, and walked to his closet, where he pulled out the green duffel bag that housed his personal armory. As long as he was going to be awake talking to himself – and watching for more midnight excursions – he could use the time to prepare for whatever lay ahead. His instincts were telling him that this job would either be extremely boring or incredibly difficult. Being prepared was the best he could do, for now.

10

"What's going on? Why are you wigging out on me?"

I slammed my bedroom door behind us without replying, and rushed to my desk to turn on my computer.

"Are you going to tell me or what?" Paul asked anxiously. "What was that all about?"

I motioned sharply for him to keep it down, then took a deep breath and tried to calm down myself. My senses had returned to normal as soon as we got in the house; I couldn't feel Paul's heart anymore, or hear a cricket scratching its legs, or smell the water in a damp wall. But my heart was still racing, so I knew I hadn't dreamt it. All of those things had been real, and they'd come from the stone. The dancing symbols had been real, too. Paul hadn't seen them, but there were a million possible reasons for that. The symbols – and what they'd told me – were true. They weren't sane, or normal, and they certainly weren't rational, but I'd never been more sure of anything in my life.

Now I just had to figure out how to use them.

I outlined for Paul what I'd seen, including as much solid detail as possible. To his credit, he sat and listened without interrupting or asking any stupid questions. I glanced at him as I finished, wondering how he was going to react. His face was completely expressionless.

"You're looking at me like I'm crazy," I observed quietly.

Paul jumped, then grinned. "You're over reacting. This is how I always look at 2AM."

I smiled at his joke and relaxed marginally, thankful for a friend who could tell jokes in the face of that kind of story.

Paul sobered then, and sat down on my bed. “You said in the shed that you knew what the symbols meant. Did they … speak to you?”

I shook my head. “They didn’t talk to me, not like you and I are talking. But they showed me something.” I shrugged awkwardly, unable to explain.

Paul grunted. “And are you going to tell me, or are you hoping I’ll just guess and save you the trouble?”

I closed my eyes, reliving the images I’d seen and heard through the stone. “I saw a medieval town, like something you’d see in a movie, and I heard … yelling. Swords clashing. Horses running. I could swear I’d been hearing a battle. When it was over, I saw the date in my mind, just as clearly as if it were on my computer screen.” I turned to stare at the screen in question, wondering.

“What was it?” Paul asked.

“What?” I asked, dazed at the strength of the memory.

“The date, smarty, what was the date?”

I looked away from the monitor and back at Paul. “August 18, 1485,” I replied. Neither of us spoke for a moment, and the words hung in the air, unanswered.

“I also saw a list of numbers, but I’m not sure what they mean,” I added, after a moment of silence. I found a pencil and wrote the numbers on a piece of scratch paper.

“37 23.516 – 122 02.625,” Paul read.

“Does that make sense to you?” I asked.

Paul smiled. “You, my friend, obviously didn’t pay attention to the movie the other night,” he replied.

“What are you talking about?”

"***Close Encounters***... remember the movie? Remember the scene when they discovered that numbers were being transmitted from space? They grabbed the big globe and figured out that they were receiving coordinates – longitude and latitude. Map coordinates from space," he concluded with a wide grin.

I snorted. "Paul, I think your obsession with movies may finally have paid off." I typed "map coordinates" into my computer, and searched the numbers imprinted on my mind. Paul got up and walked over to stand behind me. A couple of seconds later, Google maps gave me the answer.

"What the..." Paul said. He leaned over my shoulder and read the name of the town on the computer screen. "Abergavenny, England. Those are real coordinates? Where the hell is that?" He returned to the bed and sat heavily. "This just got a lot scarier."

"Tell me about it." I turned away from the monitor and looked at Paul. "This confirms it, though. Everything I read in that journal, everything Doc and Fleming talked about ... it's all true."

Paul closed his eyes and tried to take in what I'd just said. "So what do we do?"

I shook my head in response. "I have no idea. But I think we have to do it in a hurry. Doc leaves again in a few hours, and from what I've heard, he'll be lucky to make it back."

Paul and I talked about the stone and its power for the rest of the night. More importantly, we talked about what we were going to do with the information we had. I didn't get more than thirty minutes of sleep, but when we emerged at 6:15, we had a plan.

Doc was already up and making breakfast when we walked into the kitchen. Reis was with him, drinking coffee and staring out the window.

"Good morning, gentlemen. Up and ready for school I see," Doc said cheerfully, looking up from the frying pan in front of him. "Did you sleep well?"

"Not really," Paul replied quickly. He glanced at me as we slid into our chairs. I frowned back, unprepared to start any conversations.

"I'm sure a nice hot breakfast will fix you right up," Doc answered. He served us each a plate of bacon and eggs, along with wheat toast and generous glasses of orange juice. Paul began shoving the food in his mouth, signifying his inability to talk, and I turned to my grandfather.

The plan was to get him talking, lead him into a conversation about time travel theories, and go from there. I was a physics student, which meant that I had regular access to things like Einstein and his theories of relativity and alternate realities. I hoped that I could sell Doc on having come across those theories of time, and being curious about them. If I could lead him far enough and show enough interest, he might open up and tell me about his own theories. He might even tell me about the stones, and the symbols I'd seen last night. It was a long shot, but if he opened up it might give me a chance to talk him out of going back again, and putting himself in danger. It had sounded good at 4:30 in the morning, and had been the only thing we could come up with. Now, I wasn't so sure.

Still, I'd kill myself if I didn't try.

I sighed and tried to prepare myself. I knew what I wanted, but I wasn't foolish enough to think it would be easy. "Actually, Doc, I'm not that hungry. I kind of wanted to talk to you about something."

Doc looked up from his own plate of food. "Yes, Jason? You know I'm always available."

I swallowed again. I wasn't sure he was actually going to be available for what I had in mind, but plunged in. "Well, I was thinking about something I read the other day. About time travel." Doc put down his fork and looked at me with interest. So far, so good. "See, I was really interested in the stuff about wrinkles in time and all that. You know, time travel, and the idea that time exists in a different dimension. The idea that those wrinkles – black holes – could actually be holes in time. But how would that work, exactly, if mankind wanted to use them? Could you *create* wrinkles, do you think, or *find* them? Wouldn't you need –"

"Some sort of magic machine or something?" Paul interrupted. "Like a secret, super-cool tool?"

My jaw dropped, and I froze. Paul interrupting had not been part of the plan. Especially with something so obvious, and damning. If Doc realized that we'd been in his shed, in his secret room, he'd ground me until I was forty. I glared at Paul, who winked at me as though he'd just made the most brilliant move ever, and glanced back at Doc. His face, which had welcomed my questions a moment ago, was now cold, hard, and closed. He raised his eyebrows and tipped his head back to look down his nose at me. As he did, my Doc – the man I'd grown up with – disappeared, and a stranger took his place.

"I'm sure I don't know, Jason. I haven't put much thought into it," he said quietly. He stood up abruptly, knocking the table askew in his haste, and grabbed his unfinished plate of breakfast. "If you boys will excuse me, I just remembered that I have business to attend to. I'll finish my breakfast at my desk."

I gasped and grabbed at his arm. He couldn't leave, not now. This definitely wasn't going the way I'd envisioned. "But Doc, I just wanted to talk to you about –"

Doc pulled his arm from my grasp and looked evenly at me. I thought I saw his face soften for a moment, then go back to its cold façade. "Jason, I appreciate that you want to know more about things like that, and I applaud your creative theories on the subject. But I don't have time to answer your questions right now. I'm sorry, son, but I'm busy, and I must be ready for a 7 o'clock appointment."

I gulped. The stone's next window opened up at 7AM. I'd seen the time last night, in the symbols. He was still going. "But Doc –"

He interrupted again, this time nodding toward Reis. "Mr. Slayton, would you mind driving the boys to school today? I'm afraid I have plans, and if the boys wait any longer, they'll be late."

Reis blinked at Doc in confusion, then nodded slowly. "Of course. We're all going to the same place, after all." He frowned, then folded the paper in front of him and looked at me. "Are you boys ready?"

I glanced at Paul, then at Doc. "Actually, I –"

"Jason, I must insist," Doc said, his voice hard and his hand on the door. "Now, I'll see you after school. Have a good day." He didn't leave any room for discussion, but turned and walked briskly away, his back straight and angry.

I stared after his vanishing back, shocked. This definitely hadn't played out like I thought it would. And now he was on his way into the den, to await his jump back in time. And where did that leave me? What was my move now? What about my plan?

Before I could think any farther, though, Paul grabbed my arm and mumbled something about getting out while we could. He pushed me out the door and into the back of Reis' green Volvo. I climbed in, still stunned, and slumped down in the back seat.

"Are you with us?" Paul asked, turning from the front seat to stare at me.

"Yeah, I'm okay," I lied. The truth was, I was far from okay. I was confused and alone, and growing more desperate by the moment. The 'plan' that was supposed to open up a conversation with Doc had managed to do the exact opposite, and now I was on my way to school and he was waiting to jump back in time, where a war awaited him.

I looked from Paul up to the rear view mirror, to meet Reis Slayton's eyes. He held eye contact for a moment then glanced behind me to stare at the house. When he looked at me again, his eyes held a note of concern and suspicion.

I blinked slowly in agreement, then leaned my forehead against the cool, icy glass of the window. I was exhausted and worried, and couldn't think. The episode with the stone the night before had thrown me out of balance, and this thing with Doc wasn't helping. It wasn't like him to push me out of the house, or ignore my questions. If I could just pull myself together for a moment, think rationally…

The smell of grass was unmistakable, rich and heavy around me. I cracked one eye open and saw bright green landscape in every direction. The grass around me was long, up to my waist, and rolled like waves in the wind. I was standing atop a bluff, and could see for miles in every direction. I saw millions of flowers, in every color of a Crayon box, and gasped at the beauty of it. A shockingly cloudless blue sky floated overhead, and the air was so clean that it hurt to breathe. The landscape was vibrating with a low humming sound, which gave it a hazy, underwater feeling. I didn't know where I was, but I didn't think I was dreaming. I certainly wasn't in Kansas – or New Hampshire – anymore.

A low drumming sound drew my attention away from the landscape and toward my left. At least a dozen horses emerged from the tree line and galloped hard up the hill, directly toward me. Men sat high atop the animals, decked out in what looked to be full sets of armor. They were dressed in colorful uniforms, with long cloaks covering their chests and backs. Some of them carried banners, and all had swords at their sides and battle shields on their saddles. Several had designs stitched into their cloaks or stamped on their shields. I searched my memory and came up with a word: coats of armor. These were knights, then, or lords. Whoever they were, they were hard men, with expressions that showed no emotion. I took an involuntary step back and turned as I heard the sound of thunder once again, this time coming from the other direction.

A cloud of thick, heavy dust rose from the feet of eleven more horses as they slid to a stop several feet away. These men were dressed just as impressively. They too appeared to be armed and ready for combat.

I swallowed silently, wondering where I was and what I'd wandered into. I was sure that this wasn't a dream, and if it wasn't – if I was actually in this place, with these men – then I was probably in just as much danger as they were. More, I corrected myself, as I didn't have armor, a sword, or a shield. I took another step backward, to distance myself from the two groups.

For several minutes, none of the men spoke. The horses breathed heavily, but didn't move. Finally, a man wearing a dark red cloak embroidered with a black hawk legged his horse forward, away from his companions, and made his way to the clearing between the two groups. Before the man's horse stopped, another soldier from the opposite side nudged his mount forward to intercept him. The second soldier, who came from the right, wore a cloak of white and dark blue. He had short blond hair and a sharp goatee, with intense black eyes that gave his features a sharp, sinister edge. He was short, but exuded a twisted, powerful aura. He wasn't a man I would want to meet.

"You are Lord Stanley?" he asked, smiling faintly.

The man in red nodded slowly. "And you are Richard's lead council. Lord Dresden, I presume?"

I gasped, then clapped my hand over my mouth to shut out the sound. Lord Dresden. John Fleming's son. The man with the evil smile was the man trying to kill Doc and change the world.

The two men gazed at each other, their horses dancing nervously. They obviously disliked and distrusted each other. They were just as obviously working to keep their tempers in check.

"I trust my brother is well?" Lord Stanley asked finally.

"He is being treated as a respected guest should be treated, I assure you," Dresden answered quietly.

Stanley snorted. "You'll forgive my impatience. I am in no mood for civilized conversation. Set out the terms of my brother's release and have done. I do not wish to waste your time, or my own."

A bark of laughter escaped Dresden's mouth. "A man of my own heart, then. Very well, let us discuss terms. I do not want money for your brother. I wish to offer you an alliance. An alliance that would assure your family twice as much land as you already hold, as well as Richard's word that your lands to the north will be protected."

Stanley's face paled in shock. "Are you mad, man? You abducted my brother and now you expect me to ally with you?"

"You must choose a side, Lord Stanley. My sources tell me that you lean toward allying your house with the Earl of Oxford, and the house of Tudor."

I gasped again. The Earl of Oxford. Doc.

Before I could draw any conclusions, though, Stanley interrupted me.

"What I do with my men — and my house — is none of your concern, Dresden."

Lord Dresden quickly raised his right hand and pointed toward one of the knights near Lord Stanley. A flash of flame and smoke erupted from under Dresden's right sleeve, accompanied by a thunderous clap of sound. The men jumped and then froze, watching as Stanley's knight rocked backward off his mount and fell, clutching his chest. He landed with a hard thump at the feet of his horse.

"You were questioning my powers?" Dresden asked with a cold smile. "Everything in this country is my concern. And you will do as I say."

"What is it you want?" Lord Stanley asked solemnly, looking down at his dying knight.

Dresden nodded slowly, accepting the victory, and placed both hands on the saddle in front of him. "The battle for the crown will take place outside the village of Bosworth two week from now. I had thought to delay it, but Oxford has forced my hand. You will fight on our side, rather than Tudor's. Assemble your army and assist Richard in defeating the pretender, thus keeping the crown where it belongs. Your brother will stay with me to ensure that our alliance is maintained. I will release him when I am satisfied that you have performed your duties. If you fail, or if you desert us, he will die a slow, unpleasant death. Is this clear?"

Lord Stanley nodded his head quietly.

"One more thing, Stanley." Dresden paused dramatically. "I want the Earl of Oxford delivered to me. By the end of the battle."

"Dead?"

Dresden shook his head. "I need him alive. He has information I require. Afterwards..." He flexed his hand and smiled wolfishly. "Well, that is none of your concern. But it will not be pleasant for him."

Stanley gave Dresden a look of pure hatred, but nodded curtly. "Richard will maintain his crown." His voice dropped with regret. "I will deliver the Earl to you, and leave him to your mercy. I will expect my brother's release the day after the battle." He and his band of knights wheeled their horses and galloped away, leaving Dresden smirking and victorious.

The humming sound around me intensified, and then everything went dark.

"NO!" I screamed. I opened my eyes and popped up, staring wildly around me. I saw a tangle of metal, glass, and upholstery, scenery flashing by … and then the back of Reis' head. Paul turned in his seat to stare at me. I was back in New Hampshire, safely driving to school. Back from … what had that been, exactly? Not a dream – I was sure of that. And not fiction, either. A flash of the present, or the future. Of a meeting that had taken place – or would take place – in the past. A meeting about Doc's capture and death. I gasped as I remembered the details – Stanley, Earl of Oxford. And Dresden's smile. It never occurred to me to question the vision. I knew, beyond a shadow of a doubt, that it had been the truth, and that it had come from the stone. They were going to kidnap and kill Doc, and he had no clue. I had to get home. Had to tell him.

"Jesus," Paul gasped. "You scared the hell out of me. Why're you yelling?"

I ignored him, turning to Reis. "Reis, you have to turn around, please. We have to go back." I tried to sound calm and rational.

Reis glanced at me in the rearview mirror. "What are you talking about, kid? We're already running late."

I glanced at my watch. It was already 6:47, and Doc would be leaving at 7. "Please, Reis, we don't have much time."

By this time, Paul had turned around in his seat, to hang over the back. He looked at me anxiously. "What is it? What's wrong?"

"I had a dream. I think Doc's in trouble. Please, I have to warn him before he leaves."

"A dream?" Reis asked skeptically. "Before he leaves?"

I transferred my gaze to Paul, hoping for an ally. "The stone spoke to me again, Paul. Doc's in trouble. There are people trying to kill him. We have to go back, Reis, please! Turn around. I need to go home, NOW!" I closed my mouth on the panic in my voice.

"Holy cow, he's right. We have to go back!" Paul turned to Reis and grabbed his arm. "Dude, Doc could be in trouble!"

Reis sighed heavily, but nodded; it was, after all, his job to ensure our safety. The car's speed, though, left something to be desired.

"Could you maybe go a little faster?" I asked anxiously.

"No kidding, senior citizens drive faster than this!" Paul agreed.

Reis shook his head and accelerated slightly. "Are you two always this high strung?" he asked, glancing again at the rearview mirror. This time, his worried glance went past me and to the road behind us.

"We're teenagers. We survive on Mountain Dew and Slim Jims. What do you want from us?" Paul replied.

I ignored them both, willing the car forward, and praying that I'd get home in time to stop Doc from jumping back in time. Or at least warn him about what was waiting for him in the past. I knew what the stone had told me, and after my experience last night, I didn't doubt the story. This time, death was waiting for Doc in the past.

The man in the light blue minivan nodded, then disconnected the call and dropped his cell phone in his pocket.

"What did he say?" the man seated in the passenger seat asked.

The man behind the wheel flashed a toothy grin and turned over the ignition. "It looks like we're through watching. Now that the old man's alone, we're to move in and grab him. The organization wants to take him in, figure out exactly what he knows."

"And the boy?" the passenger asked.

The driver shook his head and put the vehicle in drive. "The kid's at school, and we don't know how important he is yet. He can come later. Right now our boss has some questions for the old man." He glanced in his rearview mirror to see another colleague pulling an assault rifle from its case and inspecting the gun's magazine. "Are you ready back there?" he asked.

"Ready," the man replied tersely.

"How much force can we use?" the passenger asked.

"As much as it takes," the driver replied. He pulled the minivan out of Harvey's Truck Stop and onto Heater Road. "Our superiors want him for questioning. If we can get the journal as well, we have orders to do so. We need him alive, but we don't need him in good shape. He won't be going home anytime soon. Not until he tells us what he knows."

11

The Volvo handled the sharp turn onto Heater Road like a German sports car coming off the Autobahn. We flew past Harry's Truck Stop, barely slowing at the stop sign. Reis was taking my request to hurry at face value, now, and we were making record time. Paul glanced back at me in shock, then transferred his gaze to the back window.

"That's funny," he mumbled.

"What's that?" I asked impatiently.

Paul shrugged. "Nothing. Just seems like I see that blue minivan everywhere lately."

Reis looked at Paul and glanced in the rearview mirror. "Do you know the driver, or recognize him at all?" he asked tersely. "Is he from around here?"

"No, I don't think so," Paul replied.

I turned to look at the van myself, and studied the driver carefully. Nothing stood out about the man, but I was sure I didn't know him. "I've never seen him either."

Reis' demeanor changed, and his voice hardened. He straightened and seemed to grow, suddenly all business. A military man in action. I could almost see the green beret on his head.

"I was afraid of that," he answered. "Hold on, boys, this may get a bit bumpy." He downshifted and stamped on the accelerator, throwing Paul and I back into our seats. The Volvo tore forward like a real sports car, its engine roaring to life.

"When we get home, get out of the car on Paul's side and run to the garage, quick as you can. Understood?" he snapped.

"What are you talking about?" Paul asked. He lunged forward to grab the dashboard as we rounded onto Bank Street.

"When we hit the driveway, run toward the garage. That's an order! How difficult is that?" Reis barked. He glared at Paul, then glanced back at me in the rear view mirror. I nodded wordlessly, confused.

Then I threw myself down onto the seat next to me. Reis had driven the car over a curb and onto the sidewalk, missing an oncoming truck by inches. Paul grabbed for the dashboard again and shouted a pointless warning at the oncoming traffic. A second later, Reis had pulled the car off the sidewalk and back onto the road, just in time to miss Baker Glasgow, who was delivering newspapers on his bike. If I hadn't been scared to death, I would have laughed at the sight of Baker flipping his bike in panic, dozens of papers flying through the air behind him.

"I'm going to get sick," Paul groaned as the car picked up speed once again.

I nodded silently, stunned at the sudden action, and saw Paul duck as we flew through a row of shrubbery. The Volvo roared down Bank Street, and I turned to look out the rear window. I was stunned at what I saw.

Instead of falling behind, as it should have, the blue minivan had sped up. It was gaining on us, and the passenger was now hanging out his window and motioning wildly toward our car.

"Hold on!" Reis shouted. He downshifted the sedan and applied the brakes, simultaneously spinning the steering wheel hard to the right. The Volvo whipped violently around, its wheels chewing up asphalt and burning rubber as the car spun. We lurched forward again, onto Patriots Drive and into our driveway, where we screeched to a violent stop.

"RUN!" Reis yelled, ducking down and pulling a gun from below the seat.

Paul and I opened our doors and jumped out. I had no idea what was going on, or whether we were even in danger, but I didn't plan to stick around and find out. My feet were moving before they hit the ground, propelling me toward the garage. Behind us, I heard the sharp squeal of breaks and the peeling of rubber tires. I turned to see the minivan slide to a violent halt in the street in front of our driveway, and three men jump out. Before I could see any more, Paul pulled me in the side door of the garage.

He slammed the door shut behind us, and we ran to press our faces against the garage's lone window. We got there just in time to see Reis hurtle over the hood of his car, pulling another large handgun from under his sports jacket. He hit the ground on our side of the car and knelt, taking careful aim with both guns over the hood of the car. One of the men from the minivan walked purposefully around the hood of the van, clutching a gun at his side. In his other hand he held a badge and a set of credentials.

"FBI … we have warrants!" the man yelled. "I'm going to come around your car. Don't shoot. Give up your weapons and no one gets hurt."

"Don't move!" Reis shouted back. "I wasn't born yesterday, and I know you're not FBI! You come any closer and I'll shoot!"

The man ignored the threat and walked slowly toward the Volvo. I couldn't hear what Reis was saying anymore, but I could see him shake his head and square his shoulders. I held my breath.

Suddenly, three loud shots sounded out and the minivan's passenger dropped to the sidewalk, clutching his stomach. A second gunman moved away from the van and walked toward the Volvo, carrying what looked to be a grenade launcher. This man didn't speak, but brought the weapon up to his shoulder and pulled the trigger.

Our driveway exploded in smoke and fire. Glass shattered as pieces of metal, plastic, and leather erupted from Reis's car, turning the Swedish automobile into Swiss cheese. Reis flew through the air and landed heavily several feet from the garage, in the flowerbed that bordered our driveway. I watched him fly through the air, then dragged my eyes from what I was sure was his dead body to watch the assassins. Instead of charging forward to press his advantage, the second gunman seemed content to stand his ground beside the minivan. His fallen companion dragged himself back to the vehicle, holding his stomach with one hand. The third man helped him inside. The second gunman pulled out a handgun, pumped several rounds into what was left of Reis' car, and then jumped into the van. The van's tires squealed as it pulled away, tearing up Mrs. Grey's yard on its way back to the road. I blinked and it was gone, leaving the driveway bloodied and burning.

Paul and I were quiet for a moment, staring at the driveway and what was left of Reis' car.

"What the hell was that?" Paul asked dully.

I shook my head and looked back at Reis. What on earth were we going to do with one dead body guard? I'd only known him a day, but I'd started to like the guy, and I'd never done well with death. I let my eyes run over his body, shocked at what had just happened, and Reis' part in it. Before I could turn away, though, one of his hands shot out, followed by the other. He pushed himself up off the pavement, brushed the debris from his clothes, and walked casually toward us, shaking his head.

Paul and I glanced at each other, dumbstruck.

"That's one hell of a substitute teacher," Paul muttered.

I nodded in agreement, then slapped my hand to my forehead. "Damn it!" I shouted, glancing down at my watch. I sprinted to the door, threw it open, and ran full speed toward the garden shed. I didn't have time to wonder if Paul was coming with me.

"Stop! Where are you going?" Reis shouted. I could hear him pounding after me, but I was already at the door of the shed. The lock was gone, which meant that Doc was inside. I flung the door open, nearly ripping the flimsy thing off its hinges, and sprinted the four steps it took to get to the back of the shed. My hand slammed down on the wooden dowel, and I turned to watch the trap door open.

This time I knew exactly where I was going, and what to expect. I scrambled down the metal ladder, skipping the last two rungs and falling to the floor. The room was fully illuminated, but not from overhead lights. Turning, I saw that the glow came from the stone itself. It was glowing far more brightly than it had been the night before, with thousands of symbols dancing in the air above it. And on the stone, quickly disappearing, sat my grandfather's shadow.

Brilliant light danced over the stone in a million different colors, tracing the outline of a human form. Doc had been lying on the stone. I could still see the outline there, like an impression on a blanket. My heart lurched, and I reached toward the stone. The bright, multifaceted light sharpened, as though it sensed my presence, and began to pulse. The beat of the stone's heart reached into my chest and pulled at my own, and I felt the pulses echoing in my bones. As I drew my hand back, though, the symbols faded, and the glow began to dim. It was speaking to me, trying to tell me something. I was sure of it. I just hadn't learned how to speak the language yet.

A bump and gasp behind me broke the spell, and I turned to see both Reis and Paul standing beside the ladder, staring.

"What on God's green earth is that?" Reis asked quietly. "And what are you doing standing so close to it?"

I opened my mouth to reply, found that I didn't have any words, and closed it again. *Think, Evans,* I told myself impatiently. Doc had just disappeared into the past, destined for an encounter with armed – and very dangerous – men. This wasn't the time to start stuttering.

I took a deep breath and tried again. "This? Well, it's…" I paused, looking around helplessly. How exactly did one explain what this was? Or what we were up against?

"What is this place?" Reis asked again. "And what's going on?"

"Let's pretend that you're more than just a substitute teacher, looking for a place to stay, and start from there," Paul said.

Reis shot a look at Paul before turning his attention back at me. "Didn't buy the substitute teacher line?" he asked quietly.

"You don't exactly blend in with the others," Paul replied.

Suddenly I made my decision, and my explanation came out in a rush. "Reis, I don't know whether you're going to buy any of this – and I'm not sure why you would, to be honest – but I need your help. Doc's gone, and he's walking right into some big trouble, and we have to do something about it. Only we don't have a lot of time. And it might be a bit … complicated."

Reis crossed his arms over his chest and settled into a wide stance. "I'm listening, Jason. I can't guarantee that I'll believe you, or that I'll be able to help. But I am listening."

I looked down at my feet, searching for the right place to start. After a moment, I decided to go with the quick, simple, and absolutely honest version, to save time. I looked up to meet Reis' eyes as squarely as I could.

"Reis, this stone allows people to travel through time. I don't know how exactly it works, or how many people use it. I don't even know how many stones there are, or where they go. I do know that my grandfather can use them. I know that he's managed to get himself involved with some pretty nasty people – one of whom seems hell bent on changing the world – and that it's important for him to succeed. I also know – and don't ask me how, because I can't explain it – that he's in trouble. Someone's going to try to kill him. He doesn't know that, and without knowing it, how's he going to defend himself?" My voice was shaking with emotion and stress, and I didn't like it. I took a deep breath and squared my shoulders. "I don't know what I'm going to do, but I know for damn sure that I have to do something. I can't just sit back and wait to see if he comes home."

Reis grunted, and some of the tension left his shoulders. "You know, your grandfather told me that exact same story. Either you're both crazy, or I'm in way over my head here." He sighed, then continued. "Let's just say, though, that I've taken a liking to you, and I'm willing to believe your story. It would go a long way to explaining some of the weird action going on around here." He glanced at the stone, and added, "Plus, it's hard to ignore something that I can see with my own eyes. So what's our next move?"

That certainly wasn't the reaction I'd been expecting. Condescension, disbelief, and scorn, maybe, but not acceptance. My jaw dropped open and my mind went blank with surprise. "What?" I gasped.

"He said he believes you, genius," Paul snapped. "What's the plan?"

Reis nodded. "It doesn't make a lot of sense, but this situation has been off since I got here. Given your grandfather's behavior, John Fleming's insistence on the most bizarrely secretive contract I've ever signed, and those faux FBI agents in the yard, I'm willing to bet that this deal is bigger than I realized. That glowing stone behind you certainly says so. Your little friend is right. What's the plan?"

Reis' agreement brought down the blockages in my head, and kicked my brain back into action. I walked quickly over to the desk and booted up the PC.

"We don't have much time. The next trip, or window, or opening, or whatever, is at noon today."

"What on earth does that mean?" Reis asked sharply. "Trip to where?"

I finished typing coordinates into the computer, glanced at the results, and looked up at the map. "The next time the stone opens for business. The next trip it plans to make."

"Going the same place?" Paul cut in.

"No," I replied quietly. I'd found what I was looking for on the map – it sat halfway between York and London, smack dab in the middle of nowhere. I jabbed my finger at the village on the map and turned back to Paul and Reis, who had moved to stand behind me. "This time it's going to Doncaster, England."

Reis shook his head slowly. "I don't even want to ask. But what exactly are we supposed to do with that information?"

I shrugged back. "Reis, I don't have the answers. I don't even know the questions. But I'm willing to bet that John Fleming does." I began to walk toward the ladder, my mind already made up.

Reis' hand snaked out to grab me on my way by. "This is all more than a little nuts, kid. You know that, right? What makes you think John Fleming will help you?"

I pulled my arm from his grasp. "Reis, my grandfather's in trouble. We've had people chasing us, breaking into our house, and trying to blow us to hell, for who knows what reason. John Fleming is the only one still here who knows what's going on. Don't you think it's time he told us what he knows?"

12

The tall, dark-haired man bit his lower lip and shook his head in frustration. He reached for his BlackBerry and made the call. "Tell the medical team to get ready, ETA in less than sixty seconds."

The blue minivan was tearing along the frontage road that ran parallel to Lebanon's small airport. The security team opened the duel gate when the van reached the driveway, allowing it to maintain its velocity as it pulled into the airport and raced toward the designated hangar. The driver screeched to a halt just inside the doors, and the dark-haired man got slowly out of the van. Briegan was already striding toward them, his face set.

This wasn't going to be pretty, the dark-haired man thought.

Briegan looked back toward the road, then scanned the airport's perimeter, watching and listening for any unwanted attention. Satisfied that the van had made it to the hangar without being followed, he turned back to the man standing by the van.

"What the hell happened?" he snapped. "I hired you to bring in a civilian, an old man at that, and you blow up half the town?" His voice was low and calm, but undeniably dangerous.

"Your *civilian* has professional help, and someone who knew an awful lot about guns," the man spit back defensively. "You neglected to mention that he'd hired a body guard!"

Briegan took a deep breath, and released it. "What happened out there?" he asked evenly.

The dark-haired man shook his head. "Raymond took two bullets to the stomach. He's dead. We didn't get into the house. No sign of the old man, or anything else."

"And the boy and his … body guard?" Briegan demanded.

The man shrugged again. "We didn't wait to see where they went. They could be anywhere by now."

13

We tore down the back roads for several miles, avoiding other cars, and made our way onto Interstate 89. We'd lifted Doc's keys and taken his car, since Reis' Volvo was now out of commission, and I was squeezed into the passenger seat next to Paul. Neither of us had wanted to ride in the back by ourselves. Reis was driving the car faster than Doc ever had, the engine whining in protest and effort.

As we drove, my mind began to assimilate the things that had just happened. And I began to wonder at the lack of surprise on Reis' face when people started shooting. I was no expert, but it seemed to me that a normal person would have been at least a little shocked in that situation. Reis, though, had reacted quickly and naturally, like he'd been expecting it. Or dealt with that sort of thing on a regular basis. He'd handled it like a pro.

"How did you know?" I asked finally, breaking the tense silence in the car.

"Know what?" Reis asked sharply.

"Those guys back there. How did you know they weren't Federal agents?" I stopped, thinking. "In fact, are you sure they *weren't* Federal agents?"

Reis nodded once. "Positive, for a few reasons. First, they would have called local support if they were actually FBI. That's standard protocol."

"Reis, I don't speak government. English, please."

"Real FBI would have had local cops with them. These guys just came charging in, unannounced. It's unprofessional."

Paul grunted, impressed. "What else?"

"Quebec license plates," Reis answered, warming to the conversation. "No way Feds are driving a car with Canadian plates."

"You noticed an awful lot about guys firing guns and rocket launchers at you," Paul answered. "Anything else?" I could see him getting interested, filing the info away for future use.

"That wasn't a rocket launcher. It was a grenade launcher. Big difference." Reis paused, thinking. "The whole thing felt off. They didn't feel legit to me. When you've been in the business as long as I have, you learn to trust those gut feelings. And Fleming hired me for a reason."

I sat back, thinking. "But why were they after us? What on earth do we have that they want?"

Reis grunted. "They might not have been after us at all."

"Doc?" I asked.

"Or the stone. If what you say is true…" He shook his head as he tried to connect the dots. "Then there's no telling who's looking for it, or what they'd do to get it."

After a moment of silence, Paul spoke again. "Is Reis Slayton your real name?"

Reis threw Paul a quick a glance. "Why do you ask?"

"Well you have all this crazy experience. You say you're in 'the business.' And you have to admit that the name sounds … well, made up, really."

I groaned. Here we were, our lives in danger, fighting against people who were evidently bent on changing the course of history, about to confront the man who could tell us what we needed to know, and Paul was wondering whether Reis used a code name.

"Paul, really?" I asked. "You think now's the time for this sort of nonsense?"

Reis ignored me. "Made up?"

"Like Race Banon in ***Johnny Quest***, or Tony Stark or James Bond. You know, the super-cool guy name."

Reis snorted, and a corner of his mouth turned up. I couldn't be sure, but I thought it was the start of a smile. It would have been one of the first I'd seen from him. "The next time I visit my parents, I'll get a copy of my birth certificate. Will that satisfy you?"

Paul held his hands up in mock surrender. "Not necessary, captain, I was just curious. Now if you told me your name was something like Jake Stonefist or Rock Steelhead, I'd really have a hard time believing you."

A bark of surprised laughter escaped Reis' mouth and Paul smiled, proud of himself. Before he could answer, though, we got off the interstate and turned onto Route 4, and then onto a private road just outside of Woodstock.

Paul whistled quietly. "The swankiest neighborhood in two states," he remarked. "Not too shabby."

We drove slowly down the private road, through a tunnel of old trees. I looked around anxiously, but could see only dense vegetation, marked periodically with signs warning that trespassers were unwelcome. No clues about what – or who – was to come. After a few moments of driving through the hushed forest, we drifted to a stop in front of a large wrought iron gate, bordered by 10-foot brick walls. Reis rolled his window down and leaned out the window toward a speaker in the wall.

"Reis Slayton to see Mr. Fleming," he called casually.

Paul elbowed me in the ribs as the gate opened, and I nodded wordlessly. John Fleming was loaded. The entrance was bigger than anything I'd ever seen, and this was just the driveway. This man had more money and power than anyone I knew, and I was about to go into his house making demands. My stomach clenched with nerves, and I sucked in a deep gulp of air as we drove through the gate. The view was incredible; we could see the White Mountains of New Hampshire to our left and the Green Mountains of Vermont to our right. As we crested the hill, the oak and pine trees in front of us disappeared to reveal the estate. The scene before me did little to settle my nerves.

"Holy smokes," Paul murmured. "I knew there was old money in Woodstock, but that's really something. Who is this guy, anyhow?"

Paul was right. John Fleming's home made the White House look pedestrian. The house had been built in the colonial style – or age – with a portico in the front and a massive porch along the second floor, looking out onto the private drive. The driveway alone was bigger than our entire house. The whole thing was painted white, with lemon yellow shutters and trim, and flowerbeds and green lawns covered the grounds around the house. Two separate buildings stood behind the main home; I assumed that these were a fancy guesthouse and an equally impressive barn. My eyes moved on to the land behind the house, where white fences ran for miles, surrounding pastures full of horses. This was a full-blown horse ranch, complete with a mansion, circular drive, and creepy guesthouse. The main house probably had secret rooms, hidden stairwells, and a dungeon underneath. Maybe even a ghost or two.

I realized I'd been holding my breath, and let it out. Who the hell was this John Fleming, and how had Doc met him? Doc didn't belong in this world; the house was about one hundred times bigger than ours, and I couldn't imagine Doc ever being interested in horses or bushes shaped like animals. What did John Fleming have to do with my grandfather? And would he know anything about his disappearance this morning?

Reis must have been wondering the same thing, because he revved the engine and shot down the hill to the driveway. He pulled quickly into the circular drive, where a man I could only assume to be the butler met us.

"This way gentlemen. Mr. Fleming will take you in the study." The man was larger than a butler had a right to be, and had a creepy foreign accent. I stepped carefully past him, and followed Reis up to the front door.

The foyer of the home was even more impressive than the exterior had been. Two large semi-circular staircases rose from the right and left to meet one another in a wide landing on the second floor. The paneling on the walls was done in dark, glossy mahogany, and a crystal chandelier hung golden and sparkling from a domed ceiling at least four stories above us. Old paintings, maps, and tapestries covered the walls, which ended in a black and white marble floor. My eyes jumped from one spot to another, desperately trying to take everything in.

Drawing my eyes back down to ground level, I noticed Reis and the butler moving through the foyer to a set of French doors on the left. I shoved Paul, who was staring up at the ceiling, and scuttled after them.

The butler opened the doors grandly and moved aside, motioning for us to enter, but I paused. John Fleming had drawn Doc into this, asked for his help, and then let him walk into danger. To my mind, he was directly responsible for Doc's current situation. Part of me wanted to throttle the man for being so selfish and irresponsible.

My more grown-up half realized that discretion might be the better part of valor. After all, John Fleming was also the man who knew where Doc had gone, and why. He was the only one who could tell me what I needed to know. The question was whether he would.

I took a deep breath and stepped through the doorway.

I had always liked our little den, but this library put it to shame. The room was straight off the pages of an architectural magazine, and made me even more curious about the man who lived here. These walls had mahogany panels as well, with fancy crown molding at the top, and held hundreds of pictures of John Fleming. Some pictures featured him by himself, while others showed him shaking hands with people I didn't recognize, but assumed to be famous, powerful, or important. I snorted, amused. What kind of man kept that many pictures of himself? Then I saw the built-in bookshelves. Miles of them, lining two sides of the long room, and full of at least ten thousand books. It was a bookworm's dream. The bookshelves ended in an expansive fireplace, which took up an entire corner on its own, and looked like it could house a small family. A large stuffed moose head sat over the fireplace, presiding over the large, somewhat pretentious "study." To our right, a desk the size of a small automobile centered itself against the back of the room, right next to a small bar.

Compared to the house and room, John Fleming was small and relatively unimpressive. He turned from the window behind the desk and strode forward to greet us. As I watched him walk toward us, the fear and anxiety I'd felt for the last hour, the worry over Doc, and the apprehension about approaching this rich, powerful man shifted and coalesced into a large lump of ice, sitting right below my heart. I had promised myself that I could be reasonable and handle this situation rationally, in the name of getting the information I needed. I had told myself that I'd be confident and persuasive, eloquent even, in explaining to him why I needed answers to my questions. By the time John Fleming had crossed the carpet to stand in front of me, I wasn't sure I could do any of that. I was coldly angry.

"Jason, it's nice to see you again. I don't believe I've had the pleasure of meeting your friends," he said, his eyes hooded.

I almost laughed. This wasn't the same friendly, doddering old man I'd met the other night. This man was suspicious of us. And he was lying. A small part of my fear fell away at his words, and I shook my head.

"Mr. Fleming, this is my friend Paul Merrell. I believe you already know Reis Slayton. He is, after all, your employee," I answered softly.

Paul squirmed and coughed at my unpleasant reply, and Reis grunted in agreement. John Fleming's expression didn't change, though I could see his eyes narrow in displeasure.

"Please have a seat," he answered quietly. He motioned to a large leather sofa, and sat opposite the sofa in a plush leather chair. Once he was comfortably situated, he turned a false smile on me again.

"What can I help you with, son?"

I pulled air in through my teeth and gathered myself. I needed this to go quickly, and as smoothly as possible, so I started with the polite version. "Mr. Fleming, my grandfather is missing. I know that you know where he is, and how I can get to him. I came here to get answers. And I don't have a lot of time." I glanced at my watch meaningfully.

Fleming sat back in his seat but said nothing, so I charged on.

"I know about the stones, sir. I know that Doc's used them to go to Medieval England. What I don't know is why. That's what I'm here to find out."

That got Fleming's attention, and I sat back myself, satisfied. His expression of serene condescension turned to shock, then to crafty denial.

"I'm afraid I don't know what you're talking about, son," he replied quietly.

I paused. I'd expected denial, but I hadn't exactly come up with a plan to deal with it. My confidence waivered, and the silence drew out.

"Oh come on!" Paul muttered, surprising everyone in the room. He glanced at me, raised his eyebrows, and nodded toward Fleming. "Tell him, Jay," he murmured. "We don't have time, right?"

I nodded, speaking quickly at Paul's goading. "Paul's right. I've only got a few hours to figure out what's going on, and that's it. I need to know what I'm looking at. Specifically."

Fleming held his hands up. "Boys, perhaps you'd better –"

Paul cut in before he could finish. "Listen, buddy, perhaps *you'd* better," he snapped. "My friend here heard the conversation between you and Doc the other night. He heard everything! We know about the stone, and we know what it does. We know about your nut job son, and his war with Doc." He paused and glanced at me, questioning. I shrugged back, willing to let him do the dirty work, and he continued. "I think you believe in your son more than you believe in Doc, and that it's put him in terrible danger. You may not care about saving him, but we do. We need to know what you know. Now."

Fleming shook his head and looked angrily from Paul to me. "I'm afraid you misunderstood our conversation, son." His voice shook with emotion, and his cheeks turned a bright red. This man didn't like being questioned, and he was losing his temper.

Paul laughed. "Misunderstood? Really? Is that why armed men just happened to run us down and blow up Reis' car and half of Jason's driveway?

Or why they broke into their house last week? Why exactly did you hire Reis Slayton to protect Jason, Mr. Fleming? Afraid he was getting bullied in school? Come on! What's going on here?"

Instead of answering, Fleming turned to gaze at me for a moment, then moved his eyes to Reis. Reis took a deep breath, nodded, and spoke.

"The boy's right. I don't like being screwed around with, Mr. Fleming, no matter how much I'm making. You obviously know a lot more than you're letting on. I suggest you tell us what we're dealing with."

Fleming shook his head and stood abruptly. "Boys, Mr. Slayton, I'm afraid I have other business to attend to this morning. This conversation is over. I assume you can show yourselves out?"

Suddenly a soft, husky voice joined the conversation from the other side of the room. "If you don't tell them, John, I will. They certainly have a right to know."

Fleming's face went from red to a ghastly pale color, and his jaw dropped open. Reis, Paul, and I turned our heads in unison to see a tall, dark-haired girl standing, hip cocked and confident, next to a previously concealed door behind the bar. The girl had the darkest eyes I'd ever seen, with olive skin, long, straight black hair, and features as sharp and angular as a hawk's. She was beautiful, but unspeakably frightening. She studied each of us unapologetically, her eyes moving from Reis to Paul and me, her expression burning coldly as though we were her next prey. Raising her eyebrows at what she saw, she settled back onto the desk, and began tossing a green apple from hand to hand.

I gulped, unnerved by this girl's cool arrogance, and tried to collect my thoughts. Paul stared. John Fleming coughed in embarrassment and closed his eyes.

"Gentlemen, this is my granddaughter, Tatiana. Tatiana, this is –"

The girl named Tatiana interrupted her grandfather in an even, bored voice. "I heard the introductions, John."

Fleming's mouth turned down, and his face grew two shades darker. "Tatiana, I believe I've asked you not to listen to – or interrupt – my private meetings. This kind of behavior is completely unacceptable, and if it continues –"

She interrupted again before he could complete his threat. "What's unacceptable, *John*, is that you keep these nice people waiting for their answers. Now, as I said, let them in on your little secret, or I will. When it comes to the subject of Nicholas Fleming, I have every right. And you know it." She turned to look at me and bit slowly into her apple, narrowing her eyes. "I believe they were asking about Dr. Evans' whereabouts."

Fleming coughed again, and narrowed his eyes. "It seems, gentlemen, that I have little choice. I am, however, unsure where to start –"

This time it was Reis who interrupted. "Why not the beginning?" He glanced at me, and at the large grandfather clock on the wall. "And keep it short."

Fleming nodded his head and paused for a moment before speaking. "Several years ago, my son became involved with treasure speculation."

"What's that?" Paul asked.

A ghost of a smile passed over Fleming's face. "To be blunt Paul, it's an excuse for wealthy people to spend millions of dollars on treasure hunts, pretending that they're doing it in the name of history and science. The expedition that discovered the Titanic, located the Bismarck, and stumbled onto King Tut's tomb … all of those adventures costs untold millions of dollars. My son wanted to be one of those treasure hunters, and he turned to me for support." Fleming paused. "I gave my son what he asked for, and sent him on his way."

"Get on with the explanation," Reis growled. "We're not here to explore your relationship with your son."

Fleming nodded, beaten into submission. "Yes, yes. Several years ago, my son came across a stone identical to the one your grandfather has in his possession. This stone was in Romania, buried under a 1200-year-old Greek temple. He found the stone interesting, but had no use for it at the time, and put it in a storage facility. Two years later, he found another stone in the Sudan, virtually identical to the first. Same markings, same polish and color, same ... sense of power."

I squirmed in my seat, already impatient with the story. Fleming was evidently used to people hanging on his every word, and enjoyed drawing it out, giving the play-by-play version. I needed to know what had happened, but I could see the clock ticking on the other side of the room, and had a running countdown in my head. The stone opened again at noon today. I still didn't know what I was dealing with – or have a plan for moving forward – and this old man was going to take the rest of the morning answering a simple question.

"For nearly a year, my son and his colleague studied the stones, concentrating on the symbols they contained. They tried to interpret the language of the symbols, and find the tools used to inscribe them, to no avail. Seven months ago, another stone was discovered, this time in our own backyard in Plainfield, New Hampshire. Again, same markings, color..." Fleming let out a deep sigh before continuing. "I purchased the stone from a local developer for a moderate sum and brought it to Dartmouth for my son to study." He paused, rubbing his temples, and I lost my patience.

"Enough of the history lesson! Will you cut to the chase, already?" I snapped. I wanted answers, and this guy was babbling like I had all the time in the world. "I need answers, and I don't have all the time in the world!"

"Hear, hear," Tatiana agreed from the desk.

Fleming held one hand up. "I'm getting there, son. Nicholas was convinced that the stones were significant, most likely the greatest find of our time. But he couldn't unravel their secrets. After several months of study, he decided that the symbols were mathematical rather than linguistic, and that we needed the help of a physicist or mathematician." He looked directly at me. "When I brought your grandfather to see the stones, everything changed."

14

I straightened up. Now we were talking. If Fleming was going to describe Doc's involvement with the stones, maybe I'd finally get some useful information.

The old man took a moment, walked to the bar, and poured himself a glass of what appeared to be scotch. He took a long swig and closed his eyes, as if the discussion was more than he could stand.

"I'd offer you some, but I don't believe that would be appropriate," he said with a smile. "Where was I?"

I didn't think scotch was appropriate for anyone at 9:30 in the morning, but I let it go. "You said things changed when my grandfather came around. And you were going to tell us why. Quickly."

Fleming nodded. "Oh yes, I should say that it all changed. Up until that point, no one had been able to read the symbols. We'd had specialists, linguists, archeologists…" He sipped from his glass, then sat back and sighed.

"Your grandfather, on the other hand, understood the symbols the moment he laid eyes on them. He said that they … spoke to him."

The hair along my neck and arms sprang up at his words. This, then, was where it had all started. Doc had known that quickly. What had the stone said to him? And where had it led?

"What happened then?" I asked breathlessly.

"We were, of course, in shock when he told us what he thought the stones had said to him. He was talking about the ability to travel through time. We couldn't believe it, but how could we discount what he said he'd seen?" He took another long, slow sip of scotch. "So we decided to test it."

I gasped. "You sent someone back?"

"Not at all. Your grandfather devised a simple – and harmless – test. We placed a digital clock on the stone, complete with the day, month, and year, along with two high-speed digital cameras, programmed to monitor the clock. Then we waited. For nearly two days, we left the clock sitting, and changed the digital cameras every other hour. The clock didn't move, and we thought that our initial theory was wrong. Then your grandfather noticed something."

"The time on the clock had changed," I guessed.

Fleming nodded. "Not in the hour, or the minute, or even the second, but in the days. Nearly a month had elapsed on the clock, and we hadn't even seen it leave."

Reis grunted in response, and I nodded. That was on par with what I'd read in Doc's journal. The time conversion didn't match – time moved more quickly in the past than it did here in the … present. "And then?"

"You must understand; at this point, only four of us knew what happened to the clock – myself, my son, his assistant, and, of course, your grandfather."

"And my grandfather and your son disagreed about what to do," I guessed again, speaking softly. The pieces were beginning to fall into place.

"Exactly. My son wanted to make the discovery public. After all, what's the point of being a treasure hunter if you don't get to reveal your discoveries to the world?"

"And Doc, on the other hand…"

"Your grandfather was more cautious. We didn't know how the stones worked, where they would lead us, or how the time difference happened. We didn't know what effects traveling would have on the human body. If someone *did* manage to go back safely, and enter a separate timeline, how were they to get back? He thought there were too many questions still unanswered. He thought that revealing the stones would be too dangerous, at that point."

"That wasn't all he was afraid of, was it?" I asked, thinking of what I'd read in the journal.

Fleming looked at me for a moment, then bowed his head once. "Your grandfather understood something that I did not. He saw that my son would try to use the stones for his own purposes. He saw that my son wanted power in any form."

"What exactly does that mean?" Paul asked.

"My son saw opportunities for change. He saw a chance to travel into and through history to amend it. To right wrongs, and change the balance."

"Is that so bad?" This came from Paul as well.

"I supposed that depends on whether or not you're *sane*," Tatiana replied.

Fleming winced at his granddaughter's remark, then responded to Paul's question. "When Doc first came to me with this concern, I didn't see any problem with it. I felt, like my son, that the world could use some improvements. Doc, as always, was the voice of reason. He knew instantly how dangerous such a move would be. He knew that tampering with the past would throw all of history – and our present world – into chaos. He knew that upsetting the balance would lead to catastrophic outcomes."

"And your son didn't want to hear it."

"No, he didn't. He was impatient, and took matters into his own hands. The following day, without telling us, and without consulting your grandfather about the symbols, he climbed onto the stone and disappeared into history. Your grandfather was able to read the symbols to see where he went, and we knew that he was in York, England, in the year 1468. We knew also that he had no way of getting back."

"But Doc said he was going back to 1485," I cut in. Had the man called Dresden found a way to use the stones after all? Was he still jumping through time?

Fleming shrugged. "Moving through time alters the passage of time. I don't know why, but time moves more quickly in the past than it does here. My son left here four months ago. He's been living in the past for nearly seventeen years. He went to 1468. In that timeline, it's now 1485. Doc has been going back whenever he can, trying to stop him."

"Stop him from what, exactly?" Reis asked.

Fleming sighed. "I'm afraid my son has shown a propensity for violence in the past. He sometimes becomes ... confused."

Tatiana snorted, and stood from the desk to walk into our circle. "He's not confused, John. He's insane. There's a difference."

"Honey, you know I don't like it when you say negative things about your father."

"And you know that he stopped being my father about ten years ago. I don't know why you continue to lie to yourself. Are you trying to protect him? To save him? You know as well as I do that he doesn't deserve to be saved. And he won't accept interference."

At that moment, the pieces finally fell into place, and I began to understand. I ignored the shock of Tatiana's statement about her father, and picked up where she'd left off. "He doesn't want to be saved, because he's doing what he believes to be in his own best interest. When Doc jumped into the past to try and reason with him, Dresden refused to listen. He wanted my grandfather for one reason – to teach him to use the stones. So he could go where he wanted. So that he could jump through time as often as he wanted." I stopped and looked at Fleming, then Tatiana. "Doc refused. He doesn't know how it works himself, and even if he did, he wouldn't tell him. He knows that Dresden would use the power to alter history. To bend it to his will, and remake it as he wishes." My voice faded in shock as I realized the magnitude of the plot.

"Bravo," Tatiana murmured, smiling faintly. "Tricky, isn't it?"

A deep silence followed, broken only when Paul coughed and spoke up.

"So what's Doc going to do, then?"

This time it was Tatiana who answered, not Fleming. "Doc's gone back to stop my father, once and for all. Nicholas Fleming – the man you call Dresden – wants to use Doc and then kill him, or destroy the world, or both. He won't listen to reason, and he doesn't want to be saved. So that only leaves the one option."

"War," Paul murmured, awestruck. "Doc's going to kill Dresden in order to stop him."

Another light went off in my head, and I saw exactly where it was all leading. "Except that they're not going to be on an even playing field," I broke in, rising. "Dresden – I mean Nicholas – isn't going to let it come to that. He's going to try to capture Doc first, and Doc has no idea."

Fleming shook his head. "Son, Nicholas may be confused, but I assure you that he's entirely honorable. He would not deceive your grandfather."

I laughed. "I assure you that he would, and he has. He's made a deal with a man my grandfather considers to be an ally. A deal for my grandfather's life."

Paul, Reis, Tatiana, and Fleming turned to stare at me, their mouths hanging open, and I straightened, ready for their doubt.

"How on earth do you know that?" Paul asked.

I shook my head. "That's not even remotely important, Paul. What is important is getting to Doc in time to warn him."

Fleming stood up and came to rest a hand on my shoulder. "Son, your grandfather can take care of himself. I admire your desire to help him, as I'm sure he would, but let's face the facts. He's beyond your reach."

I brushed his hand from my shoulder and turned to face him, my plan crystallizing in my mind as I spoke. I hadn't considered it before, but now that I did, I realized that my path was as clear as day. I'd never been more sure of anything in my life.

"With all due respect, Mr. Fleming, my grandfather is well within my reach. And he needs my help."

Fleming chuckled. "But, my boy, the fact is –"

"Oh, the stone?" I interrupted. "You're wondering how exactly I would get to him? I'm sorry, did I forget to mention that I can read the stone? That I believe I can, in fact, ride it?"

Fleming's face went blank with shock, and I heard Tatiana gasp behind me. I turned in the face of the silence and strode toward the door, counting on Paul and Reis to follow me.

"What … what are you saying?"

Fleming's whisper was barely audible, but I turned to face the old man, who stood pale, shaking, and alone in the middle of the room.

"I'm saying, Mr. Fleming, that I can read the stones. I know that the next window to the past opens this afternoon. And I plan to be there when it does. I'm going after my grandfather, and there's nothing you can say or do to stop me."

Part II

15

Doncaster, England
August, 1485

The room's only source of illumination came from the twenty wax candles in their gothic iron stands along the wall. The stands were as tall as most men, and had served as weapons more than once. The cavernous room had a dark, mildewed feel, the air thick with the scent of dank soil. It had been built long ago, over 30 feet beneath the castle's floor. Its walls, set within the foundation itself, curved to form thirteen individual arches in the ceiling. These arches towered 20 feet above the floor, supported by wide oak beams that stretched from one end of the room to the other. It was a room built for secrecy and intimidation, for muffling the screams of the men and women unlucky enough to find themselves there.

The current occupant cared little for the architecture, though he valued the hidden secrecy of this room. There were, after all, some things that should not see the light of day. Like the artifact that sat before him now. Nicholas Fleming, known in this world as Lord Dresden, chief councilor to King Richard III in the year of our Lord 1485, sat slumped over in his gilded, straight-backed chair, staring morosely at the black stone in front of him. He wasn't happy.

He had both loved and loathed the stones in the last seventeen years, though neither emotion had helped him. He could feel this stone's power coursing through the room now, and had been able to feel its strength almost from the start. He could not, however, harness the power for himself. Not completely. He'd been trying to do so for as long as he could remember, and still didn't know the secret. He'd been lucky to travel at all on his first and only attempt, and had yet to successfully repeat the action. The stones had brought him here, to an ancient castle in Medieval England, and left him to rot. He didn't know how to go anywhere else, though he'd thought about it often enough. He couldn't tell when the stones were going to open, or where they might take him, and wasn't willing to risk the jump without knowing these important facts.

He snarled suddenly in frustration and threw the cup in his hand at the stone. Secrets. That fool Richard Evans had known them immediately, and had kept them to himself. How he hated the man. He had refused to share the knowledge, no doubt seeking to garner the power for his own uses. Even in this time, when the old man posed as the Earl of Oxford, he maintained his self-righteous, old-fashioned belief that the stones should go unused, and be protected.

Dresden knew better. He knew that the stones offered the impossible – a chance to correct mankind's mistakes, an opportunity to make right a world that had surely lost its way. If he could use the stones as he meant to … but no. He looked around the foul-smelling, windowless room in disgust. He had been brought here and dropped into this God-forsaken wilderness, left to fend for himself without benefit of warmth, money, or even electricity.

But he'd found his way. Oh yes. And now it would all start here, in this backward time before time. His new world order. His grand plan. He would use his power and technological advantages here to win the War of the Roses. With his careful guidance, Richard III would maintain the throne, thus denying Henry Tudor's reign, and with it, Great Britain's dominance over Europe for the next half millennia. This simple sequence of events would take England out of its place of prominence in the future. Make the island weak and defenseless. And easily ruled. Afterwards … he had planned it all years ago, and knew his route well. With Richard firmly on the throne – and Dresden himself in control of Richard's strings – he would begin the next stage of his plan. And from there, the next. And from there ... Dresden smiled grimly at the thought. He'd laid it all out on expensive parchment paper, several years ago, and it had been beautiful. The end, of course was still his favorite part.

A shout from the top of the staircase brought him suddenly out of his thoughts and back to the present. Before any of that could happen he needed to know how to control the stones. His recent alliance with Lord Stanley meant that the Richard Evans would soon be under his control, and with him, the secret of the stones. For the moment, at least, everything was going according to plan. He couldn't read the stones, but he held the most powerful position in the kingdom, and that was a start. Once he held Evans as well, no one would be able to stop him.

Dresden stood, rubbing his cheek and the sore jaw beneath it – he'd had an unfortunate incident with a rotten tooth the day before – and made his way toward the circular staircase. As he climbed the slippery steps, he straightened, squared his shoulders, and firmed his chin to an expression of stubborn power. He knew for himself that he possessed no physically intimidating characteristics, and did not strike a particularly powerful figure. He was relatively short, even for this time period, with fair skin and black eyes. His hair, which he kept short, was blond enough to be almost white. A trimmed goatee sculpted his chin to give his head a sharp, angular shape. His face, which had once been the soft, boyish face of an academic, had changed over the past seventeen years, and now held a cold, hard note of violence and hatred. It was not the face of a kind leader, and did not belong to a forgiving heart. His loyal subjects had spent many years learning to fear and hate him for the things he did, and the man he had become.

His face grew colder and more arrogant as he walked outside, past one of the many men currently learning to respect and fear his lord. The man, who had claimed to be the best healer in the valley, now stood on a wooden platform in the center of the public courtyard, a noose of thick, heavy rope around his neck. He had tried and failed to heal the infected molar in Dresden's mouth, and had signed his own death sentence in the failing. Dresden had, of course, had the rotten tooth pulled by someone else – the only option in this time period. That hadn't been enough to save this man's life.

He strolled through the crowd of people gathered to watch the hanging, enjoying the air of misery and fear, and entered the castle's main hall. His son was practicing his sword work in the stable yard today, and he was of a mind to watch. The boy was progressing quickly, able to take down men twice his size and age, and it pleased Dresden to watch him. Sloan Dresden was sixteen, and would soon be an accomplished swordsman and warrior. He had the strong, lean body for it, and had learned the cold craft of emotionless strategy and murder from his father. Dresden planned to take him into the coming battle to test his strength and will, though he thought that he already knew the boy's heart. His son was bred and raised to follow in his father's footsteps, trained from the day he could walk to carry on his father's battle. Today he would face one of Oxford's captured men at arms in hand-to-hand combat. Dresden had little doubt of the outcome, but wanted to be there to see it.

As he stepped out of the main hall and onto the balcony outside, one of his men stepped forward to intercept him. Dresden glanced at the man, annoyed at this new interruption, but paused when he recognized the leader of his personal spy network.

"You've returned from Abergavenny?" Dresden asked shortly.

The man before him bowed quickly. "The Earl's men were there, as you said they would be."

Dresden grunted. "And?"

"We watched for several hours, my Lord, but saw no sign of our men or the Earl himself in the village. I went to Henry Tudor's personal encampment to warn him, as you ordered."

Dresden nodded. Richard Evans had gone to Abergavenny for the same reason he had sent his own men – to seek a stone. Dresden's men had not found it, but Evans must have. He'd gone home, then, but he would be back. And when he returned…

"What did Tudor have to say? I assume he didn't recognize you as one of mine."

The soldier shook his head. "Henry Tudor does not know me as your man, my Lord. Nor did he know of Oxford's presence in Abergavenny. He was not pleased with the news."

Dresden chuckled. Evans had entered that village without permission from Henry Tudor, and had left himself vulnerable in doing so. Henry Tudor was not secure in his position yet, and disliked being disobeyed or disrespected. Dresden had seen an opportunity to bring Evans down in the Pretender's eyes, and had sent his best men to see it done.

"What does he plan to do?" he asked quietly.

"When Oxford shows himself, my Lord, he will be arrested and taken before Henry for his act of dissidence."

He nodded once at his soldier, satisfied, then turned and walked quickly toward the stairway, having already forgotten his son and the swordplay in the stable yard. A more important mission beckoned.

"Ready the men and my fastest horses," he barked. "I want to be there to see him arrested. We ride tonight."

Abergavenny, England

The stone beneath him hummed and pulsed in time with his heart, beating as it bore him through time. The world rolled around him in a mad, chaotic parade of events, people, and places, and he held tightly to both sanity and courage. When the ride came to an abrupt halt, he stilled, forcing himself to breathe. Forcing his muscles to relax. He lay on the stone in Abergavenny for longer than he'd ever had to before, filling his lungs with oxygen and slowly exhaling, counting backwards in his head to control his heart and mind.

The world finally came to a standstill around him, and Doc opened his eyes. The jumps were becoming more difficult. It had never taken him this long to recover before, and it worried him. He wondered, for the hundredth time, about the physics of jumping through time, and the effects on his body. He had come to love his role in the past, and almost depend on it, but found himself wishing more and more often for a reprieve from the pull of the stones. Perhaps...

All thoughts scattered as his memory abruptly returned. He'd jumped in a hurry this time. Jason had been asking strange questions, and had nearly made him miss the window. What was the boy on about? Why the sudden interest and the obscure questions about time travel? Surely he hadn't … Doc paused as more memory returned, and his breath caught in his throat.

The last thing he'd seen before the world went black in the jump was his grandson at the bottom of the ladder, staring at him. Jason had found his way into the hidden room. He'd seen the stone. He'd seen Doc make the jump.

Doc leapt from the stone and moved quickly to the other side of the room, turning to watch the stone for movement. No one had ever followed him through the stones before, and he wasn't sure it was even possible, but if Jason had run forward and touched the stone while the window was open…

After several minutes, though, the stone's glow faded to stark black, and the symbols returned to their places. Doc breathed a sigh of relief. Jason had stayed in the future, then. Where he was secure, and safe.

Doc, on the other hand, had work to do. He had to accomplish not one, not two, but three goals in a mere four days. He must work to gather an army, one large enough to confront Richard III. He had to lead that army into battle and defeat the old king, to ensure the safety of both history and the world. His thoughts touched gently on the idea of failure, and then moved quickly on. He didn't have the time or courage to think about that, at least not right now. The third goal … stop Dresden by any means necessary. Doc didn't understand what the man was trying to do, but he knew that it would bring danger – and perhaps devastation – to the world around him. The second goal, though, should end Dresden on its own.

Once Richard was defeated, Dresden would lose his sole supporter. His power would be eliminated. He would, in fact, be a wanted man. Left here to face justice for his actions, Dresden would end his story in the simplest way possible – by fading gently into history. Doc would return home and do his best to forget that any of this had ever happened.

At that thought, he went quickly about the process of rebuilding the Earl of Oxford. He found his heavy cloak in the corner of the room, where he'd left it prior to his trip home, then wrapped his belt around his waist and hefted his sword, measuring the weight of the heavy, thick blade. As he strode toward the door, his shoulders growing square and his hands flexing into fists, he felt the persona of the Earl settle over his body like a mantle. His face lengthened and lost the elderly softness he maintained as Doc. His mouth firmed, his eyes narrowed, and he stepped through the door into the past.

He didn't find what he'd expected. Someone had evidently told Henry of the Earl's presence in Abergavenny, and the bloody fool had taken offense. The erstwhile king's men had arrived while he was absent, attacked the Earl's own men, and laid an ambush for him. He'd already been facing an impossible task, with a scant four days to secure his goals. Now, instead of marching out to gather men and arms, plan the march, and prepare for the coming battle, he was being forced to report to Henry's encampment to satisfy that man's paranoia. The Earl shook his head in disgust. He didn't have time for this, and neither did his mission.

His men were allowed to keep their horses and arms as tokens of good will, and so rode out of Abergavenny as guests rather than prisoners. The one hundred men surrounding them, each with a hand on his sword, spoke against this position of trust, and the Earl snorted. This fickle turn of events worried him.

He glanced anxiously at the road ahead of them, wondering how long this would take, and whether he would still have time to gather the men he needed. His eyes roamed the rock-faced hills above him, seeking answers. Jagged rocks, small trees, and brush covered the hills, making them an ideal place for a hidden rendezvous.

This was not a safe road, he realized suddenly. If he were setting up an ambush himself, he would seek a location like this. The hills were covered with trees and thick brush, ideal for hiding, and the road below was exposed and vulnerable. He had already wondered at his arrest, and now the possibilities seemed frighteningly clear. An exposed road, an indefensible position… His breath began to come faster, and he bit his tongue on the last thought. If someone were to attack them here, there would be no protection, no –

A sudden movement on the hillside ahead of him caught his eye and he stiffened, ready to jump to action. He squinted toward the movement, seeking desperately to find order in the brush. Then he saw them.

A band of ten armed men sat, observing, at the top of the small hill. They were not in a position to attack, and would have failed with such a small force. They were there, then, to watch. In the middle of the band sat a small man, dressed in black or dark blue. Even at this distance, the Earl could see the sunlight glinting off the blond, nearly white hair, and recognize the arrogant bearing of the man's shoulders. Dresden, then, come to watch the arrest of his enemy. Standing in plain view, no doubt, so that the Earl would know what he'd done.

With that realization, the Earl found his true answer. Dresden had somehow managed to get into Henry's camp and capture his ear. While he wasn't putting the Earl in any true danger, he had cost him both time and strength – two things that were more important now than they ever had been. He began counting swiftly in his head, trying to estimate the damage, and making judgments and decisions as he came to them. The battle would happen in four short days. It would take a full day to get to Henry's encampment and sort through this business. After that, he would have to gather his own men and those of his king, and push them as hard as he could to reach the battle grounds.

He would have to pray that they got there in time.

A grunt of frustration passed his lips. It would be a long shot, at best, and he wasn't sure he would be able to do it. The road to battle – and the fight afterward – would be chaotic and dangerous, and many of the men there would die. They had no choice, however; if they failed to reach the battle site, Dresden and Richard would win, and history would be derailed.

Many of his men would die in the coming week, but their deaths would mean the safety of the world at large. If they got there in time.

He spared one moment to thank God that Jason was safe at home, in the future, with Reis to protect him. That, at least, guaranteed the family's future.

16

Lebanon, New Hampshire
Present Day

Reis tore out of the private drive at about 80 MPH and took the onramp to the freeway on two wheels, his hands wrapped firmly around the steering wheel. I clung to the passenger's side door, my thoughts racing along with the car, trying to make sense of what had just happened. Paul remained uncharacteristically quiet, wedged in between us.

"How long do we have?" Reis snapped. He swerved abruptly to slip Doc's car in front of a semi truck, missing its front fender by mere inches.

My thoughts stalled for a moment, trying to understand Reis's question. My head was a whirlwind, and didn't want to settle. Then the answer was there, clear and bright. "The window opens at 12 noon," I answered quietly. "That gives us..." I looked at the digital clock on the car's dashboard. "Less than two and a half hours."

Reis nodded, and his mouth settled into a grim line. "And it takes over forty-five minutes to get back to the house. That isn't going to be quick enough." He stomped on the accelerator, pushing the car to speeds it had probably never experienced, and we shot past the other cars and trucks on the freeway.

By the time we got home, my hands ached from holding onto the door, and I thought Paul might throw up. We hadn't slowed for stop signs, traffic signals, or other cars in the last twenty minutes, but we'd made it back safely, and in half the time it should have taken us.

More importantly, I had a plan.

"Your car's gone," Paul said as we pulled into our driveway. He was right; the body of Reis' car, along with the glass, plastic, fiberglass, and metal that had exploded across our driveway only hours before, had been gathered up and carted off the property. The driveway was empty, as if nothing ever happened.

If I'd thought about it, which I hadn't, I would have expected cops, a bomb squad, and half the neighborhood in our yard, courtesy of Mrs. Grey. We didn't get gunfights or grenade launchers very often on this street, and it should have drawn a crowd. Instead, the neighborhood was quiet. Doors were shut, curtains drawn. Just another Monday morning in Lebanon, New Hampshire.

"I called a clean-up crew for damage control," Reis answered casually. "Just some friends of mine. We don't have time for a three-ring circus right now."

"Cool," Paul whispered.

Reis reached up to tap the garage door opener on the visor above him, and we pulled into the darkness of the garage. The heavy metal door banged shut behind us and darkness descended, leaving us in the soft glow of the single bulb swinging overhead. For a moment we sat, eyes straight ahead, mouths shut, staring at the back wall. Then Reis broke the silence.

"We don't have much time." He looked at his watch and turned to face me. "Are you alright?"

I stared back at him for a moment before replying. "Am I alright? I'm sitting here wondering if I can believe a word of this – if *any* of us can – and you're asking if I'm al*right*? Are you *serious*?"

Reis looked away, then nodded as though he'd reached an agreement with himself. "If you'd asked me two days ago, I wouldn't have been alright either. I wouldn't have believed a word of this. But I can't ignore what I've seen and heard here. And if we're going to do this – really do it – I think we all have to believe, at least a little." He cast me a sideways grin and winked.

I hadn't thought I was waiting for his approval, but at Reis' words the world started moving again and my brain kicked back into gear.

"Right," I said, jumping out of the car. "In that case, enough of this sitting around and waiting. We have to get moving."

Paul, who'd been crushed between Reis and I, tumbled out of the car behind me. "Where are we going? What're we going to do?"

I walked quickly around the car and met Reis at the door to the house. I glanced up at the older man, then back at Paul.

"Our homework. I have a plan, but we need to know what we're getting into."

"Absolutely," Reis said with a faint smile. "Good man."

Paul whistled quietly. "I'm in, Batman. Where do we start?"

"Paul, get to anything with an internet connection. We know where we're going and when, so at least that's a start. Download as much information as you can on the Battle of Bosworth, and put it on your phone. Get into the War of the Roses, too. The players, the families, the time period. We need to know the outcomes, so we know where to go and what to do. Get anything you can on the people. How they talked, what they ate. I know a little, but we need details. We need to fit in as much as we can when we get there."

I had walked through the kitchen toward the stairs as I talked, unwilling to waste time standing around. Now Reis grasped my arm gently and broke away from Paul and me, moving toward the front door.

"Wait, where are you going?" Paul asked

Reis turned. "If we're going to go jumping into the past, I want to go prepared. I'm just going to grab the things we may need. In the meantime, don't answer the door, and stay out of sight. We've already had one set of unexpected visitors today. We don't need another."

Paul gulped at the reminder. "How do you know they won't come back once you leave?"

Reis stood quietly for a moment, thinking. He shook his head. "I don't know, not for sure. But I'd be surprised if they did. Whoever it was came for Doc, or you." Reis looked back at me and I held my breath, meeting his eyes. "I hurt them, and they'll need to regroup. Then again..." He paused, then decided. "There are things I have to get. I won't be gone for long." He nodded quickly in my direction, then turned and walked away.

Paul and I stood in the kitchen, watching the door close behind Reis.

"Do you think he'll come back?" Paul asked quietly.

I nodded. "I know he will." I moved toward the stairs, ready to start my part of the research. Paul turned toward the door.

"Okay then, I'm going home to grab a few things myself. Do some research. When I get back, I'll be ready to go."

I stopped, surprised. "What do you mean? You're not coming with us."

Paul turned to look at me, hurt. "What do *you* mean? Of course I'm coming with you."

I shook my head. "Paul, this is nuts. The only reason I'm going is to save Doc. The only reason Reis is going is to protect me. There's no reason for you to come along and risk your life." I paused, but plunged on. "I can do this without you, Paul. I don't need you to –"

"Jay, you and Doc are my family," Paul interrupted. "I haven't seen my dad in over two years, and my mother…" Paul shrugged. "Well, let's be honest, we're not exactly the Waltons. You're the brother I *should* have had. I'm not going to let you go running off into trouble without me. And I'm sure as hell not sitting at home while you have this great, life-changing adventure." He gave me a crooked smile, but I shook my head. Paul was like a brother to me too, and there was no way I was going to let him head into danger.

"But–"

Paul cut me off before I could formulate an answer. "But nothing," he said slowly. "I'm your best friend. If I were going, you'd go with *me*."

He was right, and I nodded unwillingly. "I hadn't really thought of it that way," I said quietly.

Paul snorted. "Of course you didn't, but you should." He sighed. "Jason, I'm going. I'm not letting you jump into the past without me there to watch your back. Deal with it."

He turned without waiting for an answer, and walked quickly to the door.

"Paul," I said quietly. He turned, his eyebrows raised in question, and I shrugged. "As long as you're coming along, do me one more favor. Look for my grandfather in the historical records. The Earl of Oxford. Find out where he'll be and how he gets there. When we get to the past, we need to know how to find him."

I walked quickly up the stairs, thinking. This was the first time I'd been alone in days, and the emptiness of the house echoed around me. I paused, listening to the familiar creaks and groans. This place had been my second home for as long as I could remember, and when my parents died, it had been a natural and easy transition to move here. In a time when the world itself seemed wrong, things in this house were familiar, comforting, and dependable; always in the place that made sense to both the object itself and those around it. It was, after all, the home of a physics professor. Everything had a certain order, reason, and location, put there according to the unendingly organized – and logical – mind of my grandfather.

I stopped mid-stride, one foot on a higher stair than the other, my eyes fixed on the hallway in front of me. The unendingly organized and logical mind of a physics professor. Of course. Suddenly I was running up the stairs toward Doc's room, my mind racing. I couldn't believe I hadn't thought of it before. Doc had been traveling into the past for months, interacting with the people there, building a life with every trip. And he would have gone prepared. "Measure twice, cut once" was one of his favorite mottos. No way would he have gone trudging into old England without doing his homework first. And he always wrote everything down.

I just had to find it.

I skidded to a halt just outside his room and threw open the door. The rich, familiar scent of English Leather aftershave hit me like a ton of bricks, and I gasped.

"Try not to skimp on the aftershave there, Doc," I muttered to my absent grandfather. "Never know who you might meet on the roads of old England."

I snorted at my own joke, then walked to the old oak desk in the corner. It was the obvious place to start, and Doc had never been good at subtlety. Throwing open the drawers, though, I found only old photos of my dad and grandmother, miscellaneous receipts, a broken compass, an autographed copy of a paperback novel, and a signed Ted Williams baseball card enveloped in hard plastic. I glanced twice – and then three times – at the baseball card, and made a mental note to come back to it when I got home. The only other item in the drawer was an ancient bronze pocket watch, colored and pitted with age. It had an engraving on the back from my grandmother, which read, "My love for you is timeless."

I smiled, then paused, rubbing the engraving with my forefinger and closing my eyes. This was Doc's watch. I'd seen him carrying it when I was younger, and even had a blurred memory of him teaching me to wind it up. The heavy, rounded edges pressed against my palm as my hand clenched, and I opened my eyes. This watch had gone to my father at one point, and made its way back into the desk at his death. It had been here, waiting for me, this whole time. I unclenched my hand and glanced down at the watch, then took a deep breath and wound the key on the side. This was coming with me. I dropped it into my pocket and smiled. I'd always had a thing for watches. I could watch gears turn for hours on end. More importantly, though, clocks could tell you the time. Especially ones with manual winders, like this one had. Where – and when – we were going, that would definitely come in handy.

Plus it was a piece of Doc – and my dad – traveling with me.

Traveling.

I slammed the drawer shut on that thought and rotated the swivel chair, searching the room for other potential hiding places. The place was pretty stark – a bed in the center of the room, with two nightstands at the sides. A large chest rounded out the room's décor, but I'd been through that before, and knew that it held only socks, boxers, and old shorts. If I was Doc, and I wanted to keep things organized … I stood resolutely and walked toward the closet. I didn't think he was hiding anything under his bed, and this was the only other option.

I threw open the door of the small walk-in closet and glared around. Long-sleeved shirts and dress pants hung along one bar, evenly spaced and organized into color blocks. Above the racks, stacks of sweaters and t-shirts, many still wrapped in their original plastic packaging, lined the wooden shelf that stretched the full length of the closet. In the back of the small room, dozens of skirts, blouses, and dresses clung to their familiar corner. My grandmother's clothes, kept in their place despite the fact that she'd passed away years earlier.

Nothing that looked remotely like a sword, shield, or suit of armor. No boxes of research, either.

I walked quickly into the closet, muttering. It was here, somewhere – I could almost feel it calling to me. "Come on, Doc, throw me a bone," I mumbled.

I moved his clothes from side to side and pawed my way frantically through an old leather briefcase and two cardboard boxes filled with record albums from the '60s and '70s, searching aimlessly for something that looked important. Then I dropped to my knees and began pulling the lids off the shoeboxes. After two or three boxes, I slowed down and started paying more attention. Most of the shoeboxes were clean, and starkly empty. Even the tissue was gone. On the sixth shoeless box in a row, the would-be home of size 13 Timberlands, I found what I was looking for.

The box held a stack of neatly typed, paper-clipped, and labeled papers. Doc's handwriting stood out in bold red ink at the top of the first page.

"Fifteenth-century living," I read. "Oh my God." My knees went weak and I collapsed abruptly, unable to support myself anymore. This was what I'd been looking for, but looking and finding were two completely different things. Finding research like this brought the whole thing into bright, startling reality. A reality that even the stone hadn't encouraged.

Still, I didn't have time to back out now.

I pulled the papers out of the box and leaned over them, running my hand over the Table of Contents. It was the organization of an academic mind, and no mistake. My eyes ran down the list, looking for a place to start.

"History, Traveling, Hygiene, What to Wear, The Law, The People, Currency, Dialogue, Basic Essentials, Royalty Protocol, and Pray, Work, and Fight," I read quietly. Doc had left me everything I needed, right here.

I turned to the first page and glanced at the material. The text read like a tour guide to Medieval England. Each page was meticulously spaced and typed out, with generous margins. Doc's handwritten notes filled the empty spaces. The breath caught in my throat at his familiar, well-spaced printing, and I swiped at the moisture that appeared suddenly on my cheek, thinking that I needed to mention to Doc that he had a water leak in his closet. Leaning forward, I began to read.

The War of the Roses 1455 - 1485 (circa)

- *England is caught in the middle of a power struggle between the York family (led by King Richard III), and Lancaster family (led by Henry VII).*
- *Named for the white rose of York and red rose of Lancaster. Both houses descended from royalty.*
- *At the start of the period, the York family is in firm control, with Edward IV on the throne. Henry Tudor – distant Lancaster relative – lives in France.*

- *Richard of Gloucester (York family, Edward IV's brother) takes power in 1483, after Edward's sons, Edward V and his younger brother, disappear. Common belief is that Richard killed both boys. Richard is crowned King Richard III, but not without controversy. Many powerful families are unhappy with this turn of events.*

- *Richard III does not make friends during reign. Continued movement of Lancaster family for reins of power.*

- *Henry Tudor is descended from royalty. Mother is a Lancaster heiress, grandfather was a bastard son of Henry V. His mother, Margaret Beaufort, has sent him to France for his safety. She now begins to insist he come home and take the crown.*

- *France backs Henry, who also receives assurances from many English lords. He crosses the Channel to make battle and take the throne.*

- *The Battle of Bosworth, August 22, 1485. Richard is killed, ending the War of the Roses. Henry Tudor becomes king as Henry VII. Marries Elizabeth of York, Richard III's niece and Edward IV's daughter, to unite families.*

Well that was a particularly clean-cut version. I'd heard of the War of the Roses, of course, and knew the bones of the story. It was Medieval England's version of the Hatfields and McCoys. The Yorks and Lancasters had warred for years, killing each other as often as they could despite the fact that they were cousins. When Richard III finally came to power, it was as a usurper and murderer. No one had complained when Henry took over. Of course, Henry VII had caused his own set of problems, and led straight to Henry VIII. We all knew how that turned out.

But it had all started here. The Battle of Bosworth. Dresden would try to help Richard win the war, while Doc would try to balance Dresden's influence by throwing his own weight on Henry's side. Dresden sought to change history, and change the course of England itself, while Doc sought to maintain it.

And in trying to maintain it, Doc was walking right into his own death.

I sat numb for a moment, caught on that thought, then shook myself. I didn't have time to doze off or get depressed. I had a window to catch, and time was sliding by too quickly.

I pulled Doc's watch out of my pocket and noted the time, then grabbed the research and moved to his bed. We had a little over an hour before the stone's window opened. I had to get through this stuff, and fast. My heart raced as I skipped through the notebook to find the section on people. This is what we would need to know if we were going to fit in.

I read the entire stack of paper as quickly as I could, memorizing as much of the information as possible, then moved to my room, where I shoved the papers into my printer. I hit the 'scan' function, and darted to the closet. I had packing to do. Downstairs, the door slammed shut and someone stormed into the house.

"Where are you?" Paul shouted. I heard his footsteps tearing through the living room and racing up the stairs.

"In here," I called back. I threw open my closet door and started rifling through my clothes, searching for my backpack and sleeping bag. When I found them, I heaved them into the center of the room.

"What were you doing?" Paul asked, appearing suddenly in the doorway. He glanced quickly around the room, taking in my lack of preparation. "Why aren't you packed? We don't have much time!"

"Homework," I replied. I tossed the sleeping bag and backpack onto my bed, then grabbed two pair of jeans, two rugby shirts, and a hoodie.

"What did you find out, anything useful?" Paul asked. He yanked open my sock drawer and started throwing things haphazardly on the bed.

"I think so," I replied. I caught three pairs of socks and stuffed them into the side pocket of my backpack, then ducked to let another five pairs fly past. "Paul, cool it with the socks," I snapped. "We're not having a rummage sale here, and you're stressing me out."

"Stressing you out? *I'm* stressing you out?" he muttered. "I'm just trying to help. Anyhow, I got a bunch of info too, all loaded on my phone."

I nodded. "And my grandfather?"

"Yeah I found him, too," Paul said. "You all done with this?"

I folded up one last thick wool sweater and jammed it into the backpack, then stood back. "Yep, packed in less than two minutes. That must be some sort of record." I threaded the draw string of my sleeping bag through the strap of my backpack and dropped both articles on the floor. Then I stuffed the Swiss Army knife that my father had given me for my tenth birthday into my pocket, along with a flashlight the size of a magic marker.

I glanced at Paul to confirm his readiness, and did a double take. He had on a pair of white Reebok high tops, dark jeans with a hole in the left knee, a short-sleeved Patriots jersey with the number '12' printed on the chest, and a dark blue baseball cap with a large B on it. He'd brought a dark green backpack that appeared to be bursting at the seams, and a light blue sleeping bag. The sleeping bag was held together by two bright orange shoelaces.

He must have noticed the dismayed look on my face, because he sighed in resignation. "We don't exactly blend in, do we?" he asked.

"Not exactly," I replied. "We'll just have to get in and get out again before it becomes a problem." I turned toward my desk and glanced at my computer, where the scanning software was showing an electronic copy of Doc's notes. My iPhone was already connected, and I made quick work of the transfer, then yanked the phone off the connector.

"How much time do we have?" Paul asked suddenly. He looked at his watch and I took Doc's watch out of my pocket.

"A little over half an hour," I answered, winding the watch and checking the time against my computer's clock.

Paul sighed in response. "Where's Reis? I'd feel a lot better if he was back," he said. He walked toward my window and drew my curtain to one side, glancing down at the yard and the garden shed that awaited us.

I grunted in response. I'd been so busy studying that I hadn't even thought about Reis, but Paul's words brought him quickly back to mind. A large knot began to form in my stomach. Paul was right, he had been gone for a long time. Was he really coming back? And if he didn't, would the two of us be brave enough to go through with this on our own? I looked at Doc's pocket watch once again and gulped.

Less than thirty-five minutes left, and Reis was nowhere in sight.

17

Suddenly Paul gasped and plastered himself to the window. "Thank God. He's here."

I shot to the window to stand next to him and watch as Reis climbed out of his car and made his way quickly toward the shed. He took the lock off and ducked inside, careful to close the door behind him.

"What's he doing? Leaving without us?" Paul whispered.

I shook my head. "He wouldn't do that. He *couldn't* do that." I turned and grabbed my sleeping bag and backpack, though. We needed to get down there, regardless of what the body guard was doing.

"Wait, he's back," Paul muttered, interrupting me. "And he's carrying something."

I turned back and stared out the window. He was right – Reis was carrying a long roll of paper under one arm.

"He's got Doc's map of England," I answered, already thinking ahead. The map would come in handy; I'd loaded a map of England onto my phone, but it was a modern map – none of the old cities or territories were labeled. I'd also have to look at it on the phone screen, which was less than ideal. The full-size map would give us a much better idea of what we were dealing with. Besides that, who knew if my phone would even survive the trip, or work when we got there? I shook my head at the thought. I could worry about that later. Right now we needed to finish preparing and get to the stone.

I looked down again, willing Reis to move faster. He tucked the half-folded map more securely under his arm, closed the shed's door behind him, and strode firmly toward Doc's car, which was parked in the driveway. He glanced at the house across the street, and then down the street itself, scanning the block for anything out of place. He must not have seen anything, because he turned his back on the street and bent to the trunk of the car to pull out a dark green duffel back and a long black case, then slammed the trunk and quickly made his way to the house, glancing back once before opening the front door.

"How much time do we have?" Paul asked excitedly.

"Twenty-nine minutes," I replied, looking at Doc's pocket watch for the hundredth time. The watch was already making me feel more secure, though I hadn't thought of this when I first nabbed it. It sat heavy and solid in my hand, reminding me of Doc's usual solid presence. I slipped it back into my pocket now, running my thumb over the engraving before withdrawing my hand.

Suddenly, Reis was standing in my doorway, looking like the cover of Tom Clancy's latest Black Ops video game. He wore black cargo pants with at least a thousand pockets and a stern, almost formal black turtleneck sweater. A utility belt that would have made Batman proud was clasped around his waist, and a shoulder harness of black heavy-duty nylon held his 9mm handgun. A black knit cap covered his hair, and a dark green scarf rested loosely around his neck. He looked relaxed and confident, as if he'd done this a million times, and already knew exactly how it was going to play out.

"I get the feeling we're a little underdressed," Paul muttered out the side of his mouth.

Reis nodded solemnly at me, glanced quickly at Paul, and laid the duffel bag on the floor. He set the rigid black case gently on my bed, flipped the locks, and pushed it open.

Paul gasped at what was inside. "Is that what I think it is?" he asked, awed.

"It's an HK-416 assault rifle, complete with undercarriage grenade launcher," Reis said sternly. He pulled the gun, shiny and black, from its case, leaned it against the bed, and looked at Paul. "Is that what you thought it was?"

"Heavy," Paul breathed. Suddenly he broke into a grin. "Do we each get one?"

The corner of Reis' mouth turned up in an answering smirk. "What do you think?"

I rose from my seat, anxious to get started, and in no mood for jokes. "Do you think the weapons are a good idea?" I asked hesitantly. "Don't you think they'll … stand out?"

Reis straightened. "I've been hired to protect you to the best of my ability. I'm not exactly trained in the use of a long bow or heavy sword, so…" He grabbed the assault rifle, popped open the chamber, and slammed a large magazine into its housing, then glanced back at me. "This will have to do. Now, how much time do we have?"

"About thirty minutes," I replied.

"About?" Reis asked sternly. "I don't think estimations are a good idea, do you?"

I frowned and reached into my pocket for the pocket watch. He was right. We all had to take this more seriously. "Twenty-four minutes and thirty seconds," I replied, snapping the case shut and turning toward the door.

Paul spoke into the silence that followed. "Getting close then. Do we at least have some sort of idea what we're going to do? Maybe even a plan?"

Reis walked quickly toward the desk, unrolled Doc's map, and pinned it down to keep it open. "Well we certainly don't have a lot of time. Jay, where did you say we would land?" he asked sharply.

"Doncaster," I replied, moving over to stand next to him and peer down at the map. Paul moved to my side and looked over my shoulder.

Reis jabbed his finger at the map. "Doncaster. And where are we going?"

I shuffled quickly through the papers on the desk, looking for the history section. "The Battle of Bosworth. Takes places in Leicester on August 22, 1485."

Reis nodded, then traced the route with a yellow highlighter. "Looks like we'll be traveling around 75 miles then." He stopped and looked sharply at me. "How long will we have? Where will we find Doc? What do we need to do?"

I paused as his rapid-fire questions hit, then pulled the map toward me and pointed to the south, where Abergavenny appeared as a small dot. "According to my research, Doc and his army will be coming from this area. Henry Tudor had Welsh blood, and used Wales as his staging point." I quickly circled another city to the north. "Richard III came – will come – from the north. Both armies will move toward each other to meet here," I circled Leicester several times, scribbling across the surrounding areas, "for their final battle." My voice cracked on the last word. I dropped the pen and looked at Reis, gulping my panic.

"We'll get there four days before the battle starts. That means we have three days to find Doc. Without getting caught by either army."

Reis nodded. "So we've got less than four days to travel 70-plus miles in a time period where people will most likely mistake us for wizards. We'll be on foot, hiding from Richard's army, as well as Dresden, and trying to find the assassins who're trying to find your grandfather. Should be … interesting." He folded the map into eighths and shoved it into one of his pockets.

"If either of you have to use the bathroom, I'd suggest you do it now," he said, striding from the room. "I have a few more things to gather. We leave in nineteen minutes."

Paul and I were in the living room stacking our gathered goods when Reis returned, looking at his watch and barking orders. "Okay gentlemen, we're almost out of time and I don't think we can afford to miss our ride." He unzipped his bag, pulled out three brown bundles, and threw two of them at us. "Put those over your clothes."

"What are they?" Paul asked, holding up the woolly robe.

"They're Snuggies," I replied, grinning and pulling mine over my head. "Get into it, Paul."

Paul snorted. "I can't wear this."

Reis, who had already donned a Snuggie of his own, reached over and shoved the robe over Paul's head. "I'm no historian, kid, but I don't think jeans and football jerseys fit in where we're going. These look at least somewhat authentic." He backed up and looked us over. "Besides, we're going into Medieval England. It's going to be colder there, and we'll need blankets."

Paul nodded, then glanced down at our sleeping bags and backpacks. Reis followed his eyes to the stack of stuff. He sighed.

"Hold up, let's see what you guys brought." He ducked down and started rifling through my bag, tossing t-shirts and a pair of jeans to the side. Within seconds he'd zipped up my bag and moved on to Paul's. I noticed that he was taking more out of Paul's backpack than mine, and smiled to myself as Paul's clothing went flying across the room.

"What are you doing?" Paul shrieked. "I need those, and we don't have time for you to play fashion advisor!" He stepped forward, presumably to salvage his wardrobe, and Reis held up a finger.

"Boys, we're going to be on foot and in quite a bit of danger. We'll need to move fast. That means traveling light." He held up a shaving kit, looking daggers at Paul.

Paul opened his mouth to argue, then thought better of it and shut it with a snap.

"And what is *this*?" Reis asked sharply, pulling out a purple marble bag.

"Chocolate coins," Paul replied. "Energy source. Just in case."

Reis shook his head, stuffed the chocolates back into Paul's pack, and glanced back down at the bags. "That'll have to do for now, I don't have time for a more thorough job." He zipped Paul's bag and stood up, glancing quickly at me and then his watch.

"Seven minutes … It's time to get down there," he said, his voice clipped. "If anyone wants to change their mind, now is the time to speak up."

Paul and I glanced at each other again, then nodded as one.

"We're ready, Reis," I answered quietly. "We don't have time to back out." I turned toward the door and strengthened my voice. "Let's go find my grandfather."

I rushed out the back door and turned left toward the back yard and garden shed, with Reis hot on my heels. We both stopped short at Paul's exclamation.

"What the hell is *she* doing here?!"

I turned, annoyed at the delay, and almost choked.

She looked as though she'd stepped right out of a Jeep ad tucked into the glossy pages of a *Maxim* magazine. I wouldn't have recognized her face at all, but the way she stood gave her away. Tatiana Fleming had appeared in my driveway uninvited, and now leaned casually back against a green SUV, her arms folded across her chest. She wore black hiking boots, baggy khaki-colored cargo pants, and a tight grey wool sweater. Her hair was pulled back into a bun and reflective sunglasses bridged the end of her nose to complete the picture. She lowered her chin to look at me over the rims of the glasses, then squared her shoulders. Beneath the glasses, her mouth firmed from a relaxed pout to a firm line.

"What are you doing here, kid?" Reis asked sharply. "We don't have time to chat."

Tatiana kicked at the black duffel and sleeping bag at her feet. "I'm coming with you," she answered, matching Reis' dry tone.

Reis shook his head. "Go home! This is no place for girls."

Tatiana shoved herself off the Jeep and took a quick step toward us. "You're going back, and I want to come with you," she said firmly.

Reis shook his head again and turned away from her. "I really don't care what you want to do. This isn't summer camp and I'm not a camp counselor." He began to move toward the garden shed, snapping my name as he went.

I jumped to follow him, but Tatiana moved before I could, sprinting forward to grab Reis' arm and stop him.

"At least hear me out," she said, her voice low and tense.

"We've got to go!" Paul protested, looking at his watch in panic. I nodded and started to move forward again, but Tatiana threw out a hand to stop me. She pinned Reis with her gaze and stood a bit taller.

"You're going after my father, who's going after Doc, and you're going to need to get to him quickly if you're going to stop him. No one knows more about my father than I do. Certainly not either of you two, or you, Mr. Slayton," she muttered. She'd obviously expected a refusal, and prepared her argument. She was speaking quicker now, driving her point home. "I know what my father is up to. His tendencies, his habits ... you need me Mr. Slayton, if you're going to succeed."

"Like a hole in the head," Reis replied. He turned away and Tatiana's hand snaked out to stop him again.

"I'm fluent in French and I've done extensive studies in European history, specifically as it relates to the Middle Ages." Reis, Paul, and I shook our heads and turned toward the shed, walking away from the girl.

She ran after us, breathing loudly.

"It's bad enough I'm chaperoning the boys!" Reis shouted at her. "I don't have time to look out for a girl!"

Tatiana sputtered in anger. "Girl?! I'm a fourth-degree black belt in Tai Kwon Do, I speak four languages fluently, and I've traveled the world since I was a kid! Don't judge me by my age or gender, Mr. Slayton!"

She ran ahead of us and threw her backpack against the shed's door, then stepped in front of it. "I'm coming with or without your blessing, and you don't have time to argue." Her voice dropped to a dangerous level with the next line. "You're running out of time, after all."

"The answer is still no," Reis said. He placed his hands on her arms and lifted her out of the way like a ragdoll.

For the first time, Tatiana became upset. Her expression – previously confident – grew hard and cold. "Is that so?" she asked quietly. The corner of her mouth turned up and she shrugged. "You might want to rethink that. I mean I'd hate for anything to happen to the stone while you were gone, or something. How exactly would you … get back?"

Paul and I had been rushing past her, anxious to get to the stone. We were already halfway through the door when her words hit me. I came to a skidding halt and turned slowly back to the yard. For a moment, silence reigned. Without the stone, we'd have no way back. And she knew it.

"Are you threatening us?" Reis asked, his voice ragged with tightly held anger.

Tatiana shook her head slowly. "No, not at all. But I do know where the stone is…" She paused for a moment before she spoke again. "And there are a lot of people who would do whatever they had to for that kind of information. I haven't exactly been trained to keep my mouth shut under intense interrogation. Can you take the chance that I won't talk, Mr. Slayton?"

I watched, my mouth hanging open. What was she saying? Surely she wouldn't –

Beside me, Paul hissed, interrupting my thoughts. He was jumping up and down and pointing at his watch. "Four minutes!" he mouthed, his eyes taking up half of his face.

I turned back to Reis and reached out to nudge him. "Reis, we have to go," I muttered anxiously.

He nodded and threw one last glance at Tatiana. "Looks like you're in, girl. But I don't like it, and I won't be watching out for you."

She smiled brilliantly in victory. "You don't have too. I've been on my own longer then I can remember." Tatiana grabbed her backpack and sleeping bag and brushed quickly past us, moving into the shed. "From what I've seen, it looks like I'll have to take care of *you*, rather than the other way around." She stopped and glanced over her shoulder. "Are you boys coming? I was under the impression that we were in a hurry."

We fell over ourselves rushing after her.

Once we were all in the shed, Paul slammed the door shut behind us. The trap door was already open – we hadn't closed it after we saw Doc leave. I moved toward it and peered into the dimness below, breathless.

"Here we go," I whispered to myself.

Reis appeared next to me, glancing at his watch. "We have less than three minutes, people!" he barked. "Quit staring and get your butts down the ladder!"

I scrambled down first, followed closely by Tatiana. We got out of the way just in time to avoid Paul, who missed the last several rungs in his hurry and landed belly-first on the ground.

I heard a soft roar behind me and turned from my fallen friend to the stone. The last time I'd seen it, it had been glowing brightly, its symbols dancing their ageless dance in the air above it. And it had held the fading form of my grandfather. Now it sat stark black and foreboding, waiting for us. The black of the stone pulled the light from the air around it, sucking energy and warmth to itself. It wasn't open – not yet – but it was readying itself. And it was speaking to me, whispering quietly of its power and the window it was about to open. I couldn't take my eyes off it, and my feet moved toward the stone of their own accord.

Tatiana, who hadn't seen the stone yet, walked toward it in a trance. She knelt down before it, sighing, and reached her hand toward its surface. As her fingers neared the stone, though, her hand jerked back like she'd been burned.

"Can I touch it?" she whispered.

"You won't have much choice if you want to come with us," I replied. I put my backpack quickly on the far end of the stone, wondering if it would make the jump, and turned back to the group.

"What do we do?" Paul asked quietly.

"Put your bags on the far end of the stone next to mine and get on the stone," I replied. I heard my voice – low and intense – and realized that I sounded like my father. He had always been steady and calm in emergency situations. I could only pray that I was as capable now.

I glanced down at the stone for help and breathed out slowly. The window wasn't open yet, but it wouldn't be long now; the stone was starting to glow as it had before, and the symbols were aligning themselves and taking on a distinct form.

"We're right on time," I said quietly. "The window hasn't opened, but I think the stone's ready for us. Doc was lying on the stone when he jumped. Everybody get to it."

As they moved toward the stone, my mind raced through the practical questions, casting shadows of doubt. Would we all fit? Would our stuff fit with us? Did we have to be touching the stone to travel? What would happen if someone's foot was hanging off? Would they arrive in the past without it?

And then suddenly I thought of the biggest question of all – would they be able to come with me at all? Would my friends come through safely? Or would I land on the other side of history, scared, facing enemies and a mission I didn't understand, and completely alone?

None of this occurred to Paul. "Well I say I lay next to Tatiana," he quipped, grinning at her.

"Oh my God," she muttered, shaking her head.

Reis pushed Paul to the side, growling impatiently. "We don't have time for antics, Paul," he snapped. He turned quickly to meet my eyes. "Jason, we're following your lead here. Move."

I nodded wordlessly, turning to the stone and holding my hands out over its face, palms down. A rush of energy shot up from the stone, hit my hands, and coursed through my body, and my senses grew unbelievably acute, until I could hear, see, smell, and even feel things that I hadn't a moment ago. Reis' pulse, the smell of the detergent left on Paul's shirt, and the brush of Tatiana's dusky skin against my arm. The scent of blood and deep, dank earth from the other side. The pull of the stone itself.

"It's time," I mumbled. "Everyone on. Quickly."

Paul took a deep breath, closed his eyes, and crawled onto the stone next to his bag. Tatiana took a tentative step onto the stone, and folded into position next to him. Reis turned and sat, watching me closely as I joined them.

Beneath us, the stone's hum took on a deeper tone, as if it sensed our presence and approved. The roaring in my head grew louder and began to drown out the conversation around me. I closed my eyes and tried to focus on the hum and roar, to guide the vibrations through my bones and into the jump.

"So how do we do this?" I heard Paul ask.

"Shut it, smarty," Tatiana snapped. "Can't you see he's trying to concentrate? What do you want to do, screw him up and put us all in danger?"

"Hey, I'm just trying to figure out what to expect here," he mumbled, abashed.

At his tone, Tatiana relented. "I heard Jason's grandfather talking to John once," she said quietly. "At first, you'll feel something in your stomach, like you're falling. Then confusion, lots of noise and scenery." She paused. "I don't think it's pleasant."

Paul blew his breath out with a whooshing sound. "Sounds terrific. So glad I signed on for this."

I heard a scuffling, and Reis' guttural reply. "Paul, if you'd rather stay here, this is your chance. Otherwise, shut it. The time for jokes is long past."

A deafening silence descended over the group then, and I opened my eyes. The air around us was glowing a bright, shining gold, and the symbols, finally free of the stone, danced before my face. Beyond them, and through what I assumed to be the 'mists' of time, I saw a dark room, unlit, with moss and ivy growing from the walls. That was our destination, then. Now the stone's roar became overwhelming, and everything else disappeared. My mind went absolutely blank.

"Here it comes," I breathed. I put my cheek down against the stone, closed my eyes, and braced myself. "Keep your hands and feet inside the ride. Breathe."

"What in the hell are we –"

I didn't know who was speaking, but they didn't get to finish. The world dropped out from under us and we fell sharply into a sphere of bright light and color. Images and memories of my life washed over me, one after another; the death of my parents, the loss of my first tooth, my first steps .... my birth. Mingled with my memories were snapshots of the past – knights in armor, bloody, terrible battles, a man with white blond hair and the eyes of a murderer. The images flashed and flickered, appearing and then disappearing in nanoseconds, with the exception of one. A girl, no older than myself, with long blonde hair and penetrating green eyes, stood out from the chaos behind her. I'd never seen her before, and yet I felt as if I'd known her my entire life. While the other images danced around me, jumbling together as one, hers remained steady. I looked past her at everything else, trying to take it all in, remember what I was seeing. The images began to whirl around in a tornado of sight and sound, pushing us farther and farther into the void. Then everything stopped.

18

DONCASTER, ENGLAND
AUGUST 18, 1485

I felt like I'd been on the worst roller coaster ride of my life. I didn't know how long the ride had lasted – two seconds, two minutes, two hours? – but I knew when it ended. It stopped suddenly, as though whatever cart we were in had hit a brick wall. That feeling was reinforced when I opened my eyes and found myself staring at a large expanse of rock. Dark rock, in fact, that looked distinctly … solid.

"What the…" I mumbled softly. The concrete walls of the garden shed had changed to gray, pitted stone cut in rough blocks. Ivy and moss grew haphazardly across the wall in front of my face, and a rivulet of water ran slowly down a section of wall to my right. I took a deep, gasping breath and almost choked on the thick, dank air. I didn't know what the room smelled like, exactly, but it was awful.

There was a muffled cough to my left. "Dude, I feel like we just went through a blender," Paul said, sitting up.

I gasped in relief at his voice and turned to him. "How do you feel? Is everyone okay? Are we all here?" Beside him, Tatiana was pushing herself to a sitting position and scraping the hair out of her face. Her eyes widened as she took in the room, and I turned to look at what she saw.

If I didn't know any better, I would have thought we'd stepped out of our garden shed and directly onto the set of Bram Stoker's ***Dracula***. The room was enormous – at least as big as a basketball court, and as cavernous as an empty stadium. Gothic beams crossed the ceiling and supported arches in the walls. At least a dozen large white candles sat in ornate iron candlestick holders, spread haphazardly around the room. There were no windows, though I spotted a row of manacles and chains along the far wall. The only furnishing in the room was a large straight-backed chair, sitting right next to the stone.

Reis was already off the stone, moving steadily along the wall toward the corner. He had his rifle propped firmly against his shoulder, and a flashlight attached to the side to light the way. I reached into my pocket and pulled out my own flashlight, and stepped off the stone to follow him. Paul moved next to me, brushing some of the dust from his pants.

"Right, so we have your basic creepy room, here," he noted. Then he glanced at the far wall and gulped. "Complete with chains and manacles. Holy crap, we really did it, didn't we?"

"Yeah, I guess so," I replied, stunned.

Reis strode suddenly out of the gloom to our left and laid a hand on Paul's shoulder, making him jump. "Everyone try to relax and get your bearings," he said quietly. "I think we're alone in here, so we're safe to look around. I'm going to find the borders of the room, and look for the way out."

The three of us nodded, then moved together to follow him across the room. He'd said we were alone, but that didn't mean we wanted to leave the man with the gun. I cast my narrow beam of light across the stone floor ahead of us, moving it all the way to the massive rafters that stretched overhead. The light wavered across the beams of wood, and I glanced at my hand. Until that moment, I hadn't realized how badly I was shaking. I clamped my other hand down over the flashlight to keep it still. Paul made a strangled noise to my left, seemingly in response, and my flashlight shot in his direction.

"Are you guys okay?" I asked.

Tatiana nodded her head and bit her lower lip. "Fine!" she breathed. She gave me a quick grin, showing a confidence that surprised me, and I worked to grin back.

Paul looked at Tatiana and back to me, blinked twice, and nodded slowly. "Yeah, I guess so. I just … this is pretty heavy, you know what I mean?"

"I know, it's nuts," I replied. I took a deep breath and glanced around the large room. Something about it caught my attention, and I cocked my head and looked again, with the distinct feeling that I'd been here before. Yes, I was sure of it. I couldn't have said why, or how, but something about this room was familiar, as if I'd seen it in a dream, or a movie. If I thought about it, I realized I'd already known what this room would look like. And what it would hold. In fact, if this intuition was right … I moved the beam of light to the far corner of the room and smiled. The stairwell was there, just as I'd thought it would be.

I'd felt this way before, I realized, in the shed at home. This strange sense of knowing something I couldn't possibly know. It had been the stone showing me where to go, then. Here … could it be the same? Had the stone somehow shown me what would be in this room? Or was I just imagining that I knew where everything was?

I pointed my flashlight back at the stairs and knew immediately that there were 102 steps waiting to carry us out of the basement, despite the fact that I couldn't see them. I also knew that some truly horrible things had taken place in this room. If I concentrated hard enough, I thought, I'd be able to hear the screams of the men and women who had been tortured here. The thought made me sick to my stomach, pressing in on my brain the way it did, and suddenly I needed to get out of the room, away from this dark, haunted place.

"We have to get out of here," I whispered, my voice shaking.

Paul turned his flashlight toward my face. "Hey, are you okay? I didn't even think to ask."

I took a deep breath and nodded, trying desperately to keep my emotions in check, and started walking. Reis had reached the end of the wall in front of us at that point, and was looking up. He turned quickly toward us when we reached him.

"Okay, ladies," he ground out, motioning us closer. "If Jason and the history books are correct, we've got less than ninety-six hours to find Doc and save him before the Battle of Bosworth begins." He glanced down at his watch, then back at the stairwell in front of him. "Looks like these stairs are the only way out of this room. Any questions?" He paused for a moment, waiting, and nodded curtly.

"Let's go." He bent to retrieve the bag he'd dropped, then straightened and looked at me. "Are you ready for this?"

I nodded firmly, and shouldered my way past Paul and toward the stairs. 'Ready' was a serious understatement, and Reis was right; we'd already wasted too much time in the room with the stone. We had ninety-six hours to cross a county we didn't know without a vehicle, while avoiding several armies, to find Doc. I was starting to get nervous, and I hadn't even let myself think about the fact that we were in the mid-1400s yet.

Reis put a hand out to stop me, and shook his head. "I'll go first, kiddo. I'm the one with the gun here." He adjusted the strap of his rifle and turned the weapon toward the staircase. We moved behind him to the dark opening, and looked up expectantly. The stairwell was steep and rounded, without benefit of torches or windows. Reis' flashlight cut a small swath of light across the deep shadows, but petered out at the first turn.

He sighed, then chuckled to himself. "Well, at least we won't get bored. Here we go."

I stepped onto the bottom stair after Reis, following as closely as I could without actually tripping on his heels. Tatiana and Paul edged in behind me, their shoes squelching against the moisture on the stairs. As we climbed we started moving faster, hugging the interior column and its excuse for a handrail. The stairway felt as though it was closing in on us, growing tighter as we went.

"I wish I knew where these stairs went," Tatiana huffed quietly from behind me.

"They go up," Paul quipped, laughing at his own joke.

Reis growled in front of me and quickened his pace. I rushed to catch up with him, struggling to find purchase on the wet, mossy steps. We'd been climbing the stairs for several minutes when they ended on a cramped landing with a large, oval-shaped door. We slid to a stop, staring at the door in front of us and breathing loudly. The thick wooden planks were scarred and discolored with age, and banded in corroded iron. It was exactly the kind of door I would have expected to see in a castle, and twice as creepy as I had thought it would be. It had one circular handhold and no keyhole. That meant we had no way of seeing what – or who – lay on the other side. Reis exhaled sharply through his nose, then glanced back at us and signaled for us to get against the wall behind the door. He unlatched the safety on his gun, stepped toward the door, and pushed.

The door swung open a couple of inches, revealing a large, empty hallway, and we breathed out as one.

"One point for us," Paul whispered. "It would have really sucked to come all this way and find ourselves locked in the basement."

Reis turned back toward us, scowling. "I know it won't be easy," he said quietly, "but I need you to try to stop talking for a while. It's not a request, Paul."

Paul looked over at me, eyes wide. "Yeah, sure, I think I can do that."

Tatiana snorted. "Or you could just shoot him. That would shut him up." She grinned.

Reis cast a quick glance her way. "You're not helping. In case you hadn't noticed, we're in a bit of a tight spot here. If would really help if you all started acting like grownups."

He ran his eyes over the three of us, eyebrows raised in question, and nodded at our silence, then placed his shoulder against the door and leaned until it opened enough for his body to slip through. We watched breathlessly as his head and shoulders disappeared slowly through the opening. Within seconds he was back, beckoning us forward.

"Okay, it's now or never," he snapped. "Follow me, and keep your mouths shut!"

The stench of the basement dissipated in the hallway, but not by much. Several dimly lit torches lined the walls, casting more shadow then light. There could have been a dozen soldiers standing motionless against either wall, ready to slit our throats, and we wouldn't have been able to see them. Let alone do anything to stop them. A seed of doubt crept into my head as we snuck away from the basement's door and began to inch our way forward. What were we doing here? Was it smart to be moving so slow? Shouldn't we be hurrying? I felt myself tensing up, getting ready to spring forward, but stopped when I felt Tatiana's hand on my back. I cast my eyes over my shoulder to find her shaking her head and making calming motions with her hands.

"This way," Reis said suddenly, turning left in front of us.

"Wait," I whispered. I looked at the corridor he'd chosen and shook my head. We needed to go the other direction. I was sure of it, the same way I'd been sure that the empty peg would open the door down to the stone. I pointed that way, hoping they wouldn't question me.

"The courtyard is this way," I said quietly, looking at Reis.

"How do you know?" Paul asked.

I shook my head. "There's no time for that right now. Just trust me. This leads to the courtyard. That's where we'll find the main gate." Reis stared at me for a moment, then nodded his head slightly, turned, and went in the direction of my choosing.

We stumbled our way through the hall, walking more quickly now, and keeping our shoulders against the damp stone wall of the corridor. A gust of fresh air blasted down the hall, blowing against our faces. We were close to the outside world. Close to escape. Or capture.

Suddenly a cackle of laughter shot through the air, its low pitch echoing off the stone walls around us. We froze, pressing our backs against the stone of the hallway. Reis threw his right hand up, signaling for us to be still, and we shrank back into the shadows. The laughter dissipated, but the deep tones of men speaking took its place. We stayed motionless for an eternity, trying to become one with the shadows around us, and hardly daring to breathe. I dug my fingertips into the wall behind me, hoping with all my might to avoid the owner of that laugh. Suddenly the talking became louder, along with the scraping of boots on dirt and stone, and the rattling of metal. *Swords swinging in their scabbards*, I thought. Whoever these men were, they had swords and they were coming straight toward us.

"We've got to make a run for it!" Paul whispered nervously.

Reis' turned his head slowly to glare at Paul, the word 'no' on his lips. Then, in a slow, almost rhythmical movement, he crouched even lower to the ground. He brought his arm down with him, signaling us to mimic his action. Now he brought his rifle up to his shoulder, pointed the barrel at the far end of the empty hallway, and waited.

"I said the man must have lost his mind, attempting to treat Lord Dresden like that. Anyone in his right mind could have seen that no good would come of it." The words hit me like a hammer. They were loud and crisp. And uttered by a man who had lived and died over five hundred years before I was born. My head began to spin, but snapped back into place as other men answered the first.

"He signed his own death sentence by doing so, that be for certain!" another man said. A chorus of laughter erupted in response, and the hair on my neck stood up.

"I believe Dresden would kill his own mother if she looked at him wrong," yet another man added. This man was quickly hushed by another, who whispered his response fearfully.

"You would all be well-advised to keep your voices down, if you know what's best. That man has eyes and ears everywhere, and we are all expendable."

Dresden. They were talking about Dresden. I bit my tongue hard enough to draw blood, and didn't breathe again until the crunching sounds of footsteps and metal began to subside, along with the rough voices. We crouched against the wall, waiting for them to fade completely. Only then did we come back to life. Reis stood up, glanced quickly around the corner, and motioned for us to move forward again. We crept quickly after him, our ears straining for the sound of more guards.

We hadn't gone 5 feet when Paul jumped, squeaked, and skittered backward several steps. I backed up to avoid him and ran into Tatiana, who stood just behind me. She sunk her nails into the skin of my back, and I closed my mouth on a yelp of pain. I felt rather than saw something run across my left foot, and directed my flashlight toward the floor just in time to see two rats the size of barn cats scurry into the darkness.

Rats. They were only rats. I grabbed my chest and fell back against the wall, willing myself to calm down.

"It's just a couple of rats, *calm down!*" Reis muttered. Tatiana pulled her fingernails from my skin and giggled nervously.

Reis looked at us and frowned, shaking his head with what I assumed to be disappointment. He met my eyes, muttered something to himself, and swung abruptly around to stride into the corridor ahead of us. We shuffled after him, sticking close to the shadows against the wall. After a few seconds of walking, we came around a corner to find ourselves at the end of the hallway, beneath a large stone arch. Beyond us stood a courtyard the size of my school's field. A flood of fresh air reached my nostrils and filled my lungs, giving me a rush of energy in the process. I had never realized that fresh air could both smell and feel so good.

Suddenly Reis dropped to one knee behind the wall, motioning for us to follow him. I peeked around the corner and glanced quickly around the yard, looking for enemies, friends, and anything that might tell us where to go. It was late afternoon or early evening – that time of day when light grows scarce, and things lose their depth. No darkness to hide us, then. The large courtyard was surrounded by the castle's walls, one of which was lined with colorful stained glass windows, presumably marking the location of the chapel. Another wall, directly to our left, housed a small door sandwiched in between two large stone chimneys. Several piles of firewood as tall as my head lay stacked beside the farthest chimney. A well, complete with two buckets and a rope-and-pulley system, along with a broken cart, completed the picture. My eyes flew from the door to the firewood to the well and back. It wasn't enough to hide us, I thought. We needed to get to an exit, but we'd be completely exposed until we were through it. That posed a problem.

A sudden clattering sound brought my attention back to the small door, which opened to reveal the light of the castle's kitchen. The doorway grew dark as a man passed through into the courtyard. He was massive, at least a foot taller than Reis, with long, stringy black hair and a bushy black beard. His eyebrows were straight and very low, barely leaving room for the two deep-set eyes under them. He wore a tattered, sleeveless shirt and dark trousers. His arms and legs were as big as tree trunks, and his hands looked like they could crush my skull without any trouble at all.

He was walking right toward us.

Suddenly a heavy hand dropped onto my shoulder, pulling me back around the corner and out of sight of the giant. I glanced back to see Reis putting his right forefinger against his lips and nodding in assurance. He'd seen the man, then, and knew what to do about him. I blew a breath between my teeth, trying to calm down, and turned to glance at the monstrous man again. He hadn't been coming for us, I realized suddenly. He'd stopped at the woodpile and was now making his way back into the kitchen, his arms loaded up with firewood. I closed my eyes for a moment in relief, then resumed my observations of the courtyard. We didn't have time for these kinds of shenanigans. If I was going to do anything to help Doc, I had to settle down, and fast.

The last of the three walls in the courtyard contained one massive window, broken up into six sections, and a heavy set of wooden doors. They were at least 60 feet from us. Beyond the wall and gate, the buildings of Doncaster rose into the sky. That was our way out, then.

Reis' thoughts must have run parallel to my own. "Okay, we're going to stay close to the wall on the left. First we run for the woodpiles, then we run for the well. From there, if we're lucky, we'll make it to the cart and then the main gate without being spotted," he said in a harsh whisper. "Questions?"

"You think we're all going to fit behind the well?" Paul asked.

Reis either didn't hear his question or decided to outright ignore him, because he suddenly launched into action, sprinting along the wall toward the first of the woodpiles. We followed, racing toward the wood in hunched, staggering gates. We made it to the first pile, took a couple of seconds to rest, and then ran for the second.

There, Reis held a hand up to stop us. He glanced back the way we'd come, his eyes panicked, and motioned violently for us to get down. Paul, Tatiana, and I dropped to our bellies on the ground. Reis crouched above us, staring at the corridor from which we'd just emerged. I glanced back, wondering what he'd heard, and my breath caught. We were 30 feet from the gate, but we weren't safe yet.

Four soldiers dressed in matching tattered uniforms – white with crude red crosses stitched into the front – came out of the corridor and strolled casually toward us.

"What do we do?" I asked under my breath.

"We've got to run for it!" Paul said, a little louder than I thought he should have.

"Don't move!" Reis said in a guttural whisper. His hand descended slowly onto Paul's head, pushing his face down into the dirt to keep him quiet.

The soldiers walked toward us, coming to a halt several feet from the woodpile. Tatiana, laying next to me, moved her hand onto my arm and tightened her grip. The solders in front of us ranged from an old man to a boy no older than I was. Two of them held pieces of meat, while one had a tankard of some sort of liquid. They settled themselves into comfortable stances and began to talk and laugh while they ate and drank.

"You've got to be kidding me," Paul muttered. He'd freed himself from Reis' grip and was glaring at the soldiers through a hole in the woodpile. "They're having a picnic *now?*"

One of the soldiers glanced in our direction, frowning, and I almost choked. I turned slowly to stare at Paul, willing him with my eyes to stop breathing and do his best impersonation of a rock.

Then the soldier turned back to his friends and laughed at something one of them had said, and I sighed in relief. I looked anxiously over at Reis, moving my head and eyes as slowly as I could. His eyes were racing across the courtyard toward the gate, his mouth drawn down in a frown. Suddenly his eyes met mine, and his frown deepened. He didn't have to say anything for me to know what he was thinking – we had to get to that gate, and fast, if we were going to escape. Instead, we were trapped here by the soldiers in front of us.

Suddenly he came to a decision and dropped to his knee beside me. The butt of his rifle came up against his shoulder, the nose peeking up over the firewood, and my fingers clenched involuntarily, digging into the ground beneath me. *That* was his plan? A gunshot would alert every soldier for miles to our presence, and get us captured for sure. I glanced from Reis to the soldiers and back, panicked at the thought. If we got caught now, Doc was as good as dead. When my eyes flew to the soldiers again, though, I almost laughed in relief.

There was a sudden lull in the conversation, and the four of them straightened as one. Chicken legs were dropped and the tankard cast to the side as the four began a sloppy march back into the hallway. Within moments, the courtyard was empty again, and we were free to go.

My eyes flew to Reis, who was strapping his rifle back into position on his back. He grabbed his duffel bag, glanced once in our direction, and sprinted for the cart beside the gate.

I was running before I even realized I'd given my legs the order to do so. I heard two sets of footsteps pounding along behind me, and prayed that they belonged to Paul and Tatiana rather than guards or giants. We slid to a stop at the wagon, and crouched down next to Reis.

"We'll have to make a run for it from here," he hissed. He looked to his right and then to his left, motioned for us to be still, and sprinted across the open area toward the gate.

We stayed put, hiding behind the cart as well as we could, and keeping our eyes on the open space in front of us. Thirty seconds later, Reis was back. He dropped to his knees, taking in gulps of air and wiping the sweat from his eyes.

"Okay, there's a sentry just outside the gate on the right. But he's watching for people coming in, not people going out. I want the three of you to follow my lead, walk straight and confident, and act like you belong. Oh, and carry your bags and packs on your left shoulder, away from the guard," he said. He turned away, then quickly turned back to address us again.

"One more thing. If he asks you a question, don't say a word. Just let me handle it, okay?"

"What if something happens?" Paul asked.

Reis' mouth grew firm. "Then you run like hell and wait for me on the southwest side of town. If I don't find you after thirty minutes, you stick to the plan. Head to Bosworth and find your grandfather, and forget about me. Understand?"

We nodded wordlessly, watching as he turned back toward the gate. He walked forward, slipping his assault rifle under his robe and leaving us to follow at our own pace.

19

Reis crept along the path ahead of us, sticking to the wall as he approached the gate. Paul, Tatiana, and I followed, doing our level best not to be seen or heard. The gate towered above us, built from rough-hewn logs and iron spikes. More spikes lined the top to create a solid layer of razor-sharp metal, ensuring that people went through the gate rather than over it. We slid into the darkness below the wall and I gulped, the eerie silence of the shadow creeping slowly up my spine. The gate to the courtyard was where we'd find the most soldiers, I knew; it was a feature designed to keep intruders out, and was manned as such. But I had no doubt that it was just as effective at keeping prisoners in. And if we couldn't get out, if we were still here come day break…

We made it through the partially open gate and onto the path outside the castle before we were caught. I heard a sharp gasp behind me, followed by the sound of a struggle, and whirled around to look back the way we'd come. A tall, dirty soldier in a tattered red and white uniform stood behind Tatiana, his arm around her body and his hand across her mouth. He was at least a foot taller than the girl, and marked with the scars of many battles. A rusty, bent sword hung loosely at his side, but he held a sharp dagger in his hand, close to Tatiana's side.

"A lady shouldn't be out this late in the day," he slurred, turning his mouth toward her ear and grinning. "I'll need to know exactly who you lot are, and what you're about."

I sucked my breath in, glancing quickly from the dagger to the sword, then up to the soldier's face. I saw Reis to my left, moving his hand slowly toward the knife I knew he had in his boot, and heard Paul mumbling under his breath. My gaze flew back to Tatiana's face, and I caught her wide eyes.

She looked at me for a moment, raised one eyebrow, and then winked.

"Oh no," I breathed, my voice catching in my throat.

Before anyone else could move, Tatiana threw her hand over her shoulder and grabbed the man's wrist, crouching down and spinning in the same movement. The soldier flew over her folded body, hitting the ground on the other side with a sickening, bone-crunching thud. He shouted and jumped to his feet, snarling in surprise and anger. Tatiana pressed her lips together in displeasure and circled her opponent, looking for another opening. When she saw him pause, she dove in and grabbed his dangling left arm, shoving it up toward his shoulder. The shoulder popped loudly as it dislocated, and the man screamed. She drove her foot into the soldier's knee, bringing him to the ground, and finished him off with a solid blow to the head with her other foot. The solder fell on his back, out cold.

Tatiana looked down at the man, her mouth quirked to the side. "The name's Tatiana, mister," she said clearly. "I'm no lady, and I stay out as late as I want."

"What the –" Paul cut his statement short as another soldier came rushing from the wall next to us, armed with a 6-foot lance. Reis swore under his breath and stepped quickly between Tatiana and the second soldier. He sidestepped the soldier's strike, planted his right foot in the dirt, and swung his left leg up toward the man's face. His foot connected with the soldier's temple and sent the man crumbling to the ground, the lance falling harmlessly at his side.

For a moment, no one moved. Then we whirled as one toward the wall, waiting breathlessly for a third attack. Reis kicked the lance away from the unconscious soldier, swung his rifle from his back to his chest, and aimed the weapon at the half-open gate in anticipation. Tatiana remained in a fighting stance, both hands held up in front of her and legs slightly bent. I bent down and picked up two likely looking rocks, trying to remember anything I'd ever learned about throwing. Beside me, Paul stood slack jawed and staring.

No one else emerged from the gate, though, and I wondered how long they would take to notice their missing comrades.

"Let's not stick around to find out," Reis mumbled, echoing my thoughts. "Run."

We broke and ran like startled deer, racing toward the town in the distance and the shelter it offered. No one looked back.

We didn't stop running until we were in the center of town, and as hidden from the castle as we could hope to be. The dirt beneath our feet gave way to smooth cobblestones, and we found ourselves in the middle of a vacant street in Doncaster.

"Wow," Paul breathed, looking around.

I had to agree with him. Dozens of stone homes rose up as high as three stories on either side of the street, crowding each other and blocking out what little sun remained. They were roofed with everything from stone and wood to some sort of dull gray material, and featured large wooden doors perched atop wide stone steps. Windows were lined with colorful curtains and decorative trim.

"Definitely the rich side of town," Tatiana murmured.

To our left, a massive stone cathedral crested the skyline. Wooden scaffolding surrounded it and ran up its four towers; evidently the local church was still under construction.

"Rich enough to build quite a nice church," Paul agreed, gazing up at the buttresses.

Suddenly Reis' hands came down on our shoulders, bringing us back to reality. "Move!" he snapped. "We don't have time to take in the sights!" I looked to my left and noticed several people milling about outside their homes. They'd taken an interest in us, and were starting to point. Reis was right – we had to move.

Seconds later we were running again, racing through streets and back alleys in a mad dash to get out of the town. As we moved away from the center of the city, the homes became noticeably smaller, two stories in lieu of three, and less impressive in their construction. Wood replaced stone, the doors became less elaborate, and the windows changed in nature; holes in the walls, with barely any covering. The streets became rougher, filled with garbage and potholes, the cobblestones slick with unnamed substances.

We were racing around a corner the first time Paul fell. He put his foot into a deep pot hole right in front of me and went down like a sack of potatoes, grunting at the impact.

"Damn it," I muttered, skidding to a stop and bending down to help him up. "Are you alright?"

He nodded, dazed, and tried to stand. "I think I twisted my ankle, but I'll be okay."

"What the hell are you two doing, playing in the mud?" Reis shouted from the street ahead of us. "Get up, get *moving!*"

I broke into a sprint again, Paul hobbling along next to me, and glanced at the buildings around us, looking for possible enemies. On either side of the street, large wooden signs protruded from the doorways to identify the occupant's trade. An arm wrapped in a bandage depicted a doctor's office, a bushel on a pole with a pint of ale no doubt marked the location of a tavern, a large pig identified a butcher, a dress for a tailor, and so on. The shops, of course, were closed for the night, but it wasn't hard to imagine how busy and full of life this part of town became during the daylight hours. No one was around at the moment, though, and I thought that we were probably safe.

A loud explosion sounded suddenly behind me, disabusing me of that notion. I stumbled at the concussion, and Paul fell to the ground again. This time, Reis raced back to help us.

"Canon fire," he snapped.

"They're shooting at us?" I gasped. "With canons?"

"No, it's a warning. They're letting everyone in town know that we're here. This way!"

He threw Paul's arm over his shoulder and darted forward, half dragging my friend into the closest alley. We raced toward the opening at the end, where we could see fields and trees. If we could get out of the town, I thought, we'd be safer.

The canon fired again and I instinctively ducked, then increased my speed. Tatiana appeared suddenly at my side, matching my pace. We raced past piles of garbage and rats the size of small dogs, barely noticing our surroundings in our panic.

Then the alley, along with the densely packed buildings around it, was gone, and we were outside the city. Reis pushed us over the small wooden bridge beyond the last building, and we sprinted forward until at last the city and its stench fell behind us.

We reached a small copse of trees several minutes later. Without a word, all four of us darted into the underbrush, paused, and collapsed.

Reis didn't let us rest long. Less than ten minutes later we were back on the road, now under cover of darkness, jogging quickly toward a farm that sat several miles from the city of Doncaster. I quickened my pace to catch up with Reis, who was moving with a long, steady stride that ate the miles. In the end, I had to sprint to keep up with him.

"What are we going to do?" I huffed quietly.

Reis grunted and pointed toward the barn ahead. "We're going to get to that barn and find some sort of cover. I don't like being on the open road when people are chasing us with canons and guns."

"I don't think canons move that fast, actually," Paul called from behind us. "They're ... you know ... heavy." His voice faded off at my quick glance, and he looked down.

"Not the point, Paul," Reis muttered. "We're fairly limited on time, here. We can't afford any delays. And that includes hiding for too long from thrill-seeking soldiers with heavy – but definitely deadly – canons."

His final words brought us abreast of the stable, and we slid down to the ground gratefully, our backs resting against the crude wall of the building. A full moon had swung into the sky, and the landscape was relatively clear before us. From this distance, we could still make out the towers of the castle, as well as the church, jutting up against the moonlit sky. The stars scattered across the darkness were brighter than any I'd ever seen in my life, with the country around us smooth and dark. The land around us was relatively flat, and appeared to be tilled for farming. Farther away, I could see stalks of wheat or corn, gently swaying in the breeze. No skyscrapers rose into the blackness, no streetlights ran along the roads. Of course there were no streetlamps, I realized suddenly. There was no electricity. These people counted on fire – candles, torches, and bonfires – to cut through the darkness. This deserted area, and the barn behind us, were lit only by the moon.

It would have been peaceful, if we weren't running for our lives.

Reis had been leaning against the wall behind me, scanning the scene for soldiers or danger. Now he jumped back into action, grabbing a compass, flashlight, and the map from various pockets in his ensemble.

"Don't move!" he snapped at Paul, scooting toward him. He grabbed the end of Paul's robe, then bent forward and threw it over his head. Within seconds he – and the flashlight – had disappeared.

Paul, Tatiana, and I were left staring stupidly at the space where he had been.

"Checking our position," I muttered, answering the question before Paul could ask. It made sense – we had to know where we were, and we couldn't risk anyone seeing the light from the torch. Not out here in the middle of nowhere.

"Well I'm glad somebody has a plan," Paul said with a shake of his head.

I snorted. He'd evidently forgotten that we'd talked about this before we left home. We waited tensely, our eyes trained on the landscape around us, while Reis figured out where we were.

"If my mother could see me now…" Tatiana murmured, pulling her hair into a tighter bun. "Running from people with guns and swords, watching a road for signs of attack… I'd be getting a strong lecture on the meaning of 'lady like.'" She laughed at some memory, shaking her head.

"Tatiana, is that a Russian name?" Paul asked suddenly, breaking the silence. "Is your mother Russian?"

Tatiana looked at him and paused a moment before answering. "It's a Russian name, but I'm Romanian," she said.

"Kind of the same thing, isn't it?"

Tatiana shook her head. "No, Russia is a Slavic country. Romania is Latin based. Also, they're different countries. For those who care about geography."

Paul nodded, trying to pretend he knew what she was talking about. "Fleming, though, that's your last name, right? Isn't that –"

"Fleming is *not* my name," she snapped, her voice low and intense. "My last name is Lazar. My mother's name."

Paul held his hands up in surrender. "Okay, wildcat, I was just asking. Sheesh." He turned to me and raised his eyebrows. "Talk about oversensitive."

I looked past him at the girl, wondering where all that anger came from. "What exactly happened between you and your father?" I asked quietly.

"What's it to you?" she snapped back.

I shrugged. "You have your mom's last name. You hate your father. Insisted on coming with us, just to make sure he was stopped. Seems like the obvious question."

She frowned and looked like she was going to snap at me again, but then sighed. Her face softened, and she opened her mouth to answer.

Before she could say anything, a scream ripped through the still night air.

Tatiana's mouth shut with a snap, and she jumped to her feet. "What on earth was that?"

"Someone's crying," I said, rising quickly to my feet as well. "Where's it coming from, can you tell?"

Reis emerged from under Paul's robe, grasping the map and flashlight to his chest. "Okay," he muttered quietly, "if the coordinates you gave us are correct, I know which direction to go, if we –"

The scream sounded again, cutting Reis off mid-sentence, and his mouth dropped open. Now that I was listening for it, I could hear exactly where it was coming from. A girl was in the barn we'd been sitting against. She'd been quiet when we first got here, but now she was sobbing. And screaming intermittently.

"Stay here!" Reis said. He stood up and made his way slowly toward the corner of the stable.

I watched him for a moment, then started after him. "Stay here," I said to Paul, pushing past him.

"What, with the ice princess? I don't think so," Paul muttered. He stepped into place beside me, and we crept along the wall. I didn't have to look back to know that Tatiana was following us; I could feel her breath on my neck.

We walked quickly around the corner of the barn, accompanied by the nameless girl's cries, and found ourselves half standing, half kneeling beside the back door of a stable, adjacent to the cottage. Now that we were closer, I could hear that the girl was actually crying for help. Begging for someone to save her. Glancing over my shoulder, I could see that the farm was deserted. The door to the house hung wide open, and broken furniture was strewn across the yard.

No one was coming to save the girl.

"Are we going to just hang out back here, or are we going to do something?" Paul whispered suddenly.

Reis turned around and was about to answer when another sound interrupted him. Several men were laughing at the girl's distress, and it wasn't pleasant. The sounds of their voices made my blood run cold and the hair on my neck stand up. Beside me, Tatiana grew tense and stifled a snarl.

We dropped as one to the ground behind the half-open door of the barn. It was built of dense, heavy boards, but the construction was poor; there were half-inch spaces between the slats. The light from inside the barn spilled though these openings, and we bent greedily to peer through. I'd never been in a barn before, but I suspected that this one held what most of them would – a horse, multiple piles of straw, two pigs, and several chickens, with some tools lining the walls. A few torches sat in holes in the bracings, throwing their light over rough dirt floors, which were strewn with manure and dirty straw. But it wasn't the tools, straw, or animals that grabbed our attention as we peered intently through the slatted door.

A short, round man dressed in bright green and blue robes, his hands flashing with jeweled rings, stood over a small girl in the center of the room. I couldn't see much of her, but she didn't look much older than Tatiana. She was certainly much smaller than the girl at my side. Two ugly, rough-looking men with dark features stood behind the fat man. They too wore robes, but in darker, more muted shades of brown and black. All three men were gazing intently at the young girl, who lay helplessly in front of them.

The girl's dress, face, and hands were covered in mud. Her hair was matted and tangled with blood and dirt, which also covered most of her face. There was blood on her knees and elbows, which she clutched against her ribs. She was down on the ground, as though one of the men had hit her and she'd fallen. She turned over now, and looked up at the three men who stood over her. Her expression was a mixture of fear, hatred, and outright rage.

20

The Bishop's mouth curled into an even uglier smirk and he swept his heavily booted foot toward her ribs again. "Your father was just hanged for treason, girl. You have no hope of salvation," he snarled.

Katherine curled inward to avoid the worst of the blow, and forced her mouth shut on the scream. It would do her no good, she knew; the men were here to beat her into submission, and her moans and cries would only goad them on. They had been here for some time already, and no amount of talking on her part had stopped them. She was bruised, cut, and bleeding in several places. She could no longer see out of one eye, and thought that several of her ribs might be broken. But her pain wasn't going to stop these men either. In fact, she believed that it would get worse before the end.

Of course she didn't plan to let it get that far. She hadn't decided what she was going to do, but she was working on it.

When she looked up again, the Bishop was still smiling. Gloating, this time. He thought he had her in his grasp. She glared at him, which only seemed to make him happier.

"Everything you had is gone. You have no choice but to follow us and beg admittance to the abbey," he smirked.

Katherine swallowed heavily, weighing her options. She was only fifteen, but had already endured more than most people her age. Her mother had died in childbirth, leaving her with only one parent. She and her father had done well enough – he as both farmer and local healer, she as midwife and housekeeper. Now, however, he was gone, hanged by the local lord, and she was an orphan. Having been born a girl instead of a boy, her options outside of wedlock were limited. The Bishop had come to her home with what he considered a charitable offer. For her own good and safety, he'd said. She snorted through her tears. A charitable offer indeed. If she agreed to sign herself into the hands of the church, as he demanded, her freedom and estate, which she had received just hours before, would be lost forever.

Suddenly the Bishop's boot struck her again, taking her unawares and sinking into her vulnerable stomach. Katherine wheezed in pain, shocked, and then turned on him with a snarl of her own.

"I will not sign papers that allow you and the church to take what is rightfully mine," she ground out, realizing that she could well be signing her own death warrant with the words. "If you want my things, man of the church, you will have to kill me for them." She got to her feet at that, meeting his eyes.

He paused for only a moment at her pointed mention of his religion. Then his mouth turned up in a cruel smile. "That can be arranged, girl."

He took the jeweled dagger from his belt and lifted it above her, savoring the moment of the kill. Katherine lifted her chin and watched his movements, waiting for the second that he began his strike. At that point, she knew, he would be off balance, and set on his path. He wouldn't be able to alter the blow.

And he wouldn't be able to stop her when she darted to the side, to get around him and out the door.

Before he could strike, though, a man's figure appeared behind him, and all hell broke loose.

I had sprung to my feet, shocked at the fat man's violence toward the girl. I'd never seen anyone hit a woman – much less a girl my own age – and my blood was burning with outrage. I knew that women had been suppressed and even abused during this time period. That didn't mean I had to stand around and watch it happen, though, and I had no intention of doing so.

I felt rather than saw Tatiana appear at my side, growling in anger. Before we could rush to the girl's aid, Reis had moved past us and into the light of the barn. He slid into place behind one of the robed men, wrapped his left arm around the man's neck, and jammed his right thumb into the flesh between the man's neck and collarbone. The man dropped to the ground, unconscious. The second man heard his companion's collapse and turned, his hand going to the dagger at his belt. Reis took one quick step forward and pivoted gracefully, swinging his foot toward the man's face. This man went down beside his companion, blood gushing from his broken nose.

The short, round man – obviously the leader of the group – turned, his mouth opening and closing in shock. He took in his fallen companions and then faced Reis, his expression dark and arrogantly angry. I glanced quickly at Reis, wondering if he had a plan, and gasped at his expression. He had been hard and professional up to this point – the ultimate cold-blooded assassin. Now he was angry. His face was a mask of barely contained rage, and he was breathing heavily.

The fat man evidently didn't notice the danger. "This girl is with me. You have no right to interfere. I am a messenger of God, and the Bishop of Fairhaven!"

Reis took one step toward the self-proclaimed Bishop and planted a quick jab into the man's nose, snapping cartilage and flattening his face. A gush of blood hit the hay below the Bishop, and he cried out in pain and shock. Reis threw one more punch and the man went down, out cold.

No one moved or said a word for several seconds, until Paul broke the silence.

"Holy crap," he whispered.

Reis had followed the fat man to the ground, and was now pulling a small roll of duct tape from his pocket. He moved quickly and efficiently, taping the three men together and then to one of the support columns of the barn. Tatiana and Paul moved toward him on silent feet, bending to help.

I shook myself into action and strode past them all, uninterested in the men on the ground, and came to a stop in front of the girl. She was standing more firmly now, and attempting to put her dress and hair back in order. She looked up at me when I stopped, then looked past me to the men on the ground. Her eyes moved back to mine, and she opened her mouth to say something. Before she could utter a word, her eyes rolled back into her head and she fell to the ground.

Katherine hadn't actually fainted, but she badly needed a moment to figure things out, and from where she stood, pretending to faint was her only option. It had worked wonders for her in the past, and gave her at least a couple minutes of peace. Now she pressed her back against the ground and focused on deep, regular breathing, trying not to let her eyes or eyelids move. The secret to a fake fainting spell was to look like you were actually unconscious – she'd learned that one the hard way once, when her father had caught her faking it. She gave herself a couple of seconds to get her body under control, then turned to the important thing. Namely, the situation at hand.

What on earth had just happened? A moment ago, her situation had been … well, difficult, really. She'd been facing a choice: join the church and lose everything, or embrace death and join her parents in heaven. Neither had been appealing. Now, things seemed to have changed. A man, obviously very powerful, had appeared out of nowhere. He had with him a girl and two young men, similar in age to her own. They were strangers to this area; Katherine had never seen their faces before, and she knew everyone in Doncaster and the surrounding villages. So who were they?

She slit one eye open to take in the scene before her, then shut it again. One of the boys had moved even closer to her, his face full of concern, and was now kneeling at her side. While that was sweet of him, it was also inconvenient, as it blocked her view of the others. What were they doing? Why had they saved her? What did they want?

Her mind darted from one possibility to the next. They certainly weren't from this area, as she'd never seen them, so she didn't think they were here for the land or property. Were they mercenaries? Kidnappers? Slave traders?

Don't be silly, Katherine, she lectured herself. They were too far inland for slave traders. Those people needed ships. Still…

Sighing, she came to the crux of the matter. Regardless of who they were, they had saved her from the Bishop. Come to her rescue when no one else had. And if they were willing to rescue her once…

What option did she have, really? She couldn't stay here, not after this, and she had no place else to go. Her life in Doncaster had ended, just as surely as her father's. She needed a fresh start, and these people might provide her with one, whether they meant to or not.

Katherine fluttered her eyelids and pretended to wake up. "Where … where am I? Who are you?" she asked, sitting up and holding a hand to her forehead. She'd found that men expected this sort of behavior when a woman was waking up from a 'fainting spell.' Personally she found it ridiculous, but as long as she was putting on a performance, she needed to do it right.

She glanced through her eyelashes at the thin boy with the kind eyes, giving him a weak smile. Something about him suggested a trustworthy kindness, and her smile grew involuntarily larger. His mouth turned up in response, and something in her heart relaxed. Perhaps these people were friends after all.

Then the girl she'd seen stepped out from behind the older man. She had beautiful black hair, smooth skin, and deep, penetrating eyes. She was also frowning in disapproval, her eyes roving along Katherine's clothing and general state of feminine distress. Her mouth turned down in deep disappointment, and Katherine narrowed her eyes. The men might be friendly. The girl, on the other hand…

She pulled herself to her feet and turned from the angry girl toward the boy, who seemed to be a leader of some sort.

"My name's Jason," he said in a soft, gentle voice. "These are my friends, Paul, Reis, and Tatiana. Are you okay? Can you walk?"

Katherine nodded and took the boy's offered hand, allowing him to pull her into the light. His hand was as soft as a young child's, and she wondered fleetingly who he was. Who *they* were, she corrected. They certainly weren't

Danes or mercenaries. *Or slave traders*, she thought, her mouth quirking to the side. Were they nobility? She was certain that they'd never done hard labor, given the state of their skin. Their dress was odd, too … not the standard traveling clothing of members of the nobility. This boy obviously traveled with a guard, though, and had no fear of the church. Their assault on the Bishop had told her that much. If he was nobility, then what – who – were the boy and girl who traveled with him?

Why had they interfered with the Bishop?

And most importantly, could they save her again?

I stood back as best I could, given the fact that she wouldn't let go of my hand, and watched her carefully. There was something vaguely familiar about her, but I couldn't put my finger on it. Her straw-colored hair was matted, dirty, and tangled, her face and neck bloody and smeared with mud. When she looked up at me, though, her bright green eyes were clear and lucid. And calculating. She was the exact opposite of Tatiana in every way – slight where the other girl was strong, bright where the other girl was dark. But there was something about her eyes that reminded me of my traveling companion. That cool, direct gaze, as though she could see right through me…

Suddenly I gasped, my memory flooding back. I had seen this girl before. I *did* know that gaze. That was why it was so familiar.

I'd seen them both on the trip through the stone. This girl's image had made the trip with me, her eyes meeting mine whenever they could. For reasons I couldn't comprehend, the stone had shown me this girl's image during my jump. Again and again. And then we'd found our way to her farm, to save her from scoundrels doing God-knew what. We'd been brought together for a reason, I could feel it in my bones and through my blood.

Of course, I had no idea what that reason actually was.

At my gasp, her eyes grew unfocused and soft, as though she'd realized that she was staring. She smiled vaguely and turned away to look at the others.

"My name is Katherine," she said in little more than a whisper. She brushed a lock of hair quickly away from her face, looking around with both curiosity and caution.

Reis grunted and gestured angrily at the men on the ground. "And what are you doing here on your own, Katherine, being beaten by this so-called Bishop? Where are your parents? Who's meant to be looking out for you?" he asked.

The girl watched him, frowning at his anger, then glanced down at the fat man. "He's the Bishop of Fairhaven," she said, her voice cold and full of hatred. "And he's a pig!" She stepped toward the three men and spit on the ground to emphasize her point, and Paul snorted.

"We noticed," he muttered. "And your parents?"

Katherine turned toward Paul, her expression softening somewhat. "The Bishop came because he knew I would be alone and at his mercy. My father was put to death today." She paused, swallowing heavily. "He came here to force me into an abbey and take possession of my estate. Failing that, he would have killed me."

"Your father was put to death?" I gasped, the unfamiliar words sticking on my tongue. "Who would do that? Why?"

Katherine's face dissolved into tears, and my heart ached for her. "My father was a good man. He helped others who were in pain. He tried to –" she choked on a sob, then swallowed and continued. "He tried to cure the lord's pain." She ducked her head, her shoulders shaking, and I squeezed her hand. My parents hadn't been put to death, but I knew what it was like to lose a father.

"The Bishop's pain?" Paul asked.

Katherine shook her head. "No … Lord Dresden!" she hissed, suddenly coming alive again. She looked up, her green eyes flashing with hatred at the name.

I shook my head in confusion and looked over at Tatiana, expecting to see the same expression. Her face, though, showed no emotion at Katherine's declaration.

"Dresden killed my father!" Katherine muttered. "Because of a toothache!" She swiped at the tears on her face and threw them away from her.

Before she could say anything else, Tatiana spoke. "Well, this is all very interesting, and quite coincidental, I'm sure, but I think we need to be going. We do, after all, have someplace to be." She looked pointedly at me, and my mouth dropped open.

"You're right, and she's coming with us," I said, surprising myself. I hadn't talked it through with myself yet, and certainly hadn't meant to say anything, but I couldn't take the words back now that that they were said. As silence descended, I realized that I was right. She *did* need to come with us, though I couldn't understand why. The stones had led me to her, and they must have had a reason. Beyond that, she was an orphan, and probably in trouble for the attack on the Bishop. The romantic in me – bolstered by the pressure of the stones – was screaming at me to protect her. If she didn't come with us, where would she go?

Reis shook his head slowly, torn. "I don't think that's a good idea, Jason. You know our situation. Perhaps she has friend or family in another village … somewhere else she could go?"

Katherine shook her head. "I have no one else," she said quietly.

"Are you both mad? She can't come, absolutely not!" Tatiana snapped. "We don't have time for this. This has nothing to do with why we're here! We've already messed with history enough, do you want to make it worse? We have to go."

"You don't get a vote in this," I replied, shocked at my own response and tone of voice. "This isn't only about you, Tatiana." I heard myself saying the words, and shook my head. I wasn't being fair to the others, but something was pushing me forward. Something that I couldn't explain. Whatever it was, it wanted me to rescue Katherine, and I wasn't strong enough to ignore it.

"Jason…" Reis started.

I didn't let him finish. "And it's not about you either, Reis. No offense to any of you, but this is *my* mission. *I'm* the one with the connection to the stones, here, and *I'm* the one who brought us into the past." I sighed, trying to decide how to say what I needed to say without terrifying everyone.

"I can't tell you how I know, or why, but she's important. I know it. We found her for a reason, I've just got to figure out what the reason is. I think we have to take her with us."

"Well that's a pretty weak motivation," Paul grumbled, putting his hand on my arm. "Jason, think about what you're asking here. Take her with us today, sure, but then what? It's not like we can take her home with us."

I turned to him, my face flushing with emotion. "I know this the same way I knew that Doc's life was in danger, Paul," I said evenly. "And if we can't take her home with us, then I guess that gives me three days to try and figure out what I *am* supposed to do with her."

I glanced at Katherine, who lifted her head and gave Tatiana a cold look. I paused for long enough to see the look returned, and turned to Reis.

"I'm bringing her with us, Reis. And that's all there is."

Reis heaved a heavy sigh, then nodded and looked at his watch. "Well, maybe she'll come in handy along the road. I'm not going to fight you on it. You've got five minutes to gather her things."

21

HEREFORD, ENGLAND
AUGUST 19, 1485

The Earl stalked past the two heavily armed guards outside the cream-colored awning and stormed into the tent. He had grown angrier as the ride went on, and paused for a moment now to look around him and allow his temper to cool. The air inside the tent assaulted his senses, making it difficult to breathe. The smell of human bodies, wet dog, and smoke merged with a heavy dose of rose petal cologne, giving the air a sickly sweet smell. It was gloomy inside the tent, with only three tallow candles burning in their sconces. Henry would have done better to open the drapes, the Earl thought, for natural light and valuable fresh air. Three old rugs of blue and white wool lined the dirt floor, and one large table, consisting of little more than a piece of wood over two crude sawhorses, dominated the small, cramped space. Eight chairs were arranged tightly around the makeshift table. All of them were occupied, leaving no space for the Earl to sit. His mouth firmed into a frown at that. Just one more sign of disrespect. He added it quickly to the growing list, wondering how exactly Henry planned to make amends with his richest ally.

For his part, Henry Tudor remained seated at the head of the table. He looked directly at the Earl upon his entrance, but said nothing. His thin, frail body, combined with gaunt facial features, made him look weaker and far older than his real twenty-eight years. It was easy to see why many men, both in England and Europe, wanted Henry Tudor on the throne. He looked like he would be easy to manipulate, and everyone, including the church, planned to take advantage of that. The Earl had to smile at the thought. If they knew how ruthless both Henry and his lineage would become, they would rethink that position.

The man in question coughed at the delay, and the Earl lowered his arms to let the two large hounds sniff his hands. After they accepted him as familiar, he took three long strides toward the table. It was European protocol to allow a country's monarch to speak first, so despite the Earl's seniority in years and position, he waited.

"You owe the church, as well as our king, a wergild," the Archbishop of Canterbury said suddenly, sneering and breaking the silence that loomed inside the tent. The Earl snorted. Evidently the church wasn't adhering to protocol today.

He looked at the future King of England and bowed slightly before turning his attention to the Archbishop. "I have forfeited much of my fortune already to ensure that our future king gains the crown. I don't have to remind your Grace of the sacrifices my men have made to guarantee success in your quest," he said quietly.

"Your sacrificed good men to take a town that was not worthy of the taking!" the Archbishop shouted.

"Don't lecture me about sacrifice, Archbishop!" the Earl snapped. He slammed his fist down on the wooden table, spilling two glasses of wine, and glared at the man. "I have given everything I own to the cause, and I'll be damned if I am to be lectured by you about not having given enough!" he barked. He paused and drew a deep breath. "Do I need to remind you what will become of this campaign should you lose me? Should you lose my men?"

For a moment, no one spoke. Seven pairs of eyes looked away from both the Earl and Archbishop. The Earl knew that he was treading on thin ice here. The Archbishop – and possibly Henry himself – had expected him to give in gracefully to this demand for a monetary fine. They hadn't expected him to flex his own muscle. This was necessary, and yet it was a gamble, for he needed Henry to claim the crown as much as anyone else in the room. And without him, Henry would surely lose. He waited breathlessly, wondering if he'd gone too far.

"It's our mission to bring order to this country," he said finally, when no one else spoke. "To bring its people a king they can believe in." He paused, his tone coming down a notch. "And I did not enter that town needlessly. Dresden's men had invaded the town, and were slaughtering its inhabitants. As king, I assumed that Henry would demand retribution. Protection for his people." The Earl let the statement linger for a moment.

"You ask for a wergild … money and land for my act of disobedience." He reached into his cloak and pulled out several small silver coins, throwing them on the table in front of the Archbishop. "Put that in your confessional box and buy yourself more henchmen. I grow tired of this conversation. We have too much work to do to quibble over such matters."

Henry took a deep breath, then nodded abruptly in agreement. The man was young and inexperienced, but he was not as stupid as the church believed, nor was he easily manipulated. He wasn't going to bend to this church official's need for attention.

The Earl sighed in relief and took a quick step back from the table. "With your permission, your Grace, I'd like to show you something."

Henry nodded again, his eyebrows quirked in curiosity.

"Trigva!" the Earl shouted.

The two guards posted outside the entrance flew to the side and the large Dane made his way immediately into the tent. Henry and his advisors drew back from the massive man, holding their breath.

"Unroll the map and place it here," the Earl said. He swept the wine goblets from the table, sending them clattering to the floor, and spread the map with his hands.

"The battle for England, your Grace, will not take place outside the gates of London as we thought," he said dramatically, jamming his forefinger down next to the town of Bosworth. "The battle for the crown will take place in the village of Leicester, in less than four days time!"

22

"Can't this horse move any faster?" Reis muttered, frustrated. "We could walk quicker than this on our *own*."

He was right. Katherine had thrown several things into a bag for herself and hitched an ancient – and emaciated – horse to a cart for the trip. Reis had argued with her at first, then given in, admitting that a horse and cart might come in handy.

Now we were all questioning the logic. My instincts were screaming for speed and secrecy, yet here we were, rattling along the road with a shocking lack of speed, behind a horse that looked like she might drop dead at any moment.

"We have to get as much distance between us and that town as possible," Reis continued, moving up to sit next to Katherine on the bench. "And we need to get to Bosworth. Four days. We have *four days*."

Suddenly he grabbed the reins from Katherine's hands.

"What are you doing?" she asked, surprised.

"Driving," he answered grimly. He adjusted the reins awkwardly in his hands, pulling experimentally on them and trying to get a feel for the leather.

Katherine grinned cheekily, amused at this change in positions, but Paul gasped.

"Do you even know how to do that?" he asked. His eyes flew from the horse to Reis and back again, quickly judging the safety of the situation. "Don't you think you should leave the driving to the, er, expert?"

Reis snorted and threw a glance over his shoulder at Paul. "Kid, right now we're bumping along a road in the middle of the night, drawing all sorts of attention to ourselves and making virtually no progress." He turned his attention back to the horse and the road ahead. "As long as we're going to make this kind of ruckus, we may as well take advantage of the tools at hand. Everyone hold onto something."

He took a firmer hold on the reins and brought them sharply down on the horse's rump. Surprised, the horse jumped and shot forward into the darkness, pulling the cart bouncing after her.

I half stepped, half fell into the bed of the wagon. I'd been sitting with Reis as he drove, watching the dark landscape slide by, and keeping an eye out for danger. Reis had even given me his assault rifle, showing me how to use the scope to scan the land around us. The day and night had taken its toll on me, though, and I'd finally admitted that I couldn't keep my eyes open much longer. I'd nearly dropped the rifle three times before Reis sent me to the back to go to sleep.

I hadn't argued with him when he suggested it, which is how I now found myself on my hands and knees in the bed of the racing cart. I reached out to pull my sleeping bag from its casing, and glanced around at the others. It was the middle of summer, but it was also the middle of the night, and the air around us was freezing. Paul was deep inside his sleeping bag, snoring, and Katherine was tucked snugly into a spare blanket next to him.

Tatiana lay on the other side of the cart, inside her sleeping bag but still wide awake. She was listening to music on her iPhone and watching the landscape fly by, lost in her own thoughts. I sighed, then swallowed heavily and made my way to her side of the cart. I knew I owed her an apology. I wasn't looking forward to it, but I also didn't want to sit by myself and stew on it.

"See anything out there?" she asked as I sat down next to her. She pulled her ear buds out and looked at me.

Well that seemed friendly enough, I thought. I shook my head and unrolled my sleeping bag, climbing into the woolly protection. "I don't know if I'd see it, even if there was anything out there. I'm exhausted. And kind of freaked out."

She grunted in agreement, but didn't answer.

I braced myself against the jolting of the cart, which seemed to be hitting every stone and hole in the road, and wondered how exactly Paul and Katherine were sleeping through this ride. Finally I cleared my throat. "I'm sorry I snapped at you earlier. I didn't mean it."

Tatiana turned to me expectantly, her eyes guarded, and I rushed forward. "It's just that I barely know you, and you're there shouting at me about wanting to bring the girl along. With Reis and Paul, at least I know where I stand. With you –"

"You don't know why exactly I'm here," she finished quietly.

I shrugged. That sounded close, at least. "Or whether you're our friend, I guess. Whether we can trust you," I added.

"You're worried about my connection to my father?"

"Is that so hard to believe?" I asked.

Tatiana shook her head. "No. But we both know that no matter what I tell you, you'll still wonder where my allegiance is."

Now it was my turn to stay silent. She was right, though I hadn't thought of it before. I'd known her for less than twenty-four hours, and she had basically blackmailed her way onto our trip. Now we were depending on her as part of our team, and I didn't know if she was on our side. Not for sure.

She sighed, resting her gaze on Paul and Katherine, then on Reis. Finally she turned back to me. "I loved my mother very much, Jason. Nicholas Fleming abused her physically and emotionally, and pushed her away. Then he left us and she killed herself. Because of him."

I gulped. "I'm sorry, that's terrible. Really. It doesn't exactly explain why you're here, though."

"I've heard the conversations between my grandfather and yours. My grandfather is wrong. Nicholas Fleming – Lord Dresden – is evil, pure and simple. I've seen him in action, and I know what he's capable of. If your grandfather thinks that Dresden is trying to hijack history for his own reasons, I believe him."

"And?"

"And I want to be there when he fails. He destroyed my mother, and tried to destroy me. Now I want to be the one that stops him. I want him to *know* that I've stopped him. I want to be the last face he sees before he dies." Her voice was cold and controlled, but broke on the last word, and I glanced quickly at her. She had clenched her jaw shut and closed her eyes. A single tear ran down her cheek.

I reached out to take her hand, unthinking. "We'll stop him," I murmured. "I promise."

A corner of her mouth turned up in answer, and she put her ear buds back in. I turned from her, my head reeling at what I'd just promised, and watched the darkness beyond the road for signs of life. As I glanced toward the horizon, I saw that the blackness was growing lighter there; dawn was near.

Which meant we were going to need a new plan soon.

I woke up several hours later. The sun was just above the horizon, sending its bright morning light shooting across the landscape and providing at least a little bit of warmth. Reis was still on the bench of the wagon, driving the horse at a shocking pace. I wondered how the old horse was still moving that fast, then glanced at Reis's face and understood. He looked like he was ready to murder someone. Possibly several someones.

The ride hadn't improved. We hit a particularly large pothole at that point, and half the contents of the wagon bed flew into the air. I took that as a sign that it was time to get up. Everyone else was somehow still sleeping, so I crawled toward the bench alone, struggling to take a seat without flying out of the cart.

After what felt like a year of working at it, I finally landed on the bench next to Reis. There, I took a firm grip on the edge of the cart and looked around. Traffic, or what passed for it, was light to say the least. We passed a large family, who appeared to be moving their entire household with one mule and a cart, and several men on horseback. The riders gave us curt nods of respect, then pressed on. The family just got out of our way. I couldn't blame them, really. Reis was driving like a man possessed. I wondered privately if he actually had any control over the horse, or if she was running away with us attached. Our bouncy and haphazard progress was very disorganized, and had the feel of a runaway train rather than orderly retreat.

We hit another deep rut then, and my focus changed to staying in said cart, rather than trying to figure out whether Reis was in control of it.

"Sheesh, Reis, you think you could hit *more* potholes?" Paul grumbled from the bed of the cart. His face appeared suddenly between Reis and I, exhibiting puffy, bloodshot eyes and hair that stuck out in every direction.

"We're in a hurry, geek," Tatiana snapped, emerging as well. "Potholes are incidental. Deal with it."

Paul's mouth snapped shut, and his face turned dark. I grimaced – I knew that look. He hated being called "geek." It was what his brother called him. I also knew his reaction – he was about to say something really stupid and hurtful in response, and get himself into even more trouble. I cut in before he could open his mouth.

"Hurry, yes. But where exactly are we going?" I glanced at Reis, who sat hunched over the reins, his mouth a grim line. "Reis? Plans?"

The body guard shook himself at my words, and glanced quickly at me. "Get to shelter," he muttered. "We're drawing way too much attention to ourselves in this contraption, and who knows who's looking for us at this point. The sooner we're under cover, the happier I'll be."

I nodded. It made sense, though I didn't see how we were going to hide and find Doc at the same time.

"And then?" Tatiana asked, mirroring my thoughts. Her face was creased into a frown of impatience – she wanted to get to the end of this journey as badly as I did, I thought.

The corner of Reis' mouth turned up at that, and he shrugged. "Then, girl, we find Doc, vanquish the bad guy, save the world, and try to get home to the future," he replied, slightly exasperated. "A more reasonable way of getting around wouldn't hurt, either."

Paul sat back thoughtfully, pulling several chocolate coins from his pocket, and the rest of us fell quiet.

"Oh my God, you actually *eat* those?" Tatiana said, glancing at him and grimacing. "What else, those disgusting marshmallow ducks they pass out at Easter? Do you think *now* is really the time to sit around having a picnic?"

Paul grinned at her, his teeth full of chocolate, and casually passed a coin to Katherine. She looked at the candy as if it were made out of magical fairy dust, then looked at Paul and me questioningly.

"It's candy," I told her quietly. "You eat it."

The girl carefully unwrapped the candy, reexamined the golden wrapper, and took a small bite. Her face lit up in surprise as the chocolate melted in her mouth.

"See, I'm not the only one who likes them!" Paul laughed.

Suddenly Reis sat up and yanked on the reins, putting an end to the conversation. The horse skidded to a quick halt, her sides heaving, and the four of us went sprawling across the cart. I looked at Reis, confused, then glanced at the road in front of us. It was pitted and badly maintained, but it was empty. No reason for him to have stopped.

"What is it?" I asked quietly. Had he seen something? Heard someone?

"Sounds ahead," he answered. "Listen. People shouting, some sort of livestock moving around. Chickens. We're going to have company soon."

Katherine's face cleared and she smiled, pushing her way forward to take a seat by Reis's side. "The town of Blythe," she chirped. "We used to have family there." She frowned at Reis' expression. "It is not a dangerous place."

Reis lowered his eyebrows at her and gestured for her to keep her voice down. "I'll be the judge of what's safe and what's not, thank you."

He took the map out of his pocket and spread it out over the seat beside him, moving his compass quickly over the paper. Katherine leaned forward and looked at the object in utter amazement. Then she noticed Tatiana's iPhone, which was sticking out of her shirt pocket.

"What is that?" she asked in wonder. She reached toward Tatiana's pocket, her fingers twitching for the iPhone.

Tatiana shoved the girl's hand away, scowling. "None of your business, missy," she snapped.

Katherine frowned, but pulled back thoughtfully. She shot a quick glance in my direction and grinned wryly at Tatiana's reaction, lifting her eyebrows in amusement.

Without thinking, I grinned back. She was right – Tatiana could be difficult sometimes.

Reis cleared his throat loudly to get our attention. "Looks to me like our best bet is to stay on this road. Keep heading south. We can't very well take this heap into the fields around the town, and we don't have any other means of getting there. Yet."

"So what's the plan?" I asked quietly. We had discussed this earlier, and agreed to avoid human contact as much as possible. Interacting with the locals would just make things … complicated. We had to assume that everyone and their brother was against us, and would try to stop us, throw us in jail, or worse. Besides, we weren't here to talk to the people of this time. We were here to save Doc.

Now it looked like Reis was changing things around on me, which made me very uncomfortable.

The man in question looked up at Katherine before glancing back at the three of us. "You three lay low in the back of the cart. You stick out like sore thumbs, and we can't afford to draw much attention. I'll sit beside Katherine up front." He took a deep breath. "We'll just have to make our way through the village, quick as we can. And you guys keep quiet. No one says anything. Right, Paul?" He turned his gaze to Paul, his eyes both commanding and pleading.

Paul gave him a quick thumbs up. "Right-oh, Captain," he muttered.

Shaking my head, I climbed into the back of the cart with Paul and Tatiana. We covered ourselves with the blankets and bags of flour Katherine had insisted on bringing along, and did our best to look hidden. The wagon lurched back into action, at a slower pace now, and we moved toward the town.

Beside me, I heard Tatiana take a deep, strained breath. Her hand found mine and squeezed it, sending along a silent message – everything would be fine. We'd be through the town and back on the road in no time.

I hoped with every ounce of my body that she was right.

23

Blythe, England

Unfortunately, fate had other plans. At first, it seemed like Reis' idea might work. After all, we had a girl from the right time period – practically a local – driving her horse and cart through a town she used to visit all the time. Perhaps no one would notice, or care, and we'd be able to pass through and get on with our mission. Just another girl, out for a drive to market or some such thing, with a cart full of various goods.

What could possibly go wrong? Aside from the four strangers she brought with her, hailing from the twenty-first century.

I couldn't see when we actually entered the town, of course, but I could certainly hear it. We passed through an atmosphere thick with the sounds of dogs barking, chickens clucking, horses calling to each other, and what sounded like a herd of five hundred angry pigs. Under it all was the deep, low hum of the people speaking to each other in English, French, and even Spanish. The accents were thick, and made the language sound more like music than our monotonous American English.

The wagon began to slow as we moved farther into the village, and some of the noise fell behind. At that point, I lifted the cloth just enough to expose one eye. This was my first time in an old English crowd, after all, and I wanted to see what the people were like. I glanced back along the road, where I saw a scattering of people, homes, carts, and animals. The people wore thick, heavy clothing in colorless browns and beiges. Most of the men wore shirts with their sleeves rolled up to their elbows, over pants that weren't much different from what I was wearing. The women were dressed in full-length tunics in varying colors, with undergarments peeking out under the hems. Some women wore veils and head dresses as well, to cover their hair. None of them showed any skin beyond their faces.

"Looks like a Renaissance fair," Paul whispered. I glanced quickly toward him to see that he and Tatiana had drawn their covers to the side as well. I could see two sets of curious eyes, taking the scene in greedily. I couldn't blame them – it was the oddest thing I'd seen in my fifteen years, and I couldn't get enough of it.

Paul was right – it looked and felt like we had ventured into an amusement park, or gone on a school field trip to a Renaissance exhibit, where people dressed up in costumes to play make believe for the day. I wouldn't have been surprised to see musicians, resplendent in velvets and lace, strolling by.

Of course there was one difference. These people weren't playing make believe. There was no parking lot in the background, or bus waiting to take us home. These were strangers, potentially violent ones, who kept things like swords and daggers in their costumes, and knew how to use them.

Further, they were people who would label us wizards – or worse – and turn us in to the authorities for a few coppers or a spare pig.

At that thought, the color and excitement drained away from the scene behind me. I settled back into the wagon, but kept one eye on the people, wondering anxiously how close we were to getting out of town. I'd seen enough.

Just then, though, we passed a row of targets, supported by haystacks. I peeked out, impressed – I'd always been secretly in love with archery, though I'd never actually seen it done. Now I gasped as the boys in front of the targets loosed a round of arrows with a sharp 'twang.' Each hit the targets at their centers. Perfect bulls eyes.

"Archery wasn't a game to these people," Tatiana whispered next to me. "The tournaments and practice were an important part of life."

"That's right," I agreed, remembering. "It was England's big advantage in war – her archers." My dad had read me a Bernard Cornwall book about it once, and become obsessed himself. For months it had been all he talked about. He'd even dressed as one for Halloween. I smiled at the memory, clearly seeing my mother's appalled – but amused – response.

The smile died on my lips when I heard Katherine gasp.

"Danes," she said, her voice low and worried. "We must hide."

"Too late," Reis answered. "I believe they've already seen us.

Seconds later, I saw what they were talking about.

Several men dressed in sleeveless leather jerkins and tattered chain mail appeared behind us, walking quickly enough to catch up with our slow-moving wagon. They were large, rough men, with hard, ugly faces and long, dirty blonde hair. They also looked distinctly unfriendly.

"I thought the Danes were kicked out of England two hundred years before this time period," Tatiana muttered, her voice low and worried.

"Apparently not all of them," Paul replied quietly.

The men were now less than 15 feet behind us. All four of them kept their eyes squarely on our cart, their hands on their battered swords. One of them had a battle axe slung across his chest. They all wore several silver rings around their arms. I cast my memory back, trying to collect any information I had on Danes. They came from the North, I knew. They wore their rings as signs of wealth and conquest. The more rings, the more potentially dangerous the man. They were traders, sometimes, but more often mercenaries and soldiers. Bullies. Raiders.

When they came peacefully, they were called Danes. When they attacked the English people, they were called Vikings instead.

The acid rose from my stomach to my throat, and I gulped heavily. The men behind us were looking less friendly with each passing moment. They meant to cause trouble, and no mistake.

"We need to move faster," Tatiana said in little more than a whisper.

"Reis, we've got a problem here," I snapped, not caring who heard. I was far more concerned about getting away from those men than confusing the townspeople at that point.

Instead of moving more quickly at my warning, though, the cart suddenly stopped.

I popped up from my hiding place, desperate to know what was going on. "What on earth are you doing?" I snapped, reaching toward Katherine. Before I could touch her, Tatiana grabbed my shoulder.

"Be careful," she murmured, nodding at the road in front of us. I turned to look, and my heart jumped into my mouth.

Two more Danes stood in the road before us. One of them had his hand on our horse's bridle. Both had swords drawn.

I glanced slowly from the men in front of us to Reis, and then to the side to meet Paul's eyes. His face had lost all color, and I didn't think his eyes could open any wider.

"Not good," he muttered out of the side of his mouth.

I nodded wordlessly, and the three of us crept forward, closer to Reis and the best protection we had.

"Is there a problem?" Reis asked casually. He carefully turned around to glance at the four men who approached us from behind, realizing just as I had that we were surrounded. He pressed his lips together at that, and shot one more sharp look in our direction. He didn't need to use words for that one – we were to be prepared. For anything.

I looked at the men at the horse's head, and then back toward the others, wondering what we were getting ourselves into. All six of the Danes were very large. Now that I looked more closely, I saw that two of them had scars across their cheeks. Several had missing teeth, and all of them had grossly unkempt facial hair hanging down their chests. Two of the men behind us had gained horses from somewhere, and now rode, their shields and long bows out. They moved forward, toward the men at the front of the wagon. These men wore heavy cloaks despite the warm summer temperature, and additional wooden shields dangled from their saddles.

They were better armed than we were.

"You're a stranger to these parts, yes?" the first horseman barked, riding closer to the wagon and notching an arrow.

For a moment Reis let the question go unanswered. I noticed that the noise from the crowd had died down. Even the chickens were quiet. The people had drawn quickly back into the alleys and buildings, hushing their children and leaving us to the mercy of the Vikings. This wasn't the first time they'd seen this kind of situation, and they didn't want to get involved.

"Did you lose your tongue, lad?" the second horseman snapped rudely, jerking his horse toward Reis and Katherine.

"I don't see how that's any business of yours, *lad*," Reis replied, his tone deep and unfriendly.

"You'll not be passing through this town without paying a tax," the first horseman said. His horse rammed into ours, knocking her to the side and nearly off her feet.

Reis snorted. "Tax? We don't need to pay your tax. We're on a mission of the church."

The two men on horseback laughed at Reis's denial, and crowded closer to the wagon.

The second horseman drew even closer, leaning toward the bench and leering at Katherine. "Your company says otherwise, boy, and your speech brands you a stranger." His eyes flicked to Tatiana, and ran quickly up and down her body. He grinned suddenly, showing a row of broken and rotting teeth. "Though I believe we can negotiate your tax, given what your companions have to offer."

Tatiana began to growl under her breath, and I saw Paul's hands flexing. Katherine had grown as still as a trapped bird on the bench, and I could practically see her thoughts racing. This situation was going from bad to worse, and I didn't think any of my companions were going to keep still much longer.

In front of me, Reis adjusted his body slightly, loosening his robe. He moved his foot slowly to the side, throwing open the bag in front of him to reveal the butt of the assault rifle.

My eyes flitted from the body guard to the rifle to the men in front us. Why oh why hadn't Reis given each of us weapons? I didn't think he could take all six of these men by himself.

"We've recently arrived from Rome," he said evenly. "As I told you, we're on a mission for the church." He carefully shifted the reins from his right hand to his left, freeing his shooting hand. It disappeared slowly beneath his robe.

Daggers, I thought. That's what he had on him. And a handgun. Perhaps that would be enough, after all.

"I do not pay homage to your God," the second horseman rasped. "Give us the church's silver, and we will allow you to pass."

Reis shook his head. "You're not listening, friend. I told you, we don't have any money." His tone was hollow, laced with an obvious warning.

"Do you wish to live?" the second horseman asked suddenly.

Reis didn't bother to answer. He yanked his hand from his robe, along with the handgun, and shouted something unintelligible.

The Vikings shrieked in response and surged toward the cart, brandishing a number of swords, axes, and daggers. An arrow flew through the air, brushing my ear, and I ducked, pulling Tatiana and Paul with me.

A thunderclap of sound erupted above us, deafening me, followed by a blur of action and blood.

In a smooth, practiced motion, the second horseman reached behind his back, retrieved an arrow, notched the 36-inch-long projectile, and brought the bow up, aimed directly at my heart.

"We'll take what we –" The Viking's words were cut short as another thunderous roar tore through the village. Fire erupted from under Reis's robe, blowing it upward to expose the assault rifle underneath. The shots ripped through the Dane's body, sending him to the ground, dead. Several of the bullets continued on past where he had been sitting to decimate the building on the other side of the road.

As he fell from his saddle, his loosed arrow cut through the warm, humid air, coming to rest in the throat of one of the Vikings behind us. He fell to the ground with a strangled cry and lay there, his body jerking in the mud. The horse belonging to the remaining rider reared up in terror at the sound of Reis's weapon, throwing its owner from his saddle. The man landed face-first on the ground and rolled quickly to the side. But he wasn't quick enough; the horse pounded him into the ground in its panic to get away from Reis and his guns. It thundered through the village, scattering chickens and pigs as it went.

I could hear the locals screaming in the alleys around us, terrified, and wondered fleetingly how long we had before they began to riot.

Reis must have had the same thought. He pushed Katherine, who was stunned and sitting absolutely still, into the back of the wagon, and grabbed the horse's reins. She was no happier about the gunshots than any of the other horses, and was lunging forward and back in panic.

Instead of trying to control her, Reis brought the reins sharply down on her rump and shouted, "Ha!"

The horse didn't need any further encouragement. She shot forward, rushing through the wide main street of the town. We weren't out of the woods yet, though. A shout from Paul drew my attention to the back of the cart, where I saw that one of the Vikings had jumped up before we left, grabbing the edge of the vehicle. He clung to the side now, one hand around Tatiana's wrist, threatening to pull her out of the cart. She glanced to me, mouthing the word 'help,' and I looked around the cart, desperate for a weapon.

Before I could move, Paul flew into action. He lugged one of Katherine's bags of flour up over his shoulder and heaved it at the Viking. Tatiana ducked at the last second, and the man took the bag across the face. He dropped like a rock to the road below us.

An ominous bump two seconds later suggested that he met a quick fate via the wheels of the wagon.

"Get down!" Reis screamed, handing the reins to me. He swung around with his rifle, looking for other enemies in the area, and covered our escape.

We stopped twenty minutes later, at a small inn by the road.

"Is everyone okay?" Reis asked. He turned to face us, breathing heavily.

"Are you?" Paul responded quickly.

Reis nodded. "I think so."

"What now?" I asked, taking in our surroundings. I didn't think we'd been followed, but I didn't trust any of the people here, now. I wanted to know who was around us at all times.

Reis rolled up his sleeve and glanced at his watch. "We've got a long way to go and very little time to get there," he said. He paused, thinking. "I'm afraid that little incident is going to draw a lot of attention, and that's not good. Word is going to get out about my guns, so our cover is blown." He jumped off the cart and gestured toward the row of horses hitched to the tying post in front of the inn. "Gather your things. Choose a horse."

"What?" Paul spluttered, jumping down. "We can't just take horses! What about the cart?"

Reis turned, his face dark. "Listen to me, Paul," he said quietly. "That little show back there blew our cover. We're labeled as people with guns, and strangers, and guess whose territory we're in right now?" He paused, waiting for an answer.

"Dresden's," I muttered. He was right – we were in a lot of danger. More now than we had been. My legs kicked into action at the thought, and I was out of the cart before I knew it.

Reis nodded. "Exactly. Now he's going to be searching for us, and he's going to know exactly who and where we are, thanks to those townspeople. We need to get moving, and we need to move a hell of a lot faster than we were doing in the wagon."

"So we're just going to go in and ask someone if we can borrow their horses?" Paul asked, shocked.

"Not at all," Reis replied, smiling. "I have a plan."

24

DONCASTER, ENGLAND

Dresden's personal chamber took up the entire room at the top of the castle's tallest tower. It stretched nearly 18 feet from floor to ceiling and housed just under 1000 square feet of living space. Six brightly colored rugs were strewn about the stone floor, with one massive rug depicting the royal crown of England lying at the foot of his bed. On top of the bed was a bright red bedspread made of silk, lavishly embroidered with silver and gold horses and birds of prey. There were dozens of multicolored pillows on the bed – rash signs of wealth in this day and age. Two tall stained glass windows stood on either side of the large desk, and paintings of stars, moons, and horses decorated the plaster walls in purple, gold, and turquoise. To anyone else, the chamber was breathtakingly beautiful, lacking nothing and even flaunting colors and materials that the royals called their own. To Dresden, these sumptuous decorations and signs of wealth were the hard-won gains of his climb to power. They were ostentatious, but they were also his due. He didn't hesitate to remind people of that.

Dresden himself was sitting at his desk, recording the day's goals, when the Bishop of Fairhaven rushed into the room, his nose swollen and bloody. Both of his eyes were blackened. He had one of his priests with him, presumably for moral support. Dresden looked up, frowning with displeasure.

"I do not recall summoning you," he said, going back to his journal. "What on earth happened to your face?"

"I was attacked!" the Bishop snapped angrily. "A ruffian attacked me without warning or reason, and I demand that he be found and punished!

No one should be allowed to strike a servant of God, not in my kingdom!"

Dresden snorted as he leaned back in his chair. Men of the church were flighty and self-righteous, and he had far more important things to do right now. A war was coming, and he needed to be prepared. If things were going to go the way he wanted…

"Make no mistake, your *Holiness*, this is not your kingdom, and you are no more a servant of God than I," he snapped. "Further, I have important business to see to, and little patience for your petty arguments. I suggest you handle this yourself, or I will finish what this other man started."

"As lord of this region, it is your duty to see justice done!" the Bishop protested. "Would you allow mercenaries to beat members of the church?" Suddenly his voice grew low and crafty. "I wonder how my superiors would feel about that. I wonder whether they would find another man … worthier of your place."

Dresden drew a long, whistling breath through his noise, his nostrils pinched. The Bishop was an idiot, but he knew how to play at politics. Just like every other self-serving church official he had met in this period. The Bishop would tell his superiors, he had no doubt, and Richard couldn't afford to lose the church's backing. Not now.

Of course the Bishop could only tell his tale if he left here alive.

Dresden's mouth quirked, and he glanced toward the drawer where he kept his personal pistol. "Well when you put it that way, Bishop, I find it hard to argue with you," he muttered, his voice smooth and slippery. "Do tell me, then, who was this ruffian?"

The Bishop smiled at the small victory. "There were four of them. I don't know who they were. They were … strange."

Dresden lifted his eyebrows in mock fascination. "Strange? How so?"

"They spoke…" The Bishop took a deep breath, his eyes sliding to the side. "They spoke like you, my Lord."

Dresden frowned, his mind trying to make sense of what the fool had said. Suddenly he noticed something hanging from the man's wrists – gray, dense material, which reflected the light back at him.

He jumped to his feet, throwing his chair against the wall behind him, and strode quickly toward the Bishop to grab his wrist.

"Duct tape," he muttered in shock, peering closely at the material. His eyes rose to the Bishop's. "What did you say about them?" he asked, his voice dangerously quiet.

"They spoke as you do, my Lord. Their accents were like yours."

Dresden's face grew dark at that. His accent … by this the man meant his speech patterns and words, as well as the sounds of them. When he first came here, his speech had been a large problem. It was, after all, from the twenty-first century. He'd taken pains to alter it and force himself into the habits of the people of this time, to fit into Medieval England.

If the Bishop was saying that these people spoke like him…

"What did these strangers look like?" he growled.

"It was dark, I don't remem–"

"Try," Dresden said, reining in his temper. If the Bishop had seen people from the future, it could mean big trouble. He needed to know as much about them as possible, regardless of whether the man wanted to talk about it or not.

The Bishop frowned, trying to regain his composure. "The man who did this to me, he was older than the others. Perhaps twenty-five years of age, perhaps older. It was dark, it was hard to tell."

"And?" Dresden asked ominously. Surely the man had seen more than *that*.

"He had short, light-colored hair, but not as fair as yours, my Lord. He was tall, as tall as Prince Sloan, and sure of himself. He came out of the shadows and attacked two of my men and myself with his bare hands."

"And? What else? You say that their speech was odd. What else, Bishop?"

"I saw ... I saw two younger men and a woman, perhaps the same age as Prince Sloan."

"Where were you? What were you doing? What were they doing there?" Dresden's questions came more rapidly as he began to lose his patience.

"I was visiting the healer's daughter. She needed my assistance in her time of need –"

"I don't care what you were doing with her," Dresden snarled suddenly. "These people you saw, what happened to them? Where did they go?"

"My Lord!" The Bishop drew himself up and looked down his nose, offended at Dresden's tone.

Dresden snorted. These men of the church – always thinking they were more important than they actually were. He obviously wasn't going to get anywhere with this man unless he pushed the issue. He moved back to his desk, where he grabbed the pistol from its drawer and raised it quickly to eye level, to point it at the Bishop's now-pale face. Then he released the safety. The Bishop jumped at the sharp click.

"You know what this is, and what it will do to you," Dresden noted quietly, his lips pinched with anger. "I suggest that you tell me exactly what I want to know, and quickly, before I am forced to use it. What were they wearing?"

The man gasped. "You would kill me … a bishop?"

Dresden smiled and shook his head. "That would rather defeat the purpose of asking a question and expecting an answer, would it not?"

He shifted the nose of the pistol to the side and smiled again, then pulled the trigger. A loud thunderclap sounded through the chamber, accompanied by a cloud of smoke. When the smoke cleared, the Bishop's priest lay on the floor, dead.

The Bishop jumped in horror, his eyes on his fallen comrade.

Dresden moved the nose of the pistol slowly back toward the Bishop and smiled wolfishly. "Now, Bishop, I believe I asked you a question."

Suddenly the Bishop found his voice. "The three men were wearing cloaks, brown cloaks. From a distance I would have mistaken them for priests," he said, his voice shaking with fear.

"And the girl, what was she wearing?"

The Bishop shook his head in confusion. "It was dark. I don't … something different, something strange. Not a cloak or armor. A shirt and light brown britches, perhaps, but nothing like I've seen before." He gulped nervously.

Dresden's heart clenched for a moment. They were from the future, then. They had to be. The men had taken some care to disguise themselves, but not enough. Who were they? And why were they here? Most importantly…

"Where did they go?" he demanded.

"They left town. I believe that they took the girl with them. North, they went north, I'm certain. I heard the older one tell one of the boys that they would head directly to York," the Bishop mumbled, squirming toward the door.

Dresden watched him closely. The man was lying, that much was obvious. He didn't know where these people had gone, and would be of no more use. Not that it mattered. If they were here to involve themselves in the coming battle – or to stop him – they would be going in only one direction.

He turned back toward his desk, tucked the gun in his belt, and unrolled the large map, jamming his finger down on the small town. "Bosworth," he murmured. "That must be where they're headed."

"My Lord?" the Bishop asked.

"Get out!" he snapped. "I have no further use for you."

The Bishop took one last look at the bloody corpse lying on the cold stone floor, and turned to flee the chamber in horror.

Dresden glanced up to make sure that the man left, and saw his son standing in the doorway. Sloan Dresden had has father's dark eyes, but that was where the resemblance ended. The boy was almost 6 feet tall, and had rich brown hair, which hung just below his shoulders. His square jaw gave him an air of power, while his shoulders and chest were broad enough to promise physical strength, his forearms well defined and muscular. He looked much older than his sixteen years would suggest.

He was also very obviously distressed at the corpse lying on the floor.

Dresden walked toward his son and stopped in front of him, raising his hand to grasp the boy's shoulder. "Why so shocked, son?" he asked coldly. The boy should not look so upset about the death of someone who had not mattered in life.

Sloan shook his head, confused. "Why kill him? What purpose did that serve, Father, except to make the Bishop dislike you even more?"

Dresden smirked. "Have you heard of the Prince of Wallachia? Ruler of Hungary? Vlad the Impaler?"

Sloan shook his head, his eyes growing cold and withdrawn.

Dresden shook himself mentally. Of course the boy wouldn't have heard of Vlad. That situation must be going on right now, he thought, rather than in ancient history, as he knew it. No amount of money spent on an education would have taught his son such things.

"He was an immensely successful count in Hungary, and ruled successfully for many years. And do you know how he did it?"

Sloan shook his head again, his expression unchanging.

"Killing meant nothing to him, son. He cared very little for human life, and eliminated anyone who dared stand in his way. Without conscience. We must take an example from him, my boy. These people that surround us are mere shadows. You must not think of them as human, but as cattle. They are nothing compared to us. Their deaths do not matter."

Dresden paused for a moment, allowing that to sink in, then squeezed his son's shoulder to get his attention. "Now, I have a mission for you."

Sloan took a deep breath and looked down for a moment. When he looked back up, his face was flat and emotionless, though something lurked in his eyes. Dresden paused for a moment. He hadn't expected to test the boy's mettle so soon, and wondered fleetingly whether his son was ready. Still, he couldn't take the trip himself, and had no more trustworthy soldier.

"You heard what the Bishop said about these strangers. It is imperative that we find them. Take your best men and follow the road from Doncaster to Bosworth."

The boy frowned in protest. "But Fa–"

"Don't question me, boy!" Dresden barked. "Take the road south, search every village, every farm, every hedge! These people *must* be found, do you understand me?"

Sloan nodded wordlessly, his lips pressed together in anger.

Dresden sighed. He had high hopes for the boy, but his son questioned his orders more often than he liked. "You heard the Bishop's description?" Another nod from the boy. "Find them, and bring them to me. If they are who I think they are..." Dresden paused. If they were who he thought they were, that made them minions of Richard Evans'. And that made them dangerous. There was only one way to deal with such people, though he didn't think his son was up to it. "Take Lawrence and his men with you, and use whatever force necessary, but bring them to me alive."

"And if they *aren't* who you believe they are?" Sloan asked, raising his chin.

Dresden's hand flew out, striking Sloan across the cheek and knocking the boy to the ground. "Mind your place, boy," he thundered. "They *are* who I believe them to be, make no mistake." He closed his eyes briefly and tried to control his anger. "I will only be a day's ride behind you. King Richard will meet me at Lord Bryer's estate in Nottingham tomorrow evening, to confirm our plans for the coming battle. Bring the strangers to me there." He watched as Sloan scrambled to his feet, and held out a hand to stop the boy.

"Do not fail me in this, son. Do not interrogate the strangers, and bring them to me alive. Meet me in Nottingham in two days, with these strangers, or it will mean your life. Do not doubt me in this. Do you understand?"

Sloan narrowed his eyes with hatred, but did not answer. He turned and stormed out the door, shouting for his horse and men, and leaving Dresden alone in the sumptuous room.

Dresden sighed, watching his son leave, and began to count the days left until the battle. If these strangers proved to be hard to find, and meant to make trouble…

25

I crouched low over the galloping horse, bringing my chest to within inches of its neck, and urged it to move faster. This also made my back a smaller target. I hoped. Looking to the side, I saw Tatiana doing the same, her face dangerously angry. The others were close behind us, their horses breathing heavily.

It had all seemed so simple when Reis explained the plan. He'd started outlining it as soon as we got out of the cart at the inn. The idea had been simple and straightforward; as long as things went the way he thought they would, everything would be fine.

As long as things went the way he thought they would. I should have known we were in trouble as soon as he'd said the words.

It had been agreed that Katherine would do the talking, and the rest of us would keep quiet. We'd already been in the inn's stable yard, which stood some distance from the inn itself. At least a dozen horses had been tied to the posts outside the stables. They'd been decked out in blankets, saddles, and bridles, practically begging for riders.

Katherine had dealt quickly with the boys who came racing around, telling them that we would be staying the night, and sending them off to ready our rooms. As soon as they disappeared, the rest of us had sprung into action, grabbing our bags and racing toward the closest horses. Tatiana and Katherine had mounted first, followed by Reis, Paul, and me. We'd been galloping toward the gate in no time.

Before we'd turned the corner and left the yard, though, the door of the inn had cracked open. Low, guttural voices had sounded through the opening, followed by shouts of alarm. We'd been too late.

As it turned out, the horses we'd chosen had belonged to a group of soldiers. And well-armed soldiers, at that. They'd been chasing us for the last twenty minutes or so. The last shout I'd heard behind us was for the men to ready their bows.

Suddenly Paul pulled abreast of Tatiana and me, breathing heavily through his mouth. He looked like he'd been through a war.

"Can you see them?" I shouted, hoping he'd looked more recently than I had.

For a moment he didn't respond, making me wonder if he'd heard me at all. Finally he turned slightly to glance behind us.

"Yeah, just over the ridge, maybe 500 feet out," he shouted, bending farther forward.

Reis caught up to us now, along with Katherine, their faces smeared with dust and sweat. Our horses were tiring quickly, and I could feel that they were beginning to slow. We needed to come up with a plan soon, or we'd be caught. How much longer would Reis run, before he decided to fight it out? Could he do it? Would he even have time to draw his weapons? We had surprised the Danes earlier in the day, but I didn't think it would work again. Were these men chasing us because of Reis and his guns? Would it even matter? We knew they had long bows; several arrows had raced past us before we'd had a chance to reach the road.

"They're gaining on us," Paul growled, bringing me back to the present. "We don't have much time!"

Suddenly a small wooden bridge appeared before us, blocking our path. Beyond the bridge was a dramatic fork in the road. One road led downstream, into the fields and valleys there. The other led directly into the forest in front of us.

Reis pulled to a quick stop, glancing at first one road and then the other. We paused restlessly, watching him.

"We don't have time for this!" Tatiana screamed, looking back at us. "They're right on our *tails!*"

Reis ignored her outburst and stood up in his stirrups, judging the road in front of us and the ravine under the bridge.

"Reis, we've got to *go!*" Tatiana implored. "Are you suicidal?"

"Wait!" Reis demanded, finally looking over at Tatiana. "Dismount, grab your horses' reins, and follow me. Quickly!"

Tatiana's face showed utter dismay at his announcement, but to her credit, she did as she was told. Without explanation, Reis led us hurriedly into the ravine and under the bridge. The structure was just large enough to hide us all from view.

"What are we doing?" I whispered. "*Hiding?* Under a *bridge?*"

Reis held up a hand for silence. "They're going to be here in a matter of seconds, so I'm only explaining this once," he snapped. "The road that forks to the left can be seen for miles without obstruction. They'll take a brief look and see rather quickly that we didn't go that way, which will prompt them to follow the road into the forest. Once they do, we'll take the road less traveled, so to speak, which, according to my compass, is the road we need to take regardless."

"And if they figure out we're hiding out down here?" Paul asked.

Reis turned his back on Paul without answering, reaching into his carrying case and retrieving his assault rifle. "Then we do it the hard way," he answered, releasing the rifle's safety.

Then we heard them, thundering up the road. We reached out and grabbed the reins of our horses, hoping our newly acquired animals would remain relatively quiet. The iron horse shoes of the soldiers' mounts moved onto the bridge over us, and came to a deafening halt in the center. I looked at my friends, took a deep breath, and waited.

My heart jumped into my throat when they finally started moving again. The bridge creaked and groaned above us at the weight, and I wondered suddenly what would happen if it broke. Would they look down and see us? Fall on top of us? I could see spaces between some of the boards – would those soldiers look down and see me looking up at them?

I glanced at Reis anxiously, but found him calm and collected. He was casually resting the butt of his rifle against his right shoulder, the nose pointed up toward the bridge above us. If anything happened, he'd be ready.

Then we heard the voices. The hair on the back of my neck stood in shock.

"Sir, what about Lord Dresden's battle? The road to Bosworth is this way," the first voice called out.

"Be damned with the battle! I want those horse thieves strung up for their crimes, and Lord Dresden would want the same," another voice answered roughly.

Reis gripped the barrel of his gun until his knuckles turned white, and I gulped. These were Dresden's soldiers? Of all the rotten ideas in the world, we'd managed to draw the attention of *Dresden's* soldiers by stealing their horses? The one man in this world we were working hardest to *avoid?*

We listened breathlessly as the horses stomped across the bridge, our eyes on the shadows above us. Obviously the leader had a decision to make. We could only hope that he decided to ride into the forest, as Reis thought he would. If he decided against the forest, we'd be trapped.

Finally, after an eternity of waiting, the man made his decision. "We find the thieves, kill them, and *then* ride to battle," he snarled. The other men grunted in agreement or acceptance, and moved after their commander. Seconds later, our pursuers had vacated the bridge and disappeared into the forest.

We were free. For the moment.

Reis nodded quickly and led his horse out from under the bridge, motioning for us to follow. Within moments, we were remounted and tearing down the open road, on our way to Bosworth.

We rode without incident, not stopping until well past sundown, when we were too tired to ride any farther. Then we led our horses far enough off the road to feel safe, and found a small clearing in the trees.

"How much farther do we have to go?" I asked once I was off my horse. I glanced at Doc's watch and noted the time. Past 10, and this would be the 19th still, as impossible as that seemed. We were making progress, but tomorrow and the day after were the only days I had to find Doc. The day after that would be far too late.

Reis grimaced at the question, then tried to put on a lighter expression. "We're moving a hell of a lot faster than we were. Tomorrow evening should put us in Bosworth, the morning after at the latest. As long as nothing comes up."

"As long as nothing comes up?" I gasped. "Reis, we have to be in Bosworth by the 21st, you know that! If we're not –"

"Jason," he interrupted, holding up one hand, "I know. You know I know. We'll get there, okay?" He watched me, waiting for a response, and I nodded grudgingly. Reis hadn't let me down yet, and he knew how important this was. If he said we'd get there, I'd just have to believe him.

"Relax, Jay," Paul cut in. "For tonight, just pretend you're Robin Hood or something. Merry men living in the forest, and all that."

I snorted. "Merry men wearing green spandex is not my idea of a good time, Paul," I grunted.

He grinned. "Maybe not, but it made you smile, and that's something."

I grinned back, relenting, and started pulling food out of my pack. We hadn't eaten anything all day, and I was famished. The others joined me, and after a brief meal of bottled water, beef jerky, and cereal bars, we curled up with whatever we had, used our backpacks as pillows, and fell asleep.

My last waking thought was of a countdown, hosted on an old bronze pocket watch. The next two days were what we'd been sent here for. The moment of truth. They had to go perfectly, or it would all be for nothing.

Katherine put the clear tube of water down, marveling at its simplicity. It was like the glass she had seen in the church, but lighter, stronger … In short, just another of the wondrous and frightening things these strangers had shown her. There had been music makers, wonderfully warm blankets, strange, pressed bars of oats, grain, and honey … and then the astonishing weapons the man named Reis had held, which spat fire and smoke and killed men.

She realized that any normal girl – any *rational* girl – would have been frightened. Terrified and running, no doubt. But she was fascinated. These people had a magic like nothing she'd ever seen before. They fought Danes, and won. And now they were after Dresden.

She'd been mulling over the same question since the night before, when they had first found her. Run or stay? She knew the decision to run would be the wise choice. These people had to be practitioners of the dark arts, and were now wanted by the law. Something inside her, though, told her to stay. Something about these people – the boy, Jason – pulled at strings deep inside her. Strings she didn't understand, but didn't feel like fighting. She wanted to see where they would go, what they would do.

Besides, she thought practically, where else would she go? She had no home. After her father's death, English law declared that his property belonged to her, but the Bishop had declared her rights forfeit. He had told her – and everyone else, for all she knew – that the church had been given the rights of her father's estate. His dying wish atop the hanging platform. In the Bishop's version, Katherine, per her father's request, was to be placed inside a convent. She knew that her father would never have said that. He loved her too much. But it was her word against the Bishop's; a losing proposition if there ever was one. She didn't stand a chance here on her own.

So she would stay, then, with these fascinating strangers, with their odd clothing and odder food. Their sticks of fire and heroic mission. She would be associated with them, she knew, and branded a witch. But she would have an adventure. Finally, for the first time in her life, she would see the world outside her home and the surrounding villages.

And she would get to take her revenge on Dresden for killing her father.

Suddenly her mood brightened and the knots in her stomach subsided. For the first time in days, she lost the confusion that had hounded her. True, it would be dangerous, but she had a direction now. A meaning.

Friends.

She glanced to the side, where Jason was already sound asleep, and wondered if they would call her friend. She hoped so. She hadn't had friends – true friends – in years. And if these friends could also save her life, and perhaps her lands … and help her find her revenge … she would do whatever she must to maintain their affection.

At that, she smiled and ducked her head, thinking it was past time for her to be asleep as well. Tomorrow, evidently, was an important day for her new friends.

26

AUGUST 20, 1485

I awoke to the feel of cold steel pressed against my cheek.

"Get up, boy," a voice above me growled.

I cringed; I'd been having a pleasant dream, where I'd been in my bed at home, waking to the smell of Doc cooking blueberry waffles downstairs...

Doc. At the thought, my heart stopped. I'd nearly forgotten when – and where – we were. I cracked one eye open, trying to adjust to reality. It was light out, and that must mean –

"Now." The rough voice cut through my thoughts, and my eyes flew open. That *hadn't* been part of the dream, then.

A dark figure stood over me, clad in black clothing and polished mail. His face was hidden in the shadow of a deep hood, though I could see the glint of his eyes. I didn't recognize the voice. Of the most immediate importance, though, was the long dagger he clutched, its side lying against my face. He moved the tip of the dagger down my cheek now, along my jaw and under my chin, to rest it finally in the soft spot at the top of my neck.

I climbed clumsily to my feet, trying to keep my chin as elevated as possible, and dropped the blanket to the ground. Shocked at this awakening, I let my eyes fly around the clearing.

Over a dozen soldiers had made their way into our camp while we slept. Rough men now held Reis, Paul, and Tatiana, though Katherine sat in the middle of the group, on her own. These were hard, brutish-looking men, currently moving with purpose through the camp, going through our things. Capes the color of blood fell just below their knees, covering the black leather jerkins and gleaming sheets of mail on their chests and arms. They bristled with knives and swords, all shining dully in the early rays of the sun. These were nothing like the soldiers we had seen in Doncaster, who had been overweight men and boys dressed in rags. These were professionals, and following precise orders. They were well fed, cleanly scrubbed, and heavily armed, and their eyes reflected a cold hunger that made me shiver.

These men would kill us if ordered to do so, and they wouldn't hesitate over the job. And I saw now that they had been at work before they woke us. Not one but two heavily woven ropes, tied in hangman's nooses, hung from a long tree limb behind my friends.

"What exactly can we do for you, gentlemen?" I asked before I lost my nerve.

There was an abrupt laugh behind me, and the dagger at my throat moved slightly as my captor threw off his hood. I glanced at him from the corner of my eye, and then did a double take. He was no older than Paul and I. His features were as striking and sharp as the men who followed him, with dramatic black eyes and dark hair, cut just below his shoulders. A thin scar on his left check turned his mouth up to give his features a joyful expression. I assumed that this was false, and almost certainly unnatural. It probably drove him crazy. My mouth turned up involuntarily at that, and I bit the inside of my cheek to keep from laughing.

Me getting killed would, after all, defeat the point.

Still, the fact that he was our age, as well as the odd feeling that I had somehow met this boy before, made me relax slightly. True, he was a soldier. But if he was our age, I might find some flexibility there. My eyes traveled slowly down his body, and back up. He wore black leather britches, with the ends stuffed into knee-high black leather boots. A black cape fell loosely by his side, completing the menacing ensemble, and in turn making him look like a fifteenth-century version of Darth Vader. I nearly choked at that thought. I'd definitely been spending too much time with Paul, to be making comparisons like that at a time like this. Still, he was barely more than a kid. Surely that made him a little less scary. A little more … gullible?

"So you're the horse thieves my men encountered yesterday," he growled. "I must admit, though, that I have never seen horse thieves so … oddly outfitted." He glanced around our camp, then yanked back on my neck. "Who are you?"

My eyes flew to Reis, who lowered his eyebrows in a silent 'no.' What was I supposed to say? I certainly couldn't tell the truth, and we hadn't come up with a real cover story. After all, the original plan had been to *avoid* the natives.

Before I could think of a reasonable reply, the boy behind me darted forward to grab Katherine, who had been sitting on the ground up to this point. He yanked her to her feet, his hand buried in her hair, and slid the flat side of his dagger across her throat.

I took an involuntary step forward, but another solider quickly grabbed my arms and yanked me back.

"Perhaps you need some encouragement to answer my questions," the leader snapped. He pressed down and Katherine gasped. A drop of blood appeared on the tip of his dagger. "Answer me, or I will kill this one and then hang the others," he drawled coldly.

"NO!" Reis yelled hoarsely. He threw his elbow into the soldier behind him and turned toward Katherine, only to be stopped in his tracks by yet another soldier. This one hit Reis in the gut with the pommel of his sword, and my erstwhile body guard doubled over in pain and dropped to the ground. In a quick motion, the same soldier brought his sword up and prepared to deliver the finishing blow.

"Stop!" I shouted desperately. My mind raced, trying to get a handle on this quick turn of events. *Stall*, I thought quickly. That was always the first step in a plan. "I'll answer your questions, just don't hurt my friends."

The young soldier nodded as though he'd expected as much, and eased his hold on Katherine. "I shall make this simple for you," he said quietly. He looked at me, then toward Paul and Tatiana. "I am going to ask you a few questions, and I expect answers. Honest ones. If I believe you to be lying, I shall kill the girl." He shrugged casually, as if to assure me that killing the girl, or anyone else for that matter, meant nothing to him. A ball of ice settled deep in my stomach, and I shivered again. I believed him.

That didn't mean that I liked it.

I nodded once, my mind racing. Where exactly were Reis' guns and daggers? Were they within reach of any of us? My eyes darted to the side, running over the clearing and searching. The last time I'd seen them...

"Who are you?" the boy suddenly asked again. "Have you heard of Lord Dresden? The lord of these lands?"

At his words, I suddenly realized why I felt as if I knew this boy. It was his eyes, the expression on his face, and the way he tilted his head when he spoke. I knew who he was. I glanced over at Tatiana, running my eyes quickly over her stance to confirm my suspicion. The young soldier stood in the same way, and I nodded to myself. He cast the same shadow as his grandfather and, in no small way, his half sister.

"Why exactly would that matter to you, Sloan?" The words shot out of my mouth before I could stop myself.

The boy said nothing at my question, though his frown deepened. He hadn't been expecting that one, I thought triumphantly.

"That's right," I continued. "You may not know who I am, but I know exactly who you are. Your name is Sloan. Your father is Nicholas Fleming, or, as he's called in this land, Lord Dresden." I knew I was right – I'd learned his name through Doc's notes, and his conversation with John Fleming. This boy had the look of his grandfather in his eyes, and the same arrogant expression as Tatiana. He would have been sent after us by Dresden, I thought, to bring us back alive – it all made sense.

Of course they never would have found us if it wasn't for the horses. That was incredibly bad luck. Still, there was nothing for it now. I glared at Sloan, who was staring back at me as though I'd just pulled out a ray gun and tried to shoot him with it. His expression had changed, if only for a moment. The cocky, arrogant look on his face had faltered and given way to confusion.

"My Lord?" the man standing next to Reis mumbled. He dropped his sword to his side and stared at Sloan, confused.

I gulped, hoping I was right. As long as Dresden wanted us alive – which he must, under the circumstances – we would be safe. I just had to convince this boy that we were who we said we were.

"I've met your grandfather," I continued, pressing my advantage. If I could keep him talking, keep him on board with the story…

"He's lying," the soldier standing behind Tatiana said in a disgusted tone. He spat on the ground in disgust, then reached up and grabbed the rope that hung above her head.

"No he's not!" Tatiana shot back desperately, speaking out for the first time and tugging against the man.

"It's true, my Lord. What they say is true!" Katherine said in a surprisingly calm voice, as if injecting reason into an unreasonable situation was going to do any good. I shot her a surprised glance, and saw her eyes slide to the side. Reis' bags lay on that side of the clearing, I remembered, complete with his personal armory. I saw now that Reis had somehow managed to inch his way over there, on the pretense of painful writhing, and had almost reached the bags.

If we kept the soldiers occupied for another minute or two, we'd be in the clear.

I glanced back toward the group of soldiers, anxious that they not see me looking at Reis, and gasped. The soldier behind Tatiana had dropped the noose around her neck and was now tightening it. This could certainly complicate matters.

"I grow tired of these games," Dresden was saying with a shake of his head. "If you will not answer my questions in a logical manner, I have no choice but to give you more adequate … motivation. String her up!"

"Dresden is looking for me!" Tatiana shouted just before the rope went tight around her neck.

Sloan turned to her, shocked. *Another point for our team*, I thought. "And why is that?" he asked skeptically.

"Because I'm his daughter," she said in a raspy voice, gasping against the pressure of the rope.

I would have bet all the tea in China that Sloan wasn't expecting that answer. He took a step toward Tatiana and released his grip on Katherine. She, in turn, staggered back and fell against my chest, wrapping her arms around my shoulders to catch her balance. Sloan studied Tatiana with cold intensity.

"Who are you?" he repeated softly.

Suddenly Reis had his guns. A roar sounded out across the clearing, and two of Sloan's soldiers flew backwards before crumpling to the ground, dead. I dropped to the ground, taking Katherine with me, and prayed that Paul had the presence of mind to do the same. The minute my knees hit the dirt, I began shuffling as quickly as I could toward Tatiana, who was still trapped by the rope wrapped around her neck. Katherine crawled next to me, her shoulder at my hip. I glanced up to catch Tatiana's gaze and saw her eyes flitting around the clearing, terrified.

Then the gunfire stopped. I paused to look for Reis and found him on the ground, a sword held to his neck. Three more soldiers appeared in front of Katherine and me, hustling us to our feet. Tatiana stood stock still, and I could see another soldier pulling Paul roughly to his feet.

"No more games," Sloan snapped. "Tell me who you are, or you will all die, right now!"

I took a deep breath. Honesty it was, then. "My name is Jason Evans."

"And where have you come from, Jason Evans?" he asked, raising his eyebrows as he took in my outfit – an orange and gray rugby shirt, battered blue jeans, and red wool socks. Evidently my attire didn't meet his approval.

"Lebanon, New Hampshire," I proclaimed, shooting him a wry smile. Something about the situation made me want to taunt him, though a part of me realized it was probably a bad idea.

"Where is that?" he asked skeptically, leaning toward me. His eyes glimmered in curiosity, and I wondered for a moment whether he actually believed me.

"About 5,000 miles east of here, across the Atlantic Ocean."

"They're lying, your Grace!" one of the soldiers repeated, making me jump. Several others grunted in agreement, and the one holding Paul pulled my friend's hands farther behind his back. Paul yelped in pain and fell to his knees.

I gulped, thinking I'd pushed too far.

"Silence!" Sloan roared. He turned back to me, locking his eyes to mine. His eyes sparked again, and I let out the breath I'd been holding. That was it – I *had* seen what I thought I'd seen. Curiosity. He was fascinated, despite himself. He didn't like what we'd done, and he didn't know if he believed me yet, but he wanted to. Now I just had to find a way to use that against him.

For a moment no one spoke. The soldiers around us stirred restlessly, looking to their leader for orders. The soldier who held me tightened his grip, bruising my arms and cutting off the circulation, and I squirmed against him.

"I'm not lying," I finally said. Waiting wasn't going to get us any closer to Doc.

"Why are you here?" he shot back.

The truth, Evans, I thought. *It's your best weapon right now*. "I'm looking for my grandfather."

Sloan studied me, trying to gauge if I was telling the truth. I looked steadily back at him, refusing to drop my eyes. Either he would believe me or he wouldn't. If he did, we had a shot at living, at least for now. If he didn't … I looked past him toward the two ropes that swung effortlessly in the breeze. Well, better not to think about that at all.

"This boy and the girl are coming with me," he said finally, gesturing to Tatiana and me.

"But my Lord –" one of the soldiers muttered, stepping toward him.

"Do as I say!" Sloan thundered. "I do not take questions from the likes of you! I was sent by my father to find these very people, and I will see it done!"

"And the others?" another soldier asked softly.

"Tie them up, throw them in the back of the cart. Take them to Lord Bryer's estate in Nottingham. I will ride ahead of you with these two."

One of the older men frowned, but nodded quietly, and the soldiers began to manhandle Tatiana and me up onto our horses. Sloan mounted his own horse, and then turned to glare at his men.

"Do not harm them, or it will mean your lives. I do not know what my father wants with these prisoners, but he wants them alive."

I looked back at my friends and shared one long, tense look with Reis, who nodded bravely at me. Then we were galloping away, prisoners of Sloan Dresden and his father.

Reis watched Jason and Tatiana vanish into the forest, sending a silent prayer after them. Then he tamped down on the rage that had been building for the last half hour; for now, he had to keep his cool and wait for his opportunity. At some point, the soldiers around him would slip up. He just had to be ready to take advantage of them when they did. He took a deep, measured breath and tried to think clearly.

Then the soldier in front of him aimed a blow at his face, bringing Reis sharply back to the present. He ducked, his mouth grim. Evidently these men didn't believe in a peaceful capture. Not that he could blame them. He had, after all, shot two of them already. A couple of the others threw some punches, but he didn't think they'd do much damage. Sloan had ordered that the prisoners arrive unharmed, and they weren't putting up a fight. Katherine was cooperating, of course, and Paul was obviously no threat. He was already trussed and laying on the ground, having taken a punch to the face and crumbled.

"Tie them up and throw them in the cart," one of the older men snapped. Reis watched carefully, filing information away in case of need. This man was the leader, then. Noted.

"What about their belongings?" another soldier asked.

The first man walked toward the duffel bag on the ground and kicked it. The soldiers had taken some of the clothing out of this bag and thrown it around the forest, but hadn't found anything of interest, and had decided not to go through the other bags. The only weapon they'd recovered was the assault rifle Reis had used in his escape attempt.

The man who had spoken lifted the rifle up now, looking closely at the safety and trigger mechanism. "Like nothing I've ever seen, though it seems to work like Dresden's weapons," he muttered quietly. Suddenly he looked up, shoving the weapon toward Reis. "How exactly does it work, stranger?" he demanded.

Reis' battered mouth stretched into a grin. "Untie me and I'll show you," he offered, lifting one eyebrow. If he could just get one more shot, now that he knew their weaknesses…

The other man lifted both eyebrows in response, his expression cold. "I think not." He slung the rifle's strap over his shoulder and turned abruptly toward his men. "Throw them and the rest of their things in the cart. Our orders are to take the prisoners to Nottingham, and that includes their baggage."

The soldier behind Reis tied a rope at his wrists, then lifted him to his feet and shoved him into the waiting cart. He fell face-first into a bag of grain and turned his face to the side, gasping. Katherine and Paul appeared next to him, tossed into the vehicle willy nilly.

"Well this is really terrific," Paul muttered darkly. The side of his face was bruised and swollen, forcing him to speak out of the corner of his mouth. "Jason and Tatiana on their way to who knows where, and we're back in a wagon, destined for another charming ride through the country to see the man we're supposed to be stopping. Only this time we're trussed up like chickens."

"I don't know, Paul, it might not be as bad as you think," Reis murmured, smiling. The soldiers had tossed the rest of their baggage into the wagon and slammed the gate shut, leaving Paul's backpack closest to Reis' face. The bag, Reis knew, was stuffed full of Paul's clothing, extra socks, and robe, along with the other pair of shoes he'd insisted on bringing.

And, of course, Reis' own 9mm Browning semiautomatic, all his daggers, and the compass, which he'd stuffed in there the previous night.

Looking up, he saw that fate was truly on his side today. The leader of the pack had evidently decided to drive the cart himself, and sat just in front of Reis. As they lurched into action, the assault rifle – loosely slung across the man's back – began swinging on its belt, mere inches from Reis' nose.

A plan began to form in his mind, unbidden, and he smiled again. This might not take as much effort as he'd thought it would. Which was lucky, considering they were on a rather tight deadline. They didn't have time to go gallivanting across the countryside. And he didn't particularly want to meet this Dresden character as his prisoner. The man seemed prone to threats, torture, and other unsavory activities. None of which Reis wanted to experience.

If this was going to work, though, they needed to move. Now.

He turned back toward the teenagers at his side, glancing from Katherine to Paul. The boy had taken the brunt of the beating, and looked miserable. Katherine, on the other hand, met his eyes with a clear, knowing gaze. After a moment she looked away, blushing. *More to that one than we realize*, Reis thought suddenly. She knew exactly what was going on. Putting that thought away for future use, he raised his voice over the cart's rattle.

"Are you two okay?" he asked.

Katherine nodded wordlessly, her eyes wide.

"Terrific," Paul snorted. "As I've already said." He paused for a moment, then spoke again, his voice cracking with tension. "What do you think they'll do to Jason and Tatiana?"

The man driving the wagon turned to glare at them, and Reis grimaced.

This wouldn't work if that guy was going to watch them that closely.

"Right now we have to worry about ourselves, and we don't have a lot of time to do it," he whispered hoarsely. "Once we get out of this, we can think about Jason and Tatiana."

"Do you think we *can* get out of this?" Paul asked nervously.

Reis ignored the question as an unproductive one, and turned on his side instead. "Never mind that right now. Do you think you can move over enough to reach my belt buckle?" He had to speak more loudly than he liked, but hoped that the creaks and groans of the cart's wheels and multiple sets of horse shoes would drown out his words. The last thing they needed was to be caught in the midst of another escape attempt now. If the soldiers had to come after them again, Reis knew, the order to keep them alive might be 'forgotten.'

Paul looked at where he was in relationship to Reis's belt buckle. "I think so, why?"

"Take your time – I don't want these guys to notice that you're moving. If you can reach my belt buckle, you should be able to slide the buckle itself up and out."

Paul squirmed to his left and scooted clumsily toward Reis. When he reached the older man, he waited for the next bump in the road, flopping dramatically over on his side when they hit it as though he'd been thrown by the wagon. Reis smiled, and looked down to see Paul's fingers working quickly at the belt buckle, fumbling with the latch. He glanced at the soldier riding by the cart, noting the man's dazed, uninterested face, and took a deep breath. The more uninterested these men were, the better. If they thought that the prisoners were well and truly defeated, they'd never see him coming.

"Okay, I think I got it," Paul muttered, turning his head so Reis could hear him.

Reis grunted. "Be careful. When you slide the buckle out, you'll be holding the hilt of a 3-inch double-edged knife."

Paul grunted back, suddenly serious. "Cool. Okay, I think I've got it out. Yeah, I can feel the blade. Now what?"

"First, don't cut yourself. Second, I'm going to roll over so my back's to you. You're going to feel around for the rope. Once you find it, start cutting. Avoid cutting my hands if you can."

It took nearly five minutes to cut through Reis' ropes. By the end, Reis had two rather deep lacerations, and two very free hands.

"Great, now what?" Paul asked.

Reis shifted his position so that he was lying diagonally across the front of the cart, with his head near Katherine's. "Katherine, can you see where we're going?" he asked.

She picked her head up and glanced toward the road in front of them. "Yes, I can see."

"Keep your eyes to the front, and let me know if you see anything useful," he said, his glance darting to the right and left of the cart. Trees, trees, and more trees. They were still in the forest, then. That worked.

"What do you mean?" Katherine asked, drawing his attention back to the cart.

"If you see people coming from the opposite direction, or if there's a hill or water. Anything that's different, let me know."

"A bridge?" Katherine asked quickly, lifting herself up for another look.

"Yes, a bridge would be perfect," Reis answered, smiling.

"I see a bridge. We should cross it soon."

Reis nodded, thinking. That was exactly what he needed. "How big is it? Is it made out of wood or stone?"

She looked again, frowning in concentration. "It's rather large. I cannot tell what it's made of, though."

"Paul, can you see anything on the other side?" Reis asked. He moved farther toward the front of the cart to make room for the boy.

"Yeah, give me a minute," Paul said, rolling to the side and throwing his body awkwardly against the wall of the cart. "Yeah, I see the bridge. She's right, it's pretty big. Maybe 30 to 40 feet long, hard to tell from here though."

"Is it made of wood?"

"Looks like it, why?"

"You're sure? No Roman arches that you can see?" Reis asked.

"What the hell are those?"

"Sorry ... big stone archways. Supports underneath the bridge."

Paul shook his head. "Nope, nothing like that. Looks like a rickety wooden bridge."

"How far away?" Reis asked. He scooted toward the knife Paul had dropped and scooped it up, raising his legs in front of him and slicing through the rope with one smooth motion.

"Maybe half a football field. Why?" Paul turned back toward Reis, frowning.

"Terrific, grab that sleeping bag with your feet and slide it over here."

Paul struggled with the bag, passing it upward toward the body guard. "What exactly are we doing?" he asked suspiciously.

Reis shook his head. "Trust me Paul, you don't want to know."

27

Riding a horse the day before had been challenging, and today I was sore in places I hadn't even known existed. Riding again at a gallop, and tied to both the saddle and the girl in front of me, was far worse.

Sloan had thrown a rope through our horse's bit and tied the other end to his own saddle, so we had little to no chance of escape. We galloped for hours, passing what felt like hundreds of small towns, carts, horses, and people. Tatiana and I tried repeatedly to speak to Sloan, to find out where we were going or what awaited us there, but to no avail. He'd evidently snapped out of the curiosity he'd felt at our camp.

I tried desperately to rein in the sense of dread growing in my stomach. Dresden's son had found and captured us, and was now taking us to an unknown destination. Most likely to see his father. Doc was out there, alone and unaware of the plot to kidnap and assassinate him. We had less than two days to find him before it all came crashing down. And that was just the plot against Doc. Never mind the plot against the world.

I needed to come up with a plan, but I was finding it difficult to think around my thirst and fear.

Suddenly we crested a hill and left the thick forest through which we'd been galloping. Sloan pulled the horses to a stop and looked out over the view.

"It's beautiful," Tatiana said quietly. I followed her gaze to the valley that lay before us, and gasped.

To one side, far below us, marshland came to an abrupt halt, the watery soil butting up against flat, lush farmland. A river sliced its way out of the marsh, ripping a ragged trail through the open terrain and traveling through the valley to disappear into another heavily wooded forest. Farmers had divided the land on each side of the river into dozens of neat plots, which sported hundreds of even rows. It looked like something out of a book.

The city, which stood at the opposite end of the valley, was built on a large bluff, giving its inhabitants a clear view of the countryside and negating the chance of a surprise attack. A cathedral with two large stone towers dominated the city's skyline. If anyone had any questions about how powerful the church was, the beautifully designed and constructed structure left little doubt. To the side of the cathedral, four smaller towers marked the location of a large castle and what I took to be the prominent homes of the city.

Sloan turned to us now, wearing an unpleasant smile. "You ask where we are going, Jason Evans of Lebanon, New Hampshire." He pointed to the castle, his face grim. "That is our destination. The castle of Nottingham, where I shall hand you over to my father, and your fate." His face changed, then, a shadow flitting across his features, and I wondered what that was. If I'd had to guess, I would say that he actually feared his father, or hated him. Possibly both.

He gave me no chance to ask. Seconds later we were off again, racing down the steep slope toward the farmlands. I clutched at Tatiana, who rode in front of me, trying to maintain my balance as trees, boulders, and then the river flew by.

Within an hour we had cut through the valley floor to reach the city. Hundreds of ramshackle homes crowded together around the perimeter of the city's high walls, their own walls tilting dangerously over the street. We careened through the streets between them, the horses' shoes sparking against the cobblestones in their mad dash.

Before long we came to the point where the river crossed the city's boundaries. Here the stench of raw sewage became overpowering, though it wasn't enough to keep the people out of the water. Three children played on the riverbank, their hands and faces covered with mud.

"Oh my God," Tatiana murmured.

I nodded, speechless. The level of poverty here, the lack of sanitation, the fact that those kids would probably die within the next week of some nameless infection...

A sudden ruckus from the bridge ahead arrested my attention, and I turned from the children. Sloan seemed to be taking offense at something the toll keeper had asked him, and was now shouting at the poor man. Seconds later, he drew his sword from the scabbard at his side, aimed, and thrust it through the man's throat. The toll keeper fell, choking, and then grew still.

Before anyone could comment, we were moving again, pounding over the bridge and through the rich part of town. *Straight toward Dresden*, the voice in my head whispered. Here, what felt like hundreds of men and women packed the streets and surrounding alleyways, slowing us down. *Marketplace*, that same dazed voice supplied. The people were buying and selling pies, loaves of bread, vegetables, rugs, knives, animal pelts, wine, grain ... the selection of goods varied as much as the people. Some sold their wares from small wooden carts, others from open wagons, tabletops, and large cloth bags. Merchants stood outside their doors, beckoning people into their shops, while children of all ages held their hands out in search of money, food, or both. It was a madhouse of activity, nearly impossible to take in. My eyes flew from one person to the next, overwhelmed by the blurs of color, noise, and activity.

After ten minutes of weaving in and out of human traffic, we arrived at a large green gate. On the other side stood the castle. Suddenly it all became real. Dresden was on the other side of that gate, waiting to do God-knew-what to us. I was, after all, the grandson of the man he called his enemy. Knowing what I knew of him, I didn't think my tender age or out-of-time status was going to do much to save me. I gulped heavily, wishing we were anywhere but here. Wishing Reis was with us. Wishing I had more than a jackknife, an old pocket watch, and flashlight in my pocket.

Three soldiers jumped to open the gate for us, and we trotted into a large courtyard. The low-lying sun reflected brightly off a massive stained glass window, which took up nearly a third of the wall in front of us. I squinted against the glare, turning to look around. The other walls sported ornate carvings in stone and heavy timber, with deep eves over the roof, windows, and doors. The whole place felt creepy and gothic.

To our right, a stone well sat next to a large wooden platform. On the other side, a massive carriage sat in front of the castle's stable. It was unlike anything I'd ever seen before, with eight large wheels reinforced by heavy iron bands to support the undercarriage of the vehicle. The axels, which held the massive weight of the carriage, looked like they were built from whole oak trees, coated in black paint and lined with heavy grease. It was easily twice the length of any of the wagons or carts we'd seen since our arrival.

Two guesses who that belongs to, I thought. That must mean that Dresden was already here. Possibly even expecting us. The thought made the lump in my stomach several sizes larger.

"Get down!" Sloan snapped, turning abruptly toward us. I saw now that he was casually wiping the blood from his sword, his face a mask of cold disgust. My stomach turned over again and my eyes darted away, unwilling to deal with the situation.

Tatiana and I slid to the ground at his urging, looking around warily, and I reached for the jack knife in my pocket. I could see Tatiana flexing her hands and knees, readying herself to do battle. We were deep in the enemy's territory, now, and deprived of most of our weapons. We hadn't discussed it but we'd both had the same thought – we needed to be ready for anything.

It was then that I felt the stone. The feeling was faint at first, a tickle in the back of my throat, the dull feeling of déjà vu. As if I had both seen and lived this exact same experience before. Then it grew stronger and expanded. A wave of calm peace washed over me, bringing with it a strength I hadn't felt moments before.

The pain in my legs and lower back disappeared, and a newfound energy coursed through my body. Suddenly I felt rejuvenated. The world, which had felt so foreign a moment ago, now felt familiar, comfortable. I knew what lay on the other side of the stable, and how to enter the royal chamber through the secret passage I wasn't supposed to know about. There was a maze of tunnels under our feet, which led into the walls, and the dungeon below them. And out of the castle. I also knew the alleys and side streets of the city. If asked, I could have led Sloan to his father, for I knew exactly where he was within the castle. I smiled at the thought, feeling as if an old and dear friend had come to visit me.

"Are you alright?" Tatiana asked.

I looked over at her and nodded at her question. I could feel everything about her as well, including her absolute fear of meeting her father unprepared. I reached for her hand, squeezing it when I found it.

"We're going to be fine," I said quietly. "Trust me."

She glanced at me, her eyes wide and her mouth grim, and gave me a single, curt nod.

Together, we strode toward the entrance and Lord Dresden.

"How close are we?" Reis asked anxiously. He looked up toward the driver's back and readied the knife, measuring the distance between himself and the man.

"In about twenty seconds we'll hit the lip of the bridge," Paul replied. A moment later, they felt the cart begin to slow down, the horse bracing itself against the downward slope leading toward the bridge. That meant it was time.

Reis adjusted his body slightly, trying to make sure that everything was out of the way.

"What are you going to do?" Paul whispered nervously, watching Reis' movements.

Reis shook his head slowly, keeping his eyes trained on the driver's back as the soldier navigated the horse down toward the bridge. He stole a quick glance at the soldiers who trailed behind; he'd counted, and knew that only three of the soldiers were in front of them. The rest conveniently followed behind. He had direct shots at all of them. Once he started shooting, though, he'd have to hit his targets cleanly. He'd have one shot at each. If he was lucky.

"I want the two of you to keep your heads down," he snapped, pinning Katherine and then Paul with his eyes. "No matter what happens or what you hear, keep your heads down. Do you understand?"

"Oh God, I knew it," Paul groaned. "You're going to do something dangerous."

"Something brave is more like it," Katherine cut in, looking calmly at Reis.

"Or something really stupid," Reis replied. He kept his head down and eyes on the man in front of them, waiting impatiently. Any minute now…

Finally he heard the change in the sound of the horse's hoofs. That was the sound he'd been waiting for. It meant that they'd reached the wooden bridge.

He sprang from the bed of the cart, pushing off with both legs to strike the driver from behind. His right arm went quickly around the man's neck, holding him for the split second it took for the knife to slip between the two vertebrae in his neck. A moment later, the man hit the bed of the wagon, dead.

The soldiers behind them shouted in alarm and surged forward, intent on over running the cart and re-capturing the prisoner. Reis bent and ripped the assault rifle from the dead man's body, bringing it up just in time to sight on the first soldier, who was nearly even with the cart. One shot sent the soldier flying from his horse, wounded.

Reis dropped to his knee, bracing his shoulders against the bench behind him, and focused on the next man. He took a quick, measured breath and squeezed off two more rounds. Each shot hit its target squarely in the chest, taking two more soldiers down.

Terrified by the sound of the gunfire, the horse hooked to the cart spooked, taking the cart with her. Reis lost his balance and crashed to the floor, losing sight of the other soldiers. Within moments he was back up, bracing his hip against the side of the bouncing cart and trying desperately to steady the rifle's site. He only had one chance to make this happen. His aim had to be true or it wouldn't work, and failure wasn't an option. Their lives were counting on this. He yanked the undercarriage of the weapon forward and drew the metallic pin back, arming the weapon's grenade launcher.

He only had one grenade – the weapon didn't support spares – so he had to make this count, or they would be toast, falling victims to the grenade themselves. He took a breath, lifted his arms, aimed his weapon at the center of the bridge … and pulled the trigger.

The rocket-propelled grenade found its mark just as the cart bounced off the bridge and onto solid ground. A thunderous explosion ripped through the valley as the bridge exploded, and debris flew across the landscape, blanketing the air in a cloud of dust and rubble.

"Awesome!" Paul shouted, popping up out of the cart to stare at the carnage behind them. Reis pushed him back down.

"Stay down!" he barked, turning his attention away from the bridge and toward the road in front of them. There had been three soldiers in front of the cart before he started, and he wasn't sure where they'd gone. If they had any brains, they were running like hell from the explosion, though he wasn't keen on the idea of them escaping either.

He frowned, then stripped the cartridge from the rifle and reloaded. If he found them, he'd be ready. In the meantime…

He turned toward Paul and Katherine, running his eyes over the two teenagers. "You two okay? Yes? Terrific. Sit down, stay down, and collect yourselves. It's going to be a bumpy ride from here on out. We're running out of time."

"Where are we going?" Paul asked, his voice hoarse from yelling. Katherine looked from Reis to Paul and back, her eyes wide and shocked.

Reis turned and sat heavily on the bench of the wagon, scanning the road in front of him. "Paul, find the map and compass. I don't know how to get to Jason, but I do know how to get to Doc. That's where we're going. Jason will … well, Jason and Tatiana, I'm sure, will head in the same direction. When they can."

Before Paul could answer, Reis brought the reins sharply down on the horse's rump, sending it quickly forward on the road to Bosworth.

28

We walked through several dank, badly lit hallways, flanked by Sloan and two of his soldiers, ducking around the water that dripped from the ceiling. A tense, heavy silence surrounded us, the soldiers to our right and left wearing identical expression of cold fear. I gulped, wondering again about the man we were going to meet. Finally we arrived at a narrow set of stairs, which ran almost vertically downward. At the bottom of the stairs we found a tall set of double doors guarded by three soldiers, all dressed in polished mail under red and white vests.

Sloan came to a firm stand in front of the doors and straightened his shoulders. "Please inform my father that I am here, and that I have brought the strangers he asked for."

One of the guards nodded silently, then slipped through the door behind him. Tatiana and I glanced at each other, and then back toward the door. The soldier was already back, motioning for us to enter.

I took a deep breath. This was it, then. We were about to meet the man who was trying to destroy the world. Change history and the future. Kill my grandfather. At that last thought, my body seemed to remember why we were here. Suddenly my skin was flushed, my breath quick, and my blood boiling in my veins. This man was putting us all in danger, and I found – much to my surprise – that I was angry with him.

I threw my chin up and marched into the room, silently hoping that Tatiana would follow my example.

At first glance, the room was somewhat less than I expected.

It was sparse and colorless, with the shutters closed against the daylight outside. The area was only dimly lit by the candles on the walls, and broken up into two noticeable spaces. One, where we stood, contained a desk and an ornately carved chair, along with a table and four smaller chairs. On the other side of the room, a bed as big as two king-sized beds back home sat against the wall. A massive fireplace occupied at least half of the far wall, and four dirty rugs the color of wet concrete lay scattered on the stone floor at the foot of the bed.

Suddenly a man stepped from the shadows beside the fireplace and walked toward us. He was shorter than I'd expected, but then the only time I'd seen him he'd been on a horse. He was easily recognizable, though, with his white-blonde hair and sharp goatee. I saw now that he plucked his eyebrows to sculpt them at an angle. It made his face harsher, more … sinister.

With those dead eyes, I wondered if Nicholas Fleming – Lord Dresden – actually needed any further demonstration of his personality.

He strolled casually toward the table that sat next to the desk, where he poured himself a glass of what appeared to be red wine. He took a sip, then turned toward us and raised his eyebrows, like he'd just noticed that we were there.

I stifled a snort.

The man lifted one eyebrow in my direction, like he'd heard it anyway, then turned toward Tatiana. He frowned and took several steps forward, coming to a stop an arm's length from her. My eyes flew to Tatiana's face, taking in the tightly clenched jaw and pale line of perspiration along her brow. She was both terrified and viciously angry, and I thought for a moment that she meant to strike the man.

Her eyes narrowed, though, and her mouth grew firm with dislike. "Monster," she breathed, the rage clear in her voice.

Dresden's hand flew out, quick as a snake, striking her in the face and sending her sprawling. I moved to help her, but stopped when she put out a hand.

"I'm fine," she muttered. "It's no more than I expected from the man who beat my mother senseless every night." She rolled quickly away from him, avoiding the kick he aimed at her head, and glared at him from behind me.

"And now you're trying to take over the world, and its history," she muttered quietly. "So cliché. So predictable, *Father*."

Behind us, Sloan gasped in shock, and Dresden looked at his son for the first time.

"So she's been telling the truth," the boy muttered. "She *is* your daughter."

Dresden's face grew dangerously dark, and his violent temper transferred from Tatiana to his son. He strode toward the boy and struck him as well, sending him to the ground next to his half sister.

"I told you not to question them, boy," he snarled.

"He didn't," I replied quickly. "I told him everything … without being asked." I tilted my chin up, daring the man to hit me as well. At least I'd taken his attention off Sloan. The kid hadn't exactly been friendly on the trip over, but I'd seen something in him in that clearing. Something light rather than dark. I wasn't going to stand by while his father beat it out of him.

I rethought that plan almost immediately, as Dresden turned and began to approach me. His eyes were cold and calculating, with no warmth or humanity in them. He looked as though his face had been poured of concrete. I saw his hands flexing at his sides and steadied myself for the blow I was sure was coming.

Instead of striking me, though, he laughed. "I don't believe it. Of all the people to stroll into my little world. I'd known that there were people from the future here, but I never expected this. Richard Evans' grandson. I'd know you anywhere. The eyes, the nose … the pure arrogance. What a wonderful – and convenient – surprise." He took a step back, placing his right hand under his chin and studying us as if we were collectable items behind a merchant's window. After a moment, a twisted smile formed beneath his angular features.

"The dear doctor doesn't know you're here, does he?" he asked quietly.

My stomach dropped into my feet. He was right. I'd just fallen into Dresden's lap, and my grandfather didn't even know I was in this time period. Very little to hope for in terms of rescue, there, even if Doc was going to be around for more than one more day. What on earth had I done?

Dresden nearly giggled. "Oh this is too good to be true. For years I've been trying to capture the old man for the information he kept from me, but you … you've just made it so much easier. And so much sweeter." He began to laugh. Slowly, at first but then more loudly, as if he'd lost control of his emotions. Or his sanity. His laugh echoed through the stone chamber, off the ceiling and down the hallway. It was a sick, revolting laugh, lacking all humanity. Lacking any type of joy. The hair stood up on the back of my neck and I glanced wordlessly at Tatiana. She stared back, her eyes wide. The man was absolutely mad.

Suddenly the laughter stopped. Dresden strode slowly back toward the desk, coming to a stop in front of it.

"You came back to help your grandfather, but instead, your actions will lead to his ultimate demise," he said, his tone cold and hollow now. He turned around, his eyes burning with malicious fire. "And what's more … you didn't just happen to arrive here. And Evans certainly wouldn't have brought you." He paused, and began walking slowly back toward me. My stomach clenched in anticipation.

"I believe," he breathed, his face now inches from mine, "that you must have followed him. And that means … that means you can read the stones on your own." His voice faded away, as though he was fascinated – or disgusted – by this revelation.

His eyes snapped up to my own, clear and malevolent, and his hands reached out and wrapped around my throat, closing slowly to block off my air. I gasped, surprised, and felt my throat closing up, the oxygen coming in shorter and shorter bursts. I struggled against his grip, but he was far stronger than I, and didn't budge.

"You can read the stones, can't you, boy? Tell me and I shall spare your life," he growled, his eyes burning.

I choked in response, unable to breathe or answer.

"Stop it!" Tatiana screamed. "You're killing him! Yes he can read them!"

Suddenly Dresden flung me to the side. I hit the floor and slid into the wall with a sharp grunt, then lay still. Tatiana cried out and I looked up, dazed, to see that Dresden was walking slowly toward his desk again.

"Of course I can't *kill* you," he murmured. "Just like I couldn't kill your grandfather in the past. He had, you see, the knowledge I required. Just as you do. Now, of course…" he turned back toward me and smiled again, and my blood turned to ice. I'd known him for about five minutes and I already knew that his smile meant trouble.

"Now," he continued, "you've released me from those particular chains. Now … I have you as my prisoner. My own private time traveling device. Which means…" he smiled grimly, amused at his own joke. "That I may finally kill Richard Evans."

He turned abruptly toward the door and shouted for his guards. When they appeared, he barked orders about assassins and killing my grandfather rather than kidnapping him. He stressed the need for urgency.

"But I don't know how it works," I gasped, trying desperately not to think about the increased danger I'd just put my grandfather in.

Dresden shook his head. "That, dear boy, is just part of the fun. You don't know exactly what you know, you see, until I force you to tell me."

A shock ripped through my body at his words. Things were going quickly from bad to worse.

"The medieval world is a waste of ignorance and filth, but they do one thing exceedingly well. They know how to inflict pain." He leaned toward me, leering, and I shrank back. "I will enjoy extracting information from you, I assure you. Of course, I can't kill you until you've told me what I need, and that may take weeks. In the end, though, you will tell me everything I wish to know, and beg me to kill you afterward."

I'd experience fear in my life, before that, but the sudden failure at our mission, the danger to Doc's life, and the gut-wrenching thought of torture was worse than anything I'd ever felt. Dresden was skipping from one thought to the next without pausing to fill in the blanks, and my head was starting to spin.

"Why?" I whispered, shocked. I collapsed, and Tatiana gathered me in protectively before turning to glare at her father.

Dresden watched us, smiling his cold, mad smile, and nodded once. "Why?" he asked. "You want to know *why*? Well, I suppose, out of everyone in this world, you're the ones who most deserve to know."

"Know what?" Tatiana snapped. "Enough of your games, Father. *What are you up to?*"

"Why, only the oldest and most cherished path of them all, dear daughter," Dresden said with another sick smile. He paused, apparently for effect, then finished grandly. "To rule the world."

Tatiana laughed out loud, causing Dresden's smile to falter. "You're absolutely mad. Alexander, Genghis Khan, Napoleon, Hitler, and now you... The list of fools who thought they could rule the world is practically endless. But you'll fail, just like they did." Her voice grew darker as she spoke, and I could feel the anger rolling off her body. I gathered it to me, pushing that anger into my own heart and forcing my mind to start moving again.

Dresden shook his head. "There's a big difference between those men and me."

We waited, speechless, for his reasoning.

"Those men were mortal. I am not," he concluded. He smiled at our confusion, and settled back onto the desk, ready to present his case.

"The stones are, after all, a fountain of youth. Surely you know that much? I've been here for seventeen years, and have yet to age a day. Why? Because I am living *outside* of time, of course. Just as I will live outside of time in every other historical period." He paused, waiting for our reactions, and nodded at what he saw on our faces.

"Yes, I planned it all out years ago, not long after I arrived here. Every time period, you see, has important elements. Large happenings that dictate the line of time. Things that have constructed our present twenty-first century. Change enough of those occurrences, though, and…" His fingers exploded outward in a 'poofing' gesture, and I gagged.

That was his plan? Travel to as many different time periods as he could, and change them to create a new future … present? One that he'd designed?

"You're *insane,*" I growled, shaking my head. "You'll destroy the world, unravel the thread of time itself. My grandfather was right. You're going to kill us all!"

"Only those who don't cooperate, boy," he snapped. "I will rewrite history, yes, using this gift I've been given. Make the world a better place. And when I'm done, when I return to what you think of as the present … the world will see me as its god, its true ruler, its savior, and will be ready to welcome me with open arms."

His words fell into a deep, empty silence, Tatiana and I both too shocked to speak. His plan was so ridiculous that I had trouble holding it in my head for more than five seconds at a time. It made absolutely no sense, and reeked of insanity and desperation.

Then again, I reminded myself, it was the plan of a madman. I'd known that before, but hearing the madness coming from his mouth was something entirely new. And no matter how crazy the plan was, it would still endanger the world, and the thread of time.

Dresden nodded at our silence. "The only piece I was missing, of course, was the knowledge of the stones. I have caught a glimpse of their power, but you … you will release all of their secrets. With you, I will truly manipulate time. Truly become immortal." The last words were a whisper, as though he was speaking to himself more than us.

A knock at the door interrupted him before he could continue.

"Enter!" he barked in response.

One of the heavy doors swung open and a large soldier entered, glowering around the room before coming to rest in front of Dresden. "You sent for me, my Lord."

Dresden turned to look at me for a split second before turning his attention toward the soldier. "Yes, Sir Lancaster. I have a mission for you. Send one of your fastest messengers to Lord Stanley's army. I believe you'll find him just north of Bosworth by now. Tell him the deal has changed. I no longer require the Earl of Oxford brought to me in chains." He turned once again to look right at me while he completed his order. "Tell him I wish the Earl to be killed instead. Immediately."

My heart sank. I had signed Doc's death warrant, just by being here. Dresden had already planned to capture Doc, but now…

The soldier saluted, then turned and left the room.

"Guards!" Dresden shouted after him. Three guards appeared at the door in short order, falling over each other to obey him.

"Take these two to the dungeons. Let the boy enjoy a few hours of peace before his interrogation begins."

He smiled nastily at me, then turned away as the guards pulled us from the chamber.

29

The soldiers behind us pushed Tatiana and me down yet another dark, narrow staircase, toward what I assumed to be the dungeon. This part of the castle obviously didn't see a lot of maintenance. The stone steps crumbled under our feet, the earthen walls following suit. In places, the walls had collapsed entirely, nearly blocking our path.

The guards shoved us roughly through, giving us no time to wonder at our surroundings. The comfort and confidence from the stone was a distant memory, now, as though I'd passed out of its reach. Fear, confusion, and claustrophobia had flooded in to replace the peace I'd felt, though I tried to keep a firm hold on my emotions. Now certainly wasn't the time to lose my head. Instead, I focused on the tunnel around us, looking for anything we could use as a weapon, or areas that might foster us if we had to hide. I stared intently into the walls as well, reaching with my mind for the stone I knew was there somewhere. I'd felt its presence as soon as we entered the castle's grounds, but hadn't felt it since entering Dresden's chamber. Had I imagined it all? I looked backward, wondering if I could locate it visually.

That was a mistake. An enormous man had appeared out of nowhere, wearing nothing but a pair of ratty pants and leather vest. He was massively overweight, and stood at least 7 feet tall. The worst part was his face, which was disfigured and terrifying. The face of a monster, with eyebrows so low that they nearly covered his beady, lifeless eyes. I was beginning to wonder if he was a zombie when he noticed me staring and bared his teeth in a gruesome smile. The teeth were blackened and broken, allowing a stream of saliva to trickle through. He lifted the large cudgel he carried and shook it at me, his grin widening.

Disgusted and unsettled, I turned away. If he was our jailor, we were going to need a terrific escape plan.

We continued down, the air becoming thicker with the smell of earth, mildew, and something far less pleasant, which I couldn't quite identify. The widely spaced torches in the walls began to sputter, making me wonder whether there was enough oxygen down here for people to survive at all.

Perhaps that was Dresden's plan, I thought suddenly. Keep us down here, in the dark, until we suffocated or went crazy. Or both. But no, I remembered, he'd already told me his plan. Torture. The thought grabbed a hold of me like a clinging monkey, clutching at my heart and refusing to let go, and I started to panic. We had to get out of here. I didn't want to think of the tortures Dresden had in mind, much less experience them personally.

Before I could explore this rather dark thought any further, we arrived at our destination. The soldier in front of us snarled for us to stop, and turned toward an iron grate in the wall. It was as tall as I was, and opened into another narrow corridor. There was only one other door there, set far back and to the side. The behemoth slumped toward this door and yanked it open, shoving first Tatiana and then me through the opening. The door slammed shut behind us.

"I'll be back for you two," the jailer muttered through the bars on the door, laughing harshly. "Don't go anywhere."

A moment later he left, taking most of the light with him.

Tatiana and I stood staring into the darkness ahead of us, our hands clenched tightly together. For a moment neither of us spoke.

I was about to ask Tatiana if she was okay when a voice called out from the darkness.

"You don't look very dangerous to me," it said calmly.

My eyes shot toward the sound, struggling to see through the dark. The owner of the voice was there, in the room with us. "Who's there?" I asked, trying to sound brave. "I'm not afraid of you."

"If you're not afraid, you're a better man than I will ever be," the voice answered in a soft, friendly tone.

I listened closely. I'd been here only a couple of days, but I'd studied history, and it didn't take a genius to hear the large difference in speech patterns between upper and lower-class citizens. The Bishop's speech had been far different from Katherine's, and Dresden's had been better still. But this man's voice was the most cultured I'd heard so far. Smooth, friendly, and extremely well spoken, like he'd been educated at Harvard rather than the local junior college. My mind began to race.

"Who are you?" I asked again slowly. "I can hear that you're well educated. Does that make you a lord? Royalty?"

The voice snorted in amusement. "I only wish I could identify your accent as quickly, stranger. Still, I have been here on my own for months. I'm not going to turn my nose up at company."

The voice moved, and a man came into the sliver of faint light. He was tall for this time period, at about my height, and shockingly thin. He looked to be in his mid- to late thirties, but then again, everyone looked older in this day and age. He could have been twenty-one for all I knew.

He was also filthy and obviously very hungry, but held himself with pride and confidence. I'd been right about his heritage, then, I thought.

"May I ask your names?" he asked, looking from me to Tatiana.

"Jason," I replied. "And this is –"

"Tatiana," she interrupted, casting me a quick look of warning. I nodded slightly – she was right to be nervous. We had no idea who this man was, or whether he was a friend. He might have been some part of a trap from Dresden. Regardless, we didn't have time to sit around talking.

"Jason and Tatiana … unusual names, but I like them. My name is Sir William. However, since the three of us are locked in this cesspool together, let us dispense with the formalities. You may call me Will or William. I promise I won't take offense."

"Why are you here? Did you kill someone?" I asked suspiciously.

The man barked with laughter. "Now I know you are strangers! No, killing someone would not have led me here, and certainly would not concern *Dresden*." At the name, his voice turned ugly and sneering. *Obviously no love lost there,* I thought. Then the man continued. "No, I am here because I had the misfortune of being born second."

"Excuse me?" I asked.

William paused, and I got the feeling he was sizing us up before he replied. "May I inquire as to why *you* two are here?" he asked suddenly, redirecting the question toward us.

I pressed my lips together, thinking, and Tatiana answered for me. Evidently she'd given up on the idea of caution, because she gave William a straight answer. "Jason's grandfather is the Earl of Oxford. Lord Dresden is holding us hostage." This wasn't necessarily true, but the reason for our detention was semantics at that point.

William coughed at that – a deep, racking cough, that shook his entire body. He took a moment to recover, breathing heavily, then apologized. "I have been here for some time, and this air is hardly good for breathing." He paused again, then continued. "The Earl of Oxford, eh? I have met the man once or twice. The last time I saw the sky, he was allying himself with the Tudor boy to fight against King Richard. I was not aware he had an heir."

I sucked the thick air in through my teeth, already frustrated with the slow, measured speech and this conversation, which was getting us nowhere. "Yeah, well, I'm his heir and we're here to help him fight Dresden. But first we need to get out of here. Doc – I mean the Earl – is in terrible danger, and if he dies Dresden wins, and then we're all in a lot of trouble. You're here, so I expect you like him even less than we do. Who are you, man, and how the heck do we get out of here?"

I began to move around the room, searching for weak spots in the wall and feeling for the stone. If I could just find it again…

William chuckled again as I searched. "You are right, I do know Dresden, though it has not been a … pleasant experience." He went on to tell us his story, between fits of heavy coughing. He was the second son of one of the oldest families in Great Britain – powerful and wealthy due to his name, but subject to his brother's orders due to his birth.

"I am my brother's second-in-command, since we are close, but it falls to me to do the less rewarding jobs," he told us. He'd been sent north to gather archers for the coming battle, and had been discovered and arrested by none other than Lord Dresden.

"So you see," he finished, "I am in the same position as the two of you. Held as a hostage until someone sees fit to pay for my ransom."

By the time he was finished talking, I had completed my circuit around the room. I hadn't found a stone out of place, or even a window or slit to shout through. If we were going to get out, it would have to be through the door.

Listening to William's story, though, I'd started to build a plan to do just that.

An hour later, food – if that's what you wanted to call it – arrived at the grate in our door. It was little more than gruel, and I had no intention of eating it, but it came with a guard and a torch, and that was what I needed right now.

In the last half hour I'd discovered who William was – Lord William *Stanley* – and explained to him what I knew about his brother. When he'd heard about the demands Dresden had placed upon his brother, and the fact that they would come at the price of Doc's life, he'd jumped at the opportunity to join us.

"We must get out and warn them!" he'd muttered, pacing aimlessly. "Warn them *both*, and stop Dresden before it's too late!"

"Welcome to my personal mission," I answered. "And you only know half of it. The question is, how do we get out?"

The appearance of the solider with the food had interrupted us then, and given me a chance to look around. When he first arrived, of course, I drew back, thinking that he was there to take Tatiana or me for the aforementioned torture. He slid the food through the grate, though, and turned to leave without a word, forgetting his torch in his rush.

I dove toward the door after he left and peered out the grate, anxiously studying the hallway outside our cell. There was nothing there to help us: cold, weeping walls, an uneven dirt floor, and the gate that led out to the main hall. As I pressed my forehead to the door, though, wondering how long we had, I felt warmth begin to trickle through my veins. Behind that came the tickle in my throat, and the glowing feeling behind my eyes. I smiled quietly. The stone had found me again. Thank God.

And it had information. We had one hour before the guard came back for me. When he did, his instructions were to make sure that I gave up whatever information I had. Regardless of the cost.

Turning, I strode quickly toward Tatiana, who was looking at the gruel on her plate as though it was a toad with three heads. I kicked it away, knelt down in front of her, and pulled out Doc's old watch to glance at the time. My heart twinged at the now-familiar feeling of the engraving on the back, but I pushed the emotion away.

"Tatiana, we have a small problem," I started. "I can't tell you how or why I know, because you'll never believe me, but we have an hour – one hour – before that guard comes back to take me away. I don't know if I'll be coming back from that trip. That means we have to move fast."

Tatiana nodded, her face calmly intense. "I believe you, Jason. I assume you have a plan."

I smiled, grateful for her confidence, and nodded. "As a matter of fact, I do. But it's going to be a bit … tricky."

She paused for a moment, thinking, then shot me a quick grin. "I'm game. What do you have in mind?"

"To start with, do you have a full charge on your iPhone?" She'd come equipped with something I'd never seen before – an iPhone charger that worked off solar power. I'd laughed at it before, as something only rich people could afford. Now I hoped she'd been using it, as my own phone had died the night before.

She gave me an odd look in answer. "Yeah, it's been charging whenever we've been in the sun. Why, do you need to make a phone call?"

I ignored her question and answered with one of my own. "Would you mind if I recorded you screaming?"

She nodded again, frowning. "Not a problem. Would you mind letting me in on what you're up to?"

I outlined my plan quickly, going through the main points and what I hoped would happen. "After that," I finished, "we run. And hope to God we can find the tunnels I know are down here somewhere."

Her face broke into a clear smile. "Brilliant," she answered. "I'm in."

Suddenly William appeared next to us, glancing from me to Tatiana. "As am I," he added. "I presume the two of you are planning our daring escape. What do I need to know?"

"Either I'm about to get us out of here, or I'm about to get us killed," I replied.

"At this point, either choice is acceptable. What can I do to help?" he asked, frowning.

I took a deep breath. "I'm going to do a little bit of magic, but I swear to you that it's only a trick, and I'm not a sorcerer or a wizard or anything like that."

William laughed. "You are an odd duck, my friend. But I do not believe in witchcraft, and you have my trust. Magic us away."

I nodded, went quickly through the plan in my head again, and then glanced at Doc's watch and did some mental calculations. Finally I looked at Tatiana.

"Okay, we have forty-five minutes. Get ready to scream for me. William, get ready to act terrified and run."

The jailer and soldier were sitting together on the crumbling staircase when they heard the girl scream. Seconds later, her scream was joined by another.

Both screams cut out as quickly as they'd started, leaving utter silence behind.

The men jumped to their feet and ran toward the back cell, swords and cudgel at the ready. What they saw when they arrived stopped them in their tracks.

"Look upon me, foolish mortals, and witness the depth of my power!" I shouted, my voice as deep as I could make it. I hit 'play' on the iPhone and held it up next to my face so that they could see the screen.

The men in front of me slid to a stop, their faces masks of fear and disbelief.

"Witness the woman who wronged me as she lies in the palm of my hand!" I opined loudly, turning the phone in the jailer's direction to reveal Tatiana's fifteen-second recording. It was nothing more than her screaming at the top of her lungs, but I knew it was more than these men had ever seen. I was counting on that to be enough. The jailer and the soldier who stood beside him watched, terrified, as Tatiana's image screamed in anguish and begged for her life.

Suddenly William broke in, playing his part with a ragged, frightened voice. "Listen to him and do as he says! I saw him place the girl in that box with my own eyes! He is the bastard son of Merlin, the devil himself! Do as he says if you value your life!" He emerged from the shadows with a look of horror and pressed his face against the iron bars, pleading to be let out.

His timing was perfect, and I pushed him roughly to the side. "Open this door, mortal, or I will shrink you down and place you inside my box for all eternity!" I commanded. I turned my flashlight on and projected the thin beam of light through the bars and onto the soldier's chest.

He didn't move, though he looked down at the light on his chest and started blubbering in fear.

"Do as I say, or join the girl in the depths of hell!" I screamed. "Open this door, lay your dagger on the ground, and release me!"

The man tore his eyes away from the beam of light on his chest and moved quickly toward the door, reaching out to unlock it. I tumbled out as the door swung open, and both men retreated, doing everything they could to avoid touching me. The flashlight drove them toward the back of the hall, giving William and Tatiana time to get out of the cell and through the door to the stairway. Once my friends were out of the cell, I gestured for both the soldier and jailer to take their place. They obeyed without question.

"You will stay here and allow me to leave," I muttered, shining the flashlight on one and then the other. "Do not follow me, and I shall allow you to live."

Both men nodded their assent, their eyes trained on the floor. I paused a moment, wondering if that was really all it was going to take, then turned, retrieved the soldier's dagger, slammed the cell door shut behind me, and darted out the main door, slamming that shut as well.

I found Tatiana and William waiting on the other side of the main door. Tatiana was beaming, and threw her arms around me, planting a kiss right on my cheek.

"That was terrific!" she blurted out, laughing.

William nodded, smiling like a maniac as well. "I do not know what you did, friend, but I am glad to count you as an ally."

I smiled crookedly, still off-balance from Tatiana's unexpected display of affection. This was new territory for me, and I wasn't sure how to respond, but I shook it off, trying to think ahead to the next step.

"What do we do now?" she asked, with that unsettling ability to guess my thoughts.

"We get out of this damn castle," I said quietly. "There's a maze of tunnels right under our feet. All we have to do…" I moved my hands over the wall in front of me, looking for the loose rock I knew I'd find there. When I found it I pushed, and the wall in front of us slid away to reveal a dark, enclosed tunnel.

Grinning, I turned back to Tatiana and William. Both wore equally shocked expressions. But neither hesitated when I ushered them into the tunnel. I grabbed a torch from the wall and followed them in, then turned to the left.

Within an hour, I knew, we'd be out of the castle and on our way to finding Doc. I just hoped we had time to get there.

30

WORCESTER, ENGLAND

The Earl of Oxford would have been content to sleep under the stars for several hours, with his pack and blanket, as it would have meant a quicker start in the morning. Perhaps before the sun rose. Henry Tudor and his entourage, however, had other ideas. They'd been marching for two days, and Henry had demanded a reprieve for both men and horses. It was a hard point to argue. If they were going to intercept Dresden at the right time and place, they needed to hurry. But they were two days away from the battle, and it would not do to bring an exhausted and unhappy army to the battlefield. Demoralized soldiers didn't win wars.

The Earl had compromised, and so found himself in his own tent, pacing anxiously at the unavoidable delay.

Suddenly the flaps around the entrance to his tent moved. The Earl jumped for his sword, but relaxed when he saw that it was only Trigva.

"My Lord," Trigva muttered, stepping into the tent. "A messenger, sent by Lord Bernard of Constantine."

Another man stepped into the tent, making his way cautiously into the uncomfortably warm confines of the enclosure. The Earl glanced at him, wondering why Bernard of Constantine was overworking his messengers. This one was thin, young, and beyond exhaustion, judging by his gaunt appearance and the deep lines beneath his eyes. He looked as if he'd been riding for days. Whatever the boy had been sent to say, it was important.

"Yes?" he asked quietly, trying not to intimidate the young man.

The messenger gulped and looked up. He nodded once, then settled back into the pose all messengers adopted while relaying their statements. "My Lord Bernard of Constantine wishes for me to relay a story many of his subjects reported witnessing in the village of Blythe yesterday afternoon, my Lord. He thought – that is, my Lord Bernard of Constantine thought – that the information may seem relevant to you. His own men do not know what to make of it."

The Earl nodded, encouraging the messenger to continue. What he heard shocked him. The man spoke of a strange man who had claimed to work for the church, but had looked nothing like clergy. The man had fought with a group of Danes who had been holding the town of Blythe for days. He'd defeated them, and quickly, using a weapon more devastating than the Devil's Flame.

"He pointed this stick at the Danes and they died immediately," the messenger said quietly. "It roared with the sound of cannon fire, and shook the walls of the houses."

The Earl sat back, trying to make sense of the story. Was this one of Dresden's men with a gun, this far afield? Shooting at Danes? With a new sort of weapon? "Did he travel alone? Wear anyone's colors or badges?" he asked intently.

The messenger shook his head. "Not that was reported to me, my Lord. But he did not travel alone. He had two young men with him, as well as two young women."

The Earl nodded, and the messenger took his leave.

"Does that mean anything to you, my Lord?" Trigva asked after the young man was out of earshot.

The Earl said nothing for a moment. Someone was traveling in this time period, and drawing attention to themselves with their recklessness. They had modernized weapons, or something like them. His mind raced to his grandson, unbidden, and the look in Jason's eyes the last time he'd seen him. Surely it couldn't be ... surely Jason wouldn't have traveled back, or put his friends in danger by bringing them along.

His instincts, though, told him that the boy may have done just that.

The Earl shook his head and sent Trigva from the tent. If his instincts were right, and these strangers were Jason and Reis, it was going to make the situation – and the coming battle – far more dangerous.

31

Dresden stared at the men in the cell, horrified.

When his soldier hadn't returned immediately with Jason, he'd suspected that something was amiss, and sent Sloan down into the tunnels under the castle to track them. He'd been reluctant to leave it to the boy, though, and had rushed after him, cloth pressed against his nose to protect himself from the stench of the underground maze and dungeon.

Now he breathed heavily through the thin cloth, trying to understand what exactly he was looking at.

"Thank God you've come for us, my Lord," the jailer said, pushing his hand suddenly through the iron bars. "We've been down here in the dark for hours."

Sloan brought the torch up to eye level and leaned hesitantly toward the cell. The enormous man – and the soldier they'd sent down earlier – pressed against the door, their faces filthy and desperate.

Dresden grabbed the torch from his son's hand and pushed the flame through the bars of the door, causing the jailer and soldier to jerk back in surprise.

"Where is the boy? Where is William Stanley?" he snapped, his eyes rushing around the confines of the cell. They weren't here, that much was obvious. His erstwhile daughter was gone as well, the devil take her.

He looked back to the soldier, his eyes spitting fire, and waited impatiently for an answer.

"Gone, your Grace, through magic and trickery," the soldier mumbled.

"Gone?" Dresden screeched, shoving the flame farther into the cell. What on earth are you talking about?"

"What did you see?" Sloan asked, his voice stiff with tension.

"He placed the girl in a box in his hand, your Grace, and cast a beam of light into the darkness, using only his palm," the jailer said, his voice trembling. "He threatened to trap –"

"You allowed William Stanley and the boy to escape, because of a few simple parlor tricks?" Dresden gasped.

Suddenly he roared in anger, turning sharply from the men in the cell and striding back out into the tunnel. This was inconceivable. Those two fools had allowed his most important prisoners to escape, and in doing so had endangered all of his plans. He had lived with the people of this time for long enough to know that their incompetence knew no limits. The next steps were glaringly clear. He was counting on Lord Stanley to join Richard in the coming battle, and capture and kill Richard Evans, all because Dresden himself held the younger Stanley hostage. Now that the younger Stanley had escaped, he would go straight to his brother. If he found him quickly, neither of these important things would happen. Even if they *did* go as planned, Richard Evans would be dead, and the boy – Dresden's only other hope at controlling the stones – would be … well, wherever he would be, it wouldn't be safely and securely in Dresden's prison.

Unless…

"Father, could it be true? Could he be a sorcerer?" Sloan asked, appearing suddenly at Dresden's elbow.

Dresden drew to a stop just outside the gate and stared at the wall in front of him, a slight smile turning up the corners of his mouth.

"How they did it is of little importance, boy. The fact is that it's done, and now we must undo it. Summon Lord Bryer's son and his men, and send them to me here. Then gather my personal guard and ready the large wagon. You and I ride for Bosworth today."

"But Father –"

"Now!" Dresden thundered. He watched the boy skitter away, then turned back to the wall in front of him, where a gaping hold stood, dark and grim. They had discovered the tunnels, then, and sought to escape that way. But they had neglected to close the door behind them, and would have made other mistakes as well.

Bryer was the best tracker he had in his service. Lord William, that boy, and his impetuous, sharp-tongued daughter would be captured and back in his dungeon by nightfall. And then they would pay for having escaped the first time.

Katherine hunkered down on the bench, willing her body to stay awake. They'd been driving for what felt like hours, and she was still reeling from the destruction of the bridge. And the soldiers, before that. And the escape on horseback, before that.

All in all, the last twenty-four hours had given her more action than she'd ever seen in her life. An adventure, indeed. Perhaps in the future she should be more careful what she wished for.

Now they were tearing along the road to Bosworth, seeking a man named Doc, and leaving Jason and the girl Tatiana to their fates. The thought did not sit well with Katherine, but Reis had assured her that Jason could fend for himself. She may have believed him if she hadn't seen the doubt behind his own eyes.

She turned at the thought, seeking him out. The man was still balanced on his knees in the back of the cart, scanning the countryside through the strange metal tube atop his weapon. She gulped, remembering what that weapon had done to the bridge, and looked toward Paul. He too scanned the land around them, watching for soldiers. Both had promised that they wouldn't be taken by surprise again. This, she believed.

The horse in front of her jerked to the left, and Katherine turned quickly around to focus on the road again. They were traveling at an unsafe pace, she knew, but her new friends were intent on arriving at their destination as quickly as possible. Neither had been willing to tell her exactly where they were going, or why.

"Damn," Reis muttered quietly, drawing Katherine's attention to the back of the wagon again. The man was looking through his tube at the road behind them, his shoulders tense.

"Soldiers?" Paul asked nervously, looking backward as well.

Reis shook his head. "Not sure, but I don't exactly want to stay on the road and find out." He turned toward the land in front of them and gestured to a group of trees. "See the trees, Katherine?" he asked quietly. "How quickly can you get us there?"

"Indeed," Katherine muttered. She tugged lightly on the left rein, urging the horse in that direction, and gave him his head. "Five minutes," she told Reis. "Maybe a bit more."

"Perfect," Reis answered. "That will give us some time to spare."

"What are we doing?" Paul asked, climbing onto the seat next to Katherine.

Reis moved to stand behind them, a hand on each of their shoulders. "Hiding as they pass," he murmured. "With luck, they won't notice us, and we can avoid another nasty fight."

Reis jumped off the cart first, snapping his orders as he checked the small clearing. "Katherine, stay close to the horse and make sure he doesn't get spooked. Paul…" He looked at Paul, who simply smiled back at him, and shook his head. "Just stay close to me and try not to talk."

Katherine climbed off the cart and led the horse deeper into the grove of trees, and Reis and Paul crouched down under some low-hanging branches, where they had a clear view of the road. Reis took a knee, aimed the scope of his rifle at the road, and studied the horizon.

"I see them," Paul noted quietly. "Do you think they saw us before we got off the road?"

Reis shook his head, wishing Paul would keep quiet for once. "No telling, but they don't appear to be rushing, so I'll take that as a good sign."

"Couldn't you just, you know, take care of them if they saw us?" the boy asked excitedly.

"No." Reis frowned, but kept his concentration on the men before them. They were soldiers, judging by their weapons, though they didn't wear any type of uniform. Not that it mattered, really. At this point, as far as he was concerned, soldiers were trouble in and of themselves.

He hoped they hadn't spotted his small group.

"Why not?"

The question broke Reis' focus, and he turned sharply. "Why not what?"

"Why not take them out?"

Reis groaned. "Three reasons. First, I don't believe in killing people unless they're trying to hurt me. Second, one of them could very well be your great grandfather ten times removed, or mine for that matter, and how would that work out for us?"

Paul nodded. "Okay, good points. And the third reason?"

Reis sighed. "Third, I don't have much ammunition left. A half a magazine for the rifle and two clips of fifteen rounds for the handgun. And then we're out."

"That's all you brought?" Paul asked, visibly shaken. "And then you're out?"

"Well the plan was to *avoid* the locals," Reis said sharply. "I didn't exactly plan on shooting up the joint."

Suddenly something caught his eye. Movement closer than he expected. He shoved Paul's face into the ground and flipped the safety on his rifle, searching desperately for the source.

The group of soldiers had sent outriders ahead of them – presumably to scout the area for other dangerous characters – and one of them had decided to beat through the small group of trees. He was just beyond the tree line now, 10 to 15 feet from where Paul and Reis lay hidden.

Reis watched him tensely, his finger on the trigger, and willed the man to move on. As the man turned to do just that, though, Reis felt the boy next to him begin to squirm. He looked down to see Paul holding a finger under his nose, trying desperately to stifle a sneeze. Reis moved to cover the boy's mouth, and knelt on a stray branch in the process. Several twigs cracked, ringing out through the trees, and both Paul and Reis froze. So did the soldier in front of them. He turned to stare at the juniper trees around them, looking intently into the underbrush. For several seconds, all three were still. The soldier moved his head to the side, studying the trees and listening to the wind. Finally, after what seemed to be a lifetime to Reis, he shook his head, turned, and walked back to his horse. A moment later, he was spurring the horse away from the woods.

Paul collapsed and rolled onto his back, breathing heavily. Reis switched the safety into place and tried to still his own heart.

"That was too close," he mumbled. The sooner they reached the battlefield, the better. He hated all this sneaking around.

Before he could get Paul up and moving, another twig snapped behind them and a voice rang out.

"That was very close. What do we do now?"

Reis swung around, his heart racing again, and gasped at the vision in front of him. Katherine had taken the opportunity to change into a pair of Tatiana's cargo pants, along with a loose-fitting beige sweater. Her dirty dress lay crumpled on the ground next to her.

"What?" she asked, noticing the stares. "Tatiana wears them, and if I'm going to be of any use to you in this running around and sneaking through forests, I cannot be hampered by skirts." She lifted an eyebrow – a skill she'd perfected in the last day – daring them to question her, and Reis shrugged. At the moment, Katherine's apparel was pretty low on his list of things to worry about.

She nodded at his silence, then asked again, "So what now?"

"Now," Reis answered, "we follow those soldiers to Bosworth and hope like hell that Jason and Tatiana managed to escape too."

"And if they didn't?" Paul asked.

Reis put the rifle back into the cart and looked down at Paul, smiling grimly. "If they didn't, we'll find Doc on our own, then go get them.

32

We scrambled along for at least a mile, zigzagging our way through a tight maze of dark tunnels, and moving as quickly as we could. The walkways were dank, tight, and still, and in some places they were no taller than my head. After the first ten minutes of walking, my shoulders were soaked with water from brushing against the walls. Rats rustled by our feet and loose rock crumbled down on our heads, making me wonder how long these tunnels had been there. And how much longer they would stand.

When the torch went out, I pulled the flashlight from my pocket and used it to light our way. William questioned it once, and then accepted it. We had already discussed the likelihood of someone coming after us, and not even William's curiosity about the flashlight could delay us. We needed to get out of there, and quickly. It was only a matter of time until someone from the castle came to drag us back.

"I hope you know where you're going, my young friend," William huffed as we rounded yet another turn. Before us, the tunnel stretched on, dark and foreboding.

I didn't answer him because I didn't need too. I knew exactly where I was going. Truth be told, if I concentrated hard enough, I thought I could probably get by without any light at all. I still hadn't figured out where the stone was, but it was close enough to speak to me, and it was providing a steady flow of information. The map in my head unfolded itself in my mind as I needed it, guiding me to the right tunnels, and around the jagged rocks and dangerous drops that littered the ground of the passage. I knew every corner and crevice as if I'd been playing in these tunnels my entire life. And for the first time since my initial encounter with the stones, I was accepting and even embracing this for what it was – a gift. I was also counting on it to lead us out of the tunnels before Dresden – or whoever he sent after us – arrived.

I'd barely completed the thought when a flash of light, followed by the sound of an explosion, boomed out of the passage behind us. I jumped, and checked with the stone. I was right, I learned; Dresden had found us more quickly than I'd anticipated.

"What in God's name was that?" William gasped, looking fearfully over his shoulder.

"Gunfire," I replied grimly. "Dresden's closer than we thought. We don't have much time."

I pushed forward, increasing our pace to nearly a sprint. If the stone was going to be warning me of any dangers, it meant that we could move faster than we had been. And right now, time was of the essence.

We wove through the narrow passages without rest, crawling when we couldn't stand straight, and scrambling over rocks and gullies as we came to them. Behind us, the men on our trail had started shouting threats and promises about what would happen to us when they caught us. Dresden hadn't come himself, but he'd told his soldiers what to say to cause the most damage, and they weren't being shy about their threats.

"There are at least ten of them back there," I huffed, squeezing desperately past a boulder that had fallen to block the tunnel. "They have guns and swords, but I think they're moving slower than we are."

When I got past the boulder I resumed my sprint, my breathing rough and unsteady. I'd been caught once, and I wasn't going to let it happen again, especially with Doc out there and in danger. I squeezed the handle of the dagger I had in my pocket, wondering if I could bring myself to fight if I had to. Anything would be better than being captured again.

"What are you talking about, they sound like they're right behind us!" Tatiana gasped, catching me at the turn.

William pounded along behind us, his wasted body struggling to keep up, and I threw my senses back into the tunnel behind us. I didn't think they were as close as Tatiana believed. They were noisy, though, and the sound bounced off these walls endlessly. I was having trouble getting an exact read on where our pursuers actually were.

"Are you sure you know where this leads?" she asked now, glancing ahead into the darkness. "Are you certain this will get us out of here?"

I turned my head so she could hear me clearly. "I've never been more sure of anything in my life, Tatiana. Now are you going to keep questioning me, or are we going to get the hell out of here?"

"Okay, okay, sorry," she replied.

"Don't be sorry. Just move faster."

Suddenly, the tunnel began to grow wider around us. Natural light came from ahead, indicating that we were nearing the surface.

"Thanks be to God," William sighed. He put his hands on my shoulders, squeezing gently. Then we pushed forward with one last burst of speed. Outside, we could find trees, bushes, caves. Places to hide. We would be safer.

We came to a stop before a small wooden door, which stood partially open, and approached cautiously, unsure of where we were or who was around. When I pulled the door open, though, nothing but a wave of bright light entered. We were free.

Mostly.

Tree roots and vines as thick as my arms covered the small opening. The tunnel ended in the side of a hill, and must have been all but invisible through the thick crop of juniper trees and scrub brush it hid behind. Unfortunately, that same brush had grown across the opening, leaving only hand-sized holes in the doorway.

I couldn't believe it. We'd come this far, escaped Dresden's castle and the threat of torture, were on our way to finding Doc, and now we had to fight roots and vines? We didn't have time to delay – Dresden's soldiers were right on our tracks, coming up behind us in the tunnel. They'd be here in a matter of minutes, and we needed to be gone by then. I pulled the dagger from my pocket and started hacking at the vines, desperate to get through. Tatiana helped, pulling at the vines as they loosened until we had a hole large enough to fit our bodies. We crawled through the thorn bushes, vines, and broken roots, stopping only when we found ourselves outside, standing on the edge of a dense wood. I looked back, trying to find the door we'd just passed through, and shook my head. I couldn't see the hill itself, much less the tunnel or door. I wondered vaguely how far we'd come, and where we were now.

"Now what?" Tatiana asked, breaking into my thoughts. "Those soldiers are going to be here in a moment."

"Right," I muttered. "Well we can't just stand around here, that's for sure. Tatiana, you and I are on our way to Bosworth, quick as we can get there. William –"

"Is coming with you," the man broke in, throwing me a look that dared me to argue. "If what you say is true, my brother is most likely already there. It's imperative that I find him and tell him everything. Our world may be counting on it."

"What about Paul and Reis?" Tatiana asked.

I noticed that she had left Katherine out, but ignored it. "We can't worry about them right now. If Reis is as good as I think he is, they've already escaped on their own. With luck, they're with Doc as we speak."

A shot echoed out of the tunnel then and I whirled toward William. "If you're coming with us, can you act as our guide?"

William nodded, already bouncing on the balls of his feet with the need to be gone. Another shot sounded from the tunnel behind us, the bullet tearing through the trees above my head, and I grabbed his arm.

"Then lead the way, Will, we're wasting time!"

We stayed as close to the road as we dared, cautious of travelers and soldiers alike. If we heard anyone on the road, we darted farther into the woods to avoid being caught. I hoped that Dresden's soldiers had lost us in the woods around the tunnel, but we couldn't be sure, and caution was a better plan than recklessness, though we needed to hurry. The longer we traveled, the more traffic we encountered. Families were moving away from the battle, while soldiers and mercenaries flowed toward it. For the first time, I began to understand what people meant when they said a battle was brewing. The air around us almost boiled with the tension of the coming fight, the noise of the soldiers filtering constantly through the trees around us.

We walked deep into the night, using my flashlight to show us the way, and pausing for rest only when we couldn't go on. The men on horseback may have been able to stop for the night, but we were on foot, and had a slightly tighter deadline than those men. We had to get to Doc, and quickly. I didn't know how much farther we had to travel, but I did know that we had to get to Bosworth soon. Dresden had sent orders to have Doc killed, and it was due to happen within the next day.

Around midnight, everything changed. We were walking down the middle of the road, too exhausted for caution, when the soldiers came thundering around the turn behind us, bearing torches, swords, and large, heavy bows.

My thoughts raced through the shocking turn of events, keeping pace with the horse under me as we thundered up the road to Bosworth. The soldiers – much to my surprise and relief – had been with William's cousin Phillip, son to the baron of Cheshire. Against all odds, they had been friends rather than enemies.

This surprising news was followed quickly by further glad tidings. Phillip was going to give us horses. And a guide by the name of Michael of Cabarus, to take William's place. Our erstwhile friend and guide was going to continue on with his cousin, in his own race to reach his brother before the battle.

After a brief rest, we now found ourselves mounted on war horses – again – and racing toward the fight we'd been hoping to avoid. Again. With men we didn't know, but had been assured we could trust. At this new pace, I thought, we might get to Doc within hours. And Michael had already told us that he knew the Earl of Oxford's position, and would have no trouble locating him.

We were going to make it. For the first time in what felt like years, I allowed myself the luxury of believing that we were almost to the end of our journey. And that we'd be successful.

Then it hit me. My legs turned to jelly and all the air rushed out of my lungs. I doubled over on the horse, gasping for breath, and tried to slow the animal. Before I could stop it completely, I was falling to the ground, darkness rushing in on me. A hazy gold glow appeared at the edges of the darkness, and a humming burned through my veins.

The *stones*, I thought. The humming…

Then all thought was lost to the vision.

Fog, deeper than I'd seen on my journey, lay thick above the forest floor, making its way lazily through the trees and low-lying brush. An old soldier, wearing a blue cape that only partially concealed a shimmering coat of mail, gently guided his large gray and white horse through the undergrowth. He was meandering, unhurried. Out for a casual stroll, then, his face lost in deep thought. Completely unaware of his surroundings.

I gasped as I recognized the tilt of the head, the Roman nose, and the stubborn chin. I knew this man. The old soldier was Doc.

Looking to the side, I saw three men, less than 30 feet away from the old soldier, creeping slowly toward him. Each of them was armed, one with a long bow, another with an axe, and the last with a sword. They crept on their bellies, rising up to stand behind trees when they came across them, and sending each other quiet hand signals. They were hunting, I realized; deliberately stalking their prey. And their target was my grandfather.

"Behind you!" I shouted suddenly, desperate to warn Doc. He didn't see them, didn't know they were there. He had no idea that there was a plot against him. No clue that there were assassins in the quiet trees around him.

It was happening, and I was too late to save him.

"Doc!" I shouted again, my voice as jagged as broken glass. But my words fell on deaf ears. After all, the thought came, I wasn't actually in the clearing with him. My body – and my voice – was somewhere far away. The stones had only brought my consciousness.

Doc brought his horse to a stop in a clearing now, and stared into the forest, his back turned to the men who would try to kill him. He had no clue – no warning that they were there.

And there was nothing I could do.

I tried to turn my head, close my eyes so that I wouldn't see what happened next. But the stones wouldn't allow it. When I closed my eyes, the scene appeared in my mind. When I turned my head, the scene swung with me to remain in my vision. There was no escaping it.

As I watched, the bowman stopped moving forward, took a knee, and strung an arrow, then stood slowly up beside the trunk of a young maple tree. He drew back his string, paused for an agonizingly long moment, and released the arrow with a sharp twang. It hit my grandfather and stuck. The impact ripped Doc's body off the horse's back and to the ground, where he rolled to the base of a tree to lay motionless in the tall, damp grass. I felt the vision mercilessly begin to recede then, but not before I glanced down at the pocket watch in my hand. I was surprised – I hadn't remembered bringing it with me into the vision. Now, though, I saw that it was 6:23PM, August 21. It wasn't going to happen on the morning of the 22nd, as I had hoped. It was going to happen tonight.

I had less than twelve hours to get to Doc and save him.

My eyes flew open to find Tatiana kneeling beside me, the early morning light glowing behind her. I closed my eyes again, trying to fit myself back into my body, then jumped to my feet.

"What happened?" Tatiana asked, confused. "Are you okay?" Michael was off his horse next to her, his face concerned.

I shook my head, dismissing that question. "That doesn't matter. We have to go. Now."

Tatiana frowned. "We *are* going, Jason. We were just leaving when you –"

I waved that off as well. "Okay, well we need to go faster. We have twelve hours to get to Doc's camp, or the jig is up." I turned to Michael, who had been assigned to guide us.

"How quickly can you get us to Bosworth?" I snapped. My voice sounded intense, even to me, and I swallowed the rest of the sentence.

He shrugged. "Perhaps by sundown, if we ride hard."

I was already striding toward my horse and motioning Tatiana to hers. "Then we ride as hard as we can. In twelve hours, Doc will be dead, and I'm not going to let that happen."

33

We traveled without rest for several hours, stopping only at noon for the sake of the horses. I was beyond exhausted and sore, though I'd become more comfortable on a horse than I'd ever thought possible. We'd gone days without truly sleeping, and I was beginning to see double, but we pressed on after a short rest. We had little to no time, and a long way to ride.

Luckily, we were able to stay on easy paths and roads, avoiding the forests and fields around us. Michael and his men had a clear idea of where we were heading, and assured me that we were taking the most direct route. We saw few people in the farms and villages we passed, and experienced no trouble with those we did see. This surprised me until Tatiana noted the obvious.

"Everyone knows a battle is brewing," she said grimly when I asked. "Anyone with a sword or pitchfork – and those without them – have been called to battle. This is the war for England, after all. Everyone's going to be fighting."

I nodded quietly. The war for England. The war for Doc's life. The war for the world's safety, though few of us knew that part. They were all wrapped up into one, now. Dresden's men had given up chasing us at this point; we'd watched them pass us earlier in the morning, hidden in a copse with handkerchiefs over our horse's noses to keep them quiet.

They, too, were on his way to the battle, to meet their lord. Dresden. The thought brought a renewed sense of dread.

This led quickly to another thought. Doc. Where was he? Why wasn't he being more careful? Had Reis, Paul, and Katherine found him yet? If not, where were they? Were they safe? Even if they'd found Doc, I didn't think they'd be able to stop what was about to happen. They didn't have enough information.

Hours ticked away as we rode, and I watched the time carefully on the watch I now wore around my neck. Before long, we were down to only six hours, then four, and finally two. We were running out of time, and no matter how much I begged and pleaded, Michael insisted that the horses could only travel so far and so fast.

Then we stopped completely.

"What's wrong now?" I sputtered as Tatiana and I pulled our horses alongside Michael's. I was beyond patience or manners.

Michael and his scout stopped talking and turned in unison at my interruption.

"There are people up ahead," Michael answered, his face creased in a frown.

"So what?" I demanded impatiently. We'd seen people on this trip, and it hadn't stopped us before.

Michael drew a deep breath and placed his right hand on the hilt of his sword. Then he closed his eyes and exhaled. "Boy, I have made a pledge to bring you to Bosworth, but if we encounter Dresden's soldiers or one of the hundred well-supported bands of thieves that roam these parts, you will be going nowhere but a shallow grave. We are not the only armed men in this area, and the closer we get to the battle, the more likely we are to meeting people better armed – and far more dangerous – than ourselves. Understand?"

"Jason," Tatiana said, pulling alongside me, "he's right. And we both know what would happen if Dresden caught us again. Just sit tight for a moment."

I nodded grudgingly. She was right, but it didn't make it any easier. Showing up a few minutes late on this occasion really would mean the difference between life and death.

"Did you see anyone else?" Michael asked the scout as the two men turned their attention away from me and back toward each other.

"No, no one else," the scout replied.

"Long bows?" Michael asked.

"Not that I could see."

"How confident are you that they are alone?"

The scout shrugged. "Fairly confident."

Michael shook his head, looking back at Tatiana and me. "Only fools would travel these roads so close to evening unarmed," he said slowly. Then he shook himself. "Very well, let's move. We do not have much time."

We spurred our horses forward, anxious to continue. Our path led out of a heavily wooded area, and into a large clearing lush with tall, rolling grass and a large lake. It took us about ten minutes of riding to see the cart the scout had spoken of. Despite the distance of nearly 200 feet, I knew immediately who it was.

"PAUL!" I screamed, standing in my stirrups and waving. I put my heels to my horse and asked for more speed, intent on reaching my friends.

"Oh you idiot," Tatiana mumbled behind me. After a moment, though, I heard her horse pounding after mine.

It took me about twelve seconds to reach their position. Paul and Katherine were ecstatic when I reached them, jumping up and down like children in the back of the cart. Reis was somewhat less enthusiastic, and had his assault rifle out, aimed at Michael and his men.

"It's okay, they're with me," I muttered at him. I slid off my horse before she came to a full stop and raced toward my friends, a wide grin plastered across my face.

"Where in the hell have you been?" Paul asked, jumping off the cart and giving me a giant man hug.

"It's a long story," I said, looking up at Katherine and Reis.

Tatiana came up beside us then and slid from her horse, laughing. Then she gasped. I glanced at her and followed her shocked gaze to look more closely at Katherine. I gasped as well.

"Are you wearing my clothes?" Tatiana asked.

Katherine looked down at her outfit and grinned. "Mine got dirty. I hope you don't mind," she replied, looking up.

Tatiana frowned at the other girl, and I held my breath. Then she shrugged, one corner of her mouth turning up. "I suppose I'll survive."

I laughed at that and turned awkwardly toward Reis. Despite my assurances, he still had his weapon trained on Michael, who had now pulled up alongside the wagon.

"It's a long story, Reis, but they're with me. You can trust them. They're leading us to Bosworth," I repeated.

"And we're running out of time!" Tatiana added. This got Reis' attention. He glanced at her, and then turned to me for the first time.

"What does that mean?" he snapped.

"It's Doc, he's about to be murdered," I said. I pulled the watch from my pocket and glanced at it. "In less than thirty minutes."

Reis nodded without question and gathered the reins. "Where?"

"Outside his camp! He'll be riding alone, and three men will come after him. We've got to save him, or this will all be for nothing. If Doc dies, I'm afraid the entire plan dies with him. Henry will never win this battle without Doc's help."

"Do you know the way?" Reis asked, looking from me to Michael and back again. The distrust of a few moments ago had disappeared, to be replaced with cold calculation and expectation.

Michael nodded. "We're close." He turned and looked at his men. "Two of you leave your mounts and take the cart. I'll meet you in Bosworth." Without a word of protest, two of his men climbed off their horses.

Michael looked over at Reis, who hadn't moved. "What are you waiting for? You three, grab the horses. My men will follow us in your cart. If we hurry, we can make it."

Reis swung suddenly into action, slinging the rifle over his shoulder and grabbing Paul's bag from the cart. He jumped out, followed quickly by Paul and Katherine. The girl walked toward one of the war horses and swung herself up, gesturing for Paul to ride behind her. He didn't hesitate either, climbing awkwardly up behind her and wrapping his arms around her waist.

I glanced at Reis to see that he too was mounted, and turned back to Michael.

Then we were off, galloping toward the camp in a cloud of dust. I ducked low over my horse's neck, praying for both speed and accuracy. Katherine and Paul's horse raced alongside my own, and I looked over at Paul. He had his arms wrapped tightly around Katherine's waist, but he was looking toward the road, shouting warnings about rocks and trees. Certainly not the same Paul I'd left behind. On the other side of them, Tatiana crouched over her horse, her hair flying behind her in a dark curtain. She felt my eyes on her and turned slightly, meeting my gaze. Her mouth quirked into a cocky grin and she winked at me – we were going to make it. We would save Doc.

I looked back to the road ahead of us and prayed that she was right.

After what I guessed to be fifteen minutes, Michael began to pull up. The road we had ridden appeared to widen here, and traffic was starting to increase. We were getting close.

"There!" Michael shouted, pointing up the road. About a mile away, we saw tents numbering well over a hundred dotting the horizon, along with countless flags and pendants in a rainbow of colors. At first glance, it looked like the circus had come to town, with people and horses crowding against each other in the free space. Then the weapons came into view. Hundreds of swords, bows, spears, and shields were stacked up in the camp. Several canons surrounded them, and more lined the road beside the tents. This wasn't the circus. These men had come to kill.

Michael slowed his horse even further and looked to the sky, indecisive. I followed his glance just as a loud crack of thunder crash over our heads. It hadn't begun to rain yet, but there was a storm coming. The sun had disappeared behind a formidable bank of clouds, turning late afternoon into evening. Mist was beginning to rise from the ground.

We had found Henry Tudor's camp, but we weren't out of the woods yet. I glanced at the watch in my hand again, and a deep feeling of dread came over me. We were going to be too late. A crack of thunder broke over our heads, and my horse jumped forward. I looked down at her, and then back toward the camp, more determined. This wasn't over yet, her actions told me. We still had five minutes, at least.

"What in the hell are you waiting for!?" I shouted, more to myself than anyone else. I sunk my teeth into my lower lip and kicked my horse in the ribs, forcing her back into action. I retreated inward, trying to pass my energy and tension down to the horse, and raced to where I knew Doc would be.

I'm not sure when my fear subsided and pure exhilaration took its place. Perhaps it was the sheer beauty of seeing so many campsites decorating the hillside. It could have been the caravan of supply wagons that stretched over and beyond the hill to the east, or it may have been the site of thousands upon thousands of soldiers and horses, riding freely and unencumbered between the campsites. To be truthful, though, I don't believe it was any of those things. I believe it was the feeling of having a high-powered war horse running full gate right underneath me, nearly flying over the ground, in an effort to save the man who held the fate of the world in his hands. Knowing that in some small way, I mattered. And feeling the stones there with me, pushing me onward as though they were on my side. For that moment, I believed without any doubt that we would make it.

To our left I saw several horsemen form up ranks and break hard in our direction. Shouts of warnings rang out from soldiers on horseback as they ran to intercept us.

"Follow me!" I screamed, breaking right toward the forest. This was where we would find Doc. And I knew exactly where to look. He was just over the ridge, and he was running out of time.

The Earl of Oxford nudged his mare to the left, asking her to move forward, around two maple trees, and into the shallow stream. He didn't hear the three men behind him, didn't see one of them raise his bow and notch his arrow.

The Earl's thoughts were not on himself, but the battle that was about to take place. His mind was playing out the upcoming battle, trying to decide how they should handle the danger Dresden and his men presented. He had pushed his own army hard to arrive here before Dresden had a chance to escape, and they would force Dresden and Richard into a battle now. Before they reached the iron works of London, and Dresden's store of firearms.

But would it be enough to win the day? Would his personal knowledge of the battle – and Dresden himself – outweigh Richard's larger force? He still wasn't certain, though he knew that his presence was the only thing that gave Henry a fighting chance. Without him –

His thoughts were interrupted by the sound of a twig snapping and he turned, frowning. He saw no one, though, and had taken pains to leave his guards behind at the camp. He was alone, now, with time to think and plan.

Turning, he urged his mare slowly toward the clearing ahead of them, his thoughts going back to the battle tomorrow and the idea that had occurred to him earlier in the day.

"Stop!" several people screamed in warning. I refused to listen. Our horses raced between foot soldiers and mounted men alike as we made our way through the outskirts of the campsite and toward the tree line just beyond the crest of the small hill.

I had a problem, though. My horse was starting to lose her power underneath me and I was starting to panic. I had pushed her to the limit, though I hoped she could keep going for just a little longer.

"Almost there, girl, almost there," I repeated over and over again, willing the animal forward. I steered her over a nearly empty stream bed and past several logs before pulling up on the reins, drawing her to an abrupt stop. There was the break in the trees that I'd been looking for. Doc had been here moments earlier.

"This way!" I shouted. My horse, thankful to continue at a slower pace, made her way carefully through the narrow opening in the trees. For nearly a minute we crawled around small bushes, rocks, and juniper, small oak, and maple trees, searching for Doc.

Suddenly my mind screamed for me to stop. I pulled abruptly back on the reins and looked to my left. There, inside a small clearing, I saw a lone figure riding tall atop his large horse. It was Doc.

My body flooded with relief. Alive. He was still alive. Then I looked behind him. The three men were there, hidden in the trees. The bowman already had his bow out, the arrow notched.

"Doc!" I screamed. This time he heard me. He turned his head, searching. The archer releases his arrow at the same moment. I watched as the arrow found its mark, striking Doc in the chest and throwing him out of the saddle and to the ground.

I screamed again, this time in anguish. I was too late to save him, but not too late to watch him die…

Part III

34

"No!" I screamed, leaping from my horse to race toward my grandfather. In the last three days, I'd found my world crumbling, been shot at, split the fourth dimension like an Oreo cookie, and landed in a castle five hundred years in the past. I'd rescued a fair maiden in distress, fought barbaric Danes and Medieval soldiers, and been abducted and threatened with torture. I'd been thrown in a dungeon, which I then escaped with my own brand of magic, run from a man trying to derail history, and raced recklessly through a land I didn't know.

All to get here in time. All to save the world and its history. And *this* was how fate repaid me? By killing Doc?

That was too much, even for me.

"No, no, NO!" I shouted, my fear and sorrow turning to anger. This couldn't be how it ended – it just didn't work. I reached deep and found the strength I was searching for, and doubled my pace.

The crack of Reis's rifle made me flinch, but I pressed on, able to think of nothing but my grandfather. As I ran toward his fallen body, I realized that Reis was running with me, casually covering my path with his rifle. Footsteps pounded along behind us as well – Tatiana, Katherine, and Paul.

None of us was willing to let Doc go, not after what we'd been through to find him.

I pulled up short and fell to my knees beside the only family I had left. Doc was lying on his side, the arrow standing straight up from his ribs. I didn't touch him, at least not at first. My mind was still reeling from what had happened, and the identity of the man who now lay before me. The face belonged to Doc, but the rest of his body was that of a stranger. He wore a shimmering layer of mail over his torso and arms, and trailing down his legs to his knees. A dark red cape lay crumpled underneath him, with a black and gold leather jerkin covering his body. His mail was held together by small iron hooks, no larger than paper clips. They must have been expensive, I thought randomly – they were stamped with decorative symbols of birds, and quite beautiful. My eyes flew from this stranger's body back to his face then, seeking the familiar, and I leaned forward, looking anxiously for any movement.

"Jay… is he …?" I heard Paul's question, and felt my friend drop to his knees beside me.

I shook my head, staring at my grandfather in horror. He wasn't moving, I could see that much. The arrow had struck him squarely in the left side, right below his arm. It would have sliced through his lungs to his heart. Still, if I knew Doc…

I reached a hand hesitantly toward him, then jumped and pulled it back.

He had jerked and coughed, and was now rolling over, blinking slowly. He drew a deep, shuddering breath, as if he was coming up for air after being submerged in a pool of water. The air came out as a sharp gasp when he looked up and saw me.

"Jason?" he asked, frowning.

I nodded, smiling from ear to ear. He could breathe and he could talk, and for the moment that was more than enough. I didn't think I'd ever been happier to see him, frowning or otherwise.

He looked at me, dazed, and then glanced over my shoulder at Paul and Tatiana. I followed his gaze to see that several other soldiers had appeared, and were now sliding off their horses to surround our small group. One of the men, roughly the size of a small mountain, came straight toward us. His arms were the size of railroad ties, and each was decorated with thick silver rings, which wrapped themselves around his massive biceps. He wore his dirty blonde hair well past his shoulders and carried an immense sword. He was the spitting image of Thor.

He was also a Dane; I recognized the hair and arm rings. I whirled around, turning my back to Doc and spreading my arms protectively in front of him, and glared at the barbarian in front of me, wondering desperately who he was and what he wanted with Doc. A menacing growl grew in my throat, surprising me, and the man stopped, his eyes wide with shock.

Then I felt Doc's hand on my shoulder and heard his breathy chuckle.

"'Tis alright, son, he's one of mine," he mumbled. He released his grip on my shoulder and rolled onto his stomach. Taking one more deep, measured breath, he pushed himself to his knees and then to his feet. There he stretched to his full height, grunting as ligaments and tendons snapped and cracked.

I stood up, shocked at this sudden return to health, and stared at the man I knew as my grandfather.

"My Lord!" the giant soldier said with evident relief.

Doc looked at me and gave me a wry grin before directing his attention toward the large soldier. "Trigva, I'm alright," he said in a voice that seemed stronger than it should have been. He looked down at the arrow sticking out of his side and frowned, then grabbed it with his right hand. One twist and a sharp jerk brought the arrow out cleanly, as though it was no more than a splinter.

My mouth dropped even farther open.

"Kevlar?" Reis asked casually. I looked up at my bodyguard and friend, wondering what he was talking about. He'd made short work of the attackers, I saw, and had now come to see about Doc, bringing one of the injured assassins with him.

Doc replied with a bark of laughter, then opened his cape and pointed to the mail underneath. "Yes, under a coat of titanium mesh. I had it made at home. I found it much stronger than steel mail, and a hell of a lot lighter," he answered quietly. "With the added benefit of being conveniently arrow proof," he added after a moment.

He smiled brilliantly at Reis, quite proud of this invention, and then turned suddenly toward me, his face growing dark. I gulped audibly. I'd seen that look before.

"Now, Jason, may I ask what the hell you and your friends are doing here?" he asked, his voice dangerously quiet.

"What?" I spluttered, not ready for the question. We'd just found Doc, for God's sake, and seen him shot with a medieval arrow! Now he was standing there as if nothing had happened, asking me what I was doing here? My mind refused to deal with the quick turn of events, or the question itself.

"You heard me, Jason. What are you doing here? And while I'm at it, how exactly did you manage it?" Doc glared at me, his eyes glowing with frustration, and I gulped again. I'd never seen him so angry before, and the fact that it was directed at me – for reasons I couldn't understand – made me slightly uncomfortable. After all we'd been though, jumping through time to save him, he was going to get angry at me? It was all too much, and I found myself suddenly growing angry as well.

"I saw you jump! I knew where you were going. And I also knew you were walking straight into a trap! Into this!" I flung my arm at the clearing, the man laying at our feet, and the arrow that now lay next to him. "I came here to save you," I snapped, my voice cracking.

Doc shook his head, his frown deepening. "How could you know any of that?" He paused, then made a chopping motion with his hand. "Besides, even if you did, it doesn't give you the right to come barging in here, putting yourself at risk. Jason, you could have been killed, do you understand that, boy? And then what would I have done?" He pulled me roughly against him, crushing me to his mail in an enormous bear hug. I wrapped my arms around him, adjusting my face slightly to avoid the worst of the metal links.

For a moment, all I could think about was Doc, and the fact that we'd reached him in time. My anger and confusion faded away, and I reveled in the fact that he was alive. Then the reason for our entire trip snapped into place, and I stepped back.

"They were going to kill you, Doc, and I wasn't going to let that happen."

Doc raised his eyebrows in question, and I plunged in. "They were sent by Dresden. Or Lord Stanley." I outlined the quick version of what I knew – the kidnapping of William Stanley and subsequent blackmailing of his brother. The plot to capture Doc. And then the change in that plot, when I showed up and Dresden declared Doc expendable.

At the end I stopped, breathing heavily, and glared at my grandfather, expecting some sort of response. He stared at me as though I'd just dropped out of the USS Enterprise, though, so I pressed on.

"Doc, I had to come back," I repeated stubbornly. If I repeated it enough times, perhaps it would get through his thick head. "I knew you didn't know – that you thought Stanley was on your side – and –"

Doc interrupted me, placing his index finger suddenly over my lips, and I grew still. He shook his head slightly, glancing around him at the soldiers from his camp. Of course, I realized. I couldn't say too much in front of his men, who probably didn't know about the stones. I clamped my mouth shut, nodding my understanding.

He turned to the giant soldier now, barking orders. "Trigva, I am unhurt, and it seems that things have changed around us. According to my grandson, we may have lost a valuable ally. We must meet with the captains of our guard, and anyone Henry cares to send. Set the meeting up in Henry's pavilion, if you will." He took in a deep, measured breath before looking back at me. "And Trigva, my grandson and his group will be joining us this evening. Please inform Elizabeth of their arrival and have her prepare their accommodations. They'll be staying with me."

"Yes, my Lord," Trigva replied quickly. He bowed, and snapped for his men to mount up.

As they galloped off, Doc turned back to us. His whole demeanor had changed, and for the first time I saw why the men and women of this time followed him.

"We do not have much time," he said sternly, looking around at us. "If Stanley has truly defected to Dresden's side, he takes several thousand soldiers, as well as archers and horses, with him. This is..." he paused, searching for the words, and his mouth turned down in a grim line, "a problem. Still, I believe there is time to be civil."

He turned toward Paul, and simply shook his head in disappointment. Then he turned toward Tatiana. A corner of his mouth drew up in a wry smile.

"You must be John's granddaughter. He's told me of you. I assume that he's unaware of your whereabouts."

Tatiana lifted one eyebrow. "He doesn't know I came, if that's what you mean. He wouldn't have approved. I wasn't going to let him stop me."

Doc barked with laughter, then stalked quickly back toward our horses, snapping orders as he went. "Come, we must ride. None of you will say a word until we are back in the confines of my tent, is that understood? Once we are there, none of you will say anything about where you've come from or what you're doing here. Agreed?"

"Yes, sir," we replied in unison.

Katherine paused for a moment, glaring at the rest of us, then spoke as though she was correcting us. "Yes, *my Lord*," she said clearly.

Doc stopped at that, frowning, and glanced at Katherine for the first time. His eyes ran down her body and back up, and he glanced at me in question.

"And who, may I ask, is *this?*" he snapped.

"Katherine of Doncaster, my Lord," she replied. Her chin lifted in pride and her eyes sought his out, and I wondered again at the change in her since our first meeting. This was not the same girl we'd rescued, and it wasn't only because she was wearing Tatiana's clothes.

Doc grunted in response, then broke into his quick stride again. "Come! We have much to discuss this evening, and very little time to do it. Your timing could not have been worse, though it seems you may have brought important information."

"But –" I started anxiously.

Doc cut me off with a stern look as he swung up into his saddle. "Not here," he snapped again, plunging into the woods and disappearing. We scrambled to mount our own horses to follow him.

"I have to admit, this isn't the welcome I was expecting," Paul mumbled as he crouched behind Katherine on their horse.

"You and me both," I replied. Turning, I drove my horse forward after the man I called grandfather.

35

We galloped out of the woods and onto the plains in a tightly packed group, with Doc at the front. He was driving his horse hard, and the rest of us were struggling a bit to keep up. My initial euphoria at seeing him had quickly subsided; he seemed to be anything but pleased to see us. In fact, he seemed downright angry about it. I wondered if the stones had somehow altered his personality, and whether that was even possible. Did he truly become someone else when he traveled? Did the stones make him who they needed him to be? I didn't think that had happened to me, but the person who rode with us now certainly wasn't my grandfather. At least not the version of him I knew.

Ahead of us, hundreds and perhaps thousands of people had gathered on the gradual slope that led to Henry Tudor's encampment. I studied the camp as well as I could as we raced through, now that I'd learned – the hard way – about knowing the importance of your surroundings. Hundreds of tents, wagons, and other temporary structures covered the slope of the hill and the valley that lay beyond. I was surprised at the number of women and children among the people; they outnumbered the soldiers themselves, and gave the encampment a cheerful, almost festive air. It certainly wasn't what I'd expected of a military camp, but then I was growing used to things being unexpected.

Somewhere, far in the distance, I felt one of the stones. It wasn't here, I didn't think – its whisper was faint, as though it was traveling over a long distance. I pulled at it experimentally, wondering where it was, and it got a bit stronger. Interesting. I put that fact away for future use, and concentrated on keeping up with Doc.

I looked over at Paul, to make sure that and Katherine were keeping up, and saw that he seemed to be enjoying the attention people were giving us. Everyone was bowing and calling my grandfather "Lord" as he passed, showing respect and love for the man leading their army. Paul was taking the praise for himself, and waving at the people as if he were Snow White riding in a gilded carriage at Disney World. Reis, on the other hand, was stoic and guarded, studying the terrain and people closely. If I knew the man as well as I thought I did, he was looking carefully for escape routes. Two of them, if he could manage it. His hand rested lightly on the gun at his side, and I saw that he still had the assault rifle strapped across his back. He didn't trust this situation, or the new version of Doc, any more than I did. Tatiana rode on my other side, her shoulders tense and her face cold. I couldn't blame her. Doc hadn't exactly given us a warm welcome.

After riding through the entire camp, we finally pulled up outside one of the largest tents on the hill. The canvas structure was surrounded by at least two dozen flags, all with different colors and shapes. Birds of prey seemed to be the main theme, though other banners featured wolves, boar, large cats, and lots and lots of crosses.

"The lords who are fighting with Henry Tudor," I murmured, looking through the standards. At least twenty of them, from what I could tell. Doc had gathered a mighty army for Henry. But would it be enough to stop Dresden and his guns?

I hoped so. The world was, after all, depending on it.

Two young men, no older than twelve, ran out from behind Doc's tent to help with our horses. They were dressed in dark brown leather jerkins, with black breeches held up by yellowing rope. They wore tattered brown boots without spurs, and bowed repeatedly. They also knew what they were doing; they had all the horses by the reins in moments, ready to lead them away.

We dismounted at their urging, and looked around.

Doc's tent stood on its own, with a large open area around it, as though no one else wanted to get close to him. Given the expression on his face, I could understand why; he had turned on us again, his face dark and angry.

"Jason, Paul, Reis, into my tent, if you please. I shall deal with you first." He turned to Tatiana and Katherine, his face growing somewhat gentler. "If you ladies will wait here –"

"They come with us," I snapped, interrupting him. I'd been taught never to speak over my elders, but if he was going to treat us as hostile strangers, he'd receive the same treatment from me. "These are my friends," I continued. "Anything you have to say to me can be said to them too."

He raised his eyebrows, shocked at this turn of events, and opened his mouth to protest. Reis stepped into place behind me, though, followed by Paul, Katherine, and Tatiana, and my grandfather closed his mouth. He nodded slowly, and I thought I saw something change in his eyes. Then he turned and walked abruptly into his tent.

"Come!" he shouted over his shoulder.

I scrambled to follow, my heart racing, but looked up as we entered, just in time to feel the first drop of rain on my cheek. A flash of lightening suddenly lit up the skyline, followed by a crash of thunder, and the pile of leaves next to me exploded in the first gust of rain-borne wind. *How appropriate*, I thought grimly. I ducked into the tent before the rain could start for real, and looked around.

The cloth structure was surprisingly large inside, and comfortably decorated. Several multi-colored rugs stretched across the ground, with clumps of bright green grass poking up between them. Two round tables sat next to one another in the middle of the space, both littered with maps and countless pieces of crusty-looking paper. Eight heavy wooden chairs were arranged loosely around the tables, and a lumpy bed sat in the far corner of the tent. It wasn't exactly the Hilton, but it was certainly more than I'd expected in a war camp.

We gathered awkwardly around the two large tables, not sure of our place or reception here. Doc still had his back to us, as though he couldn't bear to face us quite yet. Finally he turned, raking his fingers through his thick grey hair, stripped off his cape and mail, and straightened to glare at us, one at a time. Even Katherine got a cold look. In the end, though, his gaze came to rest on me.

"Are you ready to explain yourself, young man?" he asked quietly. He was angry, I could see that much. He also looked incredibly tired. And sad. "I have worked so hard to keep you out of this, to protect both your life and your world. Why are you putting that at risk?"

I opened my mouth to reply, wondering how I was going to explain, but a crack of thunder rang out, interrupting me. Reis stepped forward to lay a hand on my shoulder.

"Sir, if I may," he said abruptly. "Jason had only your welfare at heart. He learned of the stones, and the danger to your life. We went to Fleming, sir, and learned what we needed to know to make the trip. Paul and I agreed to jump to the past with Jason."

"And you believed that you were doing the right thing?" Doc snapped in answer. "You were paid to protect the boy, not encourage him to run pell-mell into the first trouble he could find!"

"Sir, they would have come with or without me," Reis answered, a slight smile at his lips. "I believed, sir, that it was best for me to accompany them. To continue protecting Jason, so to speak."

"You should have stopped them!" Doc repeated, running his hands through his hair again and pacing across the tent. At this rate, I thought, he was going to have a coronary before we even got to the battle.

Besides, Reis had already shouldered enough of my grandfather's anger.

"He *couldn't* have stopped us, Doc! I knew what I had to do, and I wasn't going to let anything keep me from it," I said firmly.

Doc glanced at me, frowning, and Reis cut in again. "I believe, sir, that you'll find your grandson somewhat … changed."

For a moment, no one spoke, the only sound the pitter patter of rain on the tent around us. I held my breath, wondering what my grandfather was going to do. He couldn't send me back, that much was certain; I was already there, and there wasn't much he could do about it. It would make things a lot easier if he'd just accept that and get on with it. We didn't exactly have time to sit around arguing.

Finally Doc settled back against the table, waiting. "Changed? How?" Then he glanced at the door, seeming to remember where we were, and straightened. "And quickly. We don't have much time."

I took a deep breath. Here it was, then, the moment I'd been waiting for. The moment when I could finally tell someone who just *might* understand what I'd been through. But where to start? The beginning seemed as good a place as any.

"Well," I finally said, "it all started when I had a dream…"

I gave Doc a quick sketch of the dream I'd had about Lord Stanley and Dresden, along with Dresden's threats. I went on to tell him what I'd decided to do, and that I could feel the stones. That they'd been talking to me and even giving me information. I told him that there'd been a stone at Nottingham, and that I could feel one here, though it was far away. Then I told him that they were still sending me visions. I left out our adventures of the last few days; those weren't important to the current situation, and we were running dangerously short of time. I finished with the tale of William Stanley, though, and noted that his presence would – ideally –alter certain plans of Dresden's.

The longer I spoke, the more concerned and confused Doc's face became. I didn't bother to look at anyone else as I rushed through the story; I knew they'd believe me, and they weren't the important ones here. Finally, though, Doc held up a hand, signaling me to stop. My words died on my lips, and I waited anxiously.

"You can read the stones?" he asked breathlessly. "I thought … I had thought I was the only one." He paused for a moment, thinking. "And you say that you can hear them? Incredible…"

I blew a soft breath through my teeth at his words, thinking that I finally had his attention. Maybe now he'd listen to what I had to say, start taking me a little more seriously. I opened my mouth to continue, but stopped when the tent flaps flew open, revealing a dark, stormy sky, driving rain, and a man in armor and a cape. We turned with gasps toward the intruder.

"How long have you been standing there?" Doc asked in a strangled voice.

The man named Trigva gave Doc a startled look at his reaction, and strode into the tent.

"I have just arrived, my Lord. The war council is gathering in Henry's tent for the meeting you requested."

Doc turned to face Reis and straightened his back. "Well, here we go," he muttered. "You three come with me, and keep your mouths shut. If anyone speaks to you, tell them that you are with me. You are not – under any circumstances – to ask or answer questions. Understood?" He strode toward the opening of the tent, his mouth a grim line, and we scrambled to follow, throwing on the hooded cloaks we'd been given. Suddenly I paused.

"What about Tatiana and Katherine?"

Doc shook his head, throwing a quick glance at the girls. "They may come with us, but they will not be allowed into Henry's tent. They will have to wait for us outside." He was already striding out of the tent, throwing his own hood up over his head, and we rushed to catch up with him.

"We will not have much time," he snapped. "But I must warn Tudor of what you've told me. If the Stanleys have changed their allegiance, we must change our own plans to accommodate that."

"What exactly is the state of affairs here?" Reis asked, loudly enough to be heard over the rain.

Doc nodded at his question, but strode quickly past two knights – seemingly oblivious to the weather – before answering. He looked around to ensure that no one outside our circle was within earshot, then cleared his throat.

"Our scouts, for the most part, agree with the text books in regard to the scale of armies on both sides. Between archers, horsemen, and infantry, Tudor has close to five thousand men. Richard's numbers are greater at over seven thousand."

I gasped. Those were the numbers I'd learned in my research, but I had assumed that they were exaggerated. If Richard's army was that much larger than Tudor's *before* Stanley's defection...

"And archers?" Reis asked quickly, his long stride matching Doc's, his head bent in thought. I could almost see the gears turning in his head, trying to find a way out of this particular mess.

Doc grunted. "The one area where we have favorable numbers. We have over fifteen hundred. Richard has about two-thirds that number."

"What about Stanley?" I countered, hurrying to catch them and join the conversation. "What if he goes to the other side?"

Doc's mouth turned down at the interruption, and he closed his eyes for a moment at the thought. "Stanley has an army equal to our own in foot soldiers and cavalry alone. They lack our number of archers, but not by much. If they have joined Dresden, it will be a very large problem. Which is what we're going to discuss right now."

"But once William reaches his brother, Lord Stanley won't *have* to fight on Dresden's side," I huffed, struggling to breathe, walk so quickly, and talk at the same time. "Dresden won't have any leverage against the family. Surely Lord Stanley will turn back and withhold his men. The way he did in the text books."

"As much as I'd like to believe that," Doc said, turning toward me, "I'm not going to bet our army – or history itself – on it."

"You don't believe we've made a difference?" I asked, quirking an eyebrow at this lack of confidence.

"I don't believe you've done anything concrete, no," he muttered. "William may or may not have made it there. Lord Stanley may or may not realize that his brother is free. And finally, Stanley may change his alliance at any time. No matter what you think you've done. If history holds true, he will keep his army at bay and let the battle play itself out."

"And if that doesn't happen?" Paul asked.

"That's exactly what I have to talk to Henry and the others about," Doc answered grimly, ducking lower to clear a low-hanging branch. "If Stanley enters the fight – on Dresden's side – I do not know if our army will be able to hold them off. And if we don't – if we lose the day – then the line of history changes and..."

Suddenly he stopped, and we found ourselves in front of a tent every bit as large as Doc's. My grandfather drew his shoulders up and pushed them back down, took a deep breath, and strode into the tent.

We scrambled to follow, as usual, and ducked through the opening to start our war council with the future king of England.

36

I gagged the moment we stepped into the tent.

It was stuffy, smelled terrible, and was much too warm for any reasonable person under the age of eighty. A fire burned in the pit at the center, and several dogs lay around it, smelling distinctly wet. The men stood on one side of the tent, gathered around a large table. They were arguing loudly when we entered, but grew quiet when they saw Doc. My eyes ran around the table, trying to judge the men in front of us, and paused when I came to a familiar face. Henry Tudor. I would recognize the long, gaunt face of the historical leader anywhere. I gulped, wondering what the protocol was in this situation, and then turned to look at the other men. I didn't recognize them, though I would later learn that Lord Taylor, the Duke of Northridge, Philibert de Chandee, the Earl of Eaton, Lord Edmond, and several high-ranking men of the church were also included, awaiting my grandfather – the physics professor's – arrival.

Everyone, including Henry Tudor, stopped talking and looked up as the man of the hour strode confidently toward the table. I had always been proud of my grandfather, but the pride and awe I felt at that moment, as Doc walked forward to take his place next to those men, went far beyond anything I'd ever felt for him. He was the man they turned to, I realized. The one they trusted. England – and the world itself – was resting on his shoulders, treating him as its savior, and he was moving forward and doing what he could to serve that responsibility.

I began to regret some of my earlier words, then, but shook it off. *Action now, regrets or celebration later, Evans,* I told myself. That had to be the way of it.

Doc had already reached the table, and was now gazing down on the maps and figures there. I knew what the map held: the terrain of tomorrow's the battlefield. The positioning of the archers, the placement of the infantry, and the timing of the cavalry's charge. Doc would know all of that from his research – the best times and places to deploy men, the areas where they should attack, what Dresden and Richard's army would do…

Assuming, of course, that the historians had it right. And that Stanley's men stayed out of it.

"Therein lies the rub," I whispered, thinking suddenly of Shakespeare. Two rather large problems, and no simple answers.

"Dresden's household guards have positioned themselves atop Ambion Hill, just as you said they would," one of the lords said, pointing to a red figurine in the shape of a wooden square that sat in the center of the map.

Doc nodded vaguely, as though the man was telling him old news, but didn't answer. Instead, he continued to study the map, reaching out to adjust a figure now and then.

"What's going on?" Paul whispered suddenly in my ear. I jumped, surprised, and shot him a glare.

"Those men are waiting for Doc to tell them what to do, and he's trying to decide what to say," I whispered back. "They think they know what's going to happen, but Doc knows something they don't."

"What's that?"

"Lord Stanley," I returned, watching my grandfather intently. "That man holds the balance of power in his hands. History says that he watched the battle but didn't take part. If his brother finds him in time, he should still do that."

"And if he doesn't?" Paul asked.

I turned to face Paul, the question hanging in the air between us. "Then we're all in serious trouble."

At that moment, Doc brought his hands slowly down on the table in front of him and looked at the men around him, his eyes bleak. "My scouts tell me that the Stanley has altered his allegiance," he said clearly. "It would appear that his army is here, and prepared to go to battle for Richard." He paused, allowing the shocked silence around us to stretch on, then cleared his throat and got down to business. "It appears, therefore, that we must reassess our plans and change them where necessary, if we expect to gain a victory tomorrow."

When we returned, we gathered around the table in Doc's tent, made sure that we were alone, and did our own planning. The battle session hadn't gone well. Henry and his advisors had pressed Doc to give them more details than he could about Stanley, and had finally declared that they didn't believe him. He was still leading the army, of course, and would make the decisions in regard to the army's movement, but I got the distinct impression that it would have been easier with support.

He was now worried about Stanley's army as well as his own. Overall, the mood was grim.

There were many things that hadn't been said at Henry's battle council, though – things that *couldn't* be said – and now was the time to deal with them. We sent Katherine, who was exhausted, to her bed at the back of the tent, and then Reis, Paul, Tatiana, and I crouched in the near-darkness around the table, with a scant three candles for light, and listened as Doc started with what he knew.

"Let's begin with the girl," he said, looking daggers at me. "Why have you brought her?"

I sighed. We were supposed to be planning a battle, not talking about Katherine. And this wasn't exactly a question I wanted to answer again. Still…

"I saw her on the trip here," I answered bluntly. "When we found her, I recognized her, and I felt…" I shrugged helplessly, trying to find the right words. "I felt like we had to bring her. Like we'd found her for a reason, and that the stones had led us to her. I can't explain it, but I couldn't leave her." I met Doc's eyes and lifted my chin, wondering if he was going to question me on this too.

To my surprise, though, he nodded once in agreement. "If you saw her on your trip, then you were right to bring her. The stones may have been trying to tell you that she's important to history in some way."

"Oookay," Paul muttered, raising his eyebrows in doubt. "So what are we supposed to do with her, since you're being so clear with the details and all?"

Doc shook his head. "For now, we keep her close to us. Let me worry about her future." He leaned forward and dropped his voice, bringing the meeting to order. "We have far more important things to discuss right now."

Reis leaned forward as well, grinning. "Now you're speaking my language. What exactly are we dealing with here?"

"Let's start with the stones," Doc murmured. "I'm not sure whether we can use them to win this battle, and I'd be lying if I said I knew how they worked. Simply put, though, I believe that they're portals, or gates if you will, that either create or mark rips in time. Those rips allow individuals to journey back and forth within the parameters of the fourth dimension. To travel through time. The stones somehow facilitate that journey."

He looked around at our darkened faces and saw our confusion, but shook his head. "I don't have time to explain in further detail, I'm afraid. You will just have to take my word for it. The stones create – for whatever reason – tunnels through time."

"Wormholes," I breathed in awe. Amazing, and it made perfect sense. Areas where time grew thin. Where the boundaries between the dimensions ceased to exist. I paused for a moment, then continued that thought. "But we can move the stones. What are they, portable black holes? They *create* holes in time?"

Doc nodded, smiling faintly at this exhibition of creative thinking. "They must, for they work even when they move," he answered. "I believe that they *attract* the holes."

"And this has what, exactly, to do with my father?" Tatiana interrupted impatiently.

Doc grunted in response, calling the meeting abruptly back to order. "Right you are, my girl." He turned and walked through the darkness to the bed to grab a piece of rope, which he laid on the table in a back-and-forth pattern so that it looked like a hard ribbon Christmas candy.

"Time may fold back and forth on itself, and there may be holes in it, but it must still move forward. And as the past has already happened, there are certain things that are … set. Our present, after all, depends on certain things happening. The American Revolution, for example. The invention of the wheel and the light bulb."

"Henry Tudor becoming kind of England," I added grimly.

Doc nodded. "Exactly, Jason."

"And Dresden is trying to alter that, to do whatever it is he's doing," Reis said slowly. "What happens if he succeeds?"

My grandfather sat back until his face was hidden in shadow, and took a deep breath. A chill ran down my spine at the answer I knew was coming.

"Well that's the question, isn't it? Small changes – my presence in history, for example – don't alter events heavily enough to damage time. Larger events – like the outcome of this battle … I believe that changing them will alter the path of time. Irrevocably."

"And?" I whispered.

Doc cleared his throat. "And, Jason, damage to the ribbon of time means damage to life itself. Potentially even the end of the world."

"So my father is risking the entire world for his own glory," Tatiana said suddenly, breaking the silence that followed. "How very … predictable of him. So what do we do to stop him? What exactly is *he* planning to do?" She pushed one of the candles aggressively toward Doc, peering into his face for questions.

"Dresden will be with Richard on the battlefield tomorrow," Doc answered, his voice growing grim with contained emotion. "He's thrown his lot in with the old king, and seeks to help him win the battle. He's spent years building alliances and planning, just for that purpose. I have rushed the confrontation, to keep him from preparing any large-scale firearms, but I don't know if it will be enough."

"So what do we do to stop him?" Tatiana pushed, her face drawn into a frown. I gulped, remembering our conversation in the wagon on the first night we were there, and her fear and hatred when we met Dresden. This was deeply personal for her, and every line of her body reflected that tension.

Doc sighed. "We must make certain that he fails. When Richard's reign ends, so too does Dresden's. History will simply consume him." He looked at me before continuing. "Once the battle is finished, we find the nearest stone and get home."

"What?" she snapped, her face a mask of shock. "We're just going to *leave* him here? That's your *plan?*"

"The only other option is to bring him with us, girl, and I'm afraid he's not open to that possibility," he snapped back, his face growing dark at her question.

Tatiana glanced at me for help, and I turned toward my grandfather, virtually speechless. He was just going to leave Dresden here, to wreak havoc as he would, and damage history where and when he found an opening? What if he found another important, world-changing situation? What if he killed someone important?

What if he found a way to jump again, and showed up somewhere else in time, as he planned to do?

"When Richard is deposed, Dresden's power will be lost. He will no longer be a threat. He'll be a wanted man, with nowhere to run," Doc was saying, as though this was the most reasonable, logical thing in the world.

I hadn't yet found my tongue, but Tatiana had, and her face was bright with anger. "So that's it? Run for the hills, like frightened sheep? After all we've been through – after all *you've* been through – you'll simply leave it up to fate and hope for the best?" Her voice was loud and shrill, though she was trying to contain it. "And what, leave my father here to continue his work? Surely you have a better plan than *that*!"

She looked from Doc to me and back, shocked, and I nodded.

"She's right," I finally said. "We can't leave him here. Just because he failed once doesn't mean he won't try again. Tatiana and I have talked to him. We know his plans, and they certainly don't include fading off into the sunset. He's trying to control the *world*, Doc. Who knows what else he'll do, where else he'll go to try to manipulate people and situations! We already know that's his plan, and he doesn't exactly seem like the sort to give up just because the first attempt doesn't work out." I turned to Doc, searching his face for answers, but he only shook his head.

"He cannot read the stones for himself. I don't know what his ultimate plan is, but he cannot leave this time period on his own. That alone will handicap him and keep him from further trouble. Once Richard is dead, he'll be stranded, with no army, no friends, and no power. I have always believed that the best and easiest way to beat him is to leave him behind. Allow him to … disappear into history."

Tatiana slammed her fist on the table in disgust. "You're wrong!"

I put out a calming hand, knowing that this wasn't the way to deal with my grandfather, and tried to sound reasonable. "Doc, we heard his plans from his own mouth. Leaving him alone isn't a viable option."

His mouth drew down in a frown and he paused for a moment before shaking his head firmly. "Jason, I have spent years dealing with Dresden and preparing for this moment. Do not assume that you or your friends know more than I. This decision is made, and it's not up for negotiation. We seek to win the battle. Then we find our way home and leave Dresden behind. Understood?"

No one answered him. Reis kept his eyes locked on the table in front of us, while Paul did his best impression of a chameleon, trying to blend in with his environment. He could have been part of the tent's fabric for all he was saying. Tatiana rose and stalked toward the back of the tent, shaking her head and muttering. I sucked on my teeth, looking for the right path, and finally decided to get us all back on track. Doc was wrong, but that didn't mean we could break off from him completely. Not now.

"So where will we go? After the battle, I mean," I asked.

Doc composed himself carefully before replying. "We know that there are stones in Abergavenny and Doncaster. Doncaster is under Dresden's protection, at least for the time being, so we'll head east to Abergavenny. A window opens tomorrow evening, and we must be there and ready."

I frowned. There was a stone at the battlefield as well – I'd felt it. Could Doc not feel that? Hadn't I told him about it? Couldn't we use that one? I kept my mouth shut, trying to remember whether I'd said anything, and was about to speak when Reis beat me to it.

"You said yourself that Dresden's men have been destroying towns and villages across the country. What if he's destroyed the stone in Abergavenny? What if we get there and it's gone?"

If we were in a movie, the dark creepy music would have started to play then. A flash of lightning broke across the sky, followed by a deep, booming bout of thunder. No one spoke. Without those stones, we wouldn't have a way home, regardless of what we did with Dresden.

"If he has destroyed the stones, we will be forced to stay here," Doc finally said. "To get by as best we may."

I gulped at his words, shrinking farther into myself.

Katherine kept her breathing slow and steady to mimic sleep. She faced the wall of the tent, so that the others wouldn't notice her eyes, which were wide open. She couldn't believe what she was hearing, and yet somehow she felt as if she'd already known. Had she heard them right? Was it possible? What did it all mean? A million and one questions ran through her mind, making it difficult to think straight. The very idea that someone could travel through time, that they'd come from another world entirely … she'd known that her new friends were strange, but this went far beyond that.

This went beyond anything she'd ever imagined.

Suddenly she heard someone walking toward her, the steps and breathing angry, and her eyes snapped shut. They'd been arguing, and she didn't want to be involved. The Earl had already stated that he had a future in mind for her. But then he'd gone on to say that he planned to leave Dresden here, while he and the others ran home.

She'd already decided that this would never do, regardless of what future he'd planned for her. Dresden couldn't stay here, to continue to threaten her world. He would have to go. Or die. She had a plan – one she'd been thinking about for hours now. The only question was whether Jason and the others – who didn't seem to agree with the Earl about Dresden's future – would help her.

37

I walked out of the tent just as the rain stopped, took a deep breath, and focused on the activity swirling around in the valley below. Watching other people's actions was easier than thinking about the conversation we'd just finished. Doc had a completely different view of our path than I did, and he was dead wrong. He also wasn't interested in hearing my opinion. At some point this would become a problem, but for now the smell of long grass, wild flowers, and horse manure combined with the damp, sharp smell of rain was enough to distract me.

To the west, the full moon had emerged from the clouds to illuminate the rugged mountain range there. A chorus of crickets and bullfrogs, and the ever-present ringing of swords being sharpened on grinding wheels, blurred together as one. Lightening bugs twinkled like Christmas lights off in the distance. It was beautiful. And deadly. Tomorrow, that valley would hold thousands of dead bodies. Perhaps my own.

I hadn't heard her approach, but Tatiana was suddenly by my side, smelling of lavender. Looking over, I noticed that her shoulders were tense, her face drawn. She hadn't come for a pleasurable chat, then.

"You know your grandfather is wrong, right?" she asked quietly.

"Of course I know," I muttered. "I said as much in the tent."

"So what are we going to do about it?" she asked, her voice dropping an octave.

I laughed. I'd been wondering the same thing, though I hadn't figured anything out yet. I should have known she'd come asking.

"I'm working on it," I replied. That was the truth – I hadn't stopped thinking about it since Doc had made his ridiculous statement. I'd even called on the stones, seeking their guidance. So far I hadn't received a response. "Got any bright ideas?" I finally asked.

"I'm afraid not," she answered. "Though I assume at this point that Doc will try to keep us from going anywhere near Dresden or the battle. Of course we'll have to disobey him."

It was a test, and I saw right through it. She wanted to know if I'd go against Doc's wishes. I wouldn't have before, but when it came to the safety of the world, there didn't seem to be much choice. "Of course," I answered after a moment.

"Do you think we'll make it?" she asked then, a touch of fear coloring her words.

I turned for the first time to face her. Her hair was down, and she looked both younger and more disillusioned than she ever had. The past few days had scarred her, as had the confrontation with her father, and she was wearing her wounds in her eyes. I reached for her hand – which had become familiar in my own – and squeezed it.

"If we don't stop Dresden now," I replied, looking into her eyes, "I'm not sure there will be anything to go back too. So we don't have much choice, do we?"

We strolled back into the tent together to find that Doc had gone on some unknown errand, leaving the rest of us to our own devices. Tatiana walked toward the back of the tent without saying goodnight, parted the curtain that acted as a temporary partition, and disappeared. I plopped down on my bed and looked over at Paul.

He held a picture up, grinning. "So far so good," he quipped.

"What are you talking about?" I asked, taking off my shirt and throwing it in the corner of the tent. Someone had set up camp beds for us – or this era's version of them – and I was ready to lay down. Today had been long and extremely stressful.

Paul, who was still wide awake, handed me the picture, which featured the two of us in Little League. "Our picture is still intact," he said, smiling as if this was the greatest news in the world.

"So?"

"So .... ***Back to the Future***. You know, the movie? If things start to go bad, we'll fade out of the picture. Then we'll *know* we're in trouble."

"Oh my God, are you serious?" I groaned. Unfortunately, I already knew the answer to that question. Of course he was. Put Paul in the scariest, most dangerous situation in the world, and he would still somehow find a way to joke about it.

He nodded, confirming my fears. "I'm not saying the movie was without its flaws. I mean obviously we don't need a Delorian to go back in time, but the disappearing image in the photo makes complete sense."

I shrugged, too tired to argue with him. For all I knew, he was right. It made almost as much sense as half of the other stuff we'd talked about tonight.

The shrug evidently wasn't good enough for him, though, since he continued talking about it while we washed up with our two buckets of hot water and soap made from lard. Doc's maid – or whatever she was – had also given us fresh pants and shirts. It was the first time I'd felt clean in days, and it was glorious. I sighed happily, and Paul took that as a sign that I'd been listening after all.

"Oh come on," he said as I dunked my head under water for one last rinse. "You honestly didn't think about it? Jumping back in time, all that? I've been dying to say, 'Doc, this is heavy,' since we found him!"

"I'm actually impressed that you suppressed that urge for as long as you did," Reis replied dryly from his own bed. His eyes were closed, but I suspected that his mind was still moving feverishly, keeping him from sleep.

Paul smiled as though Reis had given him a compliment. "Thanks, Reis."

"Any time," he replied.

That brought a much-needed smile to my face, and I chuckled as I jumped into bed. The mattress was lumpy, stuffed with straw and who knew what else, but it was clean and safe. For the moment.

Tomorrow, of course, would be a whole different story. Tomorrow…

I put the thought away as too much. For tonight, I would be content with safe darkness and the comforting sound of my best friend's snoring. After a moment of listening, I fell into a deep, dreamless sleep.

38

It was warm and humid inside the tent, and stank of unwashed bodies, dirt, and crushed grass. Dresden detested being outdoors, and the state of the tent was making the experience even worse than usual. In addition, he was having to physically restrain himself at the Bishop's news.

The assassins had failed in their attempt on Richard Evans' life, and – worse – let him escape with his confederates.

Dresden paced angrily around the tent, listening to the Bishop's impossible tail of how Evans had been shot by an arrow – at a distance of less than 50 paces – then risen and walked away. According to one of the assassins, who had escaped the scene, Evans' men had shown up in the nick of time, distracting the mercenaries and essentially saving the old man's life. The assassin's description of these men – and their weapons, which emitted loud blasts and bouts of fire – left little doubt about their identities.

"Tatiana, that boy, and their associates," he growled, his lips turning down in a snarl. Damn them. He'd known when they escaped that they would be trouble, but he'd never considered that they might get to Evans in time to save him. Now they had ruined more than one plan. With Evans dead, his men would have refused to fight for Henry, and Henry would have lost a vital source of intelligence. That, coupled with Stanley's new alliance, would have guaranteed Richard – and Dresden himself – a victory.

With Evans dead, he would also have had a clear road to the next step in his new plan: recapturing Jason and forcing the boy to either reveal the stone's secrets or take him through the stones to his next destination.

Now...

With a roar, he turned and threw a chair at the Bishop and his news. "Get out, you useless pile of horse dung!" he shouted, his anger reaching the surface. "I do not need you for my victory!"

The Bishop ducked the chair, terrified, and ran out of the tent. Sloan, who was just entering, stepped to the side and looked curiously after the church man. Dresden growled at his presence. The boy was always showing up at the most inopportune times, and it was starting to annoy him.

"People would serve you more faithfully, Father, if you shouted less and listened more," the boy observed mildly. "And we now hold fewer chips than we did. You know this. My scouts tell me that Stanley is already restless. The Earl's army is ready, and far more loyal than ours. Victory is anything but guaranteed."

"Quiet!" Dresden roared. "Gather the maps, right the chairs, and keep your mouth shut!"

Sloan's eyes blazed with anger, but he did as he was told. Perhaps the boy was learning his place, Dresden thought. He was right, though; Henry's army had been here longer, and was better armed than Richard's. Evans had no doubt been in contact with Stanley, seeking to turn him. The boy must have told his grandfather that William Stanley had escaped, by now. They would think that Stanley was free to make his own decision in regard to the battle.

Dresden had planned for that, though, and had already made his move. Stanley's army was vital, after all, to his own success.

"Did you find what I sent you for?" he asked suddenly, choosing to ignore his son's observations.

Sloan took a deep breath and paused for a moment before responding. "Sir Keeler of Spring Meadows has," he replied.

Dresden nodded his head, pleased at the news. This was what he had hoped for. "Then send for him."

Sloan left the tent and returned a moment later, followed by an aging knight.

"My Lord," Keeler said, bowing respectfully.

Dresden waved a hand magnanimously, accepted the man's bow as his due, and then gestured to the front of the tent. "I assume you brought me what I requested, sir knight," he said curtly. This was no time for gentle conversation, and he'd never cared for this particular man anyhow.

Sir Keeler paused for a brief moment, as though he disliked the question or answer, but then nodded. "Yes, my Lord."

"Show me!" Dresden demanded.

Keeler bowed once again before turning his back and whistling loudly. Within seconds, two guards appeared just outside the tent's entrance, holding a bound and gagged man under the arms. The man sagged in their hands, thin and dirty. They hadn't been gentle when they took him, Dresden saw, and the man looked worse now than he had several days earlier.

Dresden smiled, nodding, and turned to his son. "Sloan, make certain that Sir Keeler is well taken care of. Guards, leave this man with me, please."

The other men turned to go, leaving the prisoner in a crumpled heap on the floor, and Dresden stepped forward, a smile curving his lips. He couldn't help it. An hour earlier, all had seemed lost. Now he had a bargaining chip again, and it was a good one.

"Why Sir William Stanley," he drawled, reaching out with a toe to roll the man onto his back. "How very kind of you to join me again."

39

I awoke suddenly, to the sound of booming thunder in the distance. My mind stumbled at the thought, still hazy with sleep, and I frowned. Not thunder, that was wrong. It was something else, if only I could remember...

I shot up to a sitting position. *Not* thunder. Canon fire. Because we were in Bosworth, on the morning of the battle, going up against one of the most hateful people I'd ever met. Fighting for the fate of the world.

I gulped at the thought and turned, glancing around the tent. Paul and Reis were already awake, as were Tatiana and Katherine, and sun was shining through the entrance of the tent. It was here, then, the dawn. And that meant the moment of truth had finally arrived.

Before I could think any farther, Doc strode quickly into the room, his eyes flying around the small space. He shouted orders over his shoulder for Trigva to station two dozen soldiers around his tent, then pulled the curtains shut with a snap.

"My men have just captured two of Dresden's spies outside," he muttered. "Dresden is sending men after you, or me, or both of us." He moved toward my bed and pulled me out of it, shoving me toward a pile of clothes in the corner. "Get dressed, we must be prepared for anything."

"What?" I gasped. I had just woken up, and was still trying to fit the current version of reality into my head. This new information was more than I could process at the moment.

"After you? Why?" Paul asked, joining Doc at the table, where he'd set up camp.

"We're his ticket back," Doc answered. "Without Jason or me, he can't get out of this time period."

"Well…" I cut in, thinking back to what Dresden had told Tatiana and me. "He *could.* He just wouldn't know where he was going. Or when the trip was going to take place."

Doc nodded, his eyes gleaming. "Well he'll need to go quickly, either way. If he loses the battle – which we hope he will – he'll need to get out of Dodge before any of Henry's men kill him. After all, without Richard, he has no political protection here."

Paul whistled quietly. "That's heavy, Doc."

I snorted at his joke, though he looked dead serious, and continued with the train of thought. "Beyond that, if he could wipe Doc out of the picture, Henry would be at a disadvantage, and Richard would win the battle." I paused, watching Doc closely. "There are a number of reasons for Dresden to be after both of us."

"So you have to be even *more* careful, then," Tatiana concluded, stepping out of nowhere to join the group. She was wearing the same clothes from yesterday, but had taken a bath somewhere and looked better than the last time I'd seen her. I gave her a half-hearted smile of welcome, and turned back to Doc.

"So what do we do? What's the plan?"

Doc became all business at that, and nodded firmly. He took out his pocket watch and glanced at it, then looked at us. "Well people, within a couple of hours, this place is going to turn into a beehive of activity. This is probably the last time we'll be able to speak freely until after the battle. Things are going to get … intense."

We nodded, waiting for him to continue. I just hoped that he'd decide to let me take part – I had more information at my fingertips than he did, and better access to the stones. I didn't know how they would help me, but I knew that they *would.* And I didn't want to have to go behind Doc's back to do what I needed to do.

"The three of you will be staying with Reis here in the camp. Don't move. After the battle, I'll send for you…" Doc paused and shook his head. "If things go wrong and the battle does not go our way, you will have to count on Reis to take you to the stone."

I frowned at this, and opened my mouth to argue, but stopped at Tatiana's hand on my arm. Looking up, I caught her eye and saw her shake her head slightly, warning me against speaking. My mouth closed of its own accord and I nodded. Doc wasn't going to give his permission, no matter how much I argued with him. Better to save my breath and plan around that particular hiccup.

"After the battle, it'll be chaos," he was saying now. "It's always that way. Men will have lost their leaders and their direction, and will run amok. It will be incredibly dangerous. When the battle starts, hang back. Stay here, no matter what you see or hear! When it's over, I will come for you, if I can. If I cannot, Reis will take you to Abergavenny. You will go with him without argument, and go home. Forget that this ever happened. Understood?"

"But you'll win. Henry's army will win the battle, and you'll be with us. Right?" Paul asked suddenly.

Doc took a deep breath. "I'm not going to lie to you, Paul. With Lord Stanley on Dresden's side, it will be a toss-up. We may still have the weapons, but Dresden certainly has the men. It will be an even match, at best. I won't know how it's going to go until we're near the end. And by then it will be far too late to change anything."

He looked at each of us, then firmed his mouth and nodded as though he'd come to a decision. "You must all stay out of harm's way as much as possible. Reis, I'm counting on you to see them safely through this."

He turned to Reis, who nodded, and clasped him by the shoulder. Then he turned toward me, his eyes glimmering with unshed tears and words that would remain unsaid. Without speaking, he tipped his head to me, turned, and strode away.

"Well that was interesting," Paul muttered as we started at the space where Doc had been. I was speechless, my mind still reeling from what Doc had said, and couldn't quite come up with a response.

The reaction was clear in my mind, though – we couldn't sit around and watch Doc ride off into battle, casually waiting for it to be over. We had to do something.

Reis must have thought the same thing, because he barked with laughter and stepped quickly toward the tent's entrance. "Care to see the battle that will shape Western Europe for the next five hundred years or so?" he asked, parting the curtains. "Let's see if we can't find something to do while we … wait." He shot a grin in my direction and I grinned back, immensely glad to have him on my team.

The four of us pushed past him and gathered just outside the tent, gazing at the war camp beyond us. It had been busy before, but was now humming with activity. Doc – or his men – had left five large, beautiful horses standing with two squires just outside the tent, and we strapped our bags to them and mounted up. The squires disappeared immediately, leaving us conveniently to our own devices, and we turned back to the camp.

"I don't know about you guys, but I don't plan to stick around here and miss out on all the fun," Reis muttered. "Let's go." He charged forward, the four of us hot on his heels, galloping past knights on horseback, women carrying loaves of bread and buckets of water, and dozens of children running in and out of an endless crowd of soldiers and civilians alike. Everyone was making their way into the heart of Tudor's camp, for their own reasons. We rode quickly through and around them, doing our best to go unnoticed, and keeping a sharp eye out for Doc and his men at arms, who would certainly turn us around and send us back if they saw us.

Once we cleared the last of the tents, the mass of people began to lighten, and a view of the battlefield opened up in the valley below. The battle lines had already been drawn, with men on horseback traveling quickly to and from their respective encampments, in preparation of the coming battle. Groups of them stopped to talk to each other every so often, gesturing wildly in all directions and then splitting up and galloping away. I could only imagine the conversations going on – the stress of the coming battle, the question of what the enemy would do. The ever-present idea that many of these men wouldn't survive the day. The entire valley was in motion, the air around the men thick with anticipation.

The storm, which had brought down a torrent of rain the night before, had ventured eastward now, leaving only mud and low-lying clouds in its wake. It was cool, but not cold, and I wondered if there was such a thing as a perfect day for fighting. If there was, I supposed these conditions were as good as any.

From our vantage point, we could see Doc – as the Earl of Oxford – in the valley below, surrounded by the thousands of men and horses that made up the bulk of Tudor's army. To our left, well over a hundred banners decorated the slope leading into the valley itself, flowing into the basin in a virtual rainbow of colors. Each banner represented a different lord, I knew, and each would have with him his full array of knights, archers, and foot soldiers. There were hundreds of knights alone, already mounted up, the early morning light shooting sparks off their armor. Behind them stood their squires, ready to assist their masters with weapons and horses as necessary. And there must have been thousands of foot soldiers. These men, lacking the money for expensive armament, were dressed in leather for the most part, though some wore nothing more than heavily padded coats. They carried swords, axes, maces, lances, and heavy wooden stakes. The poorest soldiers carried nothing more than shovels and wooden clubs. A disadvantage, I thought, though getting hit in the head with a shovel would probably knock you out of the game just as much as getting hit in the face with a pole. My grandfather had gathered over fifteen hundred archers as well, and they stood behind everyone else, armed with 5-foot-tall bows and hundreds of arrows each.

All of these men stood, now, awaiting the order to march forward and place their lives on the line. To live or die, be captured or maimed, all to kill the enemies of their lords.

Across the field, a smaller group of men stood apart from this mob of soldiers. Only one banner flew there – a white standard, with a deep red rose embroidered in the center. There, then, was Henry Tudor. The man for whom this battle was fought. The man who must win it at all costs for the world to continue as we knew it.

I turned my eyes away from him and back to the scene before us. In an odd way, it was breathtakingly beautiful. The colors and the movement of horses and people, along with the suppressed excitement that filled the air, made me breathless with anticipation. I couldn't describe it, but my body was responding to the situation; something in the pit of my stomach knew that something big was about to happen. My instincts were screaming with readiness. I didn't know what I was going to do yet, but I was sure that I had to do *something*. There were too many lives riding on his battle for me to just sit back and watch.

The soldiers, knights, and archers were all beginning to line up now, getting ready for the first charge, and the valley echoed with the calls of both horses and men. Commanders barked orders from one end of the battlefield to the other, screaming at their men about positions, strategies, and targets. Calling out last-minute encouragements, shouting to their friends for what might be the last time. The cacophony was deafening, the voices of the men intense and battle ready.

Then a dead silence fell over the valley. My gut clenched tightly at the sudden lack of sound, and what little breath I had fled, leaving me silent as well.

Across from our elevated position, Richard's army began to gather atop the hill. They controlled the high ground then, giving them a clear advantage. I wondered fleetingly why Doc and Henry had relinquished this position. It would be a huge disadvantage during the battle, and could be the difference between victory and defeat. My stomach dropped into my feet. Surely Doc had known about the position beforehand. Why hadn't he accounted for this?

"Who's that?" Paul asked suddenly, pointing. I jumped, already tensed for the battle, and turned to see a large group of at least one hundred men on horseback standing on the hill to our right. My mind ran back to my notes, seeking the positions of the different groups, and I gulped.

"Those are Lord Stanley's knights," I answered quietly. "They stood on that hill and watched the battle."

"And we're hoping they do the same today," he guessed, his voice matching mine in intensity. I glanced at him, impressed with this more mature version of Paul, and nodded.

"If William's found his brother, Stanley will stay there, watching. If William *hasn't* found his brother, and Stanley joins Dresden…"

"And what, we're just counting on luck to be on our side?" he asked sharply. "Seems like a stupid plan, if you ask me."

"Why do you think we're up here, Paul?" Tatiana snapped, urging her horse forward to join the conversation. "This is the best vantage point. If – *when* something goes wrong, we move."

I grinned at her, thinking the same thing, and was about to answer when a roar from the valley interrupted me. My eyes flew downward, and then across to Richard's army, to see that the battlefield had erupted into motion. Richard's army was charging down the hill toward the men in the valley, the knights and foot soldiers screaming at the top of their lungs. In the valley, Doc's archers leaned forward as one, grabbed their first arrows, and loosed them into the charging army. Henry's knights and foot soldiers bounded forward, yelling defiance at Richard's men.

I gasped. The Battle of Bosworth had begun. My eyes flew to the ridge next to us, then, and I gasped again.

40

"Reis," I muttered, pointing toward the hill, "Stanley's men are forming up ranks. They're going to do more than just watch."

Reis' eyes flew to the men in question, scanning the group quickly and drawing conclusions as they went. "Damn," he muttered. "You're right."

"What's going on?" Katherine asked sharply. "Who are those men? What do they mean to do?"

"If they're forming ranks, they mean to charge," Tatiana whispered in reply. "They mean to enter the battle, on Dresden's side."

Suddenly the stone at the battlefield was with me, churning through my brain and feeding me information. Telling me what I'd already suspected, and adding to it with details I could never have known. I pulled my horse abruptly toward Reis, intent on the action I knew we had to take.

"William Stanley never made it back to his brother," I snapped. Reis looked at me, frowning, and I continued. "Reis, if he'd made it, Lord Stanley would be riding away from the battle! Instead, he's getting ready to join Richard. What do you think that *means*?"

"Where's William?" Tatiana asked, pulling up beside me. She was anxious for action, I saw, and ready to follow my lead. Regardless of where we were going.

"Dresden has him," I replied curtly, sure of the knowledge the stone was giving me. "Just over that ridge, in his camp. We have to go get him, and before Stanley's men charge. If we don't –" I looked over at Reis, trying to gauge his reaction.

"What, just ride into Dresden's camp, past his soldiers and canons and who knows what else, like it's nothing?" Paul squeaked. "How do you even know he's there?"

"Paul, weren't you just saying that sitting around was a stupid idea?" I snapped. My horse pranced under me, sensing my need for action, and my voice grew stronger with conviction. "William is the key to everything. Without him, Doc loses, and the world ends. I'm going in after the man. Are you guys coming or not?"

"I'll go with you," Katherine said confidently. I glanced at her, taking in her bright eyes and flushed cheeks, and nodded. The stones had led me to her for a reason; perhaps she was going to be an ally now, when I needed it most.

I turned back toward Reis, hoping to find another ally there. Hoping I wouldn't have to leave him behind. "Reis, we don't have much time. We have to go now, or it'll be too late. Once Stanley's forces join Richard's army, Tudor will be destroyed, and Doc will be killed."

"Are you sure about this, kid?" Reis shouted, gathering his reins.

"Beyond sure," I shouted back, trying to elevate my voice over the noise of the battle raging below us. "We're living history here, Reis, and if Stanley joins Dresden, history changes. We lose Doc, and we could lose the world." I paused, waiting for him to decide, then turned my horse back the way we'd come. Tatiana and Katherine followed suit, and I glanced back one last time. "Reis, make up your mind! We're going with or without you, but I'd rather have you on my team here!"

Reis growled deep in his throat, and legged his horse forward. Behind him, Paul fell into place. "Well if we're going to die, we may as well do it saving the world. Do you know how to get there?"

I couldn't help but grin at the question. The stone had told me exactly how to get there, and I was aching to go. "Better than that. I know a short cut that will take us around the battle and up behind their camp. We'll be there in no time. It might just be quick enough. Let's go!"

I spurred my horse forward, leading us eastward, away from Doc and the relative safety of his soldiers, and into the heart of Dresden's camp, praying that we would get there and back before Stanley made his move.

The Earl held his sword aloft, listening intently to the dull roar on the battlefield. It was time. Adrenaline coursed through his veins, readying his body for battle, and he wondered if he'd ever felt so alive. This was what it was like, then. A major battle, history riding the brink of change…

History. The future. The joy vanished from his face, to be replaced by a mask of grim murder and determination. This wasn't a battle he or the world could afford to lose.

He scanned the hill above him, looking for the familiar figure. There. Just to Richard's right, and dressed in his standard uniform of dark blue. Dresden. The man who was trying to change history. The man he'd come to stop.

The Earl of Oxford screamed with fury, declaring his intentions to the world, and dropped his sword. Around him, his men surged forward to battle.

I took the lead, feeling just as comfortable on the horse now as I did on my bike back home. We flew forward, bounding over the slopes of the ridge at an alarming rate of speed, racing toward the small path that would take us toward Dresden's camp. And William. I just hoped he was still alive. If he wasn't, we were going to have a big problem.

Below us, the battle raged, complete with the sounds of clashing iron, canon fire, and arrow flight. Men screamed in defiance and pain, coloring the air with their voices, and the horses matched them. The mass of life moved back and forth across the valley floor, marked by the pendants and flags of the lords and barons, like the tide rolling and crashing on the shore. I tried desperately to find Doc's banner, but gave it up for impossible when our own path turned and took us away from the valley.

Our mounts raced through the woods for several minutes, their bellies low to the ground with their speed. Then we were free of the tree line, and less than 50 feet from the river's edge. This was where we would cross, the stone told me – there was a turn here where the river was both shallow and narrow, offering easy passage. My horse trotted into the water, reading my thoughts, and made quick work of the crossing.

Within moments we were on the other side, and racing toward Dresden's camp. Our horses crested the shallow ridgeline that bordered the river, and we pulled to a sudden stop. Before us lay the tents, wagons, and flags of King Richard's camp.

"What's the plan?" Reis snapped, pulling abreast of me.

"You're the Navy SEAL here, Reis," I said, grinning. "Isn't infiltration and kidnapping more your line of work? And let's make it quick. We don't have a lot of time."

Reis grunted in response, but nodded. "Well I don't expect much in the way of guards or soldiers within the camp," he mused. "Most of them should be at the battle. Then again, Richard or Dresden – or both – may have held a group of soldiers in reserve. We won't know until we get in there. I'll go first. Jason, follow me as closely as you can and give me directions when you have them. Everyone else, stick close. Keep your eyes open and mouths shut." He looked around, and nodded at everyone's silence. "Once we grab the hostage, Jason takes point and I bring up the rear to make sure that no one follows us. Got it?"

Everyone nodded, intensely silent and ready for action. Without a word, Reis whirled and took off, straight toward the war camp before us.

41

Luck was on our side, at first. The people we came across weren't soldiers at all, but children playing a game that appeared to be a hybrid of tag and hide-and-seek. Several of the kids stopped to look at us, but within seconds they'd decided that we were uninteresting, and turned their attention back to the game at hand.

"Try to look as though you belong," Reis said, just loudly enough for all of us to hear. "Jason, where the hell are we going?"

I gulped; Richard's camp was a mirror image of Henry's, and just as confusing. Every tent and alley looked exactly the same, making it impossible to tell which way was forward and which was back. I panicked, thinking that we'd come to the wrong place, but settled when I felt the hum of the stone in my head. It knew where William was, and it wasn't thrown off by the confusing layout of the camp.

I listened closely, then pointed to two tents on the other side of a very large clearing. "The large one on the right, with the deep blue pendent, is Dresden's. That's where we'll find William," I said quietly. *Hopefully alive and capable of traveling,* I added silently. I hadn't said anything to the others, but the stone hadn't told me whether he was alive or not, and it was making me distinctly nervous. We needed him alert and ready to go if we were going to get to his brother in time.

We might already be too late, a voice whispered in my ear. I thrust it down, unwilling to consider the possibility, and moved forward after Reis.

The Earl felt like he'd been fighting for hours, though he'd yet to see any heavy action. He looked up from the man he'd just run through to see that the body of Richard's army had reached the base of the hill. Their numbers must have been cut significantly by the Earl's archers, but there would still be thousands of them. Far more men than the Earl had provided. Some of them would be armed with guns, though they would be able to fire only once. Still, with the number of extra men he had gathered on the road here, the Earl thought that Henry's army would hold them off for the time being. And he had a better working knowledge of the battle than anyone else. That, too, would be an advantage.

He turned at the sound of hoof beats to his left, and saw the French nobleman Philibert de Chandee, head of the French mercenaries, racing his way. Hopefully bringing good news, the Earl thought grimly; the battle was progressing as it should, for now, but he wasn't counting it a victory just yet. There were still too many things that could go wrong.

"Have you heard from our friends to the east?" de Chandee asked, nodding toward the hill on their right.

Stanley's army, the Earl thought. They hadn't heard from them yet, though Stanley hadn't joined the fray, either. Perhaps Jason had been right on that score, and William Stanley had made it to his brother's camp in time.

Remembering the man next to him, he shook his head once. "Nothing," he said curtly. "Perhaps they mean to simply watch the battle, then join the victors." *Please God,* he added silently.

De Chandee's mouth turned down at the idea of this unsportsmanlike behavior, and he shook his head as well. "I suppose we shall know soon enough, for the battle is moving quickly. It appears that you were right – Richard became impatient and charged, opening his left and right flanks. We've moved in to harry him on both sides, and leave the front to you and your men. We await your orders for anything further."

The Earl grimaced. Richard had been a fool, and no mistake. As long as Stanley stayed out of it… "Shore up the eastern flank," he barked, spurring his horse forward toward his knights. "And watch Stanley. I do not trust him, and we cannot afford his interference. Movement from him – on Richard's behalf – would turn the tide, and mean defeat."

He did not wait to hear de Chandee's response. His men needed him, and they could not afford to lose the front line of their battle.

We trotted toward the tent in question, taking care not to move too fast – or too slow – to appear casual. There were more people in this part of the camp, and several soldiers racing in and out of the area, but no one seemed to notice us. The camp was, in fact, relatively quiet. Eerily so. Our path was clear, but I couldn't help glancing over my shoulder from time to time, wondering if we were walking straight into a trap.

When we reached the tent, a soldier appeared out of nowhere and grabbed Reis' reins. "Who the hell are you lot?" he growled, moving his hand to the grip of his sword. "And what are you doing here?"

Reis looked down at the soldier, who was both shorter and broader than he, and grimaced with distaste. A moment later, he'd slid to the ground, brought his knee up into the soldier's groin, and wrapped both hands around his neck, pulling him down until the bridge of his nose met his other knee. He pulled the now-unconscious guard to the side of the tent, gesturing violently for us to move, and whispered for Katherine to stay put and watch the horses.

The rest of us ducked through the tent's opening and glanced swiftly around, searching for William. A large table, much like Doc's, occupied the center of the tent, along with several bulky chairs, a small bed in the rear, and one large chest that lay beside the bed. No William.

"Where is he?" Paul asked nervously.

I closed my eyes, reaching for the stone, and asked the same question. The answer was there before I'd finished my request, and my eyes flew open.

"In the chest," I muttered, darting forward. Throwing the lid up, I found Sir William Stanley on his back, gagged, with his legs and hands bound in front of him. His eyes were open and alert, I saw, but held a note of warning I hadn't seen there before.

"Help me!" I shouted in a whisper, leaning over to remove the rag stuffed in his mouth. As I pulled it free, William took a deep, gasping breath.

"Thank Heaven, you've rescued me again," he said, his voice hoarse. "We must flee, and quickly."

"I couldn't agree more," I answered, pulling the man from the chest and cutting his ties with my pocket knife. "We need to get you to your brother. He's about to join Richard and destroy what's left of Tudor's army."

"My brother would never be so foolish as to side with Dresden and Richard, no matter my position," William said. Then the color washed from his face, the joy replaced by a look of utter betrayal and shock. I didn't have to turn around to know that we were trapped.

"Your brother," a cold, familiar voice said smoothly, "will do exactly as he is told."

A chill ran down my spine as my brain supplied the name of the speaker, and I turned slowly. Reis stood at the ready with his assault rifle raised, but I could already see that it would do little good. Eight large, fully armed men filled the entrance of the tent, led by one of the last people I'd wanted to see again.

"Brother," Tatiana murmured, glaring at the dark-haired boy in front of us.

He shot her a quick look, indicating that he still didn't believe that particular story, and grinned nastily. "My father told me to expect your arrival. I must admit, though, that I did not believe him. I told him that you'd be mad to come into this camp, no matter who we held prisoner. And yet here you are, ready to die."

"You'll go first," Reis replied in a confident, lethal voice. He flipped the safety off his rifle and adjusted the weapon on his shoulder.

"Perhaps, but all of you will perish in turn," Sloan replied apathetically. Only then did I notice that five of the soldiers had already drawn their bowstrings, each pointing an arrow at one of us. For some reason, two of the soldiers had been assigned to me. I knew Reis was good, but there was no way he could gun them all down, not before they shot us. My thoughts flew back to an earlier situation, and I kicked myself again for the lack of armor. Of all the stupid, unprepared moves, and with the fate of the world hanging in the balance, no less.

"We appear to be at an impasse," Reis said quietly. "How are your negotiation skills?"

Sloan's grin widened. "Drop your weapon."

"That's not much of a negotiation," Reis replied.

"I give you my word that you shall live. But that is the only thing I shall grant you," Sloan replied. "And my word only stands if you drop your weapon. Now."

"Still sounds like an unfair deal to me," Reis grunted. He tightened his grip on the stock of his rifle, hunching down into a shooting stance.

"So be it," Sloan snarled, throwing himself to the ground at our feet. "Kill them all!"

A shot sounded out from Reis's rifle, and Paul screamed. The archers released their grips on the strings of their bows, loosing their arrows in our direction with sharp twangs. Sloan looked up, his face anxious, his eyes full of something I couldn't identify.

With my last thought, I reached out for the stone, asking – begging – for it to stop the arrows, the bullet, the deaths. Asking it to stop time itself.

Suddenly, and quite to my surprise, it did.

42

The Earl looked to the right, now, where the Earl of Norfolk would strike with his army. Henry wouldn't have known of that attack, but the Earl did, and they were ready. He had sent Phillibert de Chandee and his men to that flank, reinforcing it by twofold, and they would withstand the attack. In order to do this, of course, he had all but stripped his left flank, relying fully on the men there to maintain their position.

As long as no one else entered the battle, this would mean their victory. Richard was sending his last surprise weapon forward, and the Earl already had his answer prepared.

He stood up in his stirrups just in time to see the two forces come together. They met with the impact of thousands of horrific car crashes. Screams of terror, pride, and battle lust erupted simultaneously, filling the air with raw emotion. Soon the horses were screaming as well.

Suddenly a voice rang through the noise. "Raise shields!"

The old warrior bought his shield up and over his head, just in time to feel the thrust of an arrow as it punched through the heavily decorated wood. He looked up to see its iron head protruding through the thin bronze shell of the shield.

"Close ranks!" he shouted, gathering his reins. He looked to the side to see Trigva crouched under his own shield, grinning from ear to ear.

"It's time to fight!" the soldier shouted, his smile growing broader.

The Earl grinned back, then lowered his shield and looked around to find his personal guard. "Attack!" he screamed.

He and his men thundered forward, swords raised. This was it, he thought. Now he was putting everything on the line. As he surged forward, one last thought flew through his brain. If Stanley's army stayed out of the battle, Henry's army would take the day. If they didn't, it would mean the end. Of everything.

The world didn't actually stop, but for a split second I thought it did. Arrows hung motionless in mid-flight, the deafening noise of Reis's rifle disappeared, and friend and enemy alike stood frozen in place. My eyes flew around the room, trying to make sense of this strange phenomenon, and I ducked automatically, coming to a crouch in front of William. A moment later I remembered what I'd done – asked the one stone in the area to hold time for me. It would seem that it was doing its best.

But the pressure to hold that flow was coming down like a tidal wave, threatening to crack the stones themselves, and my body with them. We couldn't hold it for long; the weight was already crushing my self-discipline, pressing on my mind like an entire ocean's worth of water. I bent farther to the ground under that weight, gasping for breath, and trying to recall who I was and why I was there. When I found the answer, I grasped it with both hands and held to it with all my will. The stones had combined to give me the largest gift they had, and I wasn't going to waste it.

It took every ounce of will power I had to start moving again. Slowly – so slowly – I saw my hand reach out to grab William's wrist and free him of the time constraint I'd placed on the world. He flinched, as if waking from a dream, and came suddenly back to life.

"What … what's happening?" he whispered in disbelief.

"No time," I groaned out, sliding past him. "Move."

I pressed toward my friends, trying to keep the pressure at bay. If I released it entirely, I knew that the force of time would slide out of my control. Freeing me from the pain, but also sacrificing what little chance we had of escape. Maintaining control – using those precious seconds – was the most difficult thing I'd ever done, but it was also our only hope.

I felt rather than saw William move into lock step behind me as I plodded my way toward Paul. I reached out and touched his arm, knowing it would free him, and shook off his question. I didn't have time to explain, or the strength to do so. I could only hope that he would follow my lead as William had done. I willed my way to the front of the tent, where Reis and Tatiana stood, and reached for them with the last of my strength, crying out as I did so. When I saw them come to life I fell to the ground, fighting to keep my control, and knowing that I couldn't do it for much longer.

"I can't hold it off much longer," I gasped. "Please, hurry."

Someone – probably Reis – picked me up like a rag doll and carried me out of the tent. I was thrown onto a horse, with someone behind me, and told to hold on. Suddenly we were moving, racing away from that place, with our lives somehow intact and our mission complete. I opened my eyes for a second, to see the ground rushing along below us, and closed them again. Then the entire world blurred and went dark.

Activity to the Earl's right caught his eye and he paused in his charge to glance at the hill above them. Several lightly armored soldiers, mounted atop small, fleet horses, raced toward Thomas Stanley's banner. Moments later they had turned and were racing back from whence they'd come. The Earl's stomach sank. Stanley was receiving messengers, then, and they weren't from him. That could only mean one thing.

Moments later, his fears were confirmed as Stanley's knights begin to form ranks. His forces were no longer going to simply watch the battle. They were readying themselves to join the fray, and if communications were open between Richard and Stanley, that meant that Tudor was out of the mix.

He turned to watch as his army's right flank pushed off yet another attack by Norfolk's men. If left to their own devices, the Earl was sure that his force could defeat Richard, but now … with Stanley preparing to strike, the odds were becoming too monumental to overcome.

"My Lord, are you seeing this?" Trigva asked, his horse abruptly drawing up beside the Earl's. The man was looking up at the hill, and could only mean one thing.

The Earl of Oxford looked over at his closest ally and nodded. "Stanley's army," he noted grimly. Then he firmed his shoulders, drawing them back and raising one eyebrow at his friend. "But we will not forfeit the day yet. Come! If we are to die today, we shall do it together, and we shall take as many of them with us as we can!" He lifted his sword and spurred his horse forward into the crush of men and horses, intent on doing everything he could while his life still belonged to him.

"Jay … Jason, can you hear me?"

I heard the voice and felt the jolts of pain as my body jerked back and forth to the rhythm of the horse running full tilt underneath us. Forcing my eyes open, I glanced behind me to see Reis, his hands wrapped around my waist to hold me in place in the saddle.

"Are you with us?" he shouted, squeezing me tighter in concern.

The cloud in my head began to lift then, and I remembered where we were and – more importantly – the trouble we were in. I glanced behind my body guard, and then quickly turned back toward the front. We had been trying to deliver Sir William in time to prevent his brother's attack on Henry Tudor and my grandfather. Now it seemed that we were also trying to outrun several of Dresden's soldiers. Reis and I were bringing up the rear, as we had the best weapons. In front of us, William clung to Tatiana's waist as she led the way for Paul, Reis, and I.

"How far out are we?" I cried, loud enough for Reis to hear.

Reis ignored my question. "Can you take the reins?" he asked instead.

I reached out and grabbed them, leaning over the horse's neck for better balance and protection. Whatever Reis was about to do, it would be easier for him if I was out of the way. He shifted his body to reach behind his back, and had the rifle in front of him a moment later, up and ready to fire.

Our horse leapt over a log that sat in the center of our path at that point, nearly knocking us both off its back, and I clutched at the reins for dear life. Reis grunted and worked to recover his balance, then turned in one quick movement so that his back was pressed against mine, the rifle pointed back toward the men chasing us. Without warning, he pulled the trigger.

Several loud shots ripped through the valley and rung in my ears as Reis tried desperately to slow our pursuers. I took a moment to look back, and saw that not one but two soldiers had toppled from their mounts, their lifeless bodies strewn across the ground.

Several more had taken their place.

I counted nine of them before I turned my attention forward again to concentrate on the path in front of us. I wasn't worried about guiding the horse; the animal was running full-out toward the battlefield, terrified of the gunshots and men behind us. Tatiana raced along in front of us, choosing the smoothest path and protecting William as best she could. Paul rode beside her, clutching the reins of the two extra horses, and glancing back at me now and then.

Something about that struck me as odd, and I frowned, racking my brain for the source. Now wasn't the time to worry about extra horses, but why –

Suddenly I realized why it was bothering me. As soon as I did, I was shocked that I hadn't noticed it before. Paul, Tatiana, and William rode with us. Katherine did not.

"Where's Katherine?" I asked desperately, turning in every direction in search of her.

"She's gone!" Reis shouted back, turning his head to be heard over the wind rushing past us.

"What?" I shouted, shocked. "Where is she? Is she dead?" The thought burned a hole right through my heart, and I thought suddenly of the way her eyes had lit up when we'd decided to bring her. Surely we hadn't brought her all this way – saved her from those men in the stable – to lose her to Dresden's soldiers?

Reis turned at that, reached around me, and grabbed the reins back. He leaned forward and spurred our horse harder, so that we leapt forward into the river.

"I don't think so, but –"

"But what!?" I screamed.

"I didn't know she wasn't with us until a moment ago, Jason. We rushed out of that tent when you passed out, and didn't look back. She must not have been with the horses, or she'd be with us now. And we don't have time to go back and get her!" He screamed his answer and held me steady while our horse found its footing on the shore and drove up the hill toward the small ridge, carrying us finally into the woods. I gasped, trying to think through the situation and understand it. She must have been frozen, like the others, and without me to wake her … We'd left her standing, vulnerable and alone and terribly deserted, for Sloan to find. My gut clenched at the thought and I was about to speak again when we broke free of the trees.

Below us, the battle was still raging, with Henry's rear line about 100 feet in front of us. Our pursuers broke off and raced for their leader, and I breathed a quick sigh. Safe for the moment, then, and amongst friends.

Then I saw Stanley's army. They had formed ranks and were on the march, headed straight for the center of Doc's right flank. They were close, though, not 30 paces from us, and we would reach them in moments, with William in hand. This was is it, then. Either our plan was going to work, and we would stop Stanley from attacking, or the battle for the crown would favor Richard, and ensure Dresden's victory. And if that happened…

Tatiana threw me one quick glance, then galloped forward toward Stanley's flag bearers.

43

Lord Dresden had felt fear before, but not like this. The clash of horses, men, and steel, mixed with the screams of death, overwhelmed him, the noise threatening his hold on his temper. And things were not going well. Richard had been a fool, jumping the gun with his sudden need to charge, and had opened up their army to wave after wave of attacks from Evans' men. They were weakening quickly, with Norfolk's men doing little good, thanks to Evans' advance knowledge of the battle. Stanley's men were going to have to make their move quickly, or all would be lost.

Dresden scanned the horizon, wondering desperately where the men in question were, and noticed several unexpected horses racing in his direction. His son, he realized, riding at a frantic pace and wearing a mask of worry and failure.

"What?" Dresden roared, assaulting his son before the horse had come to a complete stop. Sloan's face fell, then turned quickly to stone. A defensive measure, Dresden thought, against the news he was about to deliver.

"They have escaped," the boy answered quickly, keeping his eyes and voice steady. "But we have another prisoner."

"Is it William Stanley?" Dresden snapped, hardly daring to hope. He couldn't understand how his fool of a son had let Jason Evans and his friends escape, but if he'd managed to retain William Stanley –

"No, sir, another," Sloan replied, dashing Dresden's hopes.

Dresden roared in frustration and turned his horse sharply toward the hill to the east. To his surprise, Stanley's men were standing ready, on the brink of their attack. He smiled, his eyes running from Stanley down to where Evans fought with his men.

"Well well," he murmured. "Perhaps the brother's life was not as important as I had thought." The moment of truth was upon them, if that was true, and it was finally time to end Evans' life and take the next steps in his plan.

"Stop!" I screamed, dismissing Katherine from my mind as best I could. I saw William waving his arms frantically as Tatiana urged their horse toward the center of Stanley's formation. There, between a dozen mounted knights, a white pendent with a blue stripe marked Thomas Stanley's position. The man we'd come to see.

I glanced to my right to see Paul's horse pull up beside us, and we pushed forward behind Tatiana and William. She'd been stopped by several knights, who were busy questioning her closely, their eyes and voices rough, and their actions rougher. One had his sword out, the tip pressed to her chest.

"These men switch their alliance as easily as the wind changes direction," I remembered Doc saying. "Blood doesn't always prevail when land, money, and power are on the line." I gulped at the thought, and hoped desperately that we'd guessed right. An awful lot was riding on Stanley doing the right thing – including Doc's life – but William being free might not alter his brother's move against Henry Tudor. Not if Dresden had offered him enough.

"Thomas, it is I, your brother! Let us through!" William shouted, leaning past Tatiana and trying to stand up in the stirrups, to be both seen and heard. He knew the risks of failure here, and it colored is voice.

Instead of responding, though, the knights around the pendant closed ranks to form an even tighter knot of men, to better protect their leader. They turned toward us, bristling with swords, lances, and arrows.

"Stop, you bloody fools, it is I, William!"

I looked past the knights in front of Tatiana, and the two other knights who flanked our position, and felt a knot of ice form in the pit of my stomach. Beyond them, an army every bit as large as Henry's stood at the ready, waiting to march forward and end Henry Tudor's chances. And William was getting no response from his brother's guard. It wasn't working.

"Robert, raise your weapon and let us through!" William demanded, his voice ragged with tension.

Finally, the man in front of him raised his visor, running his eyes down over William's face and body, and then back up again. He stared for several seconds, while the army behind him began to march forward, and I held my breath. *Please, please,* I begged silently, praying to whoever would listen for this man to believe William and take him to his brother. The guard – with Sir Stanley at its center – was beginning to move, and soon it would be far too late. After a moment, though, whoever I'd been praying to heard me, and the knight's face broke into a broad, joyous grin.

He shouted something unintelligible and the group of knights behind him paused, then broke apart. A knight I hadn't seen yet emerged, arrayed in shining armor and an intricately designed helmet, and moved forward. He held one hand up, and the army bearing down on us stopped sharply.

Only then did the new knight raise his visor, to expose an older, more worn version of William's face. "By God in heaven, you're alive!" Lord Thomas Stanley muttered, his face displaying shock, dismay, and then relief in equal measures. "How on earth have you broken free?"

He dropped off his horse and strode forward, dragging William from behind Tatiana and hugging him fiercely. "We thought you dead, or worse, and had all but given up hope," he continued, his voice hoarse with emotion.

William returned his embrace, but then pulled back. "I was nearly dead when this boy and his friend found me," he replied quickly. "The grandson of the Earl of Oxford, Thomas, and I owe him a debt of gratitude and honor. Now please, in God's name, stop this madness, for I cannot allow you to join Richard, and his devil Lord Dresden!"

Thomas Stanley paused, considering his brother's words, and I held my breath. We had brought him his brother, and freed him from Dresden's hold, but would it be enough? Would he pull his men back? Or would he move forward anyhow, and kill our hope of victory?

"Brother, you do not know what you ask," he murmured. "Dresden is far more powerful than I would have anticipated, and if we stand against him and he wins this battle –"

"He *won't* win, brother," William interrupted. "I am assured of it, by men from the Earl of Oxford's camp. He has … incredible power at his fingertips. Divine guidance in his bid for victory. Besides, I have never known you to bow to another man's wishes. Why should Dresden be any different?" He glared into his brother's eyes, and I willed the older man to accept both the vague statement and the challenge.

Lord Stanley frowned at this, but finally nodded, grinning fondly at his brother. "Your will be done then, brother," he shouted, clapping William on the shoulder. "For you are right – I do not believe in Dresden's war, and had no wish to fight for him. Your life alone secured my cooperation. Now that you are free, I think this Dresden needs no more of my help. In fact, I believe that our mother may have more need of us than anyone on this battlefield."

Laughing, the two men turned away, leaving the rest of us blinking at this fairly anticlimactic finish to our mission. I could hardly believe that it was over, and so quickly. All of our planning, all of the racing around, hiding, kidnapping … and this was it? We'd won, this easily? Suddenly, though, a buzzing filled my ears, followed by a voice.

Look behind you. I felt rather than heard the command inside my head, and turned to look past Reis, down the hill toward King Richard's lines. I caught a glimpse of fair hair, followed by a frightened face, and my momentary sense of relief fled.

"Reis, can I borrow your binoculars?" I asked, honing in on the small party of men gathered just behind Richard's archers.

Reis handed me his field glasses and turned to see what I was looking at. I lifted the binoculars slowly and adjusted the focus, already knowing exactly what I'd see. My heart rose into my throat to choke me as I found the face I'd come to know so well over the last three days.

"Katherine. Dresden has her," I whispered, handing the field glasses back to Reis. He glanced at me, then put the glasses quickly to his own eyes, focusing on where I had pointed.

"Oh my God," he muttered, aghast.

I nodded. "My thoughts exactly. And one guess where he's taking her."

"Well we already knew we had to stop him, right?" Tatiana muttered suddenly, appearing at my elbow. "This is just one more reason. We've saved the battle. Now let's go save history. And our friend."

She took off, and we raced after her. I took a deep breath and let the stones' influence take hold of my mind. I would need even more guidance now than I had before. We'd saved the battle, indeed, but our mission wasn't over … not by a long shot.

44

"He's dead!" one of Richard's men screamed as he charged toward Dresden. "The Duke of Norfolk is dead!"

Dresden glanced from his position to the battlefield below, and saw that the boy was right. Norfolk's standard had gone down, trampled by the men and horses around him.

"Damn," he breathed quietly. The man had been their second best chance. Their surprise weapon, so to speak. He'd hoped that in the rush of preparing, Evans and his other commanders would have overlooked him. The last charge had proven him wrong, but he'd still hoped that the man would do *something* helpful. He certainly hadn't expected him to die without accomplishing anything.

Dresden shook his head, frustrated. The guns would have decided the battle, if he'd had time to produce more of them. But Evans had pressed the battle, and Dresden's own men hadn't had as many guns as he'd hoped. They had given Richard's army some advantage, but it had been short lived, and hadn't broken Henry's army the way it should have. Evans had prepared his men, and they'd stood by him. Now he was leading them forward, slowly and decisively breaking through Richard's defenses.

As far he could see, the battle was already over. Stanley's men had not shown, though they'd looked ready enough, and Richard's army had no other forces for the field. The day was nearly finished. And that meant it was time to make his personal exit. As he turned to flee, however, a group of war horses galloped up, skidding to a stop in front of him and blocking his escape.

King Richard's stallion reared up and screamed, kicking mud and dirt over Dresden and his mount. The king was flanked by over a dozen of his prized knights, each armed and ready for battle. They wore full suits of armor and helmets, and each bristled with weapons. The king was equally impressive, his armor and shield bearing the white rose of York. He was as strong and ruthless as the storybooks said, and intent on his rule. Dresden had worked to control and harness that anger for the last two years, to use it for his own purposes. Here on the battlefield, however, his control was beginning to slip. Had slipped, if he was being honest, at the start of the battle, when Richard had sent his men forward rather than waiting. He drew his lips back in an imitation of a respectful smile and bowed slightly, trying to hold his temper for one more conversation.

"Your Grace, you should not be this close to the fighting," he murmured.

"Lord Dresden," the king snarled, "I am here to ensure that I keep my crown. It appears that your alliance with Lord Stanley has failed, as have your fiery weapons. Tell me, *Lord,* what exactly have you done for me on this battlefield?" He was angry, and openly blaming Dresden for the turn of the tide, then.

Far past time to leave, Dresden realized, amending the earlier thought. Things were not going according to plan, and this scene was falling apart more quickly than he'd anticipated. He had known that Henry's victory would necessitate escape, but now he began to wonder if Richard was a danger to him as well. He had led the York family through fear and intimidation for over seventeen years, but it seemed Richard had suddenly found his backbone.

He bowed, thankful for his earlier planning. He had an escape route in place, though it galled him to have to use it. Now it looked as though that planning might save his life, and that of his son.

"Your Grace, look," one of Richard's knights said suddenly, pointing toward the easternmost part of the battlefield. Richard turned his attention from Dresden, releasing the other man to breathe more freely.

"It's Henry Tudor's standard. He and his personal envoy have separated themselves from the Earl of Oxford's main force!" the soldier said excitedly.

Richard nodded once and smiled, then glanced at Dresden. "We finish this battle ourselves, men," he said, pulling his sword from its scabbard and raising it aloft. "Follow me!" He and his men bounded forward, racing toward Henry Tudor's standard bearer and what they believed would be a victory.

Dresden watched the man go, shaking his head. After all his work, after all he'd sacrificed and done for that man, he was going to throw it away. It would play out exactly as it did in the history books. Richard would die in battle, trying to fight Henry in hand-to-hand combat, and Henry would retrieve the crown himself, from the ground where Richard fell.

"Fool," he muttered angrily.

"We must join him!" Sloan interrupted, his horse dancing under him, his eyes full of glory and battle lust.

"No!" Dresden snarled. He grabbed Sloan's reins and jerked. "You'll stay with me."

"But we have Tudor, and this battle will soon be over!" Sloan stared at his father, his face a mixture of confusion and disgust.

"This battle is already decided," Dresden snapped. He spun his horse around, forcing Sloan's to follow.

"What about the Earl of Oxford?" Sloan yelled in desperation.

Dresden looked at the girl, who sat prisoner in front of one of his soldiers. He turned to study the hill where Stanley's pendent flew, and saw Jason and his daughter Tatiana in the distance. They were watching him. He could feel it. After a moment, they broke into a run, heading straight for him.

He looked back at the girl, who sat stiff and terrified in front of the soldier, and then addressed his son. "We do not need to go after him. Jason Evans will do just as well, and he's coming after *us*. For her. Now move!"

The Earl of Oxford, covered in sweat, mud, and blood, accepted a hand from one of his soldiers. He stood, doing his best to dust himself off, and looked around the field. He'd lost two of his finest horses during the course of the battle, but he'd been lucky. The truth was that both horses had lost their lives defending him, and he was still alive because of them.

Suddenly his lieutenant was by his side, shaking him vigorously. "My Lord, they're leaving!" Trigva shouted, pointing up at the hill side to the east.

The Earl straightened his back and forgot the pain in his right leg as he followed Trigva's gesture. The man was right; Stanley's army had not only stopped marching, but was now turning and beginning to make its way back up the hill. Away from the battle. At the same time, Norfolk's third attack faltered, as if the wind had been released from their sails. Looking to that side, the Earl saw that Norfolk's standard had gone down, the men around it retreating hastily. He was dead, then. The Earl looked up, meeting Trigva's eyes, and gave him half a smile. No one said anything, but the experienced men on the field exchanged long, meaningful glances. The battle was all but over.

The Earl looked again to Stanley's army, thanking heaven that the man had turned back. As his eyes ran over his color guard and through his knights, he spotted a figure he recognized. Gasping, he looked again. It was definitely Jason – he'd recognize the boy anywhere. And he looked to have his friends – and that body guard – with him. What on earth was the boy doing?

Suddenly Jason and his friends broke into a gallop, racing straight for the battlefield.

45

We thundered toward the other side of the valley, where I'd last seen Dresden, Sloan, and Katherine. I'd taken my own horse back from Paul when we dropped William off with his brother, and rode on my own now, ducking down over her neck and urging her ahead of the others. The battle was still trickling along in the valley below, but I thought I knew how it would end. Doc's forces had been gaining ground throughout the morning, Stanley was out of it, and there was only one reason for Dresden to be hightailing it out of there – he knew that Richard was going to lose.

As far as I was concerned, though, the battle was just starting. Tatiana was right – it all started and ended with Dresden. I'd stood there and listened to his plans for our world, and I wasn't about to let him get away. No matter what Doc said about it. That man had to be stopped. I just had to find a way to do it.

We pushed our horses harder, anxious to get across the valley before anyone stopped us. It almost worked.

We were halfway across the high plain when a tremendous roar went up from the men on the battlefield. I risked a quick glance downward to see Henry's standard held aloft, the men around it cheering. Richard's standard was nowhere to be seen. Henry had won, then, and history held. For now. I started a small prayer of thanks, but the words died on my lips when I noticed a group of men racing toward us. My grandfather rode in the lead.

"Damn," I muttered. I wasn't sure what I had hoped for, but avoiding this fight had certainly been on the list.

Reis, Paul, Tatiana, and I pulled to a stop as Doc and his men approached, and I stared at my grandfather with a mixture of shock and awe. Patches of dried blood covered the right side of his face and his pants were torn in several places, revealing several large wounds and a gash that looked quite serious. Blood dripped from his boots, and his sword was covered in red. Trigva rode beside him, covered in gore and looking slightly more cheerful than usual.

My grandfather – seemingly oblivious to all of these factors – wasted no time with polite conversation. "I see you chose to join the battle after all," he snapped, looking me up and down. "Though you seem to have won out with Lord Stanley, and at least your were not hurt. Come! We are running out of daylight." He ended this somewhat odd speech abruptly, pulling his horse's head to the side and peeling away. Expecting to be followed without question.

But he was going the wrong way, headed toward Abergavenny, rather than Dresden. So here was the confrontation I'd hoped to somehow avoid. And it was going to have to be quick. The stone was telling me that we didn't have much time.

"Wait!" I shouted, listening intently to the voice in my head. The stone was speaking to me more easily now, as if we'd build a connection that couldn't be severed. And it was insistent. "You're going the wrong way!" I declared.

Doc turned back, a scowl on his face. "Jason, I've let you run off on your own long enough," he snapped. "Now is not the time to question me. We're going to Abergavenny, and that's final."

"Doc, that stone isn't there anymore! You'll travel to Abergavenny and find yourself trapped, and we don't have time for that!" I yelled, hoping that this prospect would at least give him pause.

Doc growled at me and ignored the warning, spurring his horse away from my group.

I held my ground. "Listen to me!" I screamed. I was right – I could feel it. The stone at Abergavenny was ... well, there was something wrong with it. Something I couldn't identify. Its hum was a faint echo, almost completely gone, and virtually overshadowed by the stone that was *here*. On this very battlefield.

He paused again and turned, his face angry.

"The stone at Abergavenny is gone, Doc. There's something wrong with it. Can't you feel that? Can't you feel the absence?"

He stared at me for a moment, then blinked slowly. "Jason, I don't have time for these games," he said finally. "We ride for Abergavenny, and I don't want to hear another word about it."

I screamed at him then. I couldn't help it. He was riding for a stone that had been moved, and – worse – letting Dresden escape in the process. Just as he had planned. And just as Tatiana and I had discussed.

I pulled my horse around, scanning the landscape desperately for the man I sought. My grandfather might be willing to let Dresden go, but I'd heard his plans – seen the madness in his eyes – and I wasn't taking any chances. We had just under an hour before the window opened, and that gave me time to find him and stop him. He had a stone here, and I was willing to bet he was riding for it now.

Suddenly my eyes found Dresden and his men thundering away, across the plateau that led from the valley. Beyond them, I could see Dresden's camp, his personal tent … and a wagon that was alarmingly familiar.

"Oh my God," I muttered. "That overbuilt wagon. *That's* where the stone is." I put my heels to my horse's sides and she shot forward, reading my thoughts. Paul, Reis, and Tatiana fell in beside me, as I had hoped, and we raced toward Dresden. Behind us, shouts of outrage indicated – I hoped – that my grandfather and his men followed.

"What the hell are you talking about?" Tatiana yelled, ducking low over her horse. "Where are we going?"

"After Dresden!" I shouted back. "He has a stone here, and he's heading straight for it!"

"Stone?" Paul asked from my other side. "Where? How?"

"He's been traveling with the stone all along! It's under the wagon he uses. It's ridiculously heavy, over built so he can tow the stone around! Why didn't I realize that before? He's brought his ticket out here! And he's planning on taking Katherine with him. We have to get there before he leaves!"

We tore across the battlefield, weaving in and out of the traffic. Many of the men who had been fighting were now lying strewn across the ground, wounded or dead, while others were gathering their things – or the valuables of their fallen comrades – and moving off. Horses, armor, and weapons littered the ground, making the battlefield a virtual minefield of sharp weapons and traps. We rode carefully, but as quickly as we could, intent on making it to the other side. No one spared a glance for our group, now composed of Paul, Reis, Tatiana, Doc and his six Vikings, and me.

Ahead of us, I could see that Dresden and his men had reached the wagon, hitched horses to it, and taken off again. They were moving it. Towing the stone toward an old abbey in the distance. But they were moving more slowly than we were, now, and I didn't think they'd have time to unhitch the stone and make the jump before we got there. The stone itself told me that we still had twenty-four minutes before the next window opened.

I could only pray that it was right.

46

It took several minutes to reach our destination. I pulled my horse to a sliding stop in front of the abbey and looking around, panting. There were six buildings here – four made of stone and two made of wood, and ranging in size from a three-car garage-sized building to a large three-story tower, roughly the size of our high school gymnasium back home. The buildings sat around a large courtyard with a small, overgrown cemetery. The entire place was deserted, and looked like it'd been that way for a very long time.

"Horses," Paul muttered suddenly, pointing to the right. I glanced in that direction and gulped. Five horses stood lazily in the shade of the largest building, grazing. Dresden was here, then, somewhere, and so were his men. The wagon – and its precious cargo – was nowhere to be seen.

"And where are the riders?" Reis muttered, glancing from one end of the courtyard to the other. "In the church?"

I glanced down at my pocket watch and shook my head. Eighteen minutes. We needed to get moving. "The stone's on the other side of the abbey, right behind the tower. That's where we'll find Dresden. The quickest way to get there is right through the front door," I replied.

"Through the building?" Paul yelped. "Isn't that a bit chancy? You know, in terms of traps and such?"

"He's right, Jason," Reis agreed. "Can we go around?"

"Not a chance," I snapped. "There's a marsh with an armada of thorn bushes between us and the tower. We'd never get through in time." I was already moving toward the church in question, unwilling to waste time. The stone was throwing me information more quickly than I could take it in, and it was taking everything I had to maintain my focus on the real world. Dresden had Sloan and Katherine near the stone, and was getting ready to jump. The stone was … unhappy with the situation.

Reis' hand shot out to stop me. "Well then I'm going first. Doc, you bring up the rear. Leave your men here to guard our backs. If Dresden gets out, orders are to shoot to kill. Got it?" Reis glanced at the Vikings and got rough nods of consent, then glanced back at me. "Okay, kid, let's go. And keep your eyes open for anything that looks wrong."

We darted between the granite statues and tombstones of the cemetery like we were in an obstacle course, ducking down behind them whenever we could. If archers were trying to target us, the last thing we wanted to do was make it easy for them. Within twenty seconds we'd made it to the base of the stone steps that led into the church. Reis looked around to make sure we were all still in tow, then sprinted up the stairs and leaned against one of the two doors leading into the church's foyer.

We followed his lead without discussion. Reis dropped to his knees against the door and looked at me, motioning to his wrist. 'How much time?' he mouthed.

My eyes dropped to the watch in my hand. This operation was taking longer than it should. 'Ten minutes,' I mouthed back, hoping we didn't have far to go. The stone *felt* close, but with my newly sensitive connection to it, I couldn't be sure whether this was a physical fact.

Reis nodded at my time estimate and leaned around the door to peer inside. A second later he pulled his head sharply back out. An arrow came screaming through the doorway – right where his head had been – and lodged itself in one of the apple trees planted several feet from the base of the church.

Before I'd had time to process this action, Reis had dropped farther down and thrown himself through the two double doors, leveling his handgun as he dove and releasing several rounds into the church. He picked himself up, took a knee, aimed, and fired three more shots into the building. For several seconds, no one moved or said a word.

Then Reis stood back up, positioning himself several feet inside the door, and waved us into the building without looking back. When we were inside, he plunged forward into the church's interior.

I glanced around, looking for the archer and any other enemies. For some reason the stained glass windows inside the foyer were covered in red cloth, making the interior difficult to see. Unfortunately, we were still able to the see the carnage that must have taken place moments before we arrived. The abbey hadn't been used by the church for some time, but a building with a working roof always has a use, and this one had become a home. Blankets and fire wood littered one corner of the church, and several bodies lay across the floor, riddled with arrows – commoners, and unarmed.

"Oh no," Tatiana whispered.

"Dresden's men," I returned, refusing to look at the bodies around us. The random – and needless – deaths didn't surprise me. It was what I'd come to expect from the man. They did anger me, though. These people had been innocent, caught in the wrong place at the wrong time. I strode forward after Reis, ready to put an end to the carnage. The stone was calling me forward, its voice close to panicked now.

"Time?" Reis asked in a whisper when I caught him.

"Six minutes!" I replied, loud enough for everyone to hear.

Suddenly Tatiana was beside me, her hand on my arm, her eyes wide. "Did you hear that?" she asked quietly. "We're not alone."

I paused, listening intently to the church around us, and tried to filter out the echo of the stone. I asked the question firmly, and sought the answer amidst the chaos.

"Dresden has sent men to kill us," I replied quickly, turning to look at Reis. Behind us, I could see that Paul had darted back to the doors of the church, and was now peeking out into the courtyard.

Then he was sprinting back toward us. "You're right," he gasped, skidding to a stop in front of me. "There are about twenty of them, and it looks like they got past Doc's men. They're on their way in. We've got to move!"

"To the stone," I grunted, turning back toward the front of the church. "We have to stop Dresden and get out of here, or we're done for."

Reis took a step after me, then stopped and looked back.

"What are you doing?" Tatiana asked, yanking on his arm.

"We need to slow them down," he replied. He placed his gun back into its holster and stepped toward a large granite statue of the Virgin Mary, which stood conveniently beside the door.

"Help me!" he shouted, putting his shoulder to the statue and pushing. "If we don't stop them, they'll get to us before we're on the stone!"

"Are you crazy?" Paul shrieked running back to help. "We have to get out of here *now!*"

Tatiana and I quickly joined Reis and Paul, and within seconds the statue, which was as large as a man, began to rock. Slowly at first, and then more obviously, until we were lifting it several inches off the floor. Just one more shove…

"They're here!" Paul shouted, glancing out the door.

At that moment, I felt a surge of strength flow through my bones, and threw all my weight behind the next push. The statue came crashing to the floor in front of the doors, blocking them entirely, and we turned to retreat.

"Four minutes!" I shouted, starting to panic. "He's out here!" We had to find Dresden, rescue Katherine, and then get to the stone to go home, and we were running dangerously short of time. I threw open the doors at the back of the church and light spilled in, blinding me momentarily. Dresden's massive wagon sat to the right, deserted, large chains hanging from the bottom of the vehicle. The stone was gone.

My eyes darted to the ground in an effort to find it. It was out there, just beyond the bushes in front of us. I didn't need to actually see it to locate it; the humming coursed through my veins and bones, telling me where it was. It was calling me through my blood, as though it had found a long-lost friend. I took a step forward, sliding past Doc and Reis to make my way to the stone … and then Reis grabbed my shoulder with a shout of warning, and pulled me back.

47

Reis' touch kept me from moving forward, but it was Dresden's voice that brought me back to reality, sending a chill down my spine in the process.

"Doctor, how very kind of you to join us," he said, his voice low and menacing.

I pulled my eyes from the stone and looked beyond it. There, in front of the wagon, stood Dresden. Sloan stood behind him, his face impassive. Katherine trembled in front of them, Dresden's hand around her throat and a modern handgun pressed to her temple. Her eyes, wide and frightened, found mine and cleared for a moment. She was unharmed, but well and truly trapped by the gun at her head. And she was too far away for me to reach her easily.

My eyes flew to Dresden's face, my heart contorting with anger. He saw the emotion in my eyes and smiled mockingly.

"I believe, given your hurried pace and this girl's word, that the stone is ready to open," he said quietly. "Am I correct in this assumption?" His eyes slid to Doc, and then back to me.

I looked at my watch; he was right – we had less than a minute before the stone opened. The second hand was ticking down the last minute now, every second pounding through my bones like a drum. Fifty-nine … fifty-eight … fifty-seven…

"Tell me I'm right!" Dresden screamed, pressing the gun tightly to Katherine's temple. She cried out in pain, and my head jerked toward them.

"Yes, you're right!" I shouted. "Now let her go!"

Dresden smiled and shook his head. "Do you think I'm a fool, boy? The moment I release her, your man will shoot me. And then – most likely – my son. No, I think she will come with me, while you and your little friends will be left here, at the mercy of my men."

I choked, surprised. He thought to escape *and* take Katherine with him? Behind us, his men hammered on the doors of the church, shouting. We were running out of time.

Dresden read the thoughts as the crossed my face and nodded, absolutely sure of himself. "Yes, you are trapped, and you *will* die. Now, where will this stone take me? WHERE?"

"I don't know," I gasped, watching in horror.

"When will it open?"

"In less than twenty seconds," I shot back. I glanced down to find the stone glowing faintly, its symbols taking on a life of their own, and studied them carefully, allowing their message into my brain. Suddenly I paused, seeing something I hadn't expected. Something that didn't quite belong. My eyes flew back to Dresden, hoping he hadn't seen this mistake.

He was looking at me closely, no doubt trying to decide whether I was telling the truth, but he hadn't seen my lapse in focus. He'd already made up his mind.

"Move!" he yelled, turning suddenly to Sloan and pushing him onto the stone. He shoved Katherine down next to the boy and slammed the nose of the pistol into her forehead. She cried out again, but stayed upright, her eyes seeking mine in panic.

Reis raised his weapon and leveled it on Dresden. "Let the girl go, or I shoot!" he shouted.

"Shoot me and the girl dies," Dresden snarled.

"Reis, don't!" I shouted, reaching out to stop him. Dresden wasn't bluffing – he was ready to shoot Katherine if he needed to, to get away. And I wasn't willing to see her die. The symbols were rising from the stone now, beginning their dance around the perimeter. A soft glow illuminated the area above the stone, and the humming increased to a dull roar.

The door behind us shattered as Dresden's soldiers made their way through, and I turned to see them running down the aisle toward us, brandishing their swords and pikes.

"What do we do?" Tatiana muttered.

"We're done for," Paul answered, his voice dramatically tragic.

I turned back toward the stone, my breath gone, to keep an eye on Dresden. But Sloan, Katherine, and he were already gone. Shocked, I checked my watch; the stone was still beating in my head, waiting to make our trip, and the watch was still ticking. Our window hadn't closed yet.

"Onto the stone!" I screamed, pushing Tatiana and Paul roughly forward.

"What are you doing?" Doc shouted. "The window has already opened and closed! Dresden is gone!"

"Don't ask questions!" I screamed back. "Just get on!"

I heard shots from Reis' gun, and felt the stone beneath my knees, its call echoing through my mind. The screams of men circled the air as Reis, Doc, Paul, and Tatiana tumbled on around me, knocking the air out of my lungs. The five of us rushed to pull our limbs onto the stone and then…

48

I have no recollection of my second trip through the stones.

We arrived home in a jumble of arms and legs, still thrown together in our haphazard pile on its surface. I opened my eyes and shoved Tatiana's hair out of my face to see rough concrete blocks around us, connected to the concrete floor and wooden ceiling of our garden shed.

Home. We were home.

The comfort of that thought lasted about seven seconds. Then the memories came flooding back and I groaned. My head hurt at the thought of the things we'd done and seen over the past three days, and that horrendous buzzing wasn't helping.

Buzzing, I realized suddenly. Still? Shouldn't it be done now that the jump was finished? I looked down to see that the stone was still glowing, the symbols rising in their dance again.

"Off!" I shrieked, shoving at the bodies around me. "Everyone off the stone! Now!" I shot up, pushing and kicking in my panic. The jump wasn't over, not by a long shot. This stone was still open, or was about to open again, in which case we'd be thrown right back into the ribbon of time.

We had to move. Fast.

"Off!" I screamed, frustrated at the sluggish reactions of my group. I kicked one shin and pushed at someone's back. "The stone is going to open another window! Unless you want to take another trip, I suggest you *move*!" I shouted.

That got people going. I tumbled off the stone, followed closely by Reis, Tatiana, Doc, and Paul, and we turned to watch the stone, breathless.

After a few moments of watching, though, the glow faded and the stone closed. It was over. We were safe … for now. I choked out a laugh, relieved.

"How did you know?" Paul asked, glancing at me.

"About what?"

"About the stone taking Dresden away, and then still bringing us home."

I shook my head in awe. "It didn't close after Dresden left like it should have. It stayed open, and told me that we could trust it."

No one answered, though we all took another long, hard look at the stone in front of us. It had gone quiet now, like none of this had actually happened, and I swallowed heavily. How long before it opened again, and pulled us all back in?

"Well, I think I could use a good shower," Reis said finally, laughing. I joined in the laughter, then stopped abruptly when the rest of my memory returned.

"What's wrong?" Tatiana asked, noticing my silence.

I shook my head as I looked at her. "I've just remembered," I answered slowly. "Dresden. He escaped, and he took Katherine with him."

Tatiana's joyful expression changed as quickly as mine had. She stood up and dusted herself off briskly. "Right, well that means we have to find them, doesn't it? So how exactly are we going to go about doing that? I don't see that we have any options."

Paul shook his head, his face pale. "We can't. It's not exactly like we know where they went."

"I know exactly where they went," I said slowly, glancing back at the stone.

"How?" Paul asked. "You told Dresden you couldn't tell."

"I lied. I saw where they were going as soon as the stone opened the window."

"So where did they go?" Tatiana asked quietly. When I didn't answer, she asked again. "Jason, where did that man take Katherine?"

I took a deep breath, then looked up at my friends, already dreading what lay ahead of us. We couldn't let him get away, it wasn't even an option. That didn't mean that I was looking forward to going after him. "Germany, 1939. He went to join the Nazis."

Historical Note

To say I took creative license in writing this book would be an enormous understatement. I have, however, to the best of my ability, tried to introduce historical fact to the story where I deemed it appropriate. As my editor said again and again and again, 'story first, history second.' What this means, in my interpretation, is that I had to tell Jason's story the way Jason wanted it told (and we all know who controls that process – the characters), within the confines of historical truth.

Complicated, I know. So here's the truth of the story.

The War of the Roses, depending on which historian you listen to, lasted from 1455 to 1499. As the book shows, of course, the Battle of Bosworth all but ended the war in 1485, with the demise of Richard III (on the York side of things). After his death, Henry Tudor dealt with small York revolts and plots for several years. Henry VIII (his son) even dealt with a couple of nasty York-ish cousins. Nothing ever came of it.

I'm not going to delve into all of the family ties here, so let's go with the shorter version. The War of the Roses featured the Yorks (Richard III, symbolized by the white rose) against the Lancasters (Henry Tudor, symbolized by the red rose). Before Henry, other Lancasters had been carrying the flag for the family. Both Yorks and Lancasters descended from one man – King Edward III. Hence the shared belief that they deserved the crown more than the other guys.

Henry Tudor was actually related to King Henry VI's family, but was in exile in France up until our story begins.

When his (French-backed) army landed in Wales in the summer of 1485, they marched inland across England, collecting English allies as they went. Henry and the Earl of Oxford had expected stronger support from local lords, as was promised to them before they set sail from France. Unfortunately, many of the lords who had promised men and gold months before suddenly forgot their previous agreements. It didn't matter as much as it could have, since many lords did the same thing to Richard III. In other words, politicians were as nasty and deceitful then as they are today (some things never change).

The Earl of Oxford, as well as Henry Tudor, Richard III, the Earls of Northumberland and Norfolk, and the Stanley brothers, were real historical figures. The Earl of Oxford lived to be over seventy years old, and passed away in 1513 (impressive when you consider that the average life span at that time was less than forty-five years). However, John de Vere, Earl of Oxford, was only in his mid-forties when he confronted Richard's army on Ambion Hill. Still not young by any stretch of the imagination, but not as old as I portrayed him to be. In this spot, it was convenient for me to take a small creative license. (Or was that actually Doc in his guise as the Earl, acting for a man who had died years earlier? I suppose we'll never know.)

Upon reading about the (real) Earl's exploits as a soldier and leader, one has to doubt whether the Battle of Bosworth would have gone Henry's way if the Earl didn't exist. I took full advantage of this in the book, and added to it where I could.

I also told the truth about Lord Stanley. Within the confines of the story, of course. Dresden never kidnapped Lord Stanley's brother. Richard III did, however, hold Lord Stanley's son prisoner at the time of the battle, with the idea that Stanley's army would assist Richard. Richard must have hoped, at least, that Lord Stanley would refrain from joining Henry Tudor's army once the battle began. This, of course, was a double-edged sword. Stanley hesitated at the start of the battle, and certainly took his time making his decision, but ended his hesitation with the famous (and real) line "I have more sons!" It would not win the man 'father of the year' honors, but it meant that he came down on Henry's side, perhaps changing the course of history. It certainly shows that living in the fifteenth century was not for the faint of heart.

Henry Tudor's army was made up of roughly five thousand men, while Richard controlled eight to ten thousand. According to historians. I've learned over the years, though, that they tend to portray the victor with less in terms of fighting men and equipment, as it makes their victory seem that much more impressive. So I take these figured with a grain of salt. They could, after all, be nothing more than fifteenth-century sensationalism.

The Battle of Bosworth, fought on August 22, 1485, is notable because it was the last time an English monarch was killed in battle. As the history books proclaim, Henry Tudor became King Henry VII on the battlefield. During his reign, he would lead England and Western Europe out of the dark ages and into the dawn of the Renaissance Era. The Tudor dynasty – Henry VIII, Bloody Mary, and Queen Elizabeth – would all spring from his line, affecting the world for both better and worse. For better, if you believe the historians. Once again, though, we have no way of knowing whether these things actually happened or not.

History is, after all, written by the victor. Often with hidden agendas and a heavy dose of personal opinion and interpretation.

Which brings me to my final point. Today, when we study history, we study the broad strokes of our world's timeline. We may or may not be dealing with absolute fact. We are almost certainly dealing with the writer's personal feelings and interpretations. The broad brush-strokes are important, of course – who won the War of the Roses, for instance. Nazi Germany. The American, French, and Russian revolutions.

But the devil, as they say, is in the details, and we in the modern age don't get to see those. Those small details – the existence of one person or another, the presence of guns in a certain time period, the path of one unimportant soldier – all lead to the broad brush-strokes that make up our ribbon of time. And if one person got it into his head to start changing those details …

Well. Let's just leave that for Doc, Jason, Paul, Tatiana, Reis, and maybe even Katherine to deal with in the next book, shall we? They are, after all, the keepers of the black stones. And with that, the guardians of history itself.

PT McHugh

About the Author

PT McHugh didn't start out as a storyteller. He was, however, born into a family of that encouraged imagination. He became a fan of history in school and then went to college to become a construction engineer, to build a world of straight lines, angles, and equations.

He was just as surprised as everyone else when he realized that he believed in magic, and might just know the secret of how to jump through time. Since then, he's been researching the possibility and learning everything he can about history. Just in case the opportunity arises.

PT was born and raised in New Hampshire and currently lives in Raleigh, North Carolina with his wife, two daughters, and a dog named Bob, daring to dream of alternate worlds and cheering for his beloved New England Patriots.

www.ptmchugh.com